KU-631-756

KING HENRY

KING HENRY

Douglas Galbraith

ISIS
LARGE PRINT
Oxford

First published in Great Britain 2007
by Harvill Secker,
one of the publishers in
The Random House Group Ltd.

Published in Large Print 2007 by ISIS Publishing Ltd.,
7 Centremead, Osney Mead, Oxford OX2 0ES
by arrangement with
The Random House Group Ltd.

Douglas Galbraith has asserted his right
to be identified as the author of this work

British Library Cataloguing in Publication Data
Galbraith, Douglas
King Henry. – Large print ed.
1. Ford, Henry, 1863–1947 – Fiction
2. World War, 1914–1918 – Fiction
3. United States – Foreign relations –
1913–1921 – Fiction
4. Historical fiction
5. Large type books
I. Title
823.9'2 [F]

ISBN 978–0–7531–7906–2 (hb)
ISBN 978–0–7531–7907–9 (pb)

Printed and bound in Great Britain by
T. J. International Ltd., Padstow, Cornwall

Ray

Billionaires have many friends and it is my privilege to serve Mr Ford by keeping them as far away from him as possible.

For me it started with the five-dollar-a-day business, which anyone could have told him would only lead to trouble. He had his own reasons — and who can say now they didn't turn out to be right? — but there was always going to be a ruckus at the time. It was in the papers one day and every drunk, bum and rif in the state was rattling the gates the next. I could have told him that — if it wasn't for the fact that he hadn't yet exchanged a word with me or learned my name.

You see — it was the five-dollar-a-day business that really made Mr Ford famous. Until then he didn't need me. Or at least he didn't know he needed me. He was just another automobileer and it was getting to seem like there wasn't much else in Detroit. But the five-dollar-a-day business? Well, that changed everything. That was what made him so many friends all of a sudden, and a good few enemies too in among the gentler folks of Detroit. They didn't take kindly to paying five for what they were used to getting for three.

These good people had their friends too — some of them police officers. And that's why the crowds in Woodward Avenue and Manchester Street, all cursing and pushing to get through to the employment office, turned into a riot and nobody did much about it. And what with all that the newspapermen got to like him just as much as everybody else.

It was some time in the first week of January and bitter cold when the reporters got the call out to Highland Park to hear the news. I knew because I saw them coming out after the meeting, though I didn't yet know what it was about.

"We're going to lead on the money," I heard one say.

"Sure — five's the story."

Well, it turned out later that two dollars and forty-three cents was the story and the rest came in only if you stuck it out for six months or more, were twenty-two years of age (unless already married), did right by your widowed mother, didn't take in too many boarders, swept, tidied and took pride in your backyard, learned English, feared God and used whatever the Sociological Department said was a sufficient quantity of soap on yourself and your children. But that wasn't a story. Like the man said — five was the story.

Well the *Detroit News* carried it that same afternoon. By midnight there was a little bunch of men huddling outside the gates and by the time it was light the next day I'd say there could hardly have been less than ten thousand. The poets of the press gave it their all — "a magnificent act of generosity", "a blinding rocket through the dark clouds of depression", "one of God's own noblemen", "God bless Henry Ford!" It looked like the whole damned thing was turning into some sort of pilgrimage.

They put out the "No Hiring" signs right away, but things only got worse. I suppose poor men quickly get used to being lied to and not one of them was willing to turn away just in case there was a job there after all.

So many came in from out of town we must have had fifteen or twenty thousand on our hands by the end of the day. Highland Park needed one in five of these men and someone — I was against it — had the smart idea of sending company agents out with hiring slips for the better prospects and then telling the rest their chance had gone. Fights broke out at once. If anyone saw you getting one of those slips you had to be a hard and strong man to keep it. Then there was talk of them changing hands for money, and before long the Poles and Italians had more than they ought and the Irish and the Armenians got organised on the other side and then a trolley-load of reds turned up and started to sound off about dignity and the means of production and pulling down the sign off the roof and putting one up saying "The People".

That was the day Dreyfus was beaten half to death. He got caught in a corner somewhere with fifty hiring slips and having no more brains than a dog wouldn't give them up and so came back with a busted nose, three broken ribs, one arm kinked halfway up his back and no hiring slips.

"Dreyfus, you moron!" I told him. "They're numbered, they're all numbered!"

So we gave all those guys jobs and we matched up the numbers and we got their names and their addresses and the names and addresses of their wives and brothers and cousins and their landlords and their creditors and the mothers of their bastard children, and then we called them in like they were going to get their bonus and we took them all out back in a group and we hosed those rats down and kicked them out and not one of them has ever earned a cent in Detroit since that day. Mr Ford likes to run a clean shop.

It was on Monday things really started to go downhill. The men were coming back to work and to watch them go by was, I suppose, just more than fifteen thousand freezing bums could stand. That was when you could really call it a riot and the police stood by with their "told-you-so" faces and I got all the boys out front and we got ready with every firehose we could find. That was the moment. Mr Ford himself was coming in his automobile through all the shouting and screaming and the air full of whatever a man could throw and he just got through the gates when I heard that voice like some sort of strange angel.

"Mr Ford, Mr Ford sir, is it true you have to pay five dollars because no one can bear to work for you for more than three months? Is it true you want to turn men into machines?"

Ford turned to the voice and it seemed he was looking at me and then I saw the mouth moving and the clean white teeth just the other side of the railings right where I was and I reached through and I turned as I grabbed him and saw Mr Ford's pale eyes looking straight into mine and I felt the shock of that bone coming back through my baton again and again and the warm blood on my hand as I twisted his collar till that red bastard couldn't breathe and all the time Mr Ford looking straight at me.

Then it was over. There was a great *shshsh* as we got all the hoses on them at once and they scattered and ran for whatever homes they had before the clothes froze stiff on their backs. They ripped up all the stalls of the lunch vendors and smashed the cigarette kiosk and trampled everything to pieces and then were gone. The police stamped their feet and folded their hands under their arms. The Captain took out his watch and nodded. The police got into their Ford wagons and then they were gone too.

That's what I remember — and the smell of tobacco trodden into the street, sweet and rich in the wet, cold January air and of the carpets in Mr Ford's office the next day when that runt Liebold showed me in past everyone waiting and them looking at me like I was a bigshot or about to get the sack and Mr Ford himself saying to me — well, never you mind what he said to me.

Since that day I've had a good life and I know who to thank for it.

Marquis

The occasion was the first on which I was driven in the back of a chauffeured car into the workplace of my parishioner, Mr Henry Ford. The timing, the place and the manner — a certain imperiousness, shall we say, a whiff of the chancellery, of the state rather than a mere man — all marked it out in my memory.

It was in early January. I was delivered to an obscure rear entrance and guided through the noise and frantic purpose of the factory to a separate office building near the front. I think I must have walked a mile or more before being taken in there. Through successive doors the clangour of metal and machines quickly fell away, and the cold too, as I was led from climate to climate as if through the halls of a hothouse towards its most precious and cosseted specimen. The anteroom was crowded and I experienced a little vainglory as I was shown straight through and ushered directly into Mr Ford's private office. Save for myself, I found the enormous room empty of any life. I took off my coat and fanned myself with my hat, conscious that I would soon be in the presence of a man no more accessible to the greater part of mankind than the Grand Lama of Tibet.

Mr Ford's desk was positioned as a barrier across the remotest corner of the room. I noticed half a dozen of the latest newspapers folded on its top. There was a smaller table in the centre. A chair was placed by it but it was intended for no practical use, the table's surface being taken up entirely by an elegant model car, a barometer in a glass case and a large ship's compass. Another roll-top desk stood against one wall and, at a right angle to this piece, a heavy settee for two persons. An expensive cabinet Victrola stood on its own as if music and dancing might break out on the achievement of the Ford Motor Company's next triumph. The whole arrangement stood on the largest Persian carpet I have seen before or since, extending to within inches of each of the four walls as if made to order for that exact space.

There were two large double windows and an increase in the noise from outside attracted me to them. I looked down on a chaotic scene. Crowds filled the wide space before the factory gates and were increasing still as more men came from both the main avenues. At the front they were pressed against the railings and I recall my fears of a general disaster if no one took control of the situation. Toward the back, where the crowd was less dense, policemen stood in groups waiting for orders. Inside the railings a double row of employees stood looking outwards like soldiers on parade. Their bodies formed a screen, but from my vantage point I could see the water pumps and the coiled hoses behind them. I saw a man struggling to make his way and handing out slips of paper as he went. There was a sudden movement and then papers and hands were all up in the air together and I could no longer tell the clerk from the crowd around him. Immediately beneath me there was shouting, pushing and a few blows as the employees struggled to close the gates behind someone who had just come in.

I remained alone for several more minutes, taking as close an interest in the contents of the office as discretion allowed. The faint sound of water came through a side door and then Mr Ford entered, drying his hands on a white flannel which he threw casually behind him before closing the door.

I was already beginning to know Henry well in those days, but I had never seen him more excited or pleased with himself. He greeted me warmly and thanked me for coming. I indicated the newspapers on his desk.

"You're a famous man now, Henry. Truly famous."

"So it seems, so it seems. It's all come as a bit of a surprise, I must say."

He shot me one of those sharp, humorous glances just to make sure I understood. We both knew that pressmen were some of the most frequent visitors to Highland Park and had been for years. A happy thought made him grin more widely.

"Here, you'll like this. Do you know what Couzens heard from one of the boys?"

"What did he hear?"

"That he meets — the journalist, I mean — that he meets people who think it's just the name of a car, that there is no Mr Ford, nothing human behind it at all. What about that?"

"Well, they won't think that now."

He tugged up one of the sashes to freshen the air and turned to sit at his desk without, apparently, having noticed the commotion outside. Throughout our interview I saw no evidence that the increasingly riotous noise ever penetrated his consciousness.

"Well, Reverend," he said to me, eager that I should add further to his pleasure. "What do you hear? What say my fellow men?"

I nodded towards the open window.

"*They* don't mind, but your own sort — they're not so happy. You double wages in a day and they see their men walking out of their shops and into yours. There are rumblings, Henry, no doubt about it. They'll have to follow suit and they feel the money coming out of their own pockets. I have heard the word 'theft'. I have even heard the word 'red' — though I believe drink had been taken."

Henry was delighted. He leaned over the newspapers covered in his own name and poked his finger at me.

"A man who doesn't know how to make profits has no right to employ others. If these firms can't afford to live, let them die. Their men can work for me."

He was in one of his unshakeable moods and I realised that I had been summoned largely to listen. I obliged with a hearty pull on the crank, setting him on his way.

"But five dollars?" I asked. "A doubling, as near as makes no odds, and all at once?"

I heard at length about the men who made his cars. Who makes them, do you think? Me? No, *they* do — we're giving the men their due, no more and no less. I heard about the dignity of the sweeper who kept the shop a fit place to work, of how his necessity to industry equalled that of the skilled man, of how he must get what was coming to him whatever the harshnesses of the market. I heard of his family's moral condition, of crowded homes, dirty homes, wives forced to work, children neglected, houses crammed with boarders, a short-changed new generation, the working men of tomorrow physically and morally underdeveloped when they came to take their own place in industry. Wrong for one thing, but inefficient too — did anyone really think there wouldn't be a bill to pay?

Phrase after phrase he coined, fell in love with, delivered and forgot. He preached to me, telling me what I already knew with the passion of one who had learned it, or at least who had learned to speak of it, for the first time that day. I told him what I had heard from my other parishioners.

"Some worry," I said, "that a doubling of these men's income will ruin as many as it will save."

He shook his lean, sharp head emphatically.

"We are not afraid of that. Men do not choose their faults. They are imposed upon them by chance. They live the way they do only because they do not have the means to be better. Give them a decent income and they will live decently — will be glad to do so. All they need is the opportunity to do better, and someone to take a little personal interest in them — someone who will show that he has . . . well, faith, I suppose. I don't say a few of them won't need a helping hand, but that's exactly what we're going to give them. We'll walk with them along the way until they can walk by themselves. Men can be trusted to do the right thing, Samuel. That's my gospel, begging your pardon, and I'm going to prove it."

As I listened to this sermon on industrial Christianity, Henry remained deaf to everything outside. He was on his feet and excitedly developing his theme, striding this way and that across his Persian carpet which, if it had an ear for rhetoric, might very well have lifted from the boards at that moment and carried him directly to his desires. Somewhere in his mental workings, as often happened, a lever was pulled apparently at random and he next treated me to twenty minutes on his new tractor and the revolution it would bring to the world's affairs. I may have wandered a little towards the end of this and Henry caught my inattentive expression.

"You don't believe me," he said abruptly.

"What?"

"You don't believe a man can change so much, that however low his position he always has the power to get out of it if only there's a helping hand. That's parsons for you — present company excepted of course, Samuel — but I've met a few in my time who had so much faith in God they had nothing left for man."

"Now that's not fair, Henry. I haven't said a word against you in the last half-hour. I haven't said a word about anything."

But he insisted all the same that he could see it in my eyes. He stood in the centre of the room near the table with the model car and the compass. The sound of something like a war was coming through the window, but Henry was concentrating on his handkerchief. He folded it into a band.

"I'll show you," he declared as he tied it about his eyes. "We'll do it scientific — no cheating."

As the riot reached its height Henry Ford stood in the middle of his office with a blindfold over his eyes, orating about hope.

"I'll prove it to you," he told me. "We can do it right now. Where are you?"

He held out his hands like a blind man.

"Take me down there now into the street. I'll lay my hands by chance on the most worthless and shiftless fellow in the crowd, I'll bring him in here, give him a job with a good wage, I'll give him self-respect and hope for the future. I'll put my trust in him and he won't let me down. I'll show you that same man a year from now and you'll swear he's a different creature entirely. I tell you — we want to make men in this factory as well as automobiles."

After some effort I persuaded him to abandon the idea of an immediate experiment. I agreed fulsomely with everything he suggested — proof would not be necessary. At last he took the blindfold off.

"This helping hand business, Samuel."

"Yes?"

"You see, that's why I wanted to talk to you. It's not really something I have time for myself. I need a good man."

I had many questions but he was reluctant to take them up in any detail. I saw that the subject had suddenly become dull to him. We agreed to talk again at some later date and I understood that the interview was over when he looked at his watch.

We stood together by the windows. It was quiet by this stage and getting dark. Henry looked down on a cleared and sodden battlefield. I watched a solitary figure struggle to his feet and hoist up a placard that had been trampled in the rush away from the firehoses. Watered ink bled down its face. I could read "Bread, Brotherhood . . ." but not the third word. A miserable scene to any ordinary man, the great industrialist regarded it with the blank serenity of one who fully expected to see perfection with his own eyes, and very much this side of the grave.

In the six months after the five-dollar-a-day riot, twenty Detroit motor firms and an unknown number of assorted machine shops were priced out of business. Some of their men did come to work for Henry Ford. Of the others, we know nothing. The cars got cheaper and poured from the production lines at an ever faster speed. They paid six dollars a day, and tuned the lines up to a six-dollar speed. The employees could buy their own product. The conundrum of perpetual motion had been solved. Henry sat on top of it all, flying up into the sky on a volcano of dollar bills. No one could touch him now.

Zero

It was six months ago, or maybe a year, when they stopped trying to collect the rent. I was lying right here when a man nailed a plank across the door and then pasted up a notice. Three days later I busted out, but no one seemed to mind. If you don't exist, you don't have to pay. Suits me.

I sleep on rags and old newspapers. There is a roll of the *New York Tribune* beneath my head. I used to read my bed, but now it gives me nightmares. Above, there is a glazed grating. The glass is three inches thick and scuffed by ten thousand feet a day — though only about two hundred on Sundays. You can't see anything but the soles of people's shoes and sometimes just the feet. When the sun shines the pattern cuts me into squares.

Pipes and wires bring me the news and I have given up putting my fingers in my ears. Gas whispers and the telephone sings in my teeth. Greetings from Kaiser Wilhelm dot the air and the day's takings wing through the ether from Wanamaker's Philadelphia to Wanamaker's New York. Autos and trolley-cars drum meanings through the street. Voices come down the tube. It is an old coal chute with the iron cover in the sidewalk long since stolen for scrap. Someone will fall down that, passers-by say once or twice every hour. But they never have yet — or not entirely. Gum wrappers fall down and at night bottles, sometimes whole, sometimes not. Once there was a shoe that came rattling down all on its own, shiny black with a grey silk bow. There was a sweet-sounding, female cry of surprise and then lamentations. I slipped three fingers inside where toes had lately wriggled and could still feel the warmth. A man called a cab and they went off to sue City Hall. But mostly it's words that come down, the words you can say in the space of three paces — four or five if the speaker walks slowly or is unusually short. Countless thousands of little speeches in all the accents and languages there are — the world's newspaper, razored to shreds line by line, an infinity of crossed wires in the Bell Telephone Company's exchange. I hear every one and when there are enough it begins to mean something.

On Sundays, if the street is clear for a moment, boys piss down the chute. The urine gathers in the Sunday bowl and mixes with my own. I stir with a spoon and cast the waters of the city. I know what's coming.

Last week someone hurt me, but I think I'm getting better now. I thought they must have come for the rent at last. Grit caught under the door and I had to drag it open as it scraped a white line across the tiles. I found a young man in a round hat, a brown checked suit, fresh shirt and bright brass pin in his tie. He was already talking as I wondered how he could have made the mistake of coming down here. There was a little hand-cart behind him, a clever folding thing, and a stack of books tied on with a cord. He didn't seem to hear anything I said, and at first I didn't hear him.

"But tell me this, sir — can you afford not to have it? Is it not more necessary than ever in these fast-moving and confusing days when a man's ignorance can so easily embarrass him before friends and colleagues? *The New International All-American Encyclopedia* solves your problem."

I pointed upwards to the more respectable door he had meant to knock on. He talked like a machine. He forced his way into my mind and the words landed like blows.

"Do you know your *mitrailleuse* from your Maxim, your machine-gun from your mortar from your siege gun from your shrapnel? Can you tell an uhlan from a cuirassier? A Walloon from a muzhik? Can you impress and assist those around you by explaining moratorium, Landsturm, Armageddon, pan-Germanism, balance of power, Reichstag, cataclysm, vodka? Hey, wait a minute! What you doing? You damage those books you gotta pay, mister. Don't touch me. You crazy?"

I chased him up onto the sidewalk and he ran off with his little cart of books at his heels and the truth ringing in his ears as the people walked by smiling and shaking their heads to see me at it again. A hopeless case.

Consider this: land used to be beneath your feet, now it's something you do in an aeroplane.

Louis

I have desires but no power. My desires keep me awake at night. They are the desires of millions and I feel them all inside me, focused on my heart like sunlight through a burning glass. I suffer with them, or at least I feel that I should. I could imagine myself as their instrument — or I could if I was to go completely nuts.

Every minute of the day is filled. I work my fingers to the bone and at night, when I am on the point of sleep, my mind snaps awake with a new thought for tomorrow. I want only for others. What I want is good and right, reason is on my side and still I have no power. There is no connection. Shouldn't there be? In my dreams I run from some danger only to find there is nothing but air beneath my feet. I go nowhere, the dog closes. Only waking holds off the inevitable. How recently did I realise how the world really works? When did I last believe in magic or that prayers are answered, virtue rewarded? Even now I waste time. How many have died since I stopped writing and started to look out of the window? Midnight here and morning in Flanders. The light comes up and the snipers can see again. They at least can see the fruits of their work. In

St Clair Street all is quiet. Just for a moment not even a hog is being butchered in Chicago.

Dear Miss Addams,

I write at the end of a long and most dispiriting evening. I can't help but think back to our work in the spring, how hopeful it was, and how distant now, all spilt and drunk down into the ground like it had never been. Sometimes I want to cry like a child. On my own I don't think I would have the strength to go on. That is when I write to you. It is over a year since I was flattered by the offer to head the Chicago Peace Society, but when I think of what has been achieved in that time I get despondent. I should not allow myself to think of the past, but only of what we must continue to do until sanity has returned to the world. I feel that if only we could . . .

A noise from the bed distracts me. Emmy turns and speaks a word in her sleep. Betty answers with a single treble vowel. The light catches the back of her plump, dimpled hand as it flexes and grasps at the lace of my wife's nightgown where it covers her breast. Betty's face is red with heat and her golden hair dark where it clings damply to her forehead and temples. Very clearly the desire to make love to my wife blocks out everything else. I imagine it perfectly. She is not fully asleep, has no objection to being woken, indeed she has been thinking, feeling just as I have and has been praying for it to become a reality. In truth, my desires have been summoned by hers. Betty turns onto her other side, making space. I lift the nightdress. I am embraced and pulled firmly down. My daughter sleeps on as her brother or sister is beautifully conceived and I, breathlessly, am healed by an enriched future. The muscles in my thigh tense and I almost believe that I am about to get out of my chair, cross the room and, with all simplicity and decision of the man I would like to be, make my wife pregnant. She turns without waking. Betty wriggles closer and whimpers.

> . . . if only we could connect the combatant experience with the mind of the peacetime civilian. Time and again I hear from some decent person, who regularly asks after his neighbours and in his daily life would never think to pass by on the other side that the war is someone else's business and no concern at all of his, as if it were nothing more than a dispute between two anthills. Immediacy is what we need in all our communications. We must penetrate! I am formulating some ideas of this sort that I believe will be of great help and would like your permission to send an outline to you for your comment and . . .

The pen stalls above the paper. I put it down, despising words for their powerlessness. Through the gap in the half-drawn curtains I watch a drunk meander along the sidewalk. He pauses in a shop doorway before moving on. The last eighteen months run through my mind and

KING HENRY

I recall the International Women's Peace Congress in the Hague — I was there with you, Miss Addams, ghost-writing your daily cables back to the *New York Times*. The resolutions made us feel good. How laughable it seems now that we were going to post them to the governments of Europe and that our ardour would somehow go with them, stir the words into rhetoric and have a . . . Well, have what exactly? An entirely supernatural effect on the human nature of those who read them? That was when Madame Schwimmer stood up.

"Contributions from the floor may be made only through the chairman. Will you respect the chairman?"

"Oh, shut up, you fool!"

She found us, as she seemed instinctively to know, hungry to be led. There would be no "pusillanimous posting". Instead, envoys of matrons, statuesque and indomitable, would be sent in person. Officials would be bearded in their lairs and shamed by the invincible advocates of peace. Reporters would be on hand to record the events for all local papers. Darkness would lift from the outraged populations and the church bells ring. Whatever was said subsequently, there was not a single vote against at the time. Direct action was the answer. And when the replies came in it was a glorious vindication. Our ideas would indeed be considered. It would all be over before it had hardly even started. Humanity would do nothing more than frighten itself into peace and reason. What children we were then — we actually thought words meant what they meant.

Memory slips back to the previous summer. Peace still, and Emmy and I together on the boat and our through train tickets to the conference in Vienna. The weather was fine and we were excited and happy. In Paris we even went to the station as if we could have carried on. A man with silver buttons on his tunic and a peaked cap shook his head and expressed his heartfelt regrets. The trains were needed elsewhere — our tickets could not be honoured.

"But we must get to Vienna."

He tugged at his moustache for inspiration.

"Have you considered joining the Russian army?"

"We are attending a peace conference. We are delegates. It is very important."

"Ah," he said, understanding everything in a moment. "You are Americans? First you must have the war, then the peace conference."

It was the humour of the day — a necessity through the heat of the afternoon as everyone waited for the evening papers. The city was busy, but hushed as a Sunday. Hour by hour taxis became more scarce and then disappeared altogether. The motor-omnibuses quickly followed. The railway stations sucked in a thickening stream of young men with suitcases and forms in their hands. When we heard that it was not yet hopeless we knew the lying had already started. The next day, too tense to stay at our hotel, we wandered aimlessly, picking up contradictory scraps of conversation. War had become like the weather — it could be neither understood nor averted. Paris had never looked more beautiful. Would it survive? Will it even now?

We left the gardens to watch a socialist demonstration march down the Rue de Rivoli. The flags of France, Austria, Belgium, Germany, Russia and England had been cut up and stitched together in new, blended patterns. Banners proclaimed the universal brotherhood of the working man and a band played the "Internationale". A complacent crowd watched them pass. From the street corners policemen looked on with stony faces and attentive camera eyes.

The next day it was a certainty. A small group stood by a noticeboard outside the Ministère de la Marine. A single strip of paper was pinned to the wood — MOBILISATION GÉNÉRALE. Flags spread across the city and here and there a banner about Alsace and Lorraine that made the whole thing seem even stranger, like an inevitability calmly awaited for a whole, vengeful generation. We watched as the mourning cloths were taken from the Strasbourg monument in the Place de la Concorde and replaced with flowers, palm branches and a tricolour sash. The tearful mayor of the *arrondissement* spoke of forty-four years of praying for restoration and justice, of the bugles of the French army sounding the charge. Emmy spoke in my ear, but someone heard her accent and stared. We left before the end.

We ate early at a little restaurant near the hotel but the meal took half the evening to complete. The owner apologised constantly and was in turn constantly congratulated as he explained that half his waiters had already been called up. Proceedings were further disturbed by the need to stand every few minutes as the band played the "Marseillaise", "God Save the King" and the Russian national anthem. The evening ended in a different mood with a mournful rendition of "La chanson du départ". An elderly regular leaned over from his table and nodded towards the band.

"And, you know," he said to me, "they are all Hungarians!"

He shrugged and made the sign for madness.

We walked back through a confused city, half darkened — Emmy looked up to check for zeppelins — and half gay. We witnessed a celebratory attack on a German-owned china shop. Plates were smashed with great delight and the broken heads and limbs of Dresden figurines were trampled into a bone-white powder. Across the country a violent persecution was launched against the advertisements of a manufacturer of dried soup stock on the grounds — as was explained to me by one patriot in Paris — that they contained treasonous messages so cunningly concealed that only Germans could detect them. At the hotel we were handed police forms and asked with very courteous and regretful formality to fill them in and return them within the next twelve hours if we did not wish to become criminals.

It was not easy to leave Paris. We spent a whole day in the Gare du Nord watching troop trains depart. At seven in the evening we were offered a cattle truck to Le Havre, which rumbled northward through the hot, short night. We were evicted from it just after first light and spent hours on a bench — me sitting, Emmy lengthwise and trying to sleep with her head in my lap

— before the first café opened to serve us breakfast. There was no morning sailing and so we found ourselves with the best part of a day in the port. Desperate for anything that might raise our spirits, we consulted our guidebook. Emmy was anxious that we might seem to be trivial at such a terrible time. We hid the book behind our menus, but then just made each other laugh with the simultaneous thought that we risked being taken for spies. We found an entry for a church on a hill overlooking the Channel. The traveller was warned not to expect too much, but the view on a fine day was said to make it worth the walk.

The path wound through patches of sea-kale and the pink spots of restharrow. Chalk-blue butterflies rose up at every step and there was the constant sound of larks from overhead. To our right the English Channel was bright, still and empty except for small fishing boats near the coast. "Can you see the white cliffs?" Emmy asked. We peered northward into the haze, trying to distinguish one summery whiteness from another. After twenty minutes we checked the book again and thought we must have passed our destination. I asked for directions from the only passer-by we encountered. We were sent off in an unlikely direction and happily climbed a hill in an inland direction, not much caring any more whether we found the church or not. I reached the top first. I took my last few steps backward, looking out over the sea before turning to the most extraordinary and sad scene. My French had been at fault and we had been directed not to *l'église* but to *les anglais* — there, in the French countryside, in pristine uniforms amid rows of tents so white and fresh they must have come straight from the laundry, were twenty thousand British soldiers. Emmy arrived by my side and slipped her arm through mine. We said nothing for half a minute and then she asked:

"Is it safe? Perhaps we should go."

The journalist in me wasn't willing to pass up such a chance.

"I'll talk to them."

"No, don't — please!"

"It's all right."

I was already running down the hill. The closest soldiers had seen me and didn't seem to care. They were in a holiday mood.

"Here comes another young man to join us."

"Steady on. Recruiting office doesn't open till noon."

I remember catching the smell of an army for the first time — canvas, leather, men, clean, lubricated metal. I can't deny it wasn't attractive, exciting. I felt its call. I was out of breath and realised that I had nothing to say and could not really explain why I was there.

"British Army?" I asked stupidly.

"The very same. Berlin bound — come to give us a hand?"

"I didn't know you were here."

"We're not. Not till Wednesday — unless Fritz blows the whistle before then and we go for an early kick-off. So we can't let you go until then, I'm afraid. Your good lady coming too?"

The sergeant pointed up the hill to where Emmy was slowly approaching.

"The ladies' facilities aren't quite what they should be, but we'll see what we can do."

"What? We're getting a boat to England. We're trying to get home. Look, I'm an American."

I handed over my passport.

"Oh, dear," said the sergeant, looking sceptically at my surname. "Whose side are they on then?"

"Neutral — it's nothing to do with us. We were going to a peace conference."

"Is that so, Herr Lochner? Where was that then?"

"Vienna."

"Well, I should think it's been cancelled now, wouldn't you?"

The sergeant turned to the small man beside him who seemed to know exactly what was going on.

"Vienna, Harry. Is that good or bad?"

"I think it's bad, Sergeant. I've definitely heard of it and I'm sure someone said it was on the other side."

"I'd say things are looking pretty black. Who's the Prime Minister of the United States?"

"Wilson."

"Harry?"

"Common enough name, Sarge. Sounds to me like he's guessing."

"But it *is* Wilson. I'm a journalist, for heaven's sake."

"Write things in the papers, do you?"

"Nothing you don't want me to."

"Still, you can't be too careful."

He shouted over to another tent.

"Bring those last will and testament forms, will you, Bill — and get another execution squad together."

I was white and trembling and Emmy beginning to cry when the soldiers burst out laughing. Seeing that they had perhaps gone too far they found us something to sit on and brought tin mugs of tea and asked us about Paris and how we liked London, which seemed to be everyone's home town and of which they were very proud. One asked when America was going to join in while another said it would all be over before we could get there. They were happy to tell everything they knew about their own movements, which wasn't much. Nothing had happened to them yet — they didn't seem to understand war any more than I did. I asked naïve, peaceable questions and they made naïve, peaceable answers. In a lull I suddenly felt the sadness of it all and we were relieved when an officer came by, dismissed everyone but the sergeant and questioned us. My name was taken down and I was searched for a camera. My notebook was read and pages torn from it and put in the fire. Emmy gave her word of honour that she had nothing about her person.

"Say nothing about what you've seen for a week. Not to anyone. Get back to the port and get out quick."

We ran most of the way back to Le Havre and for half the journey could still hear the officer shouting at his men.

We crossed the Channel then headed straight for Southampton and home, three of us — Emmy, little Elisabeth inside and myself with a bruised, but renewed purpose. I did as I had been asked by the British Army. Emmy and I went beyond the call of duty, not even saying anything to each other, as if all the absurd talk of spies might really be true. I both felt and resented the tug of loyalty. I gave myself over to earnest inner debates in the smoking saloon about breaches of neutrality and taking sides. The ship's Marconi digest was vague. Had the fighting started? Were the men who had threatened to kill us and served us tea still alive? I had never even attended a funeral. By the time we got to New York a week had passed — I ran to the telegraph office and made the most of my scoop. At least I got a story out of it, and then a new job too.

A clock strikes one and I look down at my half-written letter. Deep in the stairwell there is an argument. A door slams and the filament trembles in its vacuum. If I earned more money we would not have to live here.

Abstractions obsess me — purchase, grip, drive. How can it be so easy for one man to seize and move the world, and so hard for another? If I asked such a man could he tell me the answer? I am not wholly lacking. I am a man of ideals, and of passion too. When I speak in public I am moved by my own words. And yet I feel that something fundamental is hidden from me.

I am very tired. I turn out the light and begin to take off my clothes. I look up at the sound of an automobile outside. It slows for the corner and backfires a single shot in my direction before disappearing. A flag on a stick pokes up from the back, suddenly bright as it passes beneath a street lamp.

My mother worries about my career. My prose is purple. My wife says I am more interested in peace than in her. I am a joke.

Clara

I remember the first time Henry made me cry. I was lying there in the dark beside him being sure not to make a sound. When I closed my eyes the tears squeezed out and ran down my temples and into my ears. Something had made him want to talk about his mother. He had tried once or twice before, but had never found the right way. Perhaps it had just come to him then and so he wanted to say it straight out in case he forgot. He put the light out first and then spoke — he said that after she died the house was like a watch that had lost its mainspring. I cried because I thought he wanted me to replace that mainspring and I didn't think I ever could.

It had been a year and a half before that, at the New Year's Ball at the big Martindale house, decked out and bright and the snow around it tram-lined by the runners of the sleighs, that I found out how the skinny, shy Henry Ford danced the polka better than anyone I had ever met. Afterwards he showed me what he had just made and explained how it worked — how the two dials of the watch told standard and railway time and how it could show the days of the week as well. Was there, he wanted to know, any chance of him walking me home after midnight?

Henry was persistent, and I liked his sisters. I do remember thinking that I had hoped for more. Even when his father offered him the loan of eighty acres of timber to clear and build on and farm, it seemed I might be taking on a hard future. But the more I thought about it the more certain I became. I don't say I knew how things were going to turn out twenty — no, let me think now — good heavens, thirty years later, but I saw something and I was the first to see it and I wasn't wrong.

The eighty acres were meant to call Henry back from Detroit where he had been working in the machine shops. He took one look at those trees, cut them down, sawed them up for timber and with me up on top by his side used a huge steam-traction engine to pull out the stumps. When there was nothing left he lost interest and was sad to have to give the traction engine back. It would only have been a few weeks after that, three months before Edsel was born, when he was quieter than usual in the evening and I knew something was on his mind. I had read out a chapter from *Oliver Twist* and was then doing a little sewing when he shifted in his chair and said at last, "I'm thinking of moving back to Detroit."

I felt at once how much I had come to like everything about our modest country life. Church and family near, the quiet and the sky and the new house all fresh and smelling of clean new timber and paint and the organ in the parlour that no one, I supposed, would be willing to carry up the stairs to a city apartment. Above all it was where I had imagined my children growing up — my child as it turned out. I remember how nervous Henry looked — we have always been able to read each other's thoughts — and he put his hand up to stop me from speaking.

"Wait. Look."

He took a sheet from the music rack and drew on the back of it. He talked for hours, but don't ask me now what he said. In the end I did understand, though not so as I could have said what or how, or explained to anyone else. It was like it is supposed to be when you wade into the river and someone holds you under and everything is quiet for a few seconds. When you come up it really is different and things make sense in a way they never did before. I have always believed in my husband.

When he had finished he looked at me and asked, "Would you be willing, Callie?" And it scares me now even to think of him asking that question and what the world would have been like if I had said anything other than "yes".

Years passed in Detroit. I don't remember how many. John Street was our first place. We unloaded what little we had and I washed the place from top to toe and sang to keep my spirits up. I lived a widow's life, playing with Edsel at home or pushing him round the city when the weather was fine. I looked in on the big houses — one with an iron guard-dog in its garden and another a stag with huge antlers. Fancy Battenberg lace hung behind the tall windows and I liked to think of myself sitting behind that screen talking with friends who lived in houses just like mine, or putting down a book in the afternoon and reaching out for the electric bell to summon whatever I wanted. In winter the George McMillans would swish by in their beautiful cutter behind their two black horses. I remember we were all together so it must have been a Sunday. I was so pleased that Mr McMillan waved to us.

"Aren't they beautiful, Henry?"

"I suppose."

The next year he bought me a sleigh for the winter, but never the horses to pull it.

I wandered in Hudson's, though more for the company than to buy anything. Sometimes I would get the trolley-car down to the waterfront and watch the ships. Edsel and I went to Canada. I bought him ice-cream and watched him chase the seagulls off the deck. It only cost a nickel if you didn't get off the ferry.

"Tell Daddy what we did today, darling."

"That's fine," Henry would say. "That's just fine. Is dinner ready, Callie? There's a little extra job to do back at the works. The sooner I get back, the sooner it'll be done."

Often it would be past midnight before I would hear the key in the door downstairs. He would undress as quietly as he could before slipping in beside me. I would pretend to be asleep but wondered for hour after hour, God forgive me, what he had really been doing. In the mornings, before he woke, I would take his long, thin fingers in mine and smell the metal and the gasoline on them and see the black threads of oil pressed deep as engraver's ink into every crevice of his skin.

My evenings were reading alone and mending things that didn't yet need it. I studied Chautauqua courses and tried sometimes to discuss them with Henry in the few hours each week we were together and awake.

Christmas came again. That year we were having my people in from Dearborn. I stood in the kitchen at the end of a long day of preparations, feeling that at last I might take a few minutes' rest when Henry came back early. He struggled through the doorway backwards and as he turned I could see he was carrying something heavy and complicated bolted to a board.

"I'm baking! Don't come in here with that dirty thing while there's food about."

"I've finished it, Callie," was all he could say. "Come over here and help me."

He pushed a tray of pies out of the way and I had no choice but to hold up one end while he clamped the other to the edge of the kitchen sink and then pulled up the window despite the freezing cold. He was so selfishly excited I very nearly told him what I thought of him for bringing such a thing into my kitchen on Christmas Eve. He took hold of my arms and looked me in the eye, as happy as a boy with a secret.

"It's an engine."

"Uh-huh."

"It's going to work, Callie. I know it is. I wanted you to see it. I could have tested it at the works, but I wanted you to see it when it first goes."

Henry always knew how to win me over. He was clambering on the drying board by this time, taking the bulb out and fixing a wire to the socket.

"I made it with a gas pipe and an old flywheel off something else. It needs a spark too."

"Careful!"

There was a crackle and a blue flash as he connected the wire to the closed top of the pipe. He took a little oilcan out of his pocket and gave it to me.

"Gasoline," he said.

"You'll burn the house down."

"In here when I say go. Not too much, just steady drips. One, two, three, four — like that. Squirt in a bit to start it."

"Edsel's in the next room."

Henry stopped for a second and thought about this. Then he asked me:

"Do babies remember things from his age?"

"Well no, not generally."

"That's fine — we can leave him there then. I'll just have to tell him when he's grown. Ready?"

At arm's length I held the nozzle of the oilcan where I was told, squeezed gently and looked the other way. There was a wheezy cough and a foul-smelling blue haze.

"Oh, really, Henry. This is a kitchen. People are going to have to eat in here."

"Again."

I jumped as the damned thing fired.

"Don't move, hold it there, keep dripping it in!"

Everything else was trembling, but I did as I was told and made sure that the oilcan at least held still. The engine went off like a gun four or five times a second, flames came out with every bang and the room was full of smoke as it seemed about to shake the sink to pieces. I could see someone through the window looking up in amazement from the street. There was banging on the walls and when the engine finally stopped Edsel was screaming in fright. Henry took the oilcan from me and threw it in the sink. He took my hands and off we went in the polka again, faster than ever, round and round the kitchen table with Henry singing, "It works, it works! Didn't I tell you it would work?"

Rosika

It was raining. Passers-by shrugged their shoulders or were in too much of a hurry to stop. I think it was not, in any case, the sort of street where a respectable man could allow himself to talk to a woman he did not know. It was getting dark and colder too as we went up and down, puzzling over numbers that went from eight to twelve and back again. The other side of the street perhaps? There should have been a sign somewhere — we had been promised organisation. I looked about for my own name. Behind me Rebecca spoke with reluctant logic.

"Well, it must be in here."

I turned to see her disappearing into a narrow, lightless alleyway. A moment later her relentlessly cheerful voice issued from the darkness.

"Here it is."

She's a sweet thing, really. But how her voice grates on me — shallow, too simple by far to know real suffering. Still, I must make what I can — a poor workman with poor materials in a barbarous age. I followed her into the alleyway.

The place stank. A rat darted for the safety of the trashcans as we walked by. The placard announcing the meeting was on the door where precisely no one could be expected to see it. Inside, though we had paid a dollar extra for heat, the janitor was only then lighting two oil heaters which filled the air with an industrial smell. The place hardly seemed to have been touched for thirty years — the lighting was gas. I put down my bag and gazed disconsolately at the few rows of chairs and two or three pews. There was a stage at the far end and above it an overconfident proscenium with dubious symbols. Rebecca chirruped with all the gaiety of an over-pedalled pianola. I sat as she fussed, shuffling a more precise order into the chairs, coming back from behind the stage with a report of the scullery there and the gas ring she had lit beneath the kettle, taking the placard from the door and moving it out onto the street where it might do some good. I checked to see that the janitor had not stolen my bag. I began to feel a little better.

I found a set of enamelled stacking cups beside the kettle, a medicine bottle full of milk and a packet of sugar and coffee neatly wrapped in a page of the *Utica Observer*. Rebecca's great strength is her ability to turn anything into a picnic. There was a mirror on the wall, spotted and plainly framed and set high up for whatever male performers once frequented that place to make their final adjustments. I shifted a box over from the sink and stood on it so that I could see my whole face. Sounds from the hall suggested that Rebecca had found a broom and was working up a sweat. It would keep her happy for several minutes while I stared, wondered and refused to flinch. Cheated of feature — how true that was — not, indeed, made to court the amorous looking glass. I took off my hat, adjusted my hair and approved, somewhere inside, my long-practised immunity to disappointment. It has been said before — and about most of my associates as well as about me — that we are the sort of women who had no choice. Unmarriageable, by reason of mind as well as body, the nuns of the modern age whose habits are the suffrage sash or the anarcho-syndicalist pamphlet. I can turn my face this way and that, adjust the lamp at that dressing table and find a little something there if I try, but I don't lie any more and I don't regret. Solid, dressed for reason rather than to please and a woman of no country. Married all the same, I'll have you know. Once to a man — poor Paul, I wasn't at all what he wanted — and now to the cause, a happier bond and one from which there will certainly be no divorce. Last year I was in fashion, or at least still a novelty. I had as many speaking engagements as I could manage. I appeared on a dozen platforms with Miss Jane Addams. "Hungary's Greatest Hebrew" the papers said. I cut that one out and it's in my bag now, beside my steamer ticket — back to Europe in November before the money runs out.

I practised a few gestures then warmed up my expressions — entreaty, righteous anger, the anguish of a martyred continent. The box rumbled beneath my feet and the reflected image became indistinct as a train went by on the El.

"Ready for the show, lady?"

The noise had covered the entrance of the janitor who was looking very pleased with himself.

"What is it? Votes, pay, corset reform?"

I got down from the box and took the kettle off the gas.

"Peace," I said.

"Peace!"

He shook his head sadly as he sorted through his keys.

"I'll be back to lock up at ten. I suppose you'll be all done by then. Peace — damned Mexicans!"

Rebecca came in from the hall — slightly breathless and with that almost permanent expression of excitement that reminds me of a dog being led towards a park.

"I saw someone reading the sign."

"Did they come in?"

"No, but people are reading it."

Simultaneously, we consulted our watches.

"Plenty of time," said Rebecca.

She began to make some coffee as I caught up with the *New York Times*. I scanned the print, listlessly looking out for something useful. Speaking agents no longer competed for my business — in fact they no longer returned my letters or telephone calls. I had had to make a score of cancellations to go to the Hague for the Women's Peace Party Conference. I made my apologies with full diplomatic courtesy and was assured that I would be re-invited as soon as I returned. They had certainly needed me over there. They had gentility, faith in good intentions and a manner that would not raise its voice to make itself heard across a drawing room in London or Boston. They laboured mightily over their resolutions and decided that the war might end if they dropped them in the post. I stood up at once.

"Infirm of purpose — give me the resolutions!"

That's how I remember it, anyway. It took another hour of debate but in the end it was agreed that we would deliver them in person right across Europe. We would insist on answers — and we got them. Once again I braved the torpedo-infested ocean. Three days back in New York, sitting by a silent telephone, I already knew I had been away too long. I picked up scraps, called in all my debts, presumed on small obligations until my name fell on old friends' ears like news of an illness in the family. I pressed on, the cause justifying all, and so came to be looking at myself in the mirror of a disused masonic hall one rainy evening in New York City.

Rebecca pushed a chipped cup of coffee towards me and smiled.

"The place looks a lot better now."

There was a sudden coldness in the air and then the sound of the outer door closing. Rebecca looked into the hall hopefully but turned back to me with a dubious expression. Sure enough, the smell of whisky soon reached the scullery. She went out to give him a pamphlet anyway.

By the appointed hour there were a dozen or so — two or three derelicts, a skinny, distracted soul dressed too thinly for the season and with his own placard on a pole, a handful of women of familiar type, Mr Lochner himself in the back row, making good the promise in his telegram, and one smartly turned-out young man with a direct manner I rather liked and the confidence to look me in the eye and touch the brim of his hat when I took my place behind the lectern.

I did the usual thing — the misery and waste of the trenches, the pitiful letters home, the grief of mothers who would never see or hold or hear their sons again. They were a hard lot that night and it was all I could do to get a tear or two from the women. I went quickly through the Hague Peace Conference and the details of the mediation plan — that usually being where I lose them — and then went straight on to the bag routine, testing a few variations for the next real meeting. I explained how it contained the keys of peace, secret papers from the highest functionaries in Europe that would, when known to the world at just the right time and in just the right way, bring a swift end to the horror once and for all. The young man, who kept his hat on and made notes throughout, wanted to know more. I smiled indulgently and let him know of the heavy obligations that limit my work, being, as I am, in the highest confidence of Europe's great empires. I wound up with the outraged motherhood of Europe, my last words inaudible beneath a tremulous and exhausted sob which, though I say so myself, is one of the best in the business.

The drunks snored. That fellow with the placard talked quietly to himself throughout and the women soon became distant when true passion entered my voice. Mr Lochner made the occasional supportive interjection and I can't say, on such a thin night, that I wasn't grateful for his presence. The young man was very attentive. I could see that he followed the argument, making notes at all the most salient points. From halfway, I began to focus my efforts on him. I realised, as a fisher of peace activists, that here was a real prospect and a chance to redeem an otherwise miserable evening. He was clearly intelligent and energetic too — an excellent recruit. He was the only one to stand up at the end to ask a question. At last he took his hat off and I remember being rather struck by his appearance, as well as his youth — a soldier's age.

"Yes?" I said encouragingly. "Don't be afraid to speak up."

His pencil poised over his notebook. He smiled charmingly.

"Swinehart, *Daily News*. Madame Schwimmer, if one of my sources told me you were a German spy, could you really prove otherwise?"

"I am a Hungarian."

"So, Hungarian spy — is that what you're saying?"

Marion

Dust blows through an open window. Through it I can see the dullness of Philadelphia stretching under a bloom of early summer heat. The latest drawings are on my desk. I look through them quickly, pick out one and fan myself with another. "Ladies' auto coat in oyster linen" — there is a slender model with all her weight on one foot and the other put out to show her sturdy Searle & Baumeister court shoe beneath the hem of the lead product. In this way the costs of the advertisement can be shared. A veil trails from her shoulders and a pair of auto goggles dangle from one finger. It is understood that men will pay, and so she sees a man where I sit and looks out at me with a frank expression that is scarcely decent. This is the one they will choose — a hundred words precisely on a ladies' auto coat in oyster linen.

I watch the nib of my pen above the paper and then look out of the window again.

"Waiting for inspiration?"

It's Lola who asks, sitting across from me on the other side of the wide drawing table. Thirty-five years old and happy to be on double my pay, she has her own apartment and a cat. Lola thinks she is an inspiration. I think she is a warning.

"Auto coat," I say.

"Dash," says Lola who is valued above all for her brevity. "Always something about dash. And then fresh when you take it off at the end. Dash and fresh."

A fish swims into my mind and refuses to leave when asked. Lola adjusts her glasses and leaves her mouth open in concentration. I laugh.

"What's so funny?"

"Nothing."

I put myself into the oyster auto coat and the words begin to come. In two minutes what has been impossible is effortlessly completed. I pin the copy sheet to the drawing and prepare to leave, explaining to Lola's frowning face that I have some last-minute preparations for the trip to Chicago.

It was only a week ago that Berton told me *Collier's Magazine* had asked him to cover the races at Chicago. Speedway Park would have its first international one-hundred-mile auto race and Berton had a press pass. Happily, I was going to be in the same city to write up the summer collections for the department stores. An unchaperoned weekend was quickly planned. We would meet on Saturday from our respective hotels and have a day at the races as whoever and whatever we wanted to be. Berton told me he had booked accommodation for that night so we would not have to return until Sunday. As I walk away from the office, I rehearse scenarios where I discover that he has booked a) two rooms, one for himself and one for his sister or

b) one room for the fictional married couple. I give the question up as hopeless and realise with excitement that I cannot predict my own behaviour. I tell myself this is good because it means I won't really be to blame for whatever happens. I tell myself also that this is a very bad argument, but it will just have to do.

I can't concentrate on the show and decide to be nice to everyone rather than pay any attention to the clothes. About a third of the way through I've already finished my piece in my head, bestowing general and safely vague praise alike on the Kuppenheimer peach-basket hats (a little passé in fact), the Hart Schaffner and Marx light woollens and the assured victory of the long coat over last summer's tunic. I warmly recommend the rust-proof Goodwin girdle long before I see it and concur that Russian lines will be "in" next year as parasols and coloured ostrich feathers blur before my eyes. The advertisers will be pleased. I join a scatter of applause, offer excuses and head for the door.

At the hotel there's half an hour's work with the portable and I'm done. I sit alone in the dining room and decline an offer of company from an older gentleman. I spend the rest of the evening in my room, debating going down to the lobby to telephone and hoping that every passing footfall is a bellboy come with a message. In the end, neither side weakens and I suppose it's a good thing we're about as proud as each other. I flick through the ads in an old copy of *McClure's*. I think of tomorrow as offers pass before me, silent as a picture play — Professor Hubert's

Malvina Cream; Why Sigh for Freedom? 9 a.m. and the day's work done with the Fritz Premier Electric Cleaner $25 ($27.50 west of the Rockies); Write for the Moving Pictures — no talent or experience required; put music in your home with the Angel Player Piano; Do You Have Power of Will?; Gossamer Powder; A Good Judge of Men? — Let Me Make you Better. I go to bed and read a few pages of a serial story. "Jenny-tired-of-her-husband" slips from my hands and I sleep.

There are a dozen men in for breakfast the next morning — two with wives dressed about 1909. I say No, thank you to a waiter's offer of a newspaper and explain that I am not waiting for Mr Rubincam and will order immediately. The exchange attracts some attention so I take a magazine from the rack and pretend to be absorbed through a quick and nervous meal. Berton and I are to meet at the station. I have to stand still in the bustle for five minutes before I hear his voice. I turn and there he is, beautifully turned out too, in cream flannel, linen waistcoat with this year's large tortoisehell buttons and one of the lovely new panama hats.

"Marion!"

We kiss and then he looks crestfallen.

"What is it?"

"The trains — it's hopeless. Everything is completely booked up. They've closed the ticket office."

"They can't have."

He has his hand on my arm and is guiding me round to the side of the station, talking all the time about how he should have got tickets in advance and how the whole weekend was ruined and it was all his fault. He's leading me, so I can't see his face until he stops and turns to me, excited and slightly scared and trying not to laugh all at once.

"So," says Berton, with a flourish towards the street. "We'll just have to take this."

I look with amazement at a bright, new open tourer. Smart leather straps curve over a green hood, the seats are of scarlet leather and everywhere the brasswork is polished to perfection so that the whole thing looks unreal, like a gold and ruby beetle taken from a jeweller's window.

"What — it's yours?"

"Ours," says Berton. "For the weekend, anyway. The Model C King — 'The Car of No Regrets', or so they tell me."

"Oh dear, I could have done better than that."

"I'll tell them. All I have to do is mention it five times in my piece."

"Can you drive it?"

He reaches inside and comes up with a booklet bearing a picture of the car on the front.

"How hard can it be?"

There's a noisy fracas in the street. A horse is shying and men shouting. Another King Tourer rushes by in a cloud of smoke and honking like a giant goose. The driver waves at Berton and yells happily — "Eat dust, losers!" as he veers away from a trolley-car at the last instant.

"That's Harry," Berton explains. "*Scribner's* — great guy."

"They've all got one?"

"Marion, they're practically giving them away. Every journalist at the races will be in a new car. Look, I got everything we need."

He takes my case and puts it in the back. Everyone seems to be watching as he pulls out from the trunk a long linen auto coat, a hat with a veil —

"It can be a sort of scarf till we get out of town."

"I know what to do with it, Berton."

— and an enormous pair of goggles. We both dress for our parts and then laugh at each other with our strange saucer eyes, unrecognisable and barely human.

"Great — let's go."

There's a tingle of fear as Berton pushes the starter and the car trembles beneath us. I cry out as it twitches backwards.

"Hey, hey!" someone shouts. "Stick to a horse if you can't handle it."

"Hold on."

He works a lever and the car startles, coughs to a halt, jumps again.

"Damn it."

The engine races and then we surge forward down the street, scattering lesser beings to left and right. As we pick up speed my scarf trails straight out behind me and I grab my hat just in time.

"Careful!"

I can't see Berton's eyes through the goggles. Whatever he is feeling comes to me only through his wrestler's grip on the wheel and the tense, fixed exhilaration of his mouth and jaw. A poster flashes by, advertising the races. The hunched autonaut glares ahead and looks so exactly like Berton there is a moment of confusion and I almost expect to see white blazes of speed shooting backwards from his shoulder and cap.

"We'll catch Harry," he shouts through the din. "I'll be damned if a *Scribner's* man'll get there first."

The city is soon left behind and on the dirt roads we speed along like a little green and gold comet at the head of its own trail of dust. The air ahead gets hazy and Berton goads the car on. We round a bend and see another a quarter-mile in front.

"There he is!"

I put my hand on Berton's arm but he doesn't notice and we get faster and faster down the straight and then the corner is coming up like something I've never seen before, like we are falling towards it. Everything changes. I'm pushed forward and things rise up to one side and we tip into the corner and some very large trees appear from nowhere. I hang on with all my strength. For a moment I'm looking down on the outside of the car. I see the wheel not turning but quite still as the tyre scuffs sideways across the grit with a ripping noise. There's nothing beneath me. Car, road and posterior reconnect with a bump and off we fly along the new straight.

We never catch the other car. At Speedway Park we turn in and are marshalled to our spot by men in armbands. As the engine rattles to a stop I stand up and then climb up on the seat to get a better view. In the distance Lake Michigan is a glittering line on the horizon. Closer in there is nothing but cars, an amazing acreage of them drawn up in neat rows, a huge field of cars just like they had grown where they were and there had never been anything else before. From one direction there is an unnatural haze and a steady mechanical growl.

"You hear?" Berton asks. "The big sixes."

The smell of gasoline is in the air. Berton takes a deep breath, says it is in our blood now and declares it the perfume of the future. He makes a note in his little book. I shake a cloud of road dust from my coat and veil, take them off and get down onto the grass.

Berton puts his hands on my shoulders.

"Did I frighten you?"

I shake my head and say no.

"I'm sorry. It was stupid."

"No, really — I wasn't scared."

He looks a little sceptical.

"Really you weren't?"

"Not a bit. It was fun."

He seems very serious and happy at the same time. I think he is about to say something. I am sure this is it. Then he looks about and a passing car sounds its horn and there's another obliterating wave of noise from the track.

"Come on. Let's get on the stands."

Rickety, wedge-shaped ranks of benches line the track. Some look as if they have been put up just for this race. We climb up high to the back of the only one with any space left. It shakes with every movement of the crowd, its timbers catch the voice of the racers as they pass. The supports at one end have sunk into the ground so that the whole thing tilts and apples roll along the benches as if we were at sea. At my back I feel the pressure of a single strip of timber behind which there is a twenty-foot drop. Two cars rush by side by side. The crowd yells and a man waves a flag.

"Now it's the real thing."

Berton explains in detail as the day becomes uncomfortably warm.

"These monsters can go a hundred miles an hour."

The main event starts. The cars are lined up inert on one side of the track and their drivers on the other. There's a pistol shot and in a chaos of running and clambering they come together. Mechanics shove from behind, engines catch and they're away with a roar so loud you could shout with all you have and still not hear your own voice. One team pushes their car a hundred yards before it comes to life. As the smoke clears we see another unmoved from its starting spot. There is a minute of frantic efforts before hope is given up. The driver gets out and walks away, throwing off a mechanic's hand with a violent shrug. In no time the cars are there again, tearing by in a stormcloud of speed as the first lap ends.

The afternoon settles down. The pack of cars stretches out until only two or three pass us at a time. Later solitary racers rush past and I get confused.

"Is he winning?"

"I think he's last."

The crowd cheers anyway and the drivers don't seem to care, flying round the bends as recklessly as if they were neck and neck, as if gravity itself were the enemy. Sometimes I have my fingers in my ears, sometimes I can hear larks and there is only a distant thunder from the far side of the track. The heat rises and I alternate between wearing my hat and fanning myself with it. Vendors with trays hanging from their necks balance on the springing benches like tightrope walkers and sell us cups of lemonade. Several times a car passes us never to be seen again. I have a strange notion of them getting lost, or just going straight on for ever as fast as they can. I try to ignore the smoke rising in the distance against the brightness of the water.

"Engine fire," says Berton. "He'll be fine."

Another hour passes and the race becomes a mystery. For Berton's sake I try to stifle a yawn and it is then I wake up as something different and appalling slides in from the right. The noise is in the crowd at first — a surge of alarm that runs with the rising wave of people that hits and lifts us too so we can see a car which seems at first still to be in the race except that it is on its side. It moves across the surface of the track like it must be ice, hardly slowing at all, but there's a shrieking and a yellow-gold trail of light from where the metal tears at the ground. I can see the head and shoulders of the driver and the blank gleam of his goggles. His hands are on the wheel. He's stretching up to keep his head from the track. He's still trying to turn the wheel, but there's nothing he can do now. The car catches on something, spins and stops right in front of where we're sitting. Men run forward and there's shouting as one is almost cut down by another racer. I smell gasoline and see figures struggle in a thickening white cloud. The driver is moving, but there is brightness too. It's small at first and for a moment I don't understand before the whole car is engulfed in a gust of heat and the rescuers reel back. Berton's hand is over my eyes, but I push it away and stand on my toes. Men are running into the flames. Everything seems hopeless when the driver himself rolls out, still burning. Mechanics tip buckets of sand and they try to beat out the flames as someone even throws a cup of lemonade from the front row. There's a moment of stillness when everyone stands back and smoke drifts from the body and another car goes by, though no one sees it now, and it all seems for nothing. Then — do you know those machines at the fairs, the ones you put your hand on and they make your hair stand up on end? — well that's how it is and not just for me; the man in front's hat rises up a good half-inch. The driver moves. Even with the smoke still coming off him he begins to move his arms and legs, and then he gets to his knees and then stands up. A mechanic goes to help him but can't because he's too hot to touch. There he stands, black and smouldering like he's just been cast in a furnace. He's dazed and moves slowly. His hands, trailing smoke, go to his eyes and he takes off his goggles and there's the white skin beneath, the only white thing about him, so white it makes him look like he has two huge pale eyes. He sees the crowd. Everyone begins to cheer and he raises his arms and we scream ourselves hoarse and shout and stamp and no one cares that the stand's about to collapse. I feel so happy. Not just relieved, but happier than before, happier than if it hadn't happened at all. The smouldering driver stands in triumph, like he always knew he'd live, like it was just a trick, Houdini's latest sensation.

Eventually someone wins. Berton drives steadily on the way back. I get drowsy, wrap myself up against the dust and lean my head on his shoulder. The noise of the car travels from bone to bone. I fold my hands over my front and curl up. Berton plants a kiss on my forehead and it's like I am inside a warm, humming engine that keeps me safe and lulls me to sleep. Some time later he wakes me with a question.

"Can you read a map?"

I am surprised to be in the city already. I take the street plan Berton holds out to me and look around, but there's nothing I recognise. I see a sign for Clark Street and there's a bridge too. The car stops as I'm looking down, trying to find where we are. When I put my head up again I see that Berton has taken his hat and goggles off. He's getting out of the car, looking at something down the street and not answering me. Then I see the ambulances, and other vans too of all sorts blocking all the roads. There are exhausted fire crews resting and police officers everywhere. On some of the vans there are large red crosses and it all looks like a newspaper picture from Europe.

Berton goes towards them and I have no choice but to follow. I smell river water. Nurses guide women by, blankets about their shoulders and water dripping from their clothes. There's something strange at the end of the street, like a new, windowless building right across it where it shouldn't be. Propellers stick out at one end and there are sparks where men are cutting holes in the upturned steel. The Chicago River is full of small boats and empty life vests and picnic baskets and other things I won't look at. From the boats men fish with long poles. From somewhere in the crowd grief is suddenly loud. Priests and a rabbi walk among those who wait.

For almost an hour I am alone and then Berton comes back with "the story". I can't listen to anything he says. From where I stand I can see the edge of the quay. I see the backs of strong men straining as they lift from the boats below. Berton is talking about himself now and me and the future. He is walking very fast up and down. "I don't know," he says to himself over and again. "I don't know, I don't know." He stops and stands in front of me. He is pale and breathing hard.

"Marion . . ."

Over his shoulder I watch a man straighten slowly. His hands go under the arms of a girl and are clasped in front over her chest. He pulls her up and I see the water draining from her dress. I recognise it. I know the store and what she paid for it when it was new last summer.

"Marion Rubincam, will you . . ."

Her hair is long and fair and hangs down like a mask over her face. Water trickles from the end of her hair and the heels of her best shoes drag on the cobbles. A newsman takes a picture with a camera. Berton has stopped talking.

"No. No, Berton. No. Never!"

Clara

Life moved steadily after that smoky, noisy evening in the kitchen. Henry did well and we moved up to a place in Bagley Avenue. He was then the chief engineer at the Edison Illuminating Company. He explained to me more than once how the dynamos were driven by a steam engine. At home from the works he would sit quietly in his chair, sometimes for an hour or two at a time without saying a single word while I sewed or read a novel.

"Shall I read aloud, my dear?"

He would shake his head and go on staring at the electric lamp as it glowed with the current made by the machines he tended. It was as if he expected the steam to follow him down the wires, somehow to hold him back even in his own home.

"A steam engine was the most exciting thing I ever saw as a boy," he said to me one evening. "I hate them now. I hate everything about them."

Once, out in the town with Edsel, I saw one of the first horseless carriages putter by. I said nothing about it to Henry. But soon the great families of Detroit made a fashion of them and there were two or three, then half a dozen and I could almost rely on seeing one every other week. I began to learn these French and German names and took care never to utter them in Henry's presence. Second-hand surreys were advertised for sale in the newspaper, and the price of horses fell. The great new ambition was to turn one's stables into a garage. The Van Heerdens subscribed to *The Horseless Age* and left it about their drawing room on Saturday mornings for guests to see. Then the circus came to town and Barnum and Bailey paraded down Main Street headed by an American car, steered crazily from side to side by a clown waving to the crowds.

Henry worked harder. I fed him and slept unnoticed beside his exhausted body for the three or four hours each night he allowed himself. Meals would be snatched on returning from the plant and then it would be straight out to the shed in the back yard until the early hours of the morning. He borrowed tools from the Edison plant and spent all our money on more. I would fall asleep to the sound of the lathe turning in the shed. Once I awoke in early light to find him sitting on the edge of the bed still in his clothes. He jumped as I touched him. I watched him undress. He has always been lean, but he seemed starved then like an old picture of a saint in a desert, or a pilgrim wasted by his journey. He wrapped himself around me and held me tight — like a spanner on a nut is what he says. That was the morning I said Edsel was lonely, that a little brother would be good for him, or a little sister. There was only silence, then a slackening of his grip and snoring.

I got out of bed one night and looked down from the back window to see the shed doors open and Henry outlined against the light. He had an axe in his hand and was breathing heavily. I recognised Jim Bishop from the Edison works and even old Mr Julien from next door. Mr Bishop had a sledgehammer and I understood the noise that had woken me when he and Henry starting up again attacking the shed. Splinters of wood flew everywhere and when the door frame was done they started to knock the bricks out too, like they were going to knock down the whole thing.

"That'll do it."

Something like two bicycles hitched together or a giant's perambulator was wheeled out through the widened gap. I went down in my dressing gown, one ear listening for Edsel. It was two o'clock in the morning.

"You're just in time, Callie."

I followed them out to the alley at the back. I remember light rain. I think I had an umbrella with me and I held it over Mr Julien as we watched. The night was still and slightly humid. The smell of gasoline hung in the air. A light appeared at a window across the way and the sash was pulled up by a wary onlooker.

Henry turned something and the engine started. He and Jim Bishop looked at each other. Henry clambered on and I half expected the flimsy thing to collapse beneath him. Jim handed him his hat. A lever was pushed and the contraption juddered and began to move forward slowly, Jim walking with it and then beginning to trot at its side as it picked up speed.

"Callie," Henry shouted to me as he trundled down the alley to the main road, "This thing has no reverse and no brake!"

He let out a noise the like of which I've never heard before or since. Jim was running to keep up.

"Try the other gear."

The thing shot forward and left him standing. Away it went, careering out of sight into Grand River Avenue and down to Washington Boulevard. There was an electric doorbell on the front to warn people he was coming. Jim and I and Mr Julien stood together in silence. We could hear it — tring-tring, trrrrinnng! — sounding across the city ever more faintly.

I went inside. I kissed Edsel. I think I cried a little before I fell asleep.

More years passed. Certainly, no one could say we were at any risk of being spoiled by early success. A second car was built and I continued to sleep alone for half of every night. The *Maine* blew up in Havana harbour. There was a sort of war, but just as anyone was starting to pay attention it was over. In the streets people whistled the tune to *In My Merry Oldsmobile*. In August '99 I found Henry home in the afternoon.

"Callie," he said, "I've resigned."

There were backers, stockholders and a new plan. In the winter I met my first journalist and got the Sunday papers early to read all about it — I think it's still in my album.

> SWIFTER THAN A RACEHORSE, IT FLEW OVER THE ICY STREETS — flying along at eight miles an hour, twenty-five on asphalt, dreamlike smoothness, infinite rapidity, Whiz! Hold on! Whew! Perfect safety; spice of peril; what more could you ask? First the lion's roar, then the voice of man. Next the voice of wind in sails, the report of gunpowder and the shrill steam whistle. And now, the long, quick, mellow, not harsh, not unmusical not distressing note that falls on the ear as civilisation's newest voice.

I believe that young gentleman writes poems now.

There were delays. The stockholders wanted sales, Henry wanted a better car. $86,000 later a halt was called. They changed their name to the Cadillac Company and Henry was sacked.

"What do we live on now, Henry?"

"Callie, you have nothing to fear. Not in that department."

We moved in with Henry's father and sister to save money and Henry rented a workshop on Cass Avenue, down by the railroad tracks. For a while I made almost all of Edsel's clothes myself. I got fatter and Henry thinner.

The answer was a racing car. In September somebody shot the President and in October the Judge closed the Court in the afternoon so that he and the attorneys along with everyone else in Detroit could troop down Jefferson Avenue and out to the tracks at Grosse Pointe to cheer the hometown entry. Vanderbilt had put in for it, and Murray from Pittsburgh, but the man to beat was Winton, a mustachioed Scotsman and ex-bicycle-maker who was already making and selling thirty cars a month. No one could remember the last time he had not won a race.

I spent the evening before begging Henry not to drive the car himself. Nothing I said made any difference. Well before the end, I was talking to myself as Henry just sat there, silent and grim and not even looking at me.

The afternoon of the race Edsel and I got seats high on a bleacher by the first corner. Vanderbilt had pulled out. Murray had engine trouble and was pushed off the starting line. Only Henry and Winton were left. Don't ask me what happened next. I spent the worst thirteen minutes, twenty-three and three quarter seconds of my married life with my eyes closed and my fingers in my ears. At the end I supposed the cheering must have been for someone and when I opened my eyes I saw it was for Henry. He was covered from head to foot in oil and dust, but I hugged him anyway.

"Never again. Please, Henry — never again."

For a second time the money came in. For a second time the arguments started. Everyone in those days thought the car was for rich men and that it could never be otherwise. There was an order to things, something invisible but very strong. Men of sense understood it and respected it, fools came to grief trying to break it. Henry, they said, was trying to break the order of things.

"I know something they don't," he told me one evening. "I know it in my bones, I can see it everywhere and I've told them time and again but they don't understand. They think the car is just a machine, but it isn't — it's a new life, a revolution, it changes everything. It's not the car, you see? — it's what the car does to the man and it will do a thousand times more for the poor man than for the rich."

Well, that was one thing, but there was another too — since leaving the Edison Illuminating Company Henry's nightmare was having to go back. He could no longer tolerate the thought of anyone above him. Equals hurt him almost as much. Within a few months he was out again with nothing but nine hundred dollars and his name. More racing cars followed. The "Arrow" was wrecked on a time trial in Milwaukee. But the "999" won everything in sight and Henry himself drove it to the mile world record over the ice of Anchor Bay.

"Well, it's not a race, Callie," he said to me. "I only said I wouldn't race again."

Once more the money came in. These were different men. They understood Henry better, above all they understood how to keep out of his way. A new, cheap car was built and this time they got the words right as well as the machine. A man called LeRoy Pelletier was taken on. A colourful describer of Klondike shoot-outs for the *New York Times*, he turned the Model A into the Fordmobile, the Latest and Best, the Boss of the Road — no novelties, no tricks, no furbelows or fangles, no experiments, no mechanical hallucinations, no surprises and all at an exceedingly reasonable price within the reach of many thousands.

"The reader of an advertisement, Mr Ford, is a lock to be picked. If you cannot turn the last lever he remains as closed as if you had achieved nothing at all. 'Reach' is the key here. 'Reach' is the soul of the auto-buyer. Put this word, or its spirit, in everything you address to the American public and you will not fail."

The cars got made and sat in the factory yard waiting to be sold. More were made and the yard was full.

"That's it," Henry said to me one Friday. "That's the last time we can pay the salaries."

The change was as undramatic and senseless as a throw of the dice. We received a letter on 15 July 1903. A Dr Pfennig wanted to buy a car and enclosed his payment accordingly. Three months later I was going through the pockets of a pair of pants Henry had left out for cleaning. I felt something and took out a cheque for twenty thousand dollars. When he came home that evening he whistled the first phrase of our tune and I whistled the last. He kissed me on the cheek.

"Henry, I found this."

He took the cheque and put it away in another pocket.

"Thank you, Callie. I wondered where I'd left that."

Theodore

Disaster has been good to me. She first turned up my cards when Seth Sicherman stepped on ice while making his way out of Molloy's. That left me in the office on Friday night more or less on my own when Mrs Sicherman called.

"What?" I said to her. "Again?"

I heard this injured, indignant noise from the other end and thought I'd got myself in trouble. I started to apologise but she was already talking.

"I call that a very unkind remark. Mr Sicherman was in a state of complete sobriety, just as he was the last time it happened. A man can be unfortunate, can't he?"

I reassured her that this was certainly possible, indeed in some cases it was more than likely.

"That's right," said Mrs Sicherman. "That's exactly what I was saying."

She went on with some details I can't remember now and hoped I would be able to let Mr Pipp, my and her husband's mutual superior, know about this mishap in a suitable manner. I swore a melodramatic oath that I would give an account of complete accuracy.

Another telephone started to ring.

"I gotta go, Mrs Sicherman. Yes I will, I'll manage fine."

Two were ringing at once and then a boy came running in, his hand full of radiograms.

"It's war! War!"

"Mrs Sicherman? I really do have to go."

The news had jumped from ship to ship by Marconi and from what I could work out it seemed only to have happened a few hours before. For all I knew, it was at one and same moment that the heel of sober Seth Sicherman's shoe came into contact with a chunk of ice and, four thousand miles away, a torpedo slashed through the Irish Sea right into the side of the *Lusitania*. Anyway, it was one hell of a piece of luck.

I had often dreamed of pronouncing those greatest of words. I thought it might happen in twenty or thirty years if everything went well, but I never imagined it could come so soon. But there I was shouting into the telephone and feeling that I must be on a stage somewhere and not still in the real world. A voice had already said "Printing House" and I could hear the clatter in the background. I took a deep breath.

"*Hold the front page!*"

"Oh, yeah?" said the voice. "And who the hell are you?"

I explained. There was a shout and I heard the power of the pure, crystalline historical moment in action as the presses slowed and then fell silent. The voice came on again, changed.

"Really?"

I hung up, made some calls, read all the radiograms and everything coming off the wires. Pretty soon the boys started coming in and through the night the office was crowded, but I'd stolen an early march on all of them and when Seth Sicherman called up at three in the morning and tried to dictate something through groans of pain from his orthopaedic bed the copy somehow got lost. Anyway, by the time our new front page appeared at dawn Sicherman's name was still at the head of the column, but the words were mine. Second-Coming type took up near a third of the page — Piracy and Murder: World Waits for Wilson to Act. Below I gave them everything I'd got — the cowardliness of the U-boat, the shuddering blast of the torpedo, heroism and dignity in the evacuation, the cold, cold water and lovers' weakened hands slipping from each other's grasp moments before the end. Inside, Mr Pipp waxed indignant — world aghast at horror, can this be the twentieth century? Above, a cartoon Kaiser, swarthy and hook-nosed, held an infant Civilisation beneath the waters with his own hands. Teddy Roosevelt thundered about humanity and national self-respect and "saddling up". The President was calm. In the basement bars of Hoboken the resting crew members of the *Vaterland* toasted victory. The dachshund kicker appeared in syndicated cartoons across the nation. In short, it was a pretty good time to be starting out in the news business.

Well, there was no war. There was an exchange of telegrams, the *Lusitania* widows dried their eyes and the world moved on. I got my reward a few weeks later.

"We've got to do something on this exposition," Pipp told me one morning. "No one else will spend two straight days on a train so it has to be you. You got three days there and when you get back I'd better believe you haven't just read the brochures."

He threw down tickets and a hotel reservation.

"Go see America, young man."

I did, and there was nothing there. Plains spooled endlessly by. When I slept it was impossible to say for how long. I would awake to precisely identical scenes and could only guess as to whether I had drowsed for a minute or an hour. Mountains intervened and after them the dullness of plains was refreshed with the dullness of deserts. The window seemed like a moving picture when the projector freezes — your mind insists it must still be moving, but the eye contradicts. From time to time there were arbitrary halts at places with names stranger than those in the most remote of foreign countries. It felt like a true adventure and I understood for the first time how much I am a city boy, at home only in that coastal fringe of cities, stretched tight and thin as the skin of a balloon around a huge and absolute nothingness. I remembered that story where someone goes right through the centre of the earth in a machine and for days on end it seems hopeless and then, just in time, they break through to the other side and there's air again and light. I think they must have got the train from Detroit to San Francisco before they wrote that. At last the Sierras broke the monotony. We snaked down the far side, pushed gently forward as Mr Westinghouse's air brakes squeezed the speed from the train, wafting it to a halt in the station as smoothly as a magic carpet.

Just where the newest houses start there are two billboards, each three storeys high. The first says Panama-Pacific International Exposition 1915. On the other something like an oriole is launched into the sky with the help of friendly, finger-like flames. The wording beneath fascinated me and I turned my head as it flashed by — First the Earthquake, then the Fire and Now . . . I looked out eagerly for signs of biblical destruction, the black remains of incineration perhaps or jagged chasms where the earth had opened for the unworthy and conducted them down to their just deserts. I was disappointed — except that everything was a little newer and neater than I was used to, there was no sign that anything had ever happened. My first sight of San Francisco put me in a sombre mood. I felt diminished by such a display of recuperative powers. It lacked drama and suggested that there could be no disaster in human affairs, however great, that could not be quickly wiped away.

A Japanese taxi driver made a furious passage through the city. I was thrown off my seat at one point by a near collision with another cab. There was a spectacular exchange of oriental abuse — neither man, it seemed, in the least concerned about the impossibility of being understood by the other.

"No good," explained my driver. "Chinese dirty. Why don't you send them home?"

At the hotel I lay down on a motionless bed and instantly fell asleep.

In the morning, in bright sunlight, I flowed helplessly toward turnstiles. I showed my press pass and with a click was admitted to the future. The Tower of Jewels stood before me, Novagems of coloured glass glittering with promise as they drifted in the breeze. Everywhere there was evidence of a war on normality. The only buildings permissible were palaces — the Palace of the Liberal Arts, the Palace of Transportation and the Palace of Social Economy. I thought I would leave that one till later and took a right down the crowded Avenue of Palms. The Court of Flowers gave onto the Court of Abundance and the Court of Abundance delivered me to the Palace of Machines where a crowd stood mesmerised by the clattering rhythms of a folding machine. Paper shot in at one end and appeared at the other as an endless stream of gummed envelopes. An attendant gathered them into boxes and stacked them on the floor, the machine doing, so the sign explained, the work of twenty skilled men every hour. Six hundred boxes of envelopes were produced every day — for demonstration purposes. Further down the aisle a Hearst colour press ran out a blurring stream of magazine covers — teeth and eyes and the highlighted pearl in one ear rushed by like the face of a passenger in a train. I turned a corner and found that I had been shrunk to one thousandth of my size as I looked up at a fourteen-ton Underwood typewriter as big as a house. A dozen vestal typists catered to its every need. All of a young woman's strength was required to depress a single key, two at once strained to turn the cylinder. To return the carriage the whole team organised themselves on the end of a rope and heaved like galley slaves. Line by line the day's headlines appeared on the starched bedsheet of paper in six-inch type — Bryan's Statement Amazes Officials; Teutons Assail Foes; England's Heavy Loss; Say Frank Should Die — Prison Commission Advises no Clemency; Reply to Germany Firm but Friendly. The girls wound the paper up another two feet and were applauded for their efforts. A sign hung down from the roof beams. I heard the words spoken in the voice of a monstrous typewriter — "Exact Reproduction of the Machine You Will Eventually Buy".

I passed the display of the Cyclops Iron Works and a device that ate wire and threatened, at the other end, to bury the world beneath an infinite mound of hairpins. Girls delved into the hopper and helped themselves to handfuls which now, presumably, they would have no need to buy. Outside, between the Water Gate and the North Gardens, a crowd of men and boys pressed around the edges of a swimming pool in which a submarine dived, bubbled and resurfaced over and again. For a quarter you could go down in it and watch the water rise over the windows. On a stand nearby a polished torpedo exerted a magnetic fascination. A boy repeatedly banged the heel of his hand on its bronze tip. His father dragged him away to some fresh attraction. He followed happily enough, exploding as he went with enthusiastic noises and wide, scattering gestures.

Something began to oppress me and I followed a sign to the marina, believing that a sight of the sea was what I needed. The esplanade was busy but I found a spot at the railing at which I could look outward and be less aware of the crowds. Here was something new — my first sight of the Pacific Ocean. I imagined a line being drawn straight out from between my shoes and not stopping until it reached Japan. Was there a counterpart there, looking eastward? I tried to think of this person — in a vague way I could see that she was young and female and very beautiful. I struggled to make the picture clearer but someone jostled me and I was back with the toy submarine and the tyrant typewriter. I scanned the nearer waters of the bay, half hoping that I might be the one to spot the hostile periscope amongst the steam yachts and the visiting dreadnoughts.

A whiff of the farmyard came to me on the sea breeze. I turned to watch a fancy dress cavalcade trot down to the marina's edge. A man in pasteboard cuirasse brandished a sword, praised the sea and gave it its name on behalf of free peoples everywhere. With his three followers he rode out of sight. Balboa had discovered the Pacific Ocean as he would every hour on the hour for the next three months.

Such were the preliminaries or the mere frame, if you like, for the picture I really remember from my first day at the World's Fair. There was a disturbance in the crowd, a parting. Some way ahead there was a man cranking a moving-picture camera. Everyone understood that they must make way for three tall men. They say this country is a republic, but I doubted it at that moment when the unspoken instruction spread and the people pressed themselves to the sides to let pass this little procession which could so easily, if re-dressed in purple and ermine, have taken place in the most antique of European capitals. The older man was in the centre. In bow tie and wing collar, the others deferred to him — the man on his right in elegant grey flannels listening carefully to what he was saying, his other companion walking half a pace behind as he toyed with his cane or adjusted the flower in his button-hole until he should be called to rejoin the conversation. From my schoolbooks I recognised Thomas Edison. I soon learned that at his right hand the aquiline man in grey, with a hundred times more wealth at his command, was my first view of Mr Henry Ford. On the left, the dapper, modest attendant to these two gods was Mr Harvey Firestone. The machines of the future fascinated, but at the appearance of the men who made them there was something new, closer to reverence as if the cloth had just been pulled from the icons of a new religion. I followed and watched them stop before the camera. I must be in those pictures — hesitant with notebook in hand, failing utterly as a journalist as I let the moment pass. A child was pushed out to collect autographs. He bowed very solemnly and made people laugh before being gathered in again. America's industrial trinity moved onto a landing stage and boarded a yacht. There were other journalists there. We chatted and traded rumours until someone ran up and told us Fatty Arbuckle was filming somewhere. He had fallen down the stairs and ended up on top of Mabel

Normand. There was said to be a photograph. The new hunt started at once, but I went my own way.

That night in the hotel I finished my thousand words for the *Detroit Free Press* in an hour. I smoked too many cigarettes, went out, drank a beer in a bar, spoke to no one and got my head down early. The two days left to me I spent more as a tourist and it was a tiring business. Every display I looked at seemed to draw something out of me. If there were credits they never matched the debits. I left the working model of the Panama Canal or the miniature Grand Canyon or the Japanese Village or the Court of Abundance feeling that someone had slyly picked my pocket of what little was left in it. I refreshed myself in the Marine Café or the Bowls of Joy and went out again grimly to do battle with an invisible enemy. I craned my neck up to the Column of Progress. A bowman stood on the top loosing an arrow (so said the brochure) into the future. I tried hard not to feel that if it found its mark and went straight through the heart I would only be relieved. I accosted a guide and asked him where the English pavilion was, or the palace of Germany. He shrugged his shoulders — "I guess they didn't come." I had a headache on the Arc of Progress, my feet hurt on Olympian Way.

I stayed late on the last day, reasoning that if I was tired enough in the morning I might sleep better on the train. The biplane curved in over the bay and landed with its last farepaying passenger. Night fell — or would have done had the General Electric Company not prevented it. I have never seen such illumination, a true artificial day generated by the Exposition's own power plant. The Tower of Jewels glittered more brilliantly. From out in the bay the Scintillator, a coal barge for the rest of the year, lit up the sky with forty-eight gaudy searchlights. The night was as tiring as the day and my dejection increased. Others seemed to feel it too — a paleness, a shortness of temper, a flinching in the eyes of an animal unnaturally deprived of darkness. From Administration Avenue I turned down Sunset Court where the light was less piercing. There was one thing I wanted to see again and I soon found her — the Star Maiden, standing on her pedestal in the Court of the Universe, looking out to sea with her head slightly upward, homeward I suppose. In the welcome dimness her features were no longer clear, but I remembered them from when I first saw her. Her arms were held upwards framing her head, the fingers straight and palms together at the top. From her head-dress beams of starlight filled this space. Her eyes were serenely half closed. There was cloth, a garment of some sort around her shoulders. Hanging down a little way it described her breasts but did not cover them. Below was a lean, naked abdomen with a subtle, central indented line between the stretched muscles punctuated two thirds of the way down by a deep navel from which, no doubt, she had been umbilically attached to the heavens themselves. Slung in descending curves from hip to hip, sheer silk draped down to ankles. Feet balanced on the world and held it firmly with a wide spread of toes which had never known the confines of a shoe. The cloth was damp and pressed against her intimately as if she faced into the breeze. It flowed round hips and thighs and between the thighs, hardly less precise than the skin beneath. I thought of the model who must have stood in the studio, shivering perhaps and complaining every ten minutes that no one could be expected to stand like that for long. I could see her getting down from her stool, being rude and sulky with the artist, arguing about money, smoking a cigarette.

A woman approached from the direction of the Manufacturer's Palace. She gave every sign of recognising me and perhaps it seemed as if I recognised her too as I smiled back, only too ready for a chance meeting with an acquaintance. She said some things about the Expo and the warmth of the evening. When I apologised and asked if she would remind me where we had met before she just laughed. She looked up at the Star Maiden and then, slyly, at me.

"It's me, you know. Don't you recognise me?"

I hesitated, as if it might be true. She put her hand lightly on my arm.

"Well, almost. Are you here on your own?"

We walked together down Florentine Way and into the darkness between two candy stalls closed for the night.

On the way back the train could not go fast enough. I revised my copy, tried to interest myself in *The Pentecost of Calamity* — it went downhill after the title — and slept impatiently. I told myself that I was well and truly launched and that a happy prospect opened before me. I was a journalist, a real newspaperman, my apprenticeship served and my press pass to the future firmly in my pocket. I looked forward to a life that would combine, rather cleverly I thought, the excitement of events with the safety, physical as well as psychological, of the scribe's detatchment. These views did not last long — in particular they did not survive my third and final initiation into the journalistic mysteries.

I few weeks later I was sent to Chicago to do an easy piece on the city's newest and tallest building. There had been little of interest in the job and I had put together about as much as I could bear by the early afternoon. I misread a timetable and on account of filling the extra hour with a couple of beers, missed the next train too. I now had two hours to kill and drifted out of the station in a poor mood and with nothing particular in mind. A crowd in North La Salle Street attracted my attention. I pushed through to the front and found a police line holding everyone back. I gave a fancy name and lied about being from the *Tribune*. When I got through I expected to find nothing more than an auto accident and perhaps pick up two or three extra paragraphs to take back to Detroit if I was lucky. At first I couldn't see what the problem was — just a wide empty space leading down to the intersection and the bridge and the river. The people there moved slowly and were quiet, they moved like priests in a church. The upturned bulk of a Lake Michigan excursion steamer confused me, as did the emotionless face of the fireman coming towards the police line. He held something small in his arms. It was wrapped in a woman's coat.

Plump infant feet stuck out at one end, but when I looked to see the child's face it was covered. I went down to the quayside and stood under the monumental shadow of the *Eastland*. Covered stretchers lay in rows — feet protruding from blankets or hands that had slipped from the side lying lightly on the ground. Only then was the connection made and that odd, easy dullness I had half been aware of for the last two months finally cleared, as if something had been taken from my ears, a mist wiped clean from before my eyes. For me, you see, the *Eastland* was the *Lusitania* and a reproach for everything I had felt through that happy, excited night in the offices of the *Free Press*. Only at that moment, in the middle of Chicago, and in the middle too of my third stroke of luck, did the *Lusitania* emerge at last to become something more than words. I steadied myself, then took out my notebook and went to work.

The boys from the *Daily News* were there, and the real journalists from the *Tribune* too. I talked to all of them and soon had everything together. Then I ran into Braley from *Collier's* whom I knew a little.

"I was out covering the races at Speedway Park."

"Some crummy tall building story."

We stood side by side, dazed at the scene before us.

"You know I just saw a man crash his car and it burst into flames and then they just put him out and he walked away."

"Is that so?"

We compared and exchanged. It was what you already know, what you read in the papers that Monday morning. The employees of the Western Electric Company had come together early to set out for their annual summer picnic. They had crowded onto the *Eastland*, preferring the upper decks where the air was fresh and they could wave to their friends and family on the quay. The work of the Jenks Ship Building Company and more accustomed to the accommodation of freight than of passengers, the *Eastland* had a troubled history. Its owners knew this well, though its passengers did not. It was top heavy and its ballast system old-fashioned and hard to control. After several near accidents its owners met their responsibilities by adding more lifeboats and rafts to the top deck. Twenty-two days later it was this extra fourteen tons of safety equipment that caused it to capsize. In four minutes eight hundred people lost their lives.

"Death by lifeboat, then," I said.

"I guess."

Braley looked back up the street. A young woman was standing on her own in a hat with a lifted muslin veil and a dusty auto coat.

"I gotta go," he said, looking so white I thought he was about to faint. "I got my girl here."

"Sure."

Soldiers appeared and began removing bodies to a temporary mortuary in the barracks nearby. Stretchers were carried past me with numbers pinned to grey blankets. A man cranking a movie camera waved me out of his shot. I stepped forward almost to the edge of the quay. Hard by the top deck of the *Eastland*, now vertical and mostly submerged, a grimy salvage barge was at work. A cable ran down from its crane and vanished into the oil and water of the river. In the darkness below Arthur Loeb, king of the bell divers, blindly laid his hand on another ankle and swam back to his iron bubble of air.

I grew up at the *Eastland*. I connected words and things and began to see how many did not. I learned too that I really was the sort of man who could savour an irony, even as he stood among the dead.

Lloyd

Overdressed, I scout the street from a window table of the Powhatan Restaurant and do my best to ignore the attention I am attracting. I toy with the newspaper and count the change in my pocket by touch. Outside a gathering of police officers tells me that things are about to start. I get a refill as she goes by, and a hurtful smile.

"Cheer up, soldier. It's not your funeral."

I say nothing and look away, hoping all the same that she'll forgive me and stop again next time around. I compose a little scene for myself — her shift ends (so what if it is the middle of the morning? it ends) and she comes and sits down opposite, she props her chin on her hand, smiles once more, determined to get it out of me, and says exactly what I need her to say.

"Go on, then. Tell me your story."

And as I start she is sometimes herself and sometimes you, Amelia. At the happier, more distant moments, the ones we might still recall together one day, her features change, become a little fuller as the eyes turn to that rich brown and the movements take on that stage-trained finesse by which I could always find you in a crowd.

"I found her in Hicksville," I say. "No, really — that's what the place is called. I suppose it started a pattern — you see, my dear, my life has always been dogged by the illusion of meaning. It would be nearly twenty years ago now — I had just finished three nights at the Huber Theatre and was staying at the Swilley Hotel across the road. They were used to actors there and had laid on a late breakfast for me. I was leaving town that day and had plenty of time for my train. Well, I was served by a young lady I hadn't seen before and from the very start I couldn't take my eyes off her. I watched her carefully as she carried things to and from my table, her style all the way from the walk to her fingers uncoiling from around a cream jug. I came up with reasons to call her back and it was clear that she saw my interest and did not in the least shy away from it. I sensed that this was what she intended, a frank playing up to my one-man audience. I was excited and began to believe I had found that most precious of treasures — a natural. I ordered a fourth egg. She came with it and struggled to find a place on the overcrowded table. She spoke to me.

"You're having quite a . . . well, a titanic breakfast I would say."

My ear caught on that word right away and I became more certain that I had stumbled on a pearl nestling in the, as it were, sty of Hicksville.

"No god, madam," I demurred. "A mere man — Lloyd Bingham, an actor by profession. Actor-manager to be precise. You may have seen the show last night?"

"I was not at liberty to see it, sir."

"A pity. I would have acted better if I had seen you there, Miss . . .?"

She laughed and did modesty in that way — oh, you know — that way no man but a fool can misread, even if he is half drunk and looking on from the back row of a poorly lit provincial playhouse. Hate me for it if you will, but that was the moment my pearl turned golden.

"Swilley," she said. "Amelia Swilley."

She theatrically presented her hand and I theatrically kissed it. I was a little dizzy with the pace of it all. Just who was the spider here and who the fly? Miss Swilley observed that I had not eaten my fourth egg.

"Alas," said I, "I am discovered. I ordered it only to bring you closer."

"Not worth the price of an egg, I'm sure."

"But is not my hostess of the tavern a most sweet wench?" I asked.

The shutters opened on the limelight, the beam flooded down and I could see nothing but her, Amelia, as she replied at once and greatly to my surprise —

"As the honey of Hybla, my old lad of the castle."

"You know it?"

She made a face — disdainful, impatient.

"It's my vacation assignment — I'm at Wesleyan. I was supposed to be staying with a friend, but her mother died unexpectedly so it was no longer convenient."

"You're the daughter of the house, then?"

She cast a dejected eye about the gloomy dining room.

"I am afraid so."

I pushed the egg across the table and suggested it would be a sin to waste it. She sat down and with two neat movements crushed its skull and exposed its innards. I watched her eat and asked how long the vacation would keep her in Hicksville. She looked at me for a while, thoughtfully.

"Well, I don't really know, Mr Bingham. Why don't you tell me all about the theatre?"

I did so, and effectively too, for within half an hour Miss Amelia Swilley had decided on a new life. We agreed on a simple ruse freely adapted from *The Desperations of Dolores*, with which the company had had a good success the year before. I would leave something of great importance in my room, Amelia would discover it and feel obliged to take it personally to the station. She would deliver herself as well as my watch and telegraph her intentions back to Hicksville from the next station, thus escaping the "the triple-locked deep dungeon darkness of my life" as Dolores so feelingly refers to it in Act III as she topples from the upstage dais beneath the charging wheels of the Pittsburgh express.

That very night, scantily protected by the curtain on a second-class sleeping berth, Amelia pressed her maidenhead upon me. Her cheek lay against mine, hot and damp. Her breath was fast in my ear.

"Oh, Lloyd. I may call you Lloyd?"

"My darling."

And hidden within the rhythm of the train I heard no word of warning as she confessed to me — "Lloyd, I want *everything*."

What followed need not be recounted in detail. Suffice it to say that the fatal verities of magazine fiction were confirmed in ghastly detail. The proprieties were quickly observed, Amelia consenting to become Mrs Lloyd Bingham. The first act unfolded in spotless sunshine. Amelia excelled at minor parts and quickly graduated to the leading roles. She needed only to read her lines once to learn them and quickly became frustrated as she waited for others to catch up. At the curtain calls she was given more and accepted it all without question. The flowers were for her, the press notices and the stage-door loiterers. Within a year envy broke up the Bingham Stock Company and we were on our own. Breakfasting in her hotel bed, Amelia received the news calmly.

"We must be free, Lloyd. We must shake the dust from our feet."

She took a card from her night-stand and held it out to me.

"Last night I conversed with a gentleman from San Francisco. You might care to have a word with him."

Before the day was out we had signed for a ten-venue West Coast tour. I played Butler, Chauffeur, Fishmonger [Voice Offstage], Cyclist Passing Upstage Left to Right and the Queen of Sheba's Footstool. I counted the money and made up the accounts. Every time I caught sight of my name in the newspaper it turned out to be hers and not mine at all.

"Oh, Lloyd," said Amelia after a year. "It's so unfair — I get three times more money than you for only half the work and it's making me feel bad."

You can't say she wasn't a considerate woman.

"Why don't you just give up? You can be my full-time agent."

I travelled at her heels, was tolerated, was broken to the sound of "my husband". I watched the clocks in railway stations, then stood alone on a platform once the crowd had gone. There was a message at the telegraph office:

Dearest,
New engagement Kansas City. Stand by.
Ever Your Pearl.

I stood by. Years passed. I followed you, Amelia, in all the theatrical columns I could get. I watched your name change from Mrs Lloyd Bingham to Mrs Amelia Bingham to Miss Amelia Bingham. I read your notices for *The Power of Gold, Hearts are Trumps, The Charlatan, The Leash of Love* and felt proud. In Oshkosh I knocked a salesman down for saying he was a good friend of yours. I lay in wait for Acton Davies after he had made a beast of himself in the *Evening Sun*. I tracked him to the Hoffman Café and dealt out correction blow for blow. For you, Amelia, I damned near bit his finger off — "Lloyd the Loyal", "Cannibal Lloyd". You must have seen those stories, surely? What should I have done Amelia? The faster I ran towards you, the further away you got. We nearly met in

Washington. I had heard you were at the Garden Theatre, but the gods were ahead of me — I was arrested for exceeding the speed limit on Pennsylvania Avenue in the open Winton Six bought with your money.

She started her own company, became a producer in a small way. I began to pick up the odd little part again. They called them top-and-tail bills — one Bingham at the top and another at the bottom. I had hopes for a while and we were always together once a year to go back to Hicksville, the slate of her parents' disapproval long since wiped clean. They liked to see me driving the latest model and carrying the valises up the path. It didn't last long.

"Good news, dear. Look!"

A letter from Charles Frohman, Mr Broadway himself.

"An offer, Lloyd. And look at these figures. My goodness, Lloyd, just look at them. You won't have to do anything now."

I saw even less of her after that. I heard from a smirking acquaintance that divorce had been advised against on grounds of cost, "reputational risks" and because there didn't seem much point. She sent more money and I sent back flowers, though without ever learning if she could tell mine from the scores of others her dresser gathered up every night, stuffed into a cab and had sent to the nearest hospital. It was all New York then, and even London. Beautiful American Leading Lady fills Palace Theatre with *Big Moments from Great Plays*. I worried when the war started — I never knew if she was at sea, or on which ship. I still read the passenger lists when there's a sinking.

My spurned waitress passes, but I am unforgiven. I summon her hazy likeness all the same and make her lean her elbows on the table and rest chin in palm with that way she has and raise an encouraging eyebrow.

"It could all have been so different, Pearl. I could have been something. I met Mack Sennett in a bar once. He knew who I was."

Outside everything has gone quiet. The traffic has stopped on Broadway and the black-plumed cortège gathers before a line of police officers. Amelia is close. I shake my head at the thought and turn back to the empty chair on the other side of my table.

"You know — I could have been a Keystone Kop."

I let the enormity of the misfortune sink in and direct that a heavy, glycerine-bright, advertisement tear should gather in the corner of her eye. It's irresistibly real and I reach across to wipe it away. People look up as I put my arm out in front of me and gesture against thin air. I find the flesh-and-blood waitress standing nearby with a question on her face. I nudge the coffee cup and she slops it full of steaming black before moving on without a word.

And then what happens? What brought me here? The big news day a couple of weeks ago and I find I'm one of that ten, maybe twenty thousand in the world for whom it's also personal. I'm looking for my name again, rushing in a panic up and down the double column of First Cabin Passengers — Battersby, Bilicke, Bistio, Bloomfield, Braithwaite. She's not there, but before any calm can come to me I'm gripped by a thought so obvious, so right that I'm sure it's true. She's not a Bingham at all now, she's gone back all the way to Amelia Swilley. My eyes move right and down — Shymer, Sonneborn, Stockhouse, van Straaten, Tiberghien, Twenlo, Vanderbilt and valet. She's alive! I'm shaking and start to walk to disguise it. I get a drink at a bar, read the reports and go over the list again. And that's when I see it.

"Another whisky."

"Someone you know?"

I read the name half a dozen times, but it doesn't change. Charles Frohman, Frohman the showman, star-maker Charlie. Well, well, well. How should I feel, am I bereaved, have I lost the manager of my wife?

Wounded By Torpedoes
Appeals for Help Made
No Word of Prominent Men

I settle down at the bar and wait for the late edition. I'm the first to snatch a copy from the boy when he comes. I scan the bread-warm pages and there it is —

Frohman Lost, Theatre Mourns

And he made a good job of it too, made all his old clients proud of him at the end and left a little something for the newspaper boys as he went down. Swimming around in the waters off Kinsale with that charming little Rita Jolivet, struggling until he found the right words.

"Rita, my sweetness, take this down, won't you? Ahem! Why fear death? It is the most beautiful adventure that life gives us."

The buoyancy of inflated sentiment left him and down he went. Professional to the last. She of course survived — well they do, don't they? In the following days I read of the arrangements for the return of the sunken hero (he had bobbed up again somewhere else — I don't criticise; I've always had a weakness for the second curtain call myself). You read that too, Amelia, how could you not? I knew you would be here, not half a mile from this spot, I'm sure — this is one rendezvous not even you could break. I look out the window, sift the mourners. No, not yet — but somewhere close.

I tried to get in touch, Amelia — I mean, more persistently than usual. I got a card from your secretary — "Miss Bingham has received your communication and is grateful for your interest in her work." Perhaps you neglected to tell your secretary that you have a husband? If I embarrass you I'll change — just tell me how.

Did you read this — as you prepared over a late breakfast? I can see it. You make even black beautiful, Amelia. And your beautiful laugh as you read in your morning paper, the same one I have here, of Mrs S. R. Meissner of 1524 Thirty-First Street, Georgetown, recipient of the wisdom of Mr Charles Frohman from beyond the grave. "It is I, Charles Frohman, speaking. I want to tell everyone in the world there is no such thing as death. I called out for help and someone took my hand and they said to me, 'It is the greatest adventure in life.' I asked what they meant and they said,l 'Only what you have already said yourself.' I said I had spoken of death but my helper said to me, 'Why, this is death,' and I could hardly believe he was speaking the truth."

Should I give her a go, Amelia? Should I cross the widow Meissner's palm with silver and ask her for a few words from my wife? I suppose she'd ask me how and when you died. Tricky.

I can see that things are about to start. I leave some coins on the table, fold up my paper and leave.

The ears of the mourners, and of the horses await the signal. To the tap of a muffled drum the cortège steps out. The face I'm looking for isn't there and so I begin to make my way through the crowds down to the Temple Emanu-El at Fifth and Forty-Third. I get there in good time. Grief-featured, I am admitted to the synagogue gloom and make a search of the early arrivals. There is no one I know. All well and good — Amelia, I can be sure, would not waste her entrance by arriving too soon. I go out again and position myself carefully in the swelling audience, a spot just right to see the cars as they draw up to the steps. There is a steady stream, a few unknown faces, acquaintances mostly, a good show of my more fortunate colleagues. Now and then a famous face appears and a frisson runs through the onlookers. When it's a moving picture actor they strain forward and make a noise — urgent and inarticulate like a response at Mass. Mr Roscoe "Fatty"

Arbuckle eases himself from a covered sedan and labours up the steps with the help of an ebony cane with a black bombazine rosette. The comedian is impeccably dressed and dignified as a statesman, but habit still overwhelms someone in the crowd and they laugh crudely.

The hearse arrives and the undead remains of Charles Frohman are borne into the synagogue chattering away, for all I know, to the enterprising Mrs Meissner of Georgetown. An automobile is hard on its heels. Anytime now it could be her — my heart quickens and I feel a little sick as my hatband moistens and tightens around my head in the heat. A woman emerges from the car and the crowd reacts quietly. She is followed closely by a man. They look about themselves, count to three and slowly ascend. I am excited too — it is Rita Jolivet, Rita the survivor, the bearer of the great man's last words (from this side of the divide at least). The story of the *Lusitania* made flesh pauses by the elaborate portal. I've heard that the offers are coming in and a star is never at rest these days. Accordingly, she makes a *distrait* quarter-turn to the audience and looks down to signal that the emotion is about to go to her knees. She slumps onto the well-timed support of what will tomorrow be described as her "unknown gentleman friend". There is a low "Oohh" of sympathy. It seems to restore her. From somewhere deep within she finds the strength to go on and steps inside. Nicely done, Rita, you hard-hearted bitch.

I'm looking back up the street to get the first sight of every car that might still come. There are a few more and each one is a torment. Then there's a lull and I become certain that this is the moment. The minor cast members are out of the way, the pause is dramatic, in my head drums roll as I push my way closer to the front. Everything is right, every term of the incantation has been pronounced and must, surely, summon her. When a man looks at me strangely I realise I am saying her name out loud. At the top of the steps men take pocket-watches from their waistcoats. The doors of the synagogue are closed and the crowd goes slack and dilutes itself back into the city.

I go too, vacantly, and drift into the park to find myself a bench over which the last, brown-edged blossom of a cherry tree scatters with every turn of the breeze. It is the edge of summer, the moment at which trees are in new and immaculate leaf. Strollers and their children abound. Connections are everywhere on display — marriages, offspring, friendships. I have to take care not to turn and talk to the absence at my side.

So, Amelia — I was wrong again. And you too, Charlie. Can you see her from up there, do your files tell you where she's working tonight? Hundreds of miles away, I'm sure — maybe thousands. I feel her distance now, as intensely as I felt her closeness half an hour ago. I thought she would turn up for you, Charlie, I really did. But she didn't, no more for you than for me — ah, well. A brotherly tear for the late Mr Charles Frohman surprises me and I unfold my newspaper — President Expects Germans to Agree; Spain Opens Doors to Jews; Greeks Vote for War; Few Americans in

London — smallest consumption of cocktails and least use of ice ever recorded, but fewer spoons stolen, say hoteliers.

I turn a page now and again like I'm really reading it and so come back to that absurd column on Mrs Meissner and the dead impresario. For the first time I catch the last paragraph. In the background the trees and the sunlight, the birds and the people all come together like those bits in symphonies that change everything you feel just at the end. And exactly what was it that the dead Frohman whispered to the clairvoyant, what was the message? "I want people to understand that everything depends on the way they have tried to live, not on the way they have lived, but on the way they have most tried to live, because we cannot all attain to what we would most wish to do. I thank God for letting me write this down."

For a while I have to keep the paper steady in front of my face. When at last I can put it down, words and setting mingle — on the stage it would be the cue for the next musical number and the summer strollers would step into a pattern and dance. My heart lifts as I too receive a message — that the world is not indifferent, that the invisible hand that guides it cannot tolerate too much unfairness and must turn the fortunes of this or that man when long-delayed justice demands it. I am made a promise, an offer on easy, though admittedly uncertain, terms. A law of nature reveals itself to me, its certain operation guarantees my future. This cannot last, my life will get better — and soon.

Marquis

I must have seen Henry Ford many times before he was rich, but not once did I notice him. Henry, Clara and the growing Edsel would have been regular attenders at St Paul's long before I was able to pick them out from their fellow worshippers. It was one of my own who first drew them to my attention. The more progressive members of the Detroit clergy came together regularly in those days to disburse some modest charitable funds of which we had the trust. I believe it was at the end of one of our Monday meetings, probably on the steps of the deanery, that I felt a hand on my elbow and a discreet, envious voice in my ear.

"So, Samuel — I hear you've bagged the Fords. Play those cards right and you'll not be wanting to spend any more time with us arguing over ten dollars here or twenty there."

When I asked what he meant I received only a knowing look and a tap of the finger on the side of his nose.

"The automobile man?" I asked. "He comes to St Paul's?"

"You really don't know?"

I listened to a description of the tall, angular industrialist, the dowdy sheet-anchor wife and the neat, bright son and heir.

"Ah, yes," I said. "Now I know who you mean. So that's him, is it?"

"Be careful, Samuel. You know what they say — money is to the modern clergyman as the incense of Noah to the nostrils of God, a sweet smell indeed. If you won't have him someone else will."

My fellow pastor smiled at me, tipped his hat and went on his way with a virtuous spring in his step.

It was, however, by an entire coincidence that I received an invitation from the Fords not more than a week after this conversation. Henry was already a wealthy man, but not yet one of those half-dozen or so extreme exceptions that chance or genius throws up in every generation. He was well-rooted in his middle years and had known just enough of hard work and poverty not to have become wholly detached from his fellow human beings. That day, talking and drinking punch in the garden at Edison Avenue, I met characters in brighter plumage and more heavily freighted by far with their own self-regard. I heard the established old merchant names of the city, the senior partners of the leading law firms, the farming families whose land had become the rentable parcels of Detroit and the old French aristocrats who had first survived and then been borne up by the regrettable Anglo-Saxon flood. They seemed to be conscious of the favour they had done Henry by accepting his invitation, and also baffled and a little amused by the fact that Henry, with his easy manners and his out-of-town accent, was not at all conscious of this favour and did not even seem to be aware of who they were.

I, a poor man in such company, was the only one thinking of money that day — and then only because of what my colleague had said to me. I don't believe a single one of those guests could have imagined that within a short space of time their economic relation to their host would be so dramatically reversed. None of them, save for Henry himself, had any ability at all to see into the future. Within a year of that encounter Henry Ford would have been able to dispose of the entire wealth of one of those men with a cheque from his personal account and not notice the difference. Within three years you could have bought and sold that gathering for less than a month's interest on his capital. I can't tell you what lies at the heart of Henry Ford — that is as obscure to me now as when I first shook his hand and gave him my name — but I will say that he is the same with several hundreds of millions beneath him as he was with ten thousand and I doubt that any man in history has been less changed, for good or ill, by incalculable wealth.

I talked little to Henry on that first social occasion — I was merely introduced, complimented on the "good sound practicality" of my preaching and passed on into the throng. I exchanged pleasantries with this or that leading member of Detroit society and two or three times drifted on the edges of Henry's own conversations. I watched the shifting circles of listeners silently communicate their bemusement, eye to eye, as Henry explained the transforming power of the machine and how his gasoline tractor would extend the revolution from town to country. When they began to believe him they became uncomfortable. These were men who already had the world the way they wanted it, whereas for Henry staying still was the sin of sins — plant him in Paradise and he would go to Hell for the sake of the journey.

The afternoon would have been inconsequential had I not found myself becalmed by a bed of roses. The buds were breaking — enough for the first colours to show, but still several days from blooming. A short, rather plain woman in early middle years had just crossed the lawn to join me. I gestured over the roses with an empty punch cup.

"On the edge of glory — I think that's when I like them best."

Her face lit up. I thought at the time, though quite wrongly, that it was a little exaggerated.

"What a lovely phrase — and I'm *so* pleased you like roses."

She held out her hand.

"Clara Ford, and I'm sorry I missed you earlier — kitchen panic. Tell me, which one do you like most?"

It was apparent from the outset that I knew little of roses and my hostess a great deal. What I clumsily described by colour and size she would name with poetic relish as the Agnes, the Reine de Violettes, the Blush Damask and the Belle Poitevine, the Baltimore Belle and Shakespeare's Eglantine. She turned and pointed to something reddish clambering aggressively around the porch colums.

"My Zéphirine Drouhin. Henry didn't notice it when he bought the house, but I would have bought it just for that."

I hesitated, fearing that it might seem insincere to agree too readily with such an improbable statement.

"You must come back in a fortnight, Reverend Marquis."

"Samuel, please."

"I will show it to you then and you will understand. In fact I will show it to you blindfolded. Have you noticed that? — you only tell me what they look like. The best conversation I ever had about roses was with a blind man. He could name them by scent and was never wrong."

From such auspicious beginnings we had a long and excellent talk. The subject of the rose in literature put me on surer ground and showed how willing Mrs Ford was to be taught as well as teacher. She claimed a great love of reading and a nostalgia for those first schoolday encounters with lines she still loved. We found we were at one on the pleasures and high importance of reading and I mentioned a school in a poor quarter of the city I had long been associated with and had struggled to improve.

"Such industry! Such hope! And yet so little chance of any of it being fulfilled."

With keen interest and gentle tact, Mrs Ford obtained the name and address of this school and the name of its principal teacher, all without the slightest suggestion that anything was being asked for, or granted.

Within three weeks I had indeed returned for my further education in the matter of roses. I had also returned to my pet elementary school and found there, as I had hoped, a scene of transformation. New glass replaced the old cracked panes, bright pictures were on the walls, new books on every desk and outside in the cramped yard, a border freshly dug and planted with roses. The children too were changed — awoken by the revelation that they really were provided for by an invisible power. I stood at the back of the class. Thirty bright-green copies of the Reverend McGuffey's *Eclectic Reader* were open at the same page — the very book for which Clara and Henry particularly had such feeling, the book which had done most to form that small part of the magnate's brain not wholly possessed with matters mechanical.

"Now, children," asked the teacher. "Who can tell me about Shylock?"

Thirty hands go up as one. Small bodies squirm with anxiety to be the first to answer.

As her husband rose, Clara Ford also became prominent in Detroit society. Her house has never quite been a salon, but what figures Detroit had to muster would often be there and what they had to say would be said. I became a part of this and the Episcopalian Church and my own causes did not suffer as a result. Henry was often absent and even when he was there, on some evenings and the occasional weekend, it was usually for a short time only. We understood that he was an active part of what the rest of us were fated passively to observe. We suspected at some simple level that like a projectionist in a picture playhouse, if he failed in his work the story would stop or the next day's newspaper be blank. Sometimes I would stay on after a worthy talk in the Ford drawing room or a summer garden party that had strayed long into the evening. When she was unsure of what to think of them, Clara would raise the issues of the day or hint at her worries about Edsel or how she wished Henry would not work so hard. Her devotion to Henry was absolute and had about it something of the martyr, unwilling ever to acknowledge needs for which her husband did not provide. We knew each other well by the time she turned to me in the garden and stopped in the middle of a sentence.

"Samuel, I would like to think of you as my spiritual adviser. I already do, but I realise I haven't asked and it seems presumptious. May I use that phrase, just to myself?"

If I hesitated it was only because I was so moved. I declared that it was an honour and hoped from that day on there would be some true service she could ask of me, that I could say "yes" to and be happy.

The years passed steadily, news of other lives our only landmarks. Roosevelt went and Taft came, pulled in the presidental victoria between high, shovelled mounds of March snow. Suffragettes paraded on the same day, led by a young woman with a sword all in white on a tall white horse. After him, Wilson, waving from the back seat of an automobile. A Frenchman flew across the English Channel. Talk of war meant prohibition, then Mexico. Harriman, the great railroad man, died. Henry read the obituaries and was gloomy for a week while on the Pennsylvania Railroad the locomotives went ninety-nine miles in an hour. In May the next year we gathered out at Dearborn where the new mansion was to be built. We looked up at Halley's comet and drank to the future as we passed through its tail at 2,500 miles a minute while farmers out west locked themselves in cyclone cellars and workers stayed home to spend their last day on earth with their families. The Standard Oil Company was broken up and the *Mona Lisa* stolen. Mark Twain died — Clara and I reread his books — the *Los Angeles Times* building blew up. A Norwegian stood at the South Pole and Mrs Alice Longworth smoked a cigarette. Henry visited a slaughterhouse. He watched and calculated as the butchers stood still and the carcasses moved past them on hooks. He went to his factory and shook his head as he looked down on the wastefulness of movement. Waste was immoral. From then on the cars moved and the men who made them stood still. The price went down again and the model letter ticked up to T. Expansion gave way to explosion.

China became a republic, its Manchu dynasty living on in the opera house alone. The *Titanic* and John Jacob Astor met their end as the band played on — one of my own particular favourites which the Fords and the rest of the congregation sang in St Paul's the following Sunday.

Hold me up, mighty waters,
Keep my eye on things above.

Germany increased her naval budget and automobiles could now be started with the touch of a button. Women, for whom wrestling with the starting handle had been considered a gross immodesty, became customers in their own right. The American Suffrage Union wrote Henry to thank him for the physical emancipation of their sex and asked him for money to help finish the job. They were not the only petitioners — it was from this year that the gates of the Ford residence were closed and guarded every hour of the day. Herman Rosenthal found his death beneath a streetlight in New York. The seven police officers standing nearby saw nothing, caught no one and obtained no evidence. John Schrank took a shot at Theodore Roosevelt, only the thickness of the manuscript of the speech the great hunter was about to give saving his life.

The Ford businesses abroad were growing fast. Because Henry could call it work, this made Clara's longed-for trip to England possible at last. Edsel went too — nineteen years old in 1912 and with no more independence of thought than a be-medalled and feather-hatted crown prince awaiting his inheritance. Long Island friends saw them off on the ship and gave Clara a seal-bound *Record of My Trip* for the great adventure. She wrote in it assiduously — extracts became letters, some of them to me. I heard of the Rolls-Royce in which they were driven round the country, of Bristol and Bath, Windsor Castle, the Piccadilly Hotel, Buckingham Palace and shopping in London as the men clubbed together on their own for the sacred rites of "business". I heard of Warwick and of finding the house in Linen Street where Clara's mother had lived as a girl. A photograph was taken on the step and the sexton disturbed to show the parish records. Warwick Castle diverted them on their return. A piece of Chinese porcelain in the great hall got under Clara's skin — she yearned for it, thought of how finely it would set off her peonies and idly mentioned to Henry how nice it would be if they could find another like it. I heard of offers being made, refused, repeated and refused again. The story went quiet and I cheered inwardly for the old powers of resistance, of decency. I told myself that it must have been Clara who had called a halt to the vulgar game. And yet, a month after the Fords' return, at a charitable reception, there was the Earl of Warwick's porcelain and Clara herself making me feel a little sad as she called it a punch bowl and asked if I didn't think it was fine.

There were great floods in Indiana and Ohio. Men rowed boats in Dayton like Venetians. Three thousand were said to have died, but the waters receded before the universal cleansing some anticipated. Our time, it seemed, had not yet come. Mr J. Pierpont Morgan died, thus moving Henry a step closer to being the richest man in the world and stimulating in him another week of reflection and discontent. The President threw a switch and sent across a continent of wires the spark that would detonate beneath the

Gamboa dyke, over the remains of which the Pacific and Atlantic waters would mingle in the Panama Canal. Mary Pickford was the Queen of the Movies, her name known even to those who had never seen such an entertainment. The appearance of Broncho Billy on the streets of Cleveland caused a riot and out on the plains the cattlemen went short-handed as their cowboys rode off to find better wages in front of the camera.

It had been a good year for Ford. That Christmas the astonishing figures in the company accounts, the spirit of the season, and perhaps also a little problem with staff turnover combined to bring on the idea of the five-dollar day. Henry became a public man as never before and I sat in his office with the sound of a riot coming through the windows as I listened to a machine-shop boy's explanation of the world.

"There's something called sociology, Samuel. It's new and scientific and gets right to the heart of people. It tells you just what they're like and what you have to do to change them. If someone was starting religion today all over again this is what it would be."

The offer, as you know, was made but not at first accepted. The Ford Sociological Department came into being without me and I continued my life in the Church. I heard tell of its works, read of them in the newspapers, endured reminders from Henry and sometimes, less directly, from Clara too.

The year wound on in innocence. The news was all of things getting bigger and faster. George Westinghouse, who had quite a hand in this aspect of our history, died.

"He was only sixty-eight," I remember Henry telling me. He shook his head and looked distant as he did the alarming arithmetic in his head.

Kaiser Wilhelm radio-telegraphed his greetings straight to President Wilson. The newspapers told us of the amiable German's latest entertainment — Live Targets, a cinematographic device of some sort which allowed the user to shoot at moving projections. In one May afternoon the Kaiser destroyed three hundred aeroplanes, animals and human beings and declared himself highly delighted. He ordered the machine installed in various cadet schools and the same pleasure was soon available here at the larger travelling funfairs. Cartoonists enjoyed a great boost to their income as Josephus Daniels decided we should have a "dry" navy. The General Federation of Women's Clubs took up the prohibition fashion and pronounced a solemn ban on the tango and the hesitation waltz.

An assassination in Europe attracted little attention. The war itself unfolded slowly in the minds of most Americans. For the men at the top it arrived dramatically on the last day of July as the New York Stock Exchange was forced to close by an avalanche of sell orders from Europe, where every other means of turning paper back into gold had already been used up. The conflict was baffling, antique. Maps and tables of dates and photographs in the newspapers of men in brass helmets, swords and operatic uniforms had no meaning in our progressive republic. American business boomed, but Henry Ford was one of the few not to entertain the purchasing agents of the belligerent powers. Henry did not approve of war. It upset him. Dead men did not buy cars. In the greatest industrial plants in America there was no war.

Socially, the only change to his life was a further swelling of the ranks of petitioners. To utopianists, perpetual motioneers, paper-money nuts, workshy geniuses in need of annuities, respectable cadgers for church and college, dog doctors and the proponents of the artificial cow were now added the peace campaigners. To a few of these, the most persistent, the secrets so long withheld from the rest of humanity had been vouchsafed — they not only disapproved of war, they knew how to stop it once and for all. There were schemes of such arcane delicacy their full detail could not be revealed until funding was in place; occult elixirs of peace waiting to be stirred to life and efficacy with a liberal admixture of dollars. Against them all Henry hardened his heart. It was his conviction that no one wished to tell him anything he did not already know, or discuss any problem to which he did not already have the solution.

"I know how to stop the war, Samuel," he revealed to me one day. "Men aren't fools — give a man a car and let him drive a hundred miles this way or that whenever he pleases and he'll see for himself that men in one place are no different from men in another. If he's been told otherwise it's lies and he'll see for himself it's nothing but lies. There's nothing I could teach the great manufacturer in the sky about standardised production — humanity is a one-model range. Have people never asked themselves why you can take two people from the opposite sides of the world and still fit them together just like they were made for it? Piston and cylinder, just like they should be. Understand that and war makes no sense. When there are enough cars in the world, Samuel, there'll be no more wars."

No employee or would-be recipient of his charity could ever contradict him. His peace of mind was the particular care of twenty men, at their head the saturnine form of his private secretary Mr Ernest G. Liebold, who lay course upon course of mortar and brick between Henry and the world.

The calm that came from ignoring everything outside himself became one of Henry's chief characteristics at this time. I recall when he accepted my invitation to the most important church reception of the year. There I was, shepherding him through the press of dignitaries, when someone took my arm and drew me away for an urgent word with a colleague. When I returned I found that a line had formed in front of Henry as it might on Easter Sunday before the Holy Father himself. Each supplicant explained their case in half a minute and left calling cards with sums of money written on the back and the number and type of motor vehicles they could best use. I myself was besieged with enquiries about the nature of Mr Ford, how to ingratiate oneself with him, the flatteries to which he was most susceptible, the weak points in the vaults and strongrooms of his goodwill. Ray drove us back that evening and Henry and I sat in silence for half the journey. I was in deep embarrassment and barely articulate as I stammered out my apology — that

I had not foreseen such a crude display, there had been no improper motive in my invitation, that he must not, above all, think there was any league or compact between myself and my fellow clergy. Henry smiled and said nothing.

I learned later that not one of the supplicants from that evening received a single dollar. By various means I was let known that for me, the friend of his wife, the discusser of roses, it would be different — the offer that had been made still stood and could be accepted at any time. As I worked hard with other rich men for fifty dollars for a school or a slum clinic, I knew that the head of the Ford Sociological Department was equipped with a company chequebook on which his signature alone was good for up to a hundred times as much. My religion and Henry Ford's resources — was there anything to be said against such a marriage? It was in the drawing room of the Ford residence on Edison Avenue with the Earl of Warwick's vase gracing the window sill that I finally made my decision. So it was that I walked with the employees of Henry Ford, indeed became one of them and gave the others the helping hand he had spoken of. I became the designated conduit of their employer's personal interest, the love of Ford made flesh.

"Samuel," said Clara as she leaned forward that day and patted me on the back of the hand, "I am so pleased."

The war in Europe settled down and apart from a few cranks most people lost interest. The news repeated itself, changing little from month to month. There would be sudden flare-ups — panicky sightings of submarines in the Hudson, lurid talk of Germano-Mexican plots and angry knock-down debates on neutrality, "preparedness" and being too proud to fight.

Alexander Graham Bell spoke into a telephone the exact same words he had spoken thirty-nine years before. Only this time he spoke in New York and was heard in San Francisco. Wireless experiments were an even greater sensation — the voice of the American Telephone and Telegraph Company President waving out from New York and halfway across the ocean to Honolulu and into the ears of Lloyd Espenchied as he crouched in a hut on the shores of Pearl Harbor. A loyal German tried to blow up a bridge with dynamite. Charlie Chaplin walked into Mack Sennett's office and asked to be given a chance. Within six months few people did not know his name. Lincoln Beachy, famous for flying his plane under the Steel Arch bridge at Niagara and appearing through the mists as if from nothing, flew in circles over the San Francisco Exposition, crashed and was killed. The *Eastland* cast off and capsized in Chicago. Eight hundred and forty-four lives ended more quickly than on any battlefield.

It was a busy time for me, doing the Lord's work and not just preaching it. Once Henry had got his way and installed me at the head of his new project I saw much less of him than before. A distant master suited me well and I was able to get on according to my own ideas as much as Henry's. It pleased me to become a well-known figure in the poorer parts of the city and it is no exaggeration to say that soon there were not many streets in Detroit I could walk down without exchanging a few words with a Ford man of one rank or another. I found myself a sort of bishop presiding over seventy-seven parishes, each containing an average of five hundred and twenty-three communicants with the Ford faith. The investigators were their priests, connecting them to the bounty of the Company or threatening excommunication if they should fall by the wayside once too often. The newspapers were gloomy, but I looked forward to days of uplift, living the parable of the talents, doing what we could to ensure that every Ford dollar was spent the Ford way. We distributed *Helpful Hints for Ford Employees*. From the back cover Joe Polianski, his wife and three clean and neatly dressed children smiled at the camera and held up the banner — We Bless the Day the Investigators Entered Our House. The English language advanced across the Polish and German quarters, new furniture was bought and the sidewalks piled with the old and dirty, books appeared on shelves and new shoes on young feet, the stairwells of tenements smelled more of soap than whisky. Back at the great Highland Park plant these new men would enter shift after shift, machined to engage in the great common enterprise, turning smoothly in their allotted place as the profits of philanthropy piled ever higher.

The Sociological Department was friend and pastor to all Ford men on $200 a month or less. Thus we covered a wide range, from the simple-minded shop sweeper to the skilled men, foremen, white-collar clerks and draughtsmen. It was our job to guide and foster these ranks in the steady life of the Ford family. Less officially, I worked to protect them and repair the damage whenever there was a change in the weather. "Reorganisation" was a rumour which put anxiety, or downright fear, into everyone who heard it. Things would start with an uneasy feeling. There would be a darkening of the sky, a pitched tightness in the mind such as epileptics speak of before a fit. Henry himself would appear more deeply lined. Normally taciturn, he would become secretive, almost entirely silent and his gaze would be sharper, exhausted. The storm would certainly follow, as fearsome and arbitrary as thunder and lightning to the ancients. Policies would be changed, rules turned inside-out, men transferred from what they knew to what they did not know or discharged without warning or explanation. When the chaos died down I and a few others would man the ambulances. The sacked would be quietly re-hired, the transferred edged back to the jobs they did best and abolished departments reconstructed under the disguise of a new name.

We were in the midst of one such convulsion when I found myself in Henry's office. It was not clear why I had been summoned and in the end I never did find out, or not exactly. I found him seated behind his desk in the corner, pale and worn as he was at these times and distracted by great events elsewhere. He greeted me and waved at the chair where I should sit. He pushed the newspaper away and rubbed his eyes.

"Who was Frohman?"

I explained that he was a man of the theatre, the country's biggest Broadway producer. The information had no effect. He folded the paper and dropped it in the waste basket.

"Vanderbilt too. You know it says in there, Samuel, that it cost three million dollars to build her and only four thousand for the torpedo that sank her."

For three seconds he concentrated on the remote corner of the room.

"That's two fifteenths of one per cent. One hell of a margin — if you'll excuse me."

I agreed briefly and waited for him to get to the point. Henry looked past me, played with a pencil, pinched the bridge of his nose and screwed his eyes tight shut like it was too long since he had last slept.

"You'll have been hearing things, I expect."

I said the men were confused, that they didn't know what was coming next. The plant was full of talk.

"You must tell them there are reasons for it."

I waited.

"Just tell them there are good reasons for it. A man can't argue against a good reason, can he?"

There was a pause, a familiar vagueness in the eyes as he turned inward for what he needed.

"It's in the nature of some things to stand still, Samuel, and for others always to be moving. Change is good. Change is what made all this. What you have to understand, Samuel, is that . . . well, that in our world stillness is death. We have to . . ."

And with that borrowed phrase there followed one of those lengthy statements that collectively express the obscurity of Henry Ford's mind. It was of the times — as discordant and fragmentary as the new music, the connections between one clause and the next twisted, tenuous or, even to the most subtle thinker, wholly absent. This particular essay on inevitable progress, the greatest good for the greatest number, the best of all possible world and the breaking of eggs to make omelettes was still in its early stages when I became aware of other voices coming from the anteroom. Henry seemed nervous, but continued speaking. Outside, Liebold was suddenly loud and there was a bump against the panels of the double doors, though they did not open. Henry paused and shifted his position. He looked down and fiddled with the edge of his cuffs. He mumbled something about the drawing office before returning to his theme. The disturbance grew and as the situation threatened to become ridiculous I stood up and excused myself for a minute to deal with it.

"You do that," said Henry, getting out of his chair as if to come with me.

I found Liebold nose to nose with a man I knew well — the mild-mannered Mr Perlmann, chief clerk of the drawing office. I had never seen him in such a state before. His hands trembled and he was rigid with anger. Liebold was sweating and had his back to the door. It seemed certain that any second the dispute must go beyond words. The usual anteroom crew looked on in eager fascination.

"Well?" demanded Perlmann. "I'll not leave without an answer. I have thirty men waiting to hear what this means. Are they transferred? How are they to do their work? Where? Why are they being treated like this? When Mr Ford hears about this . . ."

He turned to me as I slipped out from Henry's office.

"Dr Marquis — your meeting has finished?"

Liebold edged to the left to block Perlmann's way. I managed to get the two men into Liebold's tiny side office and closed the door behind us. The secretary staunchly refused to say anything and Perlmann could never quite bring himself to the heart of the matter. I began to see that it would have humiliated him even to mention it. He kept repeating that Henry could know nothing about it, that he would be very angry when he found out and that a personal interview with his employer would put everything straight. At a loss for what to do, I hoped that he might be right and promised to get him his chance. I went back into Henry's office but found it as empty as when I had first been there and the side door open, the one that led to the private washroom and through that to the fire stairs beyond.

I soon learned the story of the drawing office from other sources, and then played my part in reconstructing it. In the end I don't believe there was a single man who was not rehired. The truth was the company couldn't work without them. Outwardly nothing tangible had been lost, but tomorrow was never a certainty again for those men and that must have been the purpose of the whole affair, or it had no purpose at all. Between Henry and myself the episode was never mentioned in so many words. But the preacher in me had not quite died and on a social occasion when I had him to myself for a moment I spoke a few words as if they had been said to me by someone else, not as if I agreed or approved them in the slightest but merely as a fact, and a humorous one at that, about what could be heard around the lower depths of the Ford world. I let him know how it was said that a man in the Ford organisation had but a short time to live and is full of care, that he cometh up and is cut down like a flower, that he never continueth long on the job. Henry's eyes narrowed. He looked at me sideways, played with the glass of soda water in his hands. He said nothing as that distant, calculating expression returned to his features. The burden of his wealth became clear and I saw that I was suspected, weighed sadly as nothing but another traitor in waiting. Clara came up. She chatted cheerfully but then stopped and frowned as she caught the chill between us. She smiled uncertainly. The Ford marriage is a curiosity. They are very different people, but when together there are times when they hardly seem to be individuals at all. I did not believe that Clara either could, or would, save me from another of Henry's reorganisations.

Ray

Back in the winter of '14 I roomed with Ledenev and his wife. Ledenev was an aristocrat, a fully skilled machinist earning twice what I did. It meant the apartment was better than most and I was lucky to have a place there. I made sure I got on well with them.

Sometimes we would see little of each other, at others our shifts would coincide and we went and came back from Highland Park together and ate and slept at the same hours. Going up and down the stairs of that tenement with Ledenev I learned five languages just to say "good morning" to the others in the building. In that part of town there was no fire under the melting pot — two words of each language was all I ever learned.

That winter was a hard one. Ledenev and I took all the extra work we could find and it was on account of this that his apartment was the only one never to fall short of coal. On Sundays the place would fill with eastern Jews — Russians, Germans, a few Poles. The place was full of pamphlets, newspapers and books. They piled up and we had to move round them like the place was a library. Whenever one of these books was brushed to the floor Ledenev would wince and make a show of picking it up and dusting it off. His worst fights with Shula were over which newspapers they could burn and which they must keep. Making parts for cars was a stage in Ledenev's journey. He always let you know that your paths might be crossing for a while, but that his would soon take him elsewhere.

On Sundays, the visitors would wave the pamphlets, newspapers and books at each other and the talk would become riotous, with Ledenev in the thick of it. I would sit in the corner like a child, too dead-tired from the week's work to pay any attention. He gave me things and told me I should read them. "Go on," he would say, "it's in English." But it wasn't for me. To be honest I don't know where they got the energy or why they were bothering. Two or three languages were on the go at once, but they seemed to understand each other well enough. Sometimes I got the idea they were plotting something, but they never minded me being there. I picked up only a few words that were the same or little changed in each language. For a while I thought of cracking their code, but never got very far. Of the words they had in common, "Ford" is the only one I still remember. When the noise got too much Shula would shush them down and they would all wave their hands and say sorry and start again quieter, but not for long. She would smile at me then, as if to say, "Yes, it is all nonsense. Noisy, hopeless nonsense — but it keeps them happy."

She would be sewing aprons for a little extra money, or just lying back looking up at the grimy ceiling with her hands knitted over her belly, waiting for her baby in the spring. I sat near her by the window that looked out over the back courts. The other side of the building was close and as the winter afternoons drew in the lights would come on one by one. Dim vertical stripes showed the stairwells and brighter patches on either side were the rooms. They would flicker as figures moved in front of the bulbs. The sculleries looked onto the back as well and there was one, a couple of floors down from the top, where a woman was in the habit of standing in her stone sink and washing herself from head to toe. Maybe one time in five I was lucky enough to catch her and that was a good weekend for me. Then the Jews were complaining they couldn't read in the afternoon gloom and Shula put her lights on a few minutes earlier. My picture frame lit up and my sink bather saw me looking down on her and that was the end of that.

When I came back from the riot I still had a streak of blood on my face, though it wasn't mine. Shula fussed about me as I cleaned up and kept asking about Ledenev who hadn't come back yet. I said he must be fine, that he had been inside working his lathe, that he had what the others wanted and that was why there was a riot. I told her then that I had seen Mr Ford, actually seen him. I told her the sight of him had stopped me cold and that he was a strange-looking man, but I didn't say what I was doing at the time. Then I was summoned the next morning and you know about that. Within a week I had twice the money and within a month three times more than before. I got a place of my own and packed my bag and said goodbye to the Ledenevs. They didn't pretend much that they were sad to see me go. They had the new five-dollar wage and the baby coming and the books piling up and all that, so I understood.

Now the more you have, the more some people will take from you, and that's what made so much work for me and the boys. We patrolled the perimeter as before and we kept our ears open for union talk and dealt with that too. We got friendly with the scrap-metal dealers in the city and found out who was stealing all that copper wire. We visited homes to check in tool boxes for anything that shouldn't be there and when the men stole from each other, we helped them out there as well. The old coat racks went and were replaced with pulleys. The bell rang at the start of the shift and the coats and lunch pails were hauled up to the ceiling way out of reach. Mr Ford was very pleased. "The perfect industrial solution to human nature," he called it — "if you can't fly you can't steal." The men worked the first half of the shift getting hungrier and hungrier just thinking of those lunch pails hanging above their heads. Then the bell would ring for the lunch hour and the pulleys would come down. "Manna from heaven!" one guy always joked. Thirty minutes later everything had to be back on its hook and the bell would ring again and up it went, out of the way for another four hours. It was better really — you weren't worrying who was at your things and it cut down on the ugly rumours. No one was suspected, because no one was trusted.

Mr Ford liked to walk around the plant himself to see that things were going right. In those days things were getting so much bigger so much faster it was like a completely different place every month. He used to stop by the lathes and talk to the skilled men about their work. Sometimes the men would clam up if he talked to them, wondering what it was all about really, frightened in case something wasn't right. He got used to my company and from then on whenever he walked the shop floors I was with him. It felt good walking there by his side. We passed Ledenev one day, working at his lathe. He gave me quite a look, but I didn't care. That's my advice — arrange things so a great man gets used to you being there. I'd say that's the best an ordinary Joe can get in this life.

They taught me how to drive and life speeded up. Sometimes I drove Mr Ford himself when he was going to a function in the evenings or at the weekends and he didn't want to have to bother about anything himself. That's how I met Mrs Ford who's a real lady and has always treated me well. I'd do anything for her, just as I would for her husband. They gave me money for a suit of clothes so I wouldn't look out of place and I began to see things I never thought I would and learn how to handle myself with all sorts of people. I even had Mr Thomas Edison in the back of my car once, though not everyone believes me.

There has never been a name for my job. I do what is required and whatever doesn't fit neatly with the other men. Mr Ford always likes to say he can rely on me and when he needs some special sort of reliability that's my job. One way or another I've ended up seeing most of the Ford Motor Company, and in the end that included the Sociological Department. Everyone talked about it and no one liked it and things certainly didn't get any better when the Reverend took over. According to the grapevine he was some sort of favourite of Mrs Ford but to the men he was just Slimy Sam, always poking his nose in where it didn't belong. Me — I ended up in the middle and did my best to say nothing to no one.

For a long time the Sociological men looked after themselves. Then one of their moral uplifters woke a drunken polack at the wrong time and got his hair mussed. They all ran for their new Model Ts and drove back to Highland Park. They had a conference in their office and someone took a crayon and coloured in the map on the wall. Red was those parts of the city where folks were less passionate about self-improvement. Whenever one of Slimy Sam's college boys had to take his clipboard out to a red block either me or one of my men had to go with him.

That's how I found myself back at Ledenev's a year and a half after I'd left. The Sociological Department had long since lost the element of surprise. People would know in advance which area they were heading for on any particular day, and even if they didn't whole blocks would swing into action as soon as their cars were seen pulling up at the sidewalk. Clean clothes would be placed in the top of laundry baskets, lodgers would brush themselves down, pomade their hair and rehearse their stories about being blood relatives from out of town just come on a visit. Windows would open all at once and cough dust into the air like this too was a factory and every part of it running off the same powertrain. Bibles and schoolbooks from the Ford English School would be placed on tables and opened to show how piety had been interrupted. The contents of ashtrays were tipped into drawers and water dripped from the overflow pipes as whisky bottles were lowered into lavatory cisterns. That was the deal — the investigators treated the employees like children, and the employees made fools of the investigators.

Usually I had little to do except hang around the cars in the street while the questions were being asked and the forms filled. But being in that neighbourhood made me feel kind of uneasy. I recognised some of the faces in the street and a couple of folk nodded back at me uncertainly. The word had gone out that there was a reorganisation on and it made everyone tense. Anyway, after a quarter of an hour I went in and climbed the stairs to the top apartment. The door was open. I heard Shula's voice giving short answers, and a man who spoke much more than she did. Between questions he talked on with a stagey casualness like a dentist who knew he was about to hurt you. I rapped my knuckles on the door frame and went in. There was a moment of non-recognition in Shula's face and then a look of relief. She turned her back on the investigator as we greeted each other and asked about the usual things. The other man was younger than me. You could see the care he took over his appearance. He had a sort of marble face that looked like he must have shaved it every two hours and he held a clipboard and the green fountain pen his mother gave him for his birthday. He knew who I was, of course, and it wasn't easy for him to ask me to leave. He looked sternly at his clipboard all the same, at the questions that remained to be asked and then looked straight at me and raised an eyebrow like some high-handed society doctor asking to be left alone with his patient. Shula reacted at once.

"You'll stay, won't you?"

"Sure," I said. "There's a lot to catch up on."

I glared back at the young investigator, pleased with my victory, and let him know that he should carry on without worrying about me.

The apartment had changed. A new shelf had been clumsily attached to the wall where it supported a small Chinese jar and a dozen books which were now the only ones to be seen. Prominent at the end of this short row was the Ford pamphlet *Helpful Hints*. Its advice on light and airiness had been ruthlessly followed. The stacks of newspapers had all gone. The place smelled of paint and new rose-patterned curtains hung at the window. I looked out and down two floors to see the white square of the sink I used to watch so keenly all Sunday afternoon. There was a fat armchair and a soft red rug on the floor. In the corner, in a wooden pen, a sturdy eighteen-month-old girl dropped a red wooden brick onto a green one. We eyed each other cautiously as she picked up the brick and tried to fit it into her mouth.

"Getting enough sleep? Yes? And your husband? That's good."

Shula and the investigator were just out of sight, but I could hear everything they said. He talked like he was reading out of a book, all about how the Ford way was to see factory and home as part of the same big picture, how they often found that a man who did less than his share in the factory had troubles at home. Did Mrs Ledenev have anything she wanted the investigators to know?

I moved round to where I could see them — the questioner with his back to me and Shula just visible over his shoulder. He must have been younger than her by a good few years and it grated on me to hear his worldly-wise tone and how he worked hard on her to get in where he had no right to be. Shula's answers got shorter and sometimes she said nothing at all, but I guess he thought he could get away with anything.

"You know the Ford Motor Company pays top dollar. They pay the best in the industry, Mrs Ledenev, and they feel that's what they should get from their men in return. If a man starts his day on the line and he's already tired wouldn't you say that's a problem? Another baby coming? No, no — of course. I was just wondering. So it's no, then?"

He makes a mark on his clipboard.

"And this little beauty here, she must keep you both pretty busy at home. Enough for anyone, I expect. And Mr Ledenev, he has interests? I mean things outside the home, things that take up his time and energy. Have you ever seen your husband drunk, Mrs Ledenev? Well, I'll take that as a no. I have to ask, you understand."

He makes another mark on his clipboard and writes a few words.

"So you're doing something to stop another baby coming?"

Silence. I take a step forward.

"Do you need advice on that? We've got people who can talk to you about it. The Ford Motor Company feels that a man who takes top dollar for his work should be fresh when he starts. If you think of it from our point of view, Mrs Ledenev, it's really not fair if . . ."

He moves towards her and gives an odd sort of laugh under his breath.

"Well, I mean . . . if it's all been taken out of a man before . . ."

She used the flat of her hand, but otherwise did it like a man, turning her whole body, putting everything into it and catching him square on the side of the face. His head jerked sideways and cracked off the door frame. He dropped his clipboard and stumbled backwards, nearly falling into Ledenev's armchair. After a few seconds with no one saying anything he asked if I saw what happened. I just told him it was better he should go. The best he could do was to pick up his clipboard and tick a box in as threatening a way as he could manage. We listened to his steps as he retreated down the stairwell.

When there was silence Shula spoke.

"Skid row — is that how you say it? Back on skid row again."

She looked at the armchair and the patch of carpet and the rose-patterned curtains and started to cry and then the baby started too. She went to pick her up.

"What if he tells the police?" she asked me.

"He won't. Anyway, it's easily dealt with — you just tell them he put his hand where he shouldn't've and got what he deserved. Give them my name, if you like. I'll back you up."

For a moment I thought she hadn't really understood, and it was then the whole thing started to get to me as I saw that what bothered her most was telling a lie. I remembered how it was for me before I had some cash in the bank and I told her straight.

"You can't play fair with these people, Shula — you'll always lose if you do."

She had a desperate look and I guessed she was wondering what she would say to Ledenev when he got home.

When I got down to the street I nearly jumped out of my skin when I saw the man himself coming back after an early shift. I must have looked guilty and I started to feel it. He didn't look too happy to see me and I think he would have walked right by if I hadn't spoken to him. He was cool, but I tried to keep it going until most of the investigators got into their cars and headed off back to Highland Park. I was wondering all the time if I should tell him what happened or leave it to Shula to decide what to say. When there was no one left in the street he suddenly said I should come round some time and that he was sorry if he had seemed unfriendly. A man had to take what he could get in America and no one should hold it against him.

"The truth is, Ray — if I'm seen talking to you these days I lose friends. I'm sorry, but that's how it is."

I made my own excuses, saying I was not really a part of it but just come along with my boys for safety's sake. Then I felt even more I should tell him about the investigator and I was about to when he took me by the arm, strong enough like he was about to throw me out of a bar and giving me a look that put the hair up on the back of my neck.

His daughter's voice, harsh and angry, sounded down the stairwell.

"You know what this is, don't you?" he says to me. "You know what it all amounts to?"

He nods upwards to his apartment.

"When I'm awake at night and she's sleeping, sometimes she used to say my name — now she says his."

There was nothing to say after that. I got my boys together and we went back to the plant directly. I described the investigator in Ledenev's apartment and one of them knew him by name. I told them how Shula had damned near floored him and they all thought that pretty funny and were keen to get a closer look. So we made up something as soon as we got back and we got him apart from the rest in a vacant shed. We couldn't touch him of course, but we backed him up in a corner till he looked real scared and couldn't get away. We asked him how many of the employees' wives he had touched up, why he had gone too far with Mrs

Ledenev, and if he hadn't why she had laid that big red mark down one side of his face. I knew what would hurt him most and as I got my money out I could see I was right. It was like a blow in the belly when he saw what I had in my hand — a guy like me with money like that. He could see what I was worth to Mr Ford, and I guess he knew what he was worth. Well, maybe he had some troubles at home of his own, because that bastard college boy took my money and for that I got the Ledenev Sociological Report and the pleasure of throwing it in the fire myself.

The reorganisation went on and for a while I got as jumpy as everyone else — I'd stuck my neck out pretty far, after all. When it was about a week later and I got in to find a note calling me to Mr Ford's office, I thought that was the end. Now Mr Ford doesn't always say what he means like other people and as I stood there and listened to him and wondered what he was on about I still thought I was finished. You see, you just have to wait for a few clear words among all the others and hold on tight to those words when they come.

Well they did come — somewhere in among a lot of talk about efficiency and keeping things moving and people getting too comfortable and taking advantage and some detail that passed me by about the drawing office. I told him I'd be right on it, that he could be sure I'd do a good job. I got the boys together and we went to the drawing office and before anyone else was there took all the desks and the chairs and the drawing tables out back. Then I handed out some axes and took one myself and in half an hour we had the whole lot in pieces. Perlmann turned up before we were through. He watched us and had a look on his face like he was getting fit to cry like a baby. I put my back into it then and every time I swung that axe and let it bite into the wood I just felt so happy it was him and not me.

Theodore

Things got quiet that summer. "Stalemate" was the only news from Europe and after being told of the great advances on the Western Front for the fiftieth time and still nothing happening, the story slipped back to the second and then the third pages, giving way to unexpected baseball results and local automobile accidents. When Seth Sicherman limped back into the office with a cane and a grievance things got even quieter for me. I was kicked down a few rungs to the apprentice stories — *demi-monde* weddings, arrests for drunkenness among the moderately well-known, the ready-to-wear clothing debate or being sent to hang around Windsor docks all day, asking every young man who got off the ferry if he was deserting his country in disgust to join up with the Canadians to save civilisation. Two of them said they were and that I should do the same, and one threatened to knock me down.

Our own war of words settled down in its rhetorical trenches. Pacifists were "milk-faced grubs" and the preachers of preparedness nothing but "jingoes" and "warmongers". Anxiety pitched up to hysteria when the snoozing and conspicuously sabre-slashed Dr Heinrich Albert had his briefcase stolen by a Secret Service man at the 50th Street elevated and saw its contents splashed all over the front of the New York *World*, proving that everyone's worst fears were as nothing compared to the awful truth. Mr William Jennings Bryan packed up his troublesome conscience and flounced out of President Wilson's cabinet. He got up on the stump before his fellow Americans and asked them the same question ten times a day — why should they live in a pistol-toting nation if they were not going to live by a pistol-toter's ideas? Well, that was the end of him.

With Sicherman back in harness these plums all fell on his side of the fence. That put me back on local news and it just so happened that one of the most constant sources of local news in Detroit, ever since he doubled the pay in his factory and started to preach the gospel of industrial salvation, was Mr Henry Ford. Since 1905 Sicherman had held to the view that the horseless carriage had no future, it was nothing more than a symptom of a futile and disordered restlessness, the mechanical expression of the same illness that made fools prattle on about conservation, rational dress and votes for women. By 1915 the matter had become too painful to discuss and he had decided to revenge himself on Henry Ford by ignoring him and all his works. It had become an article of faith for him that nothing of interest or importance could come from that quarter and so for me, the field was clear.

Mr Ford was known for getting on well with newspapermen. He was good copy and they listened to him the way he liked to be listened to. Because he rarely read any newspapers they could write anything they wanted and still be welcomed back a month later. During quieter periods they would go to him and, if they could get through, ask him what he thought of the great issues of the day. He would explain how an increase in the export of cars to Mexico or of tractors to Russia would make these problems evaporate like a bad dream. Like the cars themselves, it was all a bit of a joke. But somehow Ford got into people's heads. No one could quite say how it happened — America woke up one day and found that Henry Ford was, well, kind of ubiquitous I guess.

The war got beneath Mr Ford's skin and this put the whole newspaper game into a new gear. As a manufacturer he made a big thing of not supplying any of the countries involved. He started to get mail from all sorts of pacifists and cranks. I heard he never read a single letter of that sort, but he liked to make his voice heard all the same and it was heard, louder and louder through the second half of 1915. The word was that Henry Ford was bored with making cars, that he had his eye on higher things, that he was in need of a new cause, an adventure perhaps, something to soak up all that money. You can be sure there were plenty of newspapermen who lay awake long into the night trying to work out how they could arrange it for him.

As "accidental" sinkings of American ships went on Mr Ford waded into the preparedness debate. He took the view that if Belgium hadn't been prepared for war she wouldn't have, as he put it, "got her nose punched". The newspapers asked if that were so then why should people even bother to lock their doors or pay for a police force to catch thieves or, for that matter, to stop someone bigger and stronger taking Mr Ford's factory away from him? It was suggested that he would be as happy making cars under a foreign government as under one of his own countrymen. I don't suppose he was troubled by any of this, or even much aware of it. And as for the fuss caused when he pointed out that the Ford Motor Company did indeed have a factory in Germany and that the German people needed cars and tractors as much as anyone else, I truly believe he didn't even understand it. As I got closer to him I saw how he spoke to the world as if through a telephone that only worked one way. It was his privilege to use such a rare machine, for his words to be carried to the people and yet for no troubling echo ever to come back. He never heard the fury of his opponents, or their arguments. Maybe he was just bored, maybe it was just a game, but it didn't seem so to me as I happily became part of Henry Ford's one-way telephone and thrilled to see my words printed under his name.

So there I was, being sent out on slow news days to hang around the offices in the Highland Park plant hoping for a Ford quote. I got to see how the whole set-up worked and was filled in by a fellow named Swinehart who'd been there longer than anyone. There were three people who mattered, collectively known as the pack; the bull terrier, the poodle and the retriever. The first was a big guy called Ray who'd come from nowhere and was supposedly the chauffeur, though he was really a lot more than that; then there was Liebold, the personal secretary, a poisonous, hairless German who prided himself on not having a friend in the world; and finally Marquis, Mr Respectable, head of the Sociological Department and said to be the keeper of Clara Ford's secrets.

"Look out for Marquis," Swinehart told me. "Ex man of God."

"You don't say?"

This judgement turned out to be a little unfair, but it woke me up at the time, it being an axiom of our trade that the affairs of fallen clergymen are happy hunting grounds. And so I started to pay particular attention to Dean Marquis whenever he passed me in the anteroom and we soon got on a nodding acquaintance.

The anteroom was so big it was really more of a hall. Pictures of cars hung on the walls, along with six or seven clocks. Rows of chairs went down either side and there was a desk at the far end, just to one side of the large double doors that led to Mr Ford's office. Liebold worked in a small side room and also from this desk which allowed him a schoolmaster's view of everyone waiting. More than once I watched him play with people, keeping them there all day, moving them to a more hopeful chair closer to the great doors just when they seemed about to despair and head for home. That was his joke and we, as observers, soon learned that the poor fool who had worked his way up to chair two or three by five in the afternoon had only a few minutes left before being dismissed. Liebold was always impassive as he gave them the bad news — no sympathy, no joy either. But I noticed that he would always go into his private room immediately afterwards. What he liked to do in there, I'll never be sure — but from the sound of it he was either running on the spot to keep fit, or dancing.

I asked Swinehart about the clocks and learned that this was one of Mr Ford's great enthusiasms, that he had dismantled them and taught himself how to repair them as a child. I made sure to spend my next Sunday afternoon in the Detroit City Library and when Mr Ford was next passing me in the anteroom at Highland Park I happened to remark in his hearing:

"Is that not a particularly rare three-weight Chauncey Jerome of the mid-1850s hanging on the wall over there?"

Swinehart gave me a deadly look and Liebold, dogging his master's steps at the time, smirked but then looked crestfallen as Mr Ford's face came alive and he took me by the arm and guided me about the room telling me of the peculiarities of each clock and how he had acquired it. What a pleasure it was, he said, to meet a young man who takes an interest in these things. He asked my name and acknowledged me after that and when he had nothing to tell us at the end of the day his cheery, "Nothing for you today, boys" always seemed more in my direction than towards the others.

"You snake," Swinehart said to me later, "You slimy snake, Delavigne."

Through the summer and into the fall things got nowhere fast for me. The hopes for a big Ford story faded. It was agony for us — all the volatile elements were there, all that was needed was a little good luck or a touch of the newsman's art to bring them together. But "the pack" were every bit as smart as we were, and smarter than all the peacettes in the whole damned country put together. For all the truck-loads of mail Mr Ford got every week, they made sure that nothing got through to him that might set off the explosion we were all hoping for. They were good at what they did, no doubt about that — they kept Mr Ford wrapped up like a baby. People started to give up. I was assigned to other stories and by the time the starting gun finally went off I wasn't even there to hear it.

From what I could work out there was nothing unusual that day and no warning of what was about to happen. We knew the front pages of all the big papers but they weren't a lot different from what they always were around that time. That's kind of what I like about the news — sometimes things just go off for no reason at all. For a newsman, there's always hope.

The first thing anyone noticed was this voice coming from Mr Ford's office, even though there was no one in there but Ford himself. It got louder and kept repeating the same thing and so everyone was looking at Liebold as he got up and went nervously to the doors only for them to burst open right in his face and Mr Ford to be there in his shirtsleeves with a copy of the *New York Times* in his hand.

Well, according to the version I got he just walked right out into the middle and shouted in front of all those people — "Twenty thousand! Good God in heaven, twenty thousand in one day! I can't even make cars as fast as that!" and then went straight back in again without saying another word. Everyone just stared at everyone else, apart from the newspapermen — they were already running for the stairs. And that's how the gun went off — that's how all the fun started.

Soon every paper in the area was calling in and next day those from out east as well. It was all Liebold could do to keep them off. Mr Ford was determined to have his say and my guess is — don't ask me to prove it — that Liebold hoped he could satisfy him with a piece in a local paper and would then just pray the story wouldn't go much further. Well that was one thing and the other was that my boss, Mr Pipp, and Ford had some history. I never got to the bottom of it, but they went back quite a way, to before Mr Ford got to what he is now. Anyway, it was enough to put the *Detroit Free Press* at the head of the queue.

I was in the office finishing off something I don't remember now when Mr Pipp came out, swinging his spectacles around his fingers like he does. He had that sort of sly, fat look and a good lunch inside him.

"You're thick with Ford, aren't you Teddy?"

"I wouldn't say that."

Two desks away Sicherman brutalised his typewriter, but refused to look up.

"Sure you are. He likes you. You can talk clocks with each other or whatever it is he likes to go on about these days. Anyway, you'll get more out of him than most so why don't you do it? It's fixed — tomorrow at eleven. A man from the works will pick you up here. You know the sort of thing we're looking for."

So I was collected the next morning from our city offices and chauffeured through the streets of Detroit in a bright Pierce-Arrows like an important man. It was big Ray himself at the wheel. He said I would have half an hour for the interview and that he was sorry the car was not a Ford. He told me how competitors' products were bought for assessment and at busy times you had to take what you could get if you needed a vehicle in a hurry. I was excited and enjoyed being looked at by all the people on the sidewalks.

"No need to apologise."

We got into the country in no time and then swung onto a rough road that took us into the Fords' Dearborn estate. It seemed an odd, semi-wild place for a mechanic to want to live in. We passed a new building on a river that would be the powerhouse, and then the great Fair Lane mansion itself. It was half built then, covered in scaffolding and with piles of uncut timber still lying about. Beyond it was Ten Eyck Farm where the Fords were living until Fair Lane was ready. The Pierce-Arrows scudded to a stop in the dust. I was reaching for the handle when Ray opened the door for me and I got out and stood before a large, old-style farmhouse.

I tugged the bell-pull and was ushered in by the Fords' Japanese butler. Hat in hand, I waited in the hallway as instructed. Two or three minutes passed and in the end I was caught out examining myself in the hat-rack mirror.

"How're you looking today, Mr Delavigne?"

I can't say why, but it still seems extraordinary to me — there he was in the hallway, coming towards me with his hand out, just like anybody in his $20 suit and his silver watch-chain and so skinny it was like there was nothing inside but a few canes holding his pants and jacket up in a shop window somewhere. Mr Ford has an easy manner even in his office, but there in his home he made me feel like I'd known him for years. He even asked about my mother's health. I said, "Fine, thank you sir," and then right away wondered how he knew to ask. He reached for his own hat.

"Walk with me, young man. I think better on the move. How did you take to the Pierce?"

I hesitated and Mr Ford smiled.

"Isn't she smart? — A dandy little car for a young man like you."

We enthused together over this luxurious and powerful automobile.

"Did you see what was wrong with her?" he asked me.

"Well I'm no engineer, sir."

"The price, Mr Delavigne, that's what's wrong with her. Not one American in ten thousand will ever own a car like that. The men who make that car have no ambition. That car will not change the world, mine will. Let's go this way."

We turned to the left and started to walk up through the woods. I listened to him talk about how much his father had wanted to keep him on the land and had brought his son back from Detroit for a while with some new acreage to look after.

"But all I did was cut down all the lumber and when that was gone I went back to the machine shops where I'd been happy before. That was home for me. I didn't think I'd ever need this again."

We walked on, deeper into the woods. He was pleased to tell me the names of the plants and of some of the birds we saw. He talked about his good friend John Burroughs the naturalist and the pleasure he had gained from giving the old man a car so he could more easily get out to wild places. All the time I thought of the questions I had prepared, about the war and pacifism, the rumours of his political ambitions, but there never seemed to be a right moment to speak up. Mr Ford stopped all of a sudden, filled his lungs and looked up at the trees.

"You know I fought in the civil war?"

I wasn't sure I'd heard him correctly.

"Sir?"

"That's right. I mean, of course, in an earlier life — the one immediately before this one. I was born, as you may know, in 1863. A bullet hit a Union soldier fighting Freedom's fight, and I was born. That's the way it happened. Sometimes I see it like I was there myself."

"And you were," I coaxed, excited by the scent of a scoop yet anxious not to scare it away.

"I was indeed. I dream of it sometimes, you know? There are details I never read in any book — how else could you explain it?"

"Makes sense to me."

He started off again, and though he must be more than twenty years my senior I struggled to keep up with his long stride.

"I worked very hard as a young man, Mr Delavigne."

"Yes, sir."

"Then I got what I deserved, then I got so much I thought I must be lucky. But now I wonder if it wasn't all meant to be."

"May I quote you on that, Mr Ford?

"Of course. I'm not a politician, Mr Delavigne. I'm not ashamed of my private opinions. You put it all in the way you think best. You'll have heard for yourself I'm not a words man."

I reassured him on this point, but was interrupted.

"Goldfinch! There — you see it?"

"Eh, I think . . ."

"Now, isn't that beautiful? I always want to write a poem when I see a goldfinch."

"Have you written a poem, Mr Ford?"

"Not yet. I do keep a notebook with me now, just to be ready for when there's something worth preserving. I have a dozen or so at home all full up. It happens more and more these days, something worth preserving I mean. Time of life, I suppose."

I trotted along by his side as he wandered randomly through his enthusiasms — how he had bought an old farm and would preserve it just as it had been, his passion for old carts and carriages and pieces of horse harness which were already becoming hard to find, the old-time music and the dances folks were already forgetting, the school readers he had learned from and still enjoyed today and even the hard bench seats of the country schoolroom which he had rescued from the bankrupt stock sale of the company that made them. Bone by bone he exhumed that whole life of forty years ago and talked of how he was storing the pieces and would one day assemble them and bring back to life everything that had been lost. Then he stopped and leaned a hand on one of the trees and put his head down as if feeling faint.

"Mr Ford?"

He looked at me blankly until I thought he was about to ask who I was and what my business might be walking through his woods. I laughed nervously and reached for the first thing I could think of to say.

"So you're ready for that poem, sir?"

"Mm?"

"In your notebook, sir. You'll be ready for that poem when it comes to you?"

To my relief he seemed to understand again, as if something loose had suddenly been re-engaged.

"I am, Mr Delavigne, you're absolutely right. I'm ready for it whenever it comes. Dammit, there was something else. The thing I really wanted to tell you."

He pinched the bridge of his nose and assumed an expression of great effort. I got my pencil ready and sent up a newsman's prayer. A shudder shook his bony shoulders and he started off again, striding quickly through the woods. He began to speak and I stayed with him, scribbling page after page of jolted, broken script.

"What you've got to understand, Mr Delavigne, what you've got to make our people see, is that New York wants war, the moneylenders, the arms makers, all those fancy folks in the east, they want war. They know there's money in it for them. Fighting over there is none of America's business, but there are people, elements, interests, powers we can't see clearly who want to make it America's business just because of what's in it for them.

"I don't want to make guns, Mr Delavigne, I want to make cars and tractors — ploughshares and pruning hooks — and I'm going to and you can't have the gasoline tractor and war in the same world at the same time. You see, if you let people stay home and make a good living then that's what they'll do. It won't matter any more who comes round banging a drum and telling them they got to stick their noses into someone else's affairs the other side of the world. Do you know why we call the Ford the Universal Car, Mr Delavigne? Because it shows people they're all the same. The affordable car and warfare just won't go together. Try starting a war when the common man can drive into his neighbour's country any time he feels like it and take a look for himself — I tell you, the days when men only travel in an army are gone. And that's what I want you to tell your readers, Mr Delavigne. I say I would rather burn a factory down than let it be used for arms. You are the first to know that I'm going to give a million dollars for a worldwide campaign for universal peace. I'll do more — I'll give everything I possess to stop the war and the stockpiling of weapons in this country. Every last cent

I've got! This is the new work of my life — Universal Car, Universal Peace."

My prayers had been answered — more than that, I had had such a cornucopia of front-page copy emptied over my head in the space of two minutes I was momentarily speechless.

"Mr Ford, sir, do you really mean that?"

He didn't hesitate.

"Yes sir, in heaven's name, I do."

He put his long hand on my shoulder and pinned me eye to eye.

"This is what I want you to tell the people, Mr Delavigne — there may be money in war, but there's money in peace too and it's a hundred times more. And this is just for you, son — for now, I'd bet I'm the only man in the world who has any idea how big it's really going to be. This isn't just a new century, it's a new age and it doesn't have time for wars. Who can tell me what's new about war? Come on, young man — this way."

By the time I could start after him he was almost out of sight. I felt light, unsteady even, as I sensed a lifetime of scepticism being pulled from under my feet. Could all this talk mean anything — universal man, permanent peace somehow worked by the strange magic of the affordable automobile? Nonsense, surely — mere childishness. But I couldn't entirely shake it off.

I was still a little dazed when we came out of the woods and I saw that he had guided us in a loop so that we returned precisely to our starting point. The

Pierce-Arrows was rolling majestically up the driveway and I understood that my interview was coming to an end.

When I took my leave Mr Ford held me by the arm and I could hardly believe it when I heard:

"Say, Mr Delavigne, you know I've been thinking lately how important it is for the modern company to be clearly understood. You know how once a man gets a wrong idea in his head it's a tough business to get it out. It's always cheaper to stop it getting in there in the first place. To my way of thinking a bad idea in a man's head is like sand in his gasoline — the cost is out of all proportion to the size. There's a good future for people who can stop wrong ideas getting around and you and I seem pretty much of one mind — why don't you work for me?"

Of one mind did he say? Whose? I was sure I hadn't said anything all day.

"Well, Mr Ford, that's a remarkable offer, it really is, but . . ."

"But . . .?"

He was opening the door to the car and ushering me in. I was conscious of looking down on him for the first time. Ray had never left the driver's seat and his bulky head and shoulders seemed to hem me in.

"You see, Mr Ford sir, I'm rather fond of the *Free Press*."

"And why not? It's a fine little paper, perhaps I'll buy it. Promise me you'll think about it, won't you?"

"Yes sir. I will."

"I need a man like you and I pay a man his worth. You married?"

I said I wasn't married.

"Marry!" said Mr Ford. "Marry, have children, work for me."

Ray put the car in gear and as it moved off I looked back through the rear window at the shrinking image of the great industrialist. His peculiar parting words were all I could think of. They swirled round in my mind till I got scared I would forget everything else and have nothing to write when I got back to the office. I made notes as best I could in the car. Ray drove fast and violently, shaking me about. It seemed that every time I looked up all I saw were his eyes in the mirror. And then he asked me:

"So you're going to be one of us, huh?"

His tone was far from welcoming.

"Maybe."

I said no more, but started to write my piece in my head. I knew it was the best I'd ever done and I couldn't wait to get back to the office. When the car finally stopped Ray jumped out, keeping to his chauffeur role, though opening the door this time with a rather heavy irony. I believe I caught the gleam of metal under his jacket. He saw me react, but only moved his lapel very slightly before stepping back.

I ran up the stairs and went straight to my desk. I grabbed a sheet of paper and set the keys flying. It was like I was standing up there and giving a speech to a great crowd and I wanted to write it just as fast as I was speaking it.

"Look at him go!" someone shouted.

They all laughed and when Mr Pipp read it he came out of his office right over to my desk with everyone watching on account of the smile on his face and he asked me:

"So Teddy, that old witch doctor has cast a spell on you too."

I told him straight Mr Ford was a great man. Well, I don't really know what that look on his face meant, but he printed it anyway just as I had written it, even the poem I did for Mr Ford about the goldfinch.

I went back to him three days later and said that piece on Ford was the last work I would do for the *Free Press*. I regretfully informed him of my new position and he told me with that queer smile of his that he was always happy to see a young man succeed. A handful of my colleagues came down to the street to see me off. They stood there on the steps, open-mouthed as I walked towards the polished Pierce-Arrows, fired up its huge engine and took off in the direction of Highland Park.

Rosika

Time was short, money shorter still. The tide flowed strongly against us. The voices of men grew louder while the frail female voice of sanity struggled to be heard at all. Zeppelins rained bombs on London while in New York J. P. Morgan & Co. loaned $500,000,000 to the British and French governments. Not a cent of it ever left America — it all went straight to the arms makers. Somehow humanity had to raise its voice against $500,000,000. Seeing the weakness of all others, I came progressively to understand that I alone, the mother and conscience of a bleeding continent, was fit for such a task.

"Preparedness" was the weasel word of the day. It was debated in cafés, saloons and railway carriages. It filled the newspapers. In the mouths of hypocrites and ranting demagogues it lent decency to every evil. Prepare for security, prepare for safety, prepare for slaughter, prepare to get rich. Preparedness meant dreadnoughts and submarines, it meant three-shift, seven-day working in the Bethlehem, du Pont, Remington and Winchester factories. On Sundays America went to church and got down on its knees to give thanks for the work it had just done — O, Lord, give us this day our daily munitions orders from friend and foe alike. And so what did peace come to mean? It meant an end to this plenty, it meant dashing the bottle from the drunkard's lips. Good men who loved money saw it all too clearly — "Yes," they said, "let me be peaceable, let me be sober, but not yet." President Wilson heard and spoke no more of being too proud to fight. Even our own maternal sex had its traitors. Women's Navy Leagues sprang up, Security Sororities with badges of crossed cannons pinned to their clothes. Their campaigns reached the summit of madness with a sinister pledge to be imposed on every child at the start of the school day. They would chant that they were the slaves of the state, heart, mind and body, that they stood ready to be spent in the fires of war whenever their superiors thought fit. Military parades increased. Women lined the streets, urging their sons on to death. Any lesser soul would have despaired. Happily, I do not permit myself despair.

My anxieties were practical too — I had once, briefly, the uncomfortable experience of being an enemy alien in England. A declaration of war by the United States would return me to such a condition, a wanderer perforce, the natural state, as some say, of my people.

I had two dates in Detroit. Little was expected of them and I knew they might well be my last in America. My friends in Hungary wanted me back. They told me of the work to do there, how they thought they were close to winning the vote for women. They asked me if that was not the best way to peace, what government elected by women would ever give itself over to such cruelty again? I told them that if we could not stop the present war there would be no one left to vote but women.

From the slowing train I looked down on acre after acre of small factories and workshops. There was metal in the air and the occasional flash of fire as unionless labourers sweated for their bread and beer. Miss Rebecca Shelly, sitting opposite, gave me a smile of vacant cheerfulness — she had already told me that Detroit was her home town.

"Do you remember it?" I asked her.

"Oh, no — not this bit."

The train slowed more sharply, a platform appeared, then a Negro porter running — backwards it seemed at first, then level with our window and finally moving ahead as we came to a halt. I held tightly to my bag, heavy with the confidences of statesmen, treasures greater than any bank bill, promises on which the fate of millions hung. In the midst of the rushing, crowded concourse I stopped. From some hidden source a new strength suffused me. I felt refreshed, as if taking up the cause for the first time. An unreasoning hope, one might almost say a new faith, re-entered my heart. I stood still and straight. I held my arms out wide.

"Detroit!" I declared, causing no little astonishment in those around me. "Detroit, graveyard of organisers. Detroit, my Calvary!"

Rebecca caught up. Having failed to attract the attention of a porter, she laboured, red-faced and breathless, under the weight of our baggage.

"Are you all right?" she asked.

Can you believe it? I, who feel the pierce of every bullet and bayonet with my own skin, who feels as keenly as if my own life were being taken ten thousand times a day, was asked if I was all right.

"Where can we find a taxi?"

Rebecca pointed to the main exit of the station and I set off smartly. My sweet simple companion bounded after as best she could.

"Oh well," I could just hear her say. "Home sweet home."

Economy compelled us to occupy a single apartment in the Pontchartrain Rooming House. It was to this cheerless shelter that we returned after our first and particularly unrewarding meeting. Even the journalists I had contacted could no longer be bothered to come and sneer. Reviewing my scanty audience, I was forced to wonder at one point whether I was the only *compos mentis* person in the room. There were no questions at the end, only the canvassing of a number of supposed solutions to the world's moral crisis to which my own ideas were, by implication, irrelevant. These included, from what I can recall, pelmanism for all, theosophy, Christian Science, the abolition of the slavery of marriage in favour of free love, anarchism, matriarchy, the expropriation of the Jews and the annexation of Mexico. What strength had been given to me in the station seemed just as quickly to leak away, to exhaust me as violently as if I were losing my own literal lifeblood. I was quiet during our return. I considered gloomily that everyone who had attended our meeting did so merely as a preamble before moving on to other, and perhaps even more absurd, gatherings. Were these people my true fellows? When I looked down on them with — and I shan't deny it — contempt, was I looking in a mirror without realising it? I knew in my heart that the world would go mad before I did, but to carry the burden of one's certain truth is so much harder at some times than at others. I looked through a rainy window at a dark, strange city.

"Courage, my friend," said Rebecca. "Courage."

The taxi drew up at the rooming house. It was a dispiriting place indeed. Two narrow beds stood on bare boards. A pair of rugs covered the floor in part, but a creeping mange had so eaten away at their pattern that one hesitated to put one's feet on them. A finger drawn across the window glass came away black and left a thin streak of clarity. No joint in any item of furniture was quite true or sound. Table, chair and bed would lean and creak agedly whenever put to use. On the mattress an ancient stain showed through the worn translucence of the sheet. Tobacco and sour whisky breathed from the curtains and the wallpaper so that I had the uneasy feeling that the previous tenant had not entirely left. The darkened cork tips of his cigarettes lay by the bed, in a saucer commemorating the 1904 World's Fair.

Rebecca let the cases fall noisily to the floor.

"Oh, well. It'll do."

She seemed to rejoice in these circumstances, so much so that I wondered if she had chosen them deliberately. She started on a series of witless anecdotes about her life as a pupil in a boarding school where the dormitories had closely resembled the Pontchartrain Rooming House. Unpacking a case, she showed that she was indeed better adapted than I by producing a sturdy flannel dressing gown and a pair of slippers to protect her feet from the rough wood of the floor. Thus attired like a character from her own comfortable past, she padded happily down the corridor to the communal washroom. I lay back on my bed and looked up at the ceiling from which old cobwebs hung, grey with dust and hardly moving in the stagnant air. The plumbing vibrated as Rebecca made use of the facilities. I thought of home, of a ship crossing the ocean back to everything I knew. I would be returning in failure. Everyone would deny it for my sake, but it wouldn't make any difference. The old demons started to debate with me, to lay out alluringly the compensations for accepting failure, to whisper lovingly that it couldn't be half so bad as I imagined. Budapest became clear in my mind. I could smell its cafés and almost spoke aloud as I joined in the talk of good friends.

"Water's hot. Get it while you can."

Rebecca burst back into the room. She unwrapped her bathrobe and let it hang over the back of a chair then jumped into her bed with girlish athleticism and pulled the covers up to her chin. For half a minute she held her eyes tight shut like a child at prayer. When she was finished she turned to look at me and found, for a brief moment, some solemnity.

"We're right. You're right, Rosika, and they have to see it. They will see it, if only we can keep going long enough."

"Thank you, Rebecca."

She was asleep when I returned to the room. She lay on her back, her thumbs tucked under the sheet, her fingers straight and flat against the white surface, as neat as two paper clips. Her mouth was slightly open and her large front teeth just visible in a manner that suggested sharing the room with an enormous rodent. She snored very slightly. The sound would not disturb me and might, one day, be essential to the rest of a child or a husband. She had not been able to turn off her bedside lamp before falling asleep. I did it for her, hesitating with my finger on the switch, sharply caught off guard as I saw the daughter I had decided never to have. I brushed the hair from her forehead, very lightly and with fear, as if testing the delicate mechanism of a trap. I might have kissed her had I not been held back by a vision of how absurd it would be if she were to wake and question me. I climbed into my own bed and settled to read Emma Goldman's article in the latest *Mother Earth* with my spectacles on and the magazine held close in the dingy light. The scene shifted to a sad parody of marriage, and a confirmation too that my course was the right one. I concentrated on the article, marking a few phrases fit for plunder, turning over in my mind how I might arrange for myself a short and useful spell of imprisonment. At ten o'clock a noise I had not previously noticed fell silent. The room became cold. After another half-hour, and without any intervention on my part, the lights went out. The cause wrapped its arms tight around me.

In the morning we breakfasted with the single other guest — a commercial traveller in novelty cutlery who made his way noisily through a bowl of Dr Kellogg's cereal with a banana-handled spoon.

"People need a boost in the morning, a little sunshine to send them on their way. Business is good. Gotta go, ladies."

Rebecca had been out early and had returned with half a dozen newspapers. I drifted through the war news and searched automatically for any hopeful sign of change in Washington. Silently, I rehearsed passages of rhetoric for our meeting at seven o'clock that evening. Even at such a low ebb the words stirred me. Their power and humanity had always seemed to me irresistible — if only they could be properly heard. I was in search of the heart — the heart of the great neutral republic. I thought of it as a pearl locked in a safe, as a princess charmed into an age-long sleep, as a fabled city hidden behind high walls. On that particular morning I don't think I could have offered any evidence for the existence of this treasure, but I still believed in it with a perfect certainty. I was sure there was some way of opening that safe or of waking that princess. If only I could find the right way, the right words, those walls would come down quicker than anyone might think. I saw myself being received by President Wilson. "No, no!" I have to say to him,

"Please, Mr President, do not apologise — only now promise that you will do the right thing." Once again, he regrets that he had not listened to me sooner. The reverie fades. I fold the paper and place it on the table. I wipe the ink from my fingers on the edge of the cloth.

For the next two minutes there was a silence of mounting awkwardness as I looked at the crown of Rebecca's head. She seemed even to have stopped reading, to have become completely frozen. I wondered what could have so wholly absorbed her and was close to making some disobliging remark about the latest celebrity murder or the new winter fashions when she looked up and stopped me. Had she read of the death of some acquaintance or perhaps, as she looked too astonished even for that, of some miraculous recovery? She folded the *Detroit Free Press* and passed it to me across the table. There, at the top of the page in two-inch type I read the words ***Ford Repeats Pledge — All I Have For Peace***. Below, set out by Our Staff Reporter, were the words I had never dared to hope for. His opinions seemed to be my own — there was little to choose between the soldier and the murderer, war was a folly that left nothing but high taxes and crêpe at the door, take away the capitalists and you will sweep war from the world, only through misapprehension do men fight each other, it's the men sitting around the table not the men dying in the trenches who finally settle the differences. And then towards the end and perhaps most hopefully of all — "I don't read history. That's all in the past."

Here was a human decency and a courage to speak out that reminded me of nothing so much as myself — a true fellow spirit, only in this case a fellow spirit attached to a practical infinity of money. At that stage I knew little about Henry Ford but had heard it said more than once that he was no ordinary manufacturer. On that morning, over the breakfast table, I was ready to believe it when I came to the end of the article and found there a most affecting expression of compassion for all living things in the form of a beautiful poem by the great man himself. Here, I felt sure, was a man I could do business with.

Rebecca leaned across the table and tapped her finger on the newsprint.

"I know this man. I used to go to his church."

Everything seemed possible at such a moment — "Henry Ford has his own church?"

"No, no. Look — there."

I looked more precisely. There was a passing mention of Ford's wife and a dubious character described as her "spiritual adviser".

"I was in his congregation for ten years. I think he'll remember me. He'll certainly remember my parents."

As one we were struck by the same alarming thought — how many people were reading that newspaper, how many were already ahead of us in the race? We jumped from our seats and ran down the corridor to the outside door. Fortune smiled on us in the form of two taxis which immediately answered our call. We went down the steps with a grimy hall porter following and threatening to sell our baggage if we didn't come back.

I was obliged to inform him that as the fate of countless millions was in our hands at that very moment we could hardly be expected to care about our baggage. I shouted to Rebecca.

"You take Svengali, I'll take Ford."

Doors slammed. I ordered my driver to take his vehicle back to its maker with all possible speed.

Louis

I never quite worked out how she did it. I asked, of course, but Madame Schwimmer was not the sort of woman who felt much obliged always to give the same answer to the same question. Her explanations varied with her mood. Occasionally she admitted to luck but would then, in more confident passages, revert to hints involving the mastery of dark arts and deeper matters still, matters that honour would never allow her to disclose. Others had their own versions. Many just shrugged their shoulders. A muckraker by the name of Swinehart told me the credit was all his. Madame Schwimmer had gone to the offices of the *Detroit Free Press* in the hope of finding the author of the article that had set things off. It turned out the young man had resigned only a few days previously to take Henry Ford's dollar and had become as hard to find as his employer. Swinehart was on the same trail and there was an encounter on the sidewalk — a literal collision, as he has it, a contest for a cab.

"A strange old maid, kind of sad. Anyway, I'd been to one of her meetings a while back and she recognised me — we hadn't exactly been friendly. I guessed what she was there for — there was quite a pack about town that day, I kept running into them everywhere. I was looking for someone to put my money on. It had to be someone just right — not too loopy and none too sober either. Someone who would get through, but who would set the fireworks off when he got there — you know what Ford is like. Well, I picked her. And boy, did she come home!"

Swinehart knew one thing the others didn't. He had a telephone number and he knew that at the end of that line was Mr Anderson, and that Mr Anderson hated Mr Liebold. He made the call, came back with a time and a place and handed them on a card to Rosika Schwimmer.

"Thlouis —" It was years later and he was slopping his tenth whisky on the floor of some basement bar. "I tell you I was the one that got her through. That whole damned party would never have started without me. I got her through — I damned near got her a red carpet right up to his door. People forget that."

Things hadn't gone well for Swinehart after the war, but he still told a good story.

When all this was happening I was in Chicago and knew nothing about it. That changed with Rosika's mystifying telegram — "Why are you not coming to keep your appointment with Mr Ford?" At that time I was not a great believer in tycoons. Carnegie had talked peace, but had done nothing to make it real. I had been to see John Wanamaker, the department store king, but received nothing from him but platitudes and a copy of *Pollyanna*. My work with the Chicago Peace Society had taught me to recognise a false dawn when I saw one and I knew also that Ford had a liking for making headlines and had good men around him to protect him from the consequences of his enthusiasms. This was not the first time he had shown a rhetorical hatred of war, and it had never come to anything in the past. Added to all that was the fact that the telegram came from Schwimmer — I admired her energy but not her judgement, and her name at the bottom of that strange message did nothing to allay my doubts. What appointment, who had made it, did it exist at all?

In the peace business it was normal to receive a good deal of unreliable correspondence. In our case this included a sheaf of letters from a crank in New York who discerned meanings in the rattling of auto engines and offered to arrange a rendezvous with the notoriously inaccessible Ford. We had recently tried to put him off by wiring that such a meeting had already been arranged through other channels — thank you and don't write, telephone, cable or call in person ever again. Had it not been for Schwimmer's signature I would have added this new telegram to the pile and thought no more of it. Instead, I read it a dozen times and wondered. Had she really done it, had she somehow got through? I looked at my desk diary — the afternoon appointments did not excite. Outside was a dusky November morning with rain starting to streak windows the Society could not afford to have cleaned. On top of that, the arrival of the telegram fell on one of our monthly Sacrifice Days — an initiative of our treasurer which meant there would be no heating. The story began to seem more plausible. A feather of self-indulgence settled on the scales and tipped them. I declared a possible breakthrough to the secretaries in the outer office, consulted a railway timetable, drew thirty dollars from petty cash and left in a guilty rush.

The train was a welcome asylum. I kept my coat on and enjoyed the warmth as the chilly scenes passed outside. I dozed for much of the first long stretch, going back over the hopeful but unproductive days of the year and a half since Emmy and I had been stopped on a Paris station platform and told it was too late to go to a peace conference. I recalled the English soldiers near the coast — as I did every time I read a newspaper — and knew they could not all still be alive. When wakeful I had the company of my book, *The Great Illusion*, which I had snatched from the shelf at home and thrown in my bag as I gave a breathless half-explanation to Emmy before running back to the cab waiting for me in the street. Angell's phrases lifted me as they always did — obedience to primitive instincts, enslavement by catchwords, indolence before the necessary revision of old ideas. The robust, invincible logic momentarily refreshed my hopes before I turned back to the title page and the miserable date I knew I would find there — 1913. The old, needle-sharp argument followed — if they had not listened to him, what chance did I have? I returned to my obsession — power and its cryptic sources, more practically the question of where it was to be found, by what force, exactly, might our horseless carriage be coaxed into motion? The features of someone rather like Henry

Ford coalesced in my mind, borrowed uncertainly from an advertisement photograph. I struggled to make the picture clearer, worrying foolishly that I might suffer the embarrassment of failing to recognise him. The face remained general — human, certainly, but too remote to name. A fellow passenger noticed the title of my book. He guessed wrongly and bored me with an anecdote about Harry Houdini. I feigned sleep.

After the change at Toledo I had about an hour more of travelling. The approach of Detroit disturbed my concentration and I frittered away the time looking out the window or with my eyes closed, enacting a variety of scenarios, some hopeful, others more useful as preparations for disappointment, or excuses for the waste of money when I got back to the office in Chicago. As we hit the suburbs I reached out for an old magazine someone had left behind. There was the usual young woman on the coloured cover — implausible perfection, indiscriminate smile. I spent a few seconds betraying my wife in her imaginary company before moving on to the inside pages. Their cheerful trivia depressed me. Here was that stubborn, leaden resistance to anxiety that I and all my colleagues were struggling against. As a record of the world the magazine had swept reality from its bright halls with an almost perfect cleanness. If it alone survives the fire, historians will have no choice but to conclude there was no war. It strengthened my suspicion that existence consists of only two types. One, and by far the largest, is wholly absorbed in the prosecution of a loud and hilarious party. The other, a rarer and less happy breed, includes myself — and there I am, standing on the steps of this house of fun as the music beats out through the open windows and the warm night air is barley-rich with beer and whisky. I knock on the door, not to gain entrance, but only to ask, very politely, that the merrymakers look at the horror I hold in my hands and perhaps hold down the noise a little. It is no surprise that I and my kind are never welcome guests.

Beside the cover girl, I recall only a single detail from that abandoned *McClure's* — an advertisement containing one of those lines that pull you up as sharply as a fish-hook in the mouth.

Is Your Will Dormant?

> Look back upon your life. Once upon a time no doubt, you weaved great dreams of what you were going to make of yourself. Are they accomplished now? Is it not because you lacked a strong, powerful, inflexible, dominating **WILL**?

You too can be Indomitable

Send no money now

It was Frank Channing Haddock, PhD, MS, who offered these services and whose masterful features scowled from a small oval portrait beside the text. Dr Haddock could show a man, through simple exercises anyone could do, how to seize control of his own life, how to trample on the caprices of Fortune and relentlessly bend the world to his own purposes. I wondered how many could be entirely deaf to such a call — it seemed certain that Dr Haddock enjoyed a steady business.

I might have thought no more about this fraud were it not for the eerie experience of seeing the same features staring back at me through the window enlarged a hundred times. The Haddock enterprise clearly had enough turnover to engage in billboard advertising as well and there he was, repeatedly through the last mile before the station, looking down on me with a calculated blend of contempt and blandishment. Through the flickering darkness of steel girders and in the gaps between tightly packed warehouses and the newer office buildings the question repeated itself with a mesmerising rhythm — *Is Your Will Dormant?* I thought of dreams and the discouraging question of their accomplishment. I thought of my wife and daughter. I thought too of Henry Ford and the matter, unexpectedly, became hilarious. Walls veered closer, this time bearing a vast image of an automobile that seemed about to collide with our train. Beneath it I recognised, without reading, the flowing lines of the Ford Motor Company's trademark. There were four words — Ford, the Universal Car. We rumbled over an elevated section and I found myself looking down on a congested street, jam-packed with Ford cars, vans and light trucks. Fresher posters appeared, in brighter colours and with enticing pictures of the newest model.

Without a break they lined the wall all the way into the station so that it was impossible not to see them. Watch the Fords Go By; Watch the Fords Go By; Watch the Fords, Go Buy. The refrain worked simply on my appetites so that I almost felt hungry looking at them. The instruction was impossible to resist. When the train finally came to a halt I had become convinced that Detroit was his city, personally. I felt that I was arriving as the ambassador from a remote and impoverished province, an unknown and unregarded man who would have to jostle to present his credentials at the court of the most stupendous power. I put on my hat and took my case down from the rack. I realised I had made a decision. I would give it all up and join the party. This would be my last effort — it would be Mr Ford, or Dr Haddock.

That evening I felt it was too late to have any useful conversation with the Ford works. I checked into a better hotel than I had any right to and dined in genial commercial company. The next morning, in one of the telephone cabins in the lobby, I got through easily to a young woman at the Highland Park factory but had barely started on my explanation before instinct told me to hang up. I still had no confidence in the reality of this appointment and calculated, though without any great delusion about the physical presence of Louis Lochner, that I might be a little harder to reject in the flesh than as a voice over the telephone. So it was that, after a short taxi ride, I found myself in the crowded anteroom with its clocks and its pictures of birds, its huddles of press men and campaigners and a handful of bewildered salesmen who had come to talk car parts but found themselves instead at something very like the temporary centre of the world. I strained to get a glimpse over all these heads of my first goal, the private secretary, just as he was turning a dishevelled character by the shoulders and pointing him in the direction of the exit with the words "You again!" I reached the worn carpet in front of his desk.

"Louis Lochner to see Mr Ford."

The man looked up with an unexpectedly amiable expression.

"Do you have your letter with you, Mr Lochner?"

A rapt silence settled behind me. There was a sense of movement as twenty faces turned in my direction.

"Letter?"

"Mr Ford's appointments are always confirmed by letter."

I confessed I had no letter. The secretary gave a world-weary and rather disappointed sigh as if, by this late stage in the game, the very least a charlatan could do was entertain him with a more painstaking deception than this.

"Well, I'm afraid . . ."

"I'm the secretary of the Chicago Peace Society."

There was laughter at my back. No doubt an indomitable alumnus of Haddock would have found a way through, but I was already turning to leave.

"Ah," said the secretary. "A Peace Society?"

Voices could be heard through stout double doors. Mr Anderson cocked an ear in their direction, the press men leaned closer, like a row of pins pulled about by a magnet.

"I would be sorry to have to turn you away. Let me make quite sure."

We entered a small side office and I watched as Mr Anderson made a sympathetic show of consulting a diary the size of a ledger.

"My senior colleague is away, you see. I should know, really, but perhaps you made an arrangement with him? He might have failed to pass the information on? Not everyone is always perfect."

Mr Anderson paused for a moment to enjoy some private joke, then raised his eyebrow at me to repeat the question.

"I have a telegram."

"A telegram, Mr Lochner?"

I unfolded it and handed it over.

"I see," said the second secretary. "From Madame Schwimmer. Well, then — perhaps that dispels a little of the mystery. You were meant to come together. We have nothing more here than a misunderstanding as to times."

I watched his finger come to a halt in the middle of the huge page and could just make out, upside-down, a capital S followed by some less distinct letters.

"But I'm sorry," he was forced to admit. "I can't find you. You're just not here at all."

The book took on a fateful significance and I was embarrassed by my own plaintive tone as I insisted — "But I've come all the way from Chicago."

"That really is too bad. It is a shame that you seem to have made such a long journey for nothing."

A disturbance in the anteroom attracted our attention. Voices from within were suddenly louder. They had the rhythm and tone of leavetaking. Sure enough one of the doors opened abruptly — the left-hand one, blocking completely my view of who was coming out. The press went into noisy action and I thought I must be mistaken as I heard the flat, emphatic vowels of middle Europe cut through the chorus of questions. Mr Anderson took me by the arm and moved me forward. There indeed, at the centre of chaos, was the sturdy, bespectacled form of Rosika Schwimmer. Over her head I got a glimpse of the interior of Mr Ford's private office. Three men remained seated at a table strewn with papers. One of them rose from his seat and approached me only to close the door in my face and restore the privacy of these grim advisers.

"Louis!" Rosika exclaimed disapprovingly. "So you decided to come?"

The lean, angular man in his early fifties by her side could only be Ford. For the moment he ignored Mrs Schwimmer and his secretary and enjoyed a teasing exchange with the newspapermen. It was only when I got to know Swinehart later that I realised his features had been in the midst of the crush. He was smiling hopefully in the direction of his Hungarian secret weapon. He was the one who called out in his strong New York accent:

"Are you going to stop the war, Mr Ford?"

The auto king seemed not to hear. He turned to speak to Mr Anderson who, in a gap between one word and another from his employer, indicated my presence by his side and attempted an introduction. I was standing before Henry Ford, my case was being made to him, I appeared to be the sole object of his attention and felt as if I was about to faint.

"This man is a victim of circumstances," explained Mr Anderson. "He . . ."

"A victim, are you?"

I stumbled over a few meaningless syllables and appeared, indeed, to have been thoroughly victimised. Mr Ford turned to the journalists.

"What do you say to that, boys? We have a victim in our midst. Well, we can't have that."

He indicated Rosika Schwimmer whose anxious features signalled to me that now was not the time to speak. Ford must have missed Rosika's earlier remark and presented her to me as a fresh acquaintance.

"This is Madame Schwimmer. I have asked her to come out to our home tomorrow. I want her to meet Mrs Ford. Won't you come out with her? I'll arrange to have you both taken out there. Mr Anderson . . ."

Mr Anderson stepped forward.

"Arrange to have these good people taken out to Fair Lane tomorrow morning. And tell these other gentlemen they can go home. I'll have nothing for them today."

Mr Ford turned his eyes toward the exit. A path cleared before him and he took it.

* * *

I did not see Rosika again until the next morning when I found her already installed in the car sent to collect me from my hotel.

"You're Mr Ford's chauffeur?"

The large, slightly swaggering man holding open the door had not introduced himself but seemed to know who I was.

"You can just call me Ray."

Inside, Rosika was tightly wrapped in a heavy coat and flicking energetically through the pages of a small notebook.

"Good morning," I said, only to be told there was no time for pleasantries when the lives and happiness of millions weighed on our shoulders. She spoke with terse command, her heavy Central European accent making unfortunate connections in my mind with the broad comedy of the vaudeville houses.

"We have an even chance," she declared. "No better than that. If we get him, we get everything. If we don't, I go back to Hungary."

The stakes could not be higher. She closed her notebook for a moment and scowled out at the November dullness of Detroit as at the features of a personal enemy. I received a report of the meeting with Ford the day before.

"I had hoped to speak to him alone, but as you saw that was not to be. Instead I found myself in the lion's den. The lawyer was the worst. I have met that sort before — a man who would not save an infant from drowning without writing a ten-page brief on the implications of such a rash action, then charging the bereaved mother a hundred dollars for his wisdom. There was a retired banker, an old friend of Ford's I understand, and a most peculiar clergyman, a useless, mumbling old social gospeller who is said to have some sort of connection with Mrs Ford on the precise nature of which I couldn't possibly speculate. They are the 'do nothing' party. They wish Mr Ford only to make cars and money. They want to keep him within their reach. He is in thrall to these wreckers, these dwarfs. They are the Lilliputians to his Gulliver, the Delilahs to his Samson!"

I watched as her knuckles tensed about the clasps of a large, black, leather bag. She clutched it more passionately to her bosom.

"They doubted me. They questioned my integrity, my documents! I wanted to show them to Mr Ford, but of course I couldn't — not with *them* there."

"You all right, lady?"

Ray was turning slightly in his seat to get a sideways glance at his strange passenger.

"Entirely, thank you. Are we there yet?"

"Not nearly. Forty minutes without hold-ups."

Rosika placed a kid-gloved and confidential hand on my arm.

"We have time to plan, Louis. If they are there, the jailers of his greatness, I fear there will be nothing we can do. But if we can talk to him on his own we may yet win through. There is greatness in Mr Ford — from what I saw yesterday I have no doubt of that. He is a man in chains, a Prometheus on his rock, a chosen people groaning under the yoke of modern tyranny. What he needs is . . . is . . ."

Ray shifted again in his seat, eager to hear more clearly as the concept of his employer as slave came to his ears.

"A Moses?" I suggested.

"Yes!" pounced Rosika. "Or, in more modern terms, Louis — what Mr Ford needs is me."

She told me more of her meeting with the gilded slave of industry. The enemies of peace were precisely characterised and complex stratagems laid while I gave an impression of attentiveness as downtown shrank to suburb and the suburbs gave way to the wintry countryside of Michigan. We moved out of rain and into a sunny, sharp morning.

I remembered the telegram and took it from my pocket.

"Why did you send me this?"

Rosika plucked it from my fingers and read the single line.

"Why did I have to? Why get an appointment with Ford and then not come to keep it? That's what I can't understand."

"But what appointment? I hadn't made one. I assumed you had on my behalf, though when I got there no one had heard of me. Even now I don't think Mr Ford has much idea who I am."

"Nonsense. You told me yourself you had been given an appointment."

"Now, Mrs Schwimmer," I said very calmly, "you just know that isn't true."

"Then what's this?"

She snapped open the clasps on her bag and opened it narrowly. Just visible in its capacious, shadowy depths was the folded whiteness of secrets. She leaned away from me, a child jealously shielding a schoolroom slate, before finding the letter she was searching for.

"But this isn't from me," I protested.

"As good as."

"It's no such thing."

I recognised the name at the bottom of the ardent, but incoherent text. This was the very same character who sent to us in Chicago two or three times a week; the one we had recently tried to shake off with the innocent fiction of a real appointment.

"This man is a crank. He's not well."

"Who you associate with, Louis, is your business. You told him you had made an appointment with Mr Ford."

"Only to get rid of him."

"Nevertheless. The Goddess of Peace moves in mysterious ways her wonders to perform, my dear Louis. That is what you told him, he told me and I told you. I really don't see how you can object. If you were misled it was only by your own words."

Rosika was finished with the matter. When Madame Schwimmer is finished with a subject of conversation she is most emphatically finished with it. She does not end topics, she guillotines them with a stroke of the open hand and from this fate I have never known any to return.

"Mrs Ford," she asserted.

Ray's ears and the back of his head, if such a thing is possible, seemed to become more alert. I held back from too much talk and tried to give a cautious expression as the driver was surely listening to every word.

"Do you know her?"

"No," I said. "Of course not."

"That priest or whatever he is — Samuel Marquis — I have a young helper who knows him and takes to him but I most decidedly do not. If he represents her way of thinking then we have a problem. Yes, I fear Clara Ford."

"Really?"

"I understand her. Of course I do. She married a man — I have been busy in the newsaper offices; I have found out a lot, you know. Yes indeed, she married a man but now finds herself the consort of a great power, one that may be on the brink of waking to its responsibilities, of espousing the great cause. She wishes to keep him close to her, small and comfortable like he was when they were young. Ah, Louis — so often it is those we love who most keep us back from fulfilment."

A handkerchief was produced. Her glasses were slightly adjusted and there was a barely necessary dab at one eye.

"Love can be such a selfish thing, but the heart must give way to the greater good. I too have lived through these dilemmas. I must find some way of letting her know, I must commune with Clara. Leave that to me."

I assured her I would not interfere. We passed more slowly over rougher roads. I felt my chest tighten as I realised we were only minutes from arriving.

"There are some things you must know about Mr Ford. He is a great genius, no doubt, but of a particular sort. He has no taste for abstractions. I spent some time explaining our continuous mediation plan. I thought I made allowances for the fact that he is largely of a mechanical nature, but I'm still not sure he followed me. No single concept can detain him for long and the connections he makes between one topic and another are not necessarily those that would occur to a more conventionally schooled intellect. You should show no surprise when he jumps tracks, just follow a little way then give him a nudge at the next set of points. He believes he has prospered solely as result of his personal qualities. His wealth is the proof of his wisdom and it is a long time since he was contradicted by anyone. Do not smoke in his presence — he considers it witty to refer to cigarettes as 'white slavers' and believes that the products of paper combustion rust the nerves. He will explain at length how the petrol-engined tractor will end once and for all the griefs of rural humanity. You must pretend to be convinced of this. If necessary, point out that he could sell more tractors in Flanders if it was not currently a battlefield. He idolises women and is advanced on female suffrage. He will want to tell you how working in a Ford factory is all that is required to reform the character of countless inmates of Sing Sing. You will refrain from pointing out that such a life leaves a man too exhausted to commit a crime. He is a bookish man — two books from what I have been able to discover."

Rosika handed me a sheet of paper and I looked down at half a dozen lines of poetry.

"For today at least, we will admire what he admires. I'll do Emerson, you do *Locksley Hall*. Reason, I suspect, has limited power over him, Louis, but sympathy may win the day. Some of his opinions are embarrassing — you will know what I mean if that particular topic comes up. Do not react. Do not feel any obligation to defend me or my people. In any case, I heard it all yesterday. His moral conception of America is essentially geographical — east is evil, west is virtuous. You will try to sound more Chicago than New York, won't you? You will discover that you have been under a complete delusion as to the causes of the European war. It is in fact a conspiracy of New York bankers who maintain the conflict for commercial reasons only — nothing swells one's loan book like a war. All bankers are Jews. Ah, I think we've arrived."

We turned through gateposts. I learned my lines from Henry Ford's favourite poem as we bumped over a rough track through trees and then into a wide open space. The great mansion was to the right, nearly finished. Ahead of us was the building it would replace, a white timber farmhouse of pioneer simplicity, with a tall thin man already standing on the porch. Rosika leaned closer and for the first time lowered her voice.

"In short, Mr Ford is a well-intentioned simpleton. Remember, Louis, we have only one purpose here; to hitch his money to our minds — the perfect combination."

It was Mr Ford himself who opened the door of the car. He smiled warmly, held out his hand and greeted me.

"My victim!"

We found our host dressed like a character from a Fenimore Cooper novel and I feared I would be expected to tramp the Michigan countryside with him and perhaps bring down our own lunch with a musket-shot. To my relief, Mr Ford explained that he had just finished his daily walk through the woods — a practice he enthusiastically recommended to me, along with the works of his good friend John Burroughs.

"I'll send you a set — profitable reading, wonderful man. I give him a car every year."

"That's very generous of you, Mr Ford," said Rosika.

The man of business sensed a premature start to the proceedings. Rosika's eyes connected meaningfully with mine. Ford shrugged bony shoulders.

"It's nothing to me. The old fellow says it scares the birds and the deer away, but if it wasn't for that vehicle he'd just have to remember the countryside."

Clara Ford emerged and we were introduced. As we shook hands and exchanged a few words about our journey and the weather I couldn't help being reminded of my mother. Although for the rest of the day, and on a few later occasions, I was constantly expecting her ordinariness to slip, and for us both suddenly to laugh with each other and enjoy the quality of her disguise, it never happened.

“And this is Mr Delavigne, one of my latest acquisitions. He’ll be helping me handle the press from now on.”

A young man in a new suit of clothes shook Rosika’s hand and mine and treated us both to a penetrating, though not unfriendly, top-to-toe examination. Mr Ford’s voice sounded confidentially in my ear — “Let’s leave the girls to gab on. I’ve got something more exciting to show you.”

While Rosika Schwimmer and Mrs Ford got acquainted I endured the tractor factory. With Delavigne at the wheel of some extraordinary vehicle of the sort I was sure Mr Ford would never manufacture, all three of us made the drive to the new plant nearby. I was constantly on the look-out for openings on the matter of the peace campaign but the subject never came up, nor anything remotely like it. I agreed with my host that a world without intoxicating liquors would be a much better place, that the spread of the cigarette habit threatened the moral health of young men and that the latest dance fashions were distasteful foreign imports, gravely inferior to the styles of Mr Ford’s youth and, what is more, shot through with secret significances that could only end in the triumph of bolshevism. I enthused, as best I could, over countless engineers’ drawings and admired the sample machines that had already been put together. Before one of these we stood in a line of three. For quite a time Mr Ford fell silent and it seemed our role was simply to revere this object as a new golden calf. I became convinced that a long line of petitioners had gone that way before me, been treated to the same solipsistic tour, and been sent on their way empty-handed. I began to think of train timetables and whether it was still possible for me to be back home with Emma and Elizabeth before the end of the day. Mr Ford turned abruptly to his new press secretary.

"When was the plough invented, do you think?"

"Long time ago, sir."

"But when exactly?"

He turned to me and accused me of having an education.

"You must know — how long ago."

"Five thousand," I guessed. "Maybe six thousand years. It's not my field."

Delavigne reacted politely to the unintended pun.

"Six thousand years. Men pulled them first — brothers, or fathers and sons labouring like beasts just to survive. Thousands of years passed, then they harnessed bullocks, water buffalo, horses and thousands more passed. The steam engine raised hopes, but it was too heavy and costly. I ploughed behind horses when I was a boy, the same way others had for thousands of years. I was no good — furrows all squint as my mind wandered to other things."

He planted his feet more widely and put his fists on his hips. We redoubled the intensity of our gaze at this strange and revolutionary device.

"Just think — six thousand years. Then I put my hand to the problem and in twenty more years it'll all be over. Gentlemen, the muscle-powered plough will be in its grave before I am. Six thousand years of nothing and then, Henry Ford."

Delavigne fumbled in his pockets, then urgently made a note in a little book. Ford clapped him on the shoulder.

"Good man — there's a whole article in that. Write one up for me."

We moved on through the vast factory and I began to despair of ever getting to my business when Mr Ford diverted Delavigne onto some other task and I found myself in a room with him alone. He sat on a drawing table, and commended me for my patience.

"So what do you think of this Schwimmer's ideas? Will they work?"

I went through it carefully — the stalemate in the war, the desire for peace and the paralysing fear of weakness that held men back from admitting it. I told him of all our contacts in the neutral countries, of their willingness to help, how I believed that men's minds were ready, that the sides could slowly be led towards more moderate positions, that there could be peace without victory and without defeat, a peace that no one need fear. Help had to come from outside, and from where else could it come other than the great, neutral, peace-loving republic herself, from America? All it needed was . . . was . . . My speech faltered. I went through the truth in my mind — money, a figurehead, a headline-grabber, a public face and name. My eye settled coyly on the drawings on the table.

"To be thrown into gear — that's what it needs. Yes, that's it. All the parts are there — it just needs to be assembled and turned over and thrown into gear."

"Thrown into gear, eh?"

It seemed a masterstroke. I was sure the moment had come.

"That's right," I rushed on, the goal in sight. "Think of the plough, Mr Ford. For how many thousands of years has there been warfare? Put your hand to this problem and perhaps you can end war too — maybe for ever."

I received a sharp look and an unnerving, worldly smile. Mr Ford stepped out of the room and I followed.

"I wouldn't put too much faith in what Mr Delavigne writes for the newspapers. Let me show you the transmission assembly line."

That day, and through all my later dealings with Henry Ford, I found no trace of Rosika's well-intentioned simpleton.

When we returned to the house I discovered my colleague still hard at work on the business of communing with Mrs Ford.

"And you cook the cherries in a skillet with brown sugar and butter? And for the layers of bread in the casserole tin — any special type?"

"Well," said Clara, hesitantly, "just bread."

Rosika looked round and frowned to find me within earshot.

"Louis," she continued smoothly, "Mrs Ford has agreed to fund our telegraphic peace message campaign. We can send thousands of peace messages to the White House. We think $10,000 should suffice."

The figure seemed to land on Clara's consciousness like a bucket of ice water, but she had hardly begun her first word of protest when her husband waved the figure away and declared he was hungry.

At lunch we were joined by Edsel, a pale, dominated youth and the only child of the Ford union. We listened to Mr Ford's theories about the justice of poverty and wealth — how the first is an incentive to self-improvement and, failing that, a reasonable punishment for idleness and incompetence. The second is never more than fair reward for ingenuity and effort. Rosika glared at me fiercely when I debated with him on these issues. She should not have worried — Mr Ford was not at all perturbed by or even interested in any of my criticisms.

The lunch ended bizarrely when an Edison Phonograph was started and a reluctant Edsel chivvied into accompanying the music on a set of drums. We applauded his modest talent as Rosika kicked me beneath the table and mouthed the word "poem". I remained silent and left the matter to her.

"Ah — the war drums throb no longer and the battle flags are furled."

An affronted Edsel muttered something about ragtime and left the room.

"Tennyson, I think," Rosika prompted the embarrassed millionaires, "but I forget the title."

Mr Ford obligingly supplied it and confirmed it was one of their favourites. For several seconds my colleague's eyes did not leave mine. She turned at last to Clara.

"Such a fine boy, Edsel. Has he ever thought of joining the army?"

It was Mr Ford who answered abruptly.

"Edsel's future is decided."

From somewhere a clock ticked more loudly. Upstairs, a door slammed and the drapes shuddered in sympathy. I had a vision of myself with cards in hand. Call? Raise? Give the whole thing up as hopeless? I had never been much good at gambling. I began to sweat as I went over the things I would have said had I been another, better man. The war seemed very distant and our pretensions to affect its course nothing less than ludicrous. Ford sat still and silent at the head of the table. A week's interest on his capital would meet our needs several times over and yet to me it seemed an outrageous demand. This is how we misunderstand the rich — there is a scale to human lives, first it is a matter of propriety and then a tightness around the mind that forever holds back a ten-dollar man from placing fifty-dollar bets. We tremble to ask our worth, but in the end only disappoint with the smallness of our ambition. I think he wanted to be asked then. That was where we so nearly lost it, because we simply could not think as he did.

"You must see the new house before you go," said Mrs Ford. "It's too cold for me to come — I hope you understand. Henry, will you . . .?"

In the failing light we toured the magnificent shell.

"We'll have our own power plant," Mr Ford explained. "Turbines'll run in the river. They're not there yet." He idly worked an electrical switch.

We explored the place like children in a ruin, our eyes following the weak light of a battery lamp. A towering pipe organ appeared in the beam.

"Do you play?" asked Rosika.

"No."

His manner became perfunctory, absorbed. I know now that he is often this way, but at the time I was sure we had offended him and because of that lost our cause. We made our way back outside, stepping over cut timber and boxes of nails. I had resigned myself to failure, but Rosika began again on our case as we shivered our way through the gardens. We walked through a gap in some bushes and found ourselves by an empty swimming pool. The tiling had just been finished and tools still lay about the edges.

"The builders said we should have one," explained Ford. "But I don't suppose it'll see much use."

It was the only bright thing — a giant porcelain bowl holding all that was left of the light.

"Perhaps I could put fish in it?"

Rosika, who had been talking all this time about diplomacy, mediation, neutrality, borders, attrition, war aims, finally ground to a halt, accepting that Mr Ford had not heard a single word. We stared gloomily into the pristine, frivolous absurdity of the swimming pool.

"A ship," said Rosika.

"You spoke, Mrs Schwimmer?"

"A ship. That's what we need — a peace *ship*."

A hefty tonnage of steel and coal, of pistons, connecting rods, boilers, screws, funnels, smoke and hooting steam-whistles coalesced before the tiled blankness and planted a stirring kiss on Henry Ford's mind.

"A ship?"

"A peace ship. *The* Peace Ship — to take all the delegates to a mediation conference. And journalists too, to cover the story."

"Journalists, eh?" mused Mr Ford. "A peace ship, you say."

"The Henry Ford Peace Ship," I chipped in shamelessly.

Mr Ford tried the words out to see how they fitted. "The Henry Ford Peace Ship."

Have you seen an express train pick up a mail bag? They hang it out below a wide iron hoop, like a keyring but twenty times the size. Then they hang the hoop on a pole right by the track and when the train comes it scoops it up at a hundred miles an hour and carries it off. You can never quite see how it happens. One second it's there, and the next it's gone, disappeared as if the fast and the slow are too different to live in the same world. I stood in the hall of the Ford farmhouse like one of those mail bags waiting passively for its train. Mr Ford was speaking on the telephone. Clara looked worried as she searched for a warm coat for her husband. Ray was getting the car ready out front. I would not see my wife and daughter that day, or the next day or for many months, each hour of which would be lived at the dizzying, foreign pace of money.

"You work for me now, Mr Lochner. I've annexed you."

Rosika danced before the frowning Mrs Ford. She kissed me on the cheek and delivered her belated line of Emerson — "Things are in the saddle, ride mankind!"

Within an hour I was on a train to New York with Henry Ford. He talked expansively about *our* peace campaign and it was strange to hear those words that could only be prayers or mere whimsy for other men, but for him could all be turned into realities in a moment with a telephone call or a signature. Power had been hitched to our wagon, and money in abundance too. As the night rushed by I understood that if we still failed it would have to be for some other, less excusable reason.

On the seat beside my new employer his bag lay open, stuffed tight as a mattress with unread telegrams.

Marquis

It was my fault. The young lady who came to my door unannounced was charming, perhaps cleverly so. I know her parents and respect them. I remembered her from when she was a child and had no reason to be suspicious. She stated her business plainly and was not, I am sure, insincere. In the space of a few minutes' conversation we found that we had many common views on the European war. Unfortunately, I was pressed for time that day and embarrassed that I could not spend longer with her. That is why, hat in hand, I passed Miss Shelly innocently on to my wife. When I left there had not yet been any mention of Henry Ford, money or the relentless Madame Rosika Schwimmer. I gave no instruction or warning to Mrs Marquis. When I returned in the afternoon and found that the delightful visitor had obtained a passport straight to my wife's good friend Clara Ford there was no one else to blame. It was, I fear to say, the first chink in the Ford armour.

To be charitable to myself, that is not the whole story. There were other lines of attack — ones I was in no position to block. Even chance seemed on the side of this doubtful adventure. Mr Ford is a great believer in destiny. His attraction to the idea forms one of the many shallows of his mind. As a pastor it is my duty to discourage such nonsense, nevertheless, such has been the profusion and the ordering of coincidences over the last two weeks that I also have been musing on invisible forces. For one thing, it all happened when Liebold was on vacation. A man with an infinity of money and a weakness for sudden enthusiasms must be protected against himself and Mr Liebold has long been recognised as the most reliable defence against mishaps of this sort. For this very reason all Ford's intimates take great care not to let it be known when Liebold is absent or, as it was once put to me, when the lid is off the honey pot. From what I hear some journalist got wind of it anyway and passed the tip onto the Schwimmer woman. This, I am to believe, resulted from a chance encounter in the street. No doubt the truth will come out in the end.

Even at this stage nothing would have happened had Mr Anderson not proved to be another happy throw of the dice for the peacettes. Anderson has groaned under Liebold's tyranny for years. Liebold despises him and greatly fears being replaced by him. Mr Anderson greatly fears that he will not replace Liebold. Anderson would have had no difficulty in repelling the advances of Rosika Schwimmer and Rebecca Shelly — after all, he did exactly that for a dozen other petitioners on the very same day Schwimmer turned up. No indeed — it was his ambition to present Liebold on his return with a changed situation, a change of his own authorship, and what better than a new and captivating cause that would carry Mr Ford beyond the recall of his squat, balding, Germanic and — let us be frank — decidedly unpleasant personal secretary? So it was that Madame Schwimmer was ushered into the Ford presence in his office at Highland Park. Aside from the two principals, the meeting was attended by Charles Brownell, the Ford Motor Company's advertising director, Mr Ford's attorney, Alfred Lucking and myself.

Everything went well. Madame Schwimmer's case was fluent, nuanced, complex and passionate and Mr Ford's eyes quickly glazed over. After a few minutes he became absorbed in drawing a clutch plate on a notepad. The danger of a new project receded and Schwimmer finally stopped, no longer able to pretend that she was not being rudely ignored by the man she had come to see. Ford looked up then turned to Brownell.

"What do you say, Charlie?"

"No sale. Now I know I've said this before, but ambulances are the thing. Do you collect for ambulances, Mrs Schwimmer?"

Madame swelled with indignation.

"Let's face it — they gotta need 'em and we can make 'em. Ambulances is a game we can't lose."

The advertising director's eyes took on a visionary remoteness as his hands sketched the dimensions of a new poster.

"Ford First on Flanders Field, Ford to the Rescue, and then one on the way to the dressing station — Thank God it's a Ford, nurses standing by with white aprons and red crosses on them. Nurses are good."

Mr Ford showed Brownell the back of his hand — it's a gesture of his, the hand held up to the temple as if to shield the eye from a disturbing light. It means "enough" and must be instantly obeyed. Brownell sat back in his chair, accepting that the time was not yet right. The magnate turned to face his petitioner.

"I know who caused the war."

Madame Schwimmer cleared the disconsolate look from her face while the rest of us stiffened for the awkwardness to come.

"I know who's under the whole rotten business and I know who's keeping it going."

You should understand that Mr Ford has very definite opinions about the Jews. From time to time he will get relief from whatever ails him by sharing these views with anyone willing to listen and of course, when you are Henry Ford, everyone is willing to listen. His concept of Jewry is abstract and no less primitive than the evil eye or some minor deity of inconvenience who must be named and cursed whenever an engine will not start or the interest rate rises. Real men of flesh and blood do not impinge on the matter in the slightest — he sends a Christmas card and a new car every year to his good friend Rabbi Franklin. Indeed, such is the purity of his views in this field, their pristine isolation from the world of realities, that I doubt he could reliably point out a Jew in a crowded synagogue. So it was that while Brownell, Lucking and myself could all accurately interpret Madame Schwimmer's name, background, appearance, manner, accent and cast of mind, these things meant nothing to Mr Ford. The poor woman — I did not want her to succeed, but I felt for her deeply as she sat through a quarter-hour explanation of how, as a matter of scientific fact, her own people were at the root of all the world's problems, not least the war she so foolishly dreamed of stopping. I looked on with mounting discomfort as her eyes brightened and brimmed behind the heavy lenses of her spectacles and I prayed that the tear would not drop.

There the story of Henry Ford and the great peace campaign would certainly have ended had it not been for the most extraordinary mischance of all. Clara would have had her husband by her side for Christmas, hopes would not cruelly have been raised and the world's great industrialist would have done what he can instead of what he cannot. The meeting was over. Madame Schwimmer got to her feet and collected her bag, ponderous with secrets, from where it had sat beside her on its own chair throughout. She gathered herself bravely.

"Ah, well. It seems my quest is not yet over."

We did not respond when she talked of an imminent voyage back home to Hungary. I and my colleagues returned to our seats and exchanged glances of mutual satisfaction and relief. Mr Ford ushered Madame Schwimmer to the door, all danger surely passed. But as it opened, apparently against some resistance, the sound of excitement and disorder came from the anteroom. The word "Louis" was exclaimed by Schwimmer. The press men fell silent and as I looked, from where I sat, at a shadowy jostle of shoulders and the backs of heads I heard Mr Anderson's voice introduce a new actor to the drama. Whether thoughtlessly, or through a genius intuition into the mysteries of his employer's heart, he used the only word in the language that could have had such a transforming effect on the fortunes of this "victim of circumstance". Brownell, Lucking and I stared at each other with amazement and some alarm as we heard of a private invitation to Mr Ford's new home at Fair Lane, an invitation that had certainly never been mentioned before.

It was there, the next day and in the less protected surroundings of his own home, that the deed was done. Cleverly, they lured him out to the freezing grounds and away from Clara's good common sense. It was in the garden, by a swimming pool no less, that Madame Rosika Schwimmer, the quintessence of old Europe, subtle and opaque, sinfully persuasive, a refined oratorical disease to which the infant Henry had no more resistance than an Inca to smallpox, took the last steps of her long, iceberg way and convinced — oh dear, oh dear — convinced Henry Ford that he could stop the war.

The newly engaged Mr Delavigne waxed hyperbolical on the peace scheme, but did his master little good by putting the phrase, "Out of the trenches by Christmas, never to return," into his mouth. We were already deep into November, and the newspapers already laughing.

"You're going to stop the war in a month, Mr Ford?"

"Well," shrugged the engineer, "there's always Easter."

His next suggestion — that Christmas Day on the European battlefields would see a general strike of fighting men "taking the business of peace into their own hands" caused panic among the foreign delegations in Washington and briefly promoted Mr Ford to the front ranks of international revolutionary Marxism. Someone asked him if this was his new creed and the tragedy was up and running when he replied, "If it stops the war, maybe it is."

These fragments, and others still more lurid, we received at a distance, trying to interpret them as best we could. I stayed in Detroit, as did Clara, while Henry dashed from New York to Washington and back with his fresh new friends. They generated headline after headline and cartoons too, which I had to look at over my breakfast, hoping unreasonably that no one else would see them, above all that Clara would not see them. Mr Ford had had enthusiasms before and no one who knew him well believed this would come to anything. Even Liebold, who extended his vacation in Colorado to view some local plants, read the Denver newspapers without concern, certain that he could dampen his employer's ardour as soon as he got back to Detroit. A nameless inside source passed this morsel on to the local papers and there he was the Tuesday after his return — drawn as a dwarfish uniformed Prussian with a Kaiser moustache, spiked helmet and the 1915 Ford price-list poking out of his tunic pocket. He held a small fire-bucket of sand as he stood disconsolately by the edge of the blazing forest of Henry's moral passions.

It was only during my last ten days on dry land that I began to take the idea of an actual peace voyage to Europe seriously. There were reports of shipping agents brawling in the lobby of the Biltmore Hotel and then a photograph of an actual ship. A destination was announced only as "a certain central point at which delegates will congregate". Flocks of invitations flew across the land, darkening the skies. Declarations were made, so definite that even Henry Ford would have found them hard to back out of. I prayed that it would end well and, even as the telephone rang, thanked the Lord that I would have nothing to do with it myself.

Clara summoned me. On a cloudy late November morning the lamps were still lit in the main parlour at Edison Avenue. Some of the furniture had already been removed to the new house at Fair Lane and these unfamiliar spaces left us sitting in a stage-set atmosphere of disaster. Edsel was brought in for a few minutes of small-talk then sent on his way, his mother looking after her minimal family with anxious intensity. I waited for an accusation and perhaps received it when she handed me a terse letter from her husband. It talked of the packing of bags and her immediate travel to New York and embarkation.

"He really means it, then?" I said.

I felt the cold formality of her speech.

"It would appear so."

She looked again to the door through which young Edsel had just left.

"Since my marriage day I have never left my husband's side. I hoped never to do so but you will understand, Samuel, that as a mother I could never do anything that might leave Edsel an orphan."

The unworthy thought rose up in my mind — how dreadful it would be to inherit the Ford Motor Company at an early age.

"Two more ships lost last week," Clara continued. "Both of them neutral. Germany apologises and says they can't be expected to see through fog, but does anyone believe them? If you can't see and shot anyway what difference does it make? Have we forgotten the *Lusitania*?"

Her voice rose with the anger of abandonment. Why only one son? I found myself wondering. Why this sudden foreign love of Henry's, the only cause that could take him physically so far from his wife?

"It won't come to anything, Clara, surely. You know how he is. If any ship goes anywhere Henry won't be on it. A few days before departure he'll send someone else in his place and it'll be better for everyone."

"I'm not so sure, Samuel. I don't know these people, I don't understand them, I don't know what they want. Why does he need to be with them? Can't he just give them some money?"

I had never seen her so shaken or so heedless of anyone's problems but her own. For Clara, a brush with the world's great problems had brought none of that uplift the campaigners so loved to speak of and she seemed truly to have worked herself into the belief that she might never see Henry again. Her anxiety was real and drew from me a thoughtless gesture.

"If there's anything I can do, Clara. Anything at all . . ."

She reached to her sewing basket and took the letter from where it had lain in wait behind pincushions and hanks of coloured yarn. She softened, brightened as my words brought her instant relief.

"I knew I wouldn't have to ask, Samuel. I knew I could rely on you."

I took the envelope, sternly addressed to "Henry Ford, my husband" in the disciplined, country school hand I remembered well from my first invitation to the Ford residence. It was only then, holding that weighty document, that I understood how right Clara was — that this was no mere jaunt but could, quite literally, be a matter of life and death. Why not another torpedo in the night? The ghastly scene dramatised itself until Clara's words recalled me.

"You must go to him."

For an awful moment it seemed she was suggesting I share Mr Ford's madness and go with him to Europe.

"But, Clara, what could I do? And to leave you here at a time like this . . ."

It was a misjudgement and she did not spare me.

"What can you do here, Samuel? No, you must go to him at once — please. He will listen to you. That is what I ask him to do in the letter. You can stop all this nonsense before it is too late, I am sure. I would not ask anyone else. I don't even know where he is. Sometimes I read New York, sometimes Washington, sometimes both on the same day. I telephone the Biltmore Hotel and I can't get connected. *I* can't get through. Look."

She handed me a scrap of newspaper which advertised a "Mother's Day" Peace Rally to be held at the Belasco Theatre in Washington before the presentation of peace resolutions to President Wilson. Rosika Schwimmer was among the attractions as, in rather larger type, was the new, escaped Henry Ford.

"Bring him back to me, Samuel. Back to those who truly care for him."

Relieved of all thought of steaming to Europe, this was an embassy I was happy to accept. I slipped into the daily stream of my fellow citizens as Clara Ford's confidential agent, rubbing shoulders, if the newspapers are to be believed, with the spies and secret procurers of a dozen other powers all engaged on equally clandestine work. For the first time these fantasies seemed plausible to me. In trains and station waiting rooms I became self-consciously unobtrusive, avoiding eyes and anxiously questioning the motives of the most innocent glance. Faces around me turned to images from magazine stories. I became convinced I was being followed and so intimidated an elderly gentleman by turning on him and asking him his business that he actually told me, taking a worn shoe from a bag to show me as evidence of his journey to a repair shop. In the event, I proved to have some talent for the work, slipping the nets of my unseen enemies and arriving unharmed on the morning of 26 November at a scene of histrionic chaos only a few blocks from the White House itself.

The amazons of peace milled densely outside the theatre doors, my employer's lean grey head nowhere visible above the press of bonnets and the umbrellas opening as rain began to fall. Large posters proclaimed the event — Schwimmer's name in skyscraper letters and then "Henry Ford" with a generous second billing, and lower still Mrs Ethel Snowden, an obscure Englishwoman with whom I was never to exchange a word. I had not announced my arrival to the organisers, fearing they could make difficulties in my obtaining a personal interview with Mr Ford, or that they would coach him with arguments against me. Mine was to be a surprise attack and I slipped past the crowd and down an alleyway to the stage door.

Once inside, my presence was detected as quickly as that of a fox in a hen-house. The charming Miss Shelly appeared at my side and told me how delighted she was to see me. She asserted that I must have come to support their cause and I did not contradict her. When I said I had a message for Mr Ford she said, "Of course," and asked if I would like her to take it to him. When I said I must speak to him in person and that I believed he was somewhere in the building she said, "Of course," and offered to be my guide. It was some twenty minutes later and after frequent apologies for her failure to find him that we found ourselves in a sub-basement. Under the light of a single dingy bulb I looked round at the heaped costumes of harlequins, clowns, pirates, waifs, angels, imperilled princesses and pasteboard kings. Miss Shelly shrugged.

"He doesn't seem to be here either. I really am sorry — everything is a bit chaotic."

"Miss Shelly, shall we end this now? It's beneath you."

She straightened and became severe.

"Dean Marquis, I believe in what I am doing. I draw no stipend or salary for my work. We aim to succeed and will do whatever we honestly can to reach that goal."

"Honestly? Have you honestly brought me down here?"

"There is a higher honesty."

I moved some wooden swords from the top of a property basket, took off my hat and coat and sat down.

"Miss Shelly, I pray that you will succeed, as earnestly as I have ever prayed for anything."

"But you don't think we will, do you? You are not with us."

"I . . ."

I felt a sudden heaviness, as I had once before in my life in the last instant before telling a lie. I raised my hands emptily as I waited for something to say.

"I am not against you."

"That's not enough. You have come to dissuade him."

"I have come to give him a letter from his wife."

"And to talk to him."

"Yes. I have to care for Mr Ford too, and for Mrs Ford — she needs him."

"So do we. She can come with us. I know she has the invitation."

"That's impossible."

"It's her choice."

"You are harsh, Miss Shelly."

"Yes, I am. People don't understand that about us. I suppose it's because we want peace — it's a common mistake."

"He is here, isn't he?"

"Yes, he's here."

"Will you take me to him, please."

"Why don't *you* speak?"

"To whom?"

"To the meeting. To everyone. You say you are not against us. You are respected, Dr Marquis. Just say a few words at the start, then you can talk to Mr Ford."

"Are you bargaining with me, Miss Shelly?"

She smiled.

"But how could I? I'm powerless."

From above, a sound like distant thunder penetrated the floors. Miss Shelly consulted the little watch pinned to her blouse.

"Come on, we're about to start."

Perspiring in the heat, I was led quickly up several flights of stairs, the noise growing all the time, then through another door and into the bustling excitement of the wings, crowded with figures indistinct in silhouette or starkly half-lit by the brilliance from the stage. Although I couldn't see her, Madame Schwimmer's voice sounded clearly above the fray, the one sharp, irrepressible instrument no orchestra could drown. Someone was already speaking and the sound from the auditorium surged through the offbeats of their rhetoric. A confusion of excitement and panic took hold of me. As in a dream of frustration, endless stumbling blocks appeared from all around. I thought I saw something and stepped forward only to collide with Mr Lochner, late of the Chicago Peace Society. He shook my hand and congratulated me on my conversion to the cause. I shouted in his ear.

"Where's Mr Ford?"

He turned and I followed the direction of his gaze. There, on the threshold of the stage, black against its limelight was the tall, pauper-thin and unmistakable outline of Henry Ford. A stranger asked to find the odd one out would have had no difficulty. There was a poignant foreignness to his movements, the timid if hungry leaning forward to see and the quick step back to avoid being seen. Here was no actor, unless a very skilful one already in character. With an odd, barely controlled sense of urgency I felt I had to speak to him that instant — not merely that, but to get a hand on him too as if he were a child on the point of being stolen away.

"Mr Ford!"

I found Madame Schwimmer in my path. She stood very close and spoke too rapidly to be understood. My view was filled with her broad, ecstatic face, her wide, full bloom of wiry hair and, where the dark eyes should have been, only the moist obscurity of clouded lenses. A huge wave of noise came from the stage.

"Mr Ford!"

My words drowned. The glare made it hard to see. There was someone standing by Ford's side. She had her hand on his arm and just as I called a second time she stepped out with him into the light which was so intense he seemed to switch all at once from black to white. Schwimmer too went out on stage and took her seat behind the long table, skirted with the banner of the Women's International Peace Committee. She polished her pince-nez and calmly reached for a pitcher of water. Mid-stage, Ford hesitated, abruptly discovered in the stage lights. He looked to his left and I felt for him as he gauchely shielded his eyes in an attempt to see the audience. One chair behind the table was left unoccupied. As he looked longingly in its direction the cheering of the crowd resolved into a chant.

"We want Henry! We want Henry! We want Henry!"

Slowly he was drawn to the front of the stage. As the noise abated I heard a few words of the anxious exchange.

"Say it for me."

"*I* can't say it. It must be you."

Mr Ford pleaded but was inexorably moved forward. The silence became profound. Halting and weakly he spoke his fatal line.

"Out of the trenches by Christmas — never to return."

A deafening response came out of the darkness. Feet stamped and the whole building vibrated. The mystified and slightly trembling engineer was led to his place. From where she sat by his side, Madame Schwimmer raised her glass in my direction and stood to begin her work. With her hands she calmed the storm.

"The Dean of the Episcopal Cathedral of Detroit, the Reverend Dr Samuel Marquis, will start us off with a short prayer."

* * *

Late that afternoon, as the peace campaigners stood in silent vigil outside the White House while Madame Schwimmer delivered the conference resolutions, Henry Ford and I wrestled in the warmth of the New Willard Hotel. Victory often seemed close, but at times the noise and stage light of the Belasco Theatre came back into his mind and to these arguments — whatever they were — I had no answer. I persuaded him at least to return to Detroit and to Clara, and was sure, as I rode with him on the train, that she would prevail where I could not. Man and wife talked, and in an earlier age that would certainly have been enough but Lochner and Schwimmer and all that buzzed in New York came down the wires of the long-distance telephone and fought for his soul. Under Clara's eyes he spoke uncertainly into the ether.

"Do you think I really have to go?"

The other voice orated at length and we could hear its sharp crackle as it got louder. I detected Madame Schwimmer's slightly alien rhythms. Mr Ford hooked the receiver and turned to give us his decision.

"I'll talk to them," he said. "Maybe I'll just see them off."

So he went back east and for a second time I was sent after him and found myself in his room at the Biltmore at two in the morning on the day of departure. Travel-soiled and exhausted, I lay slumped in my chair, staring out at the city. The long note of a tugboat sounded from where it worked on the Hudson. Mr Ford had had a busy day with the peace campaigners. At that moment he sat opposite, as lively and restored as the winner of a bare-knuckle fight.

"So that's that."

I had nothing more to give. Over two hours all my sermons had revolted and turned against me. "You said" became Ford's refrain. "You said . . . you said . . ."

"But . . ."

"I've got it right, haven't I, Samuel? Word for word. That *is* what you said."

That was true. The parts he did remember, he remembered perfectly. They had become drawings in his mind. The parts he had forgotten, he had forgotten with equal perfection.

"Didn't you tell me that what is right cannot fail?"

"That's what I believe."

"And is it not right to try to stop the war?"

"Of course, but . . ."

"Then that's that. I got a hunch, Samuel, and I'm going through with it. I'm going to stick by these people. I'm going the whole way with them, soup to nuts and that's that."

He stood up and pushed open the window. Even at that hour, the rumble from his countless products echoed up from the streets. Lights flowed like blood around the great monuments of the moneylenders, the capitols of the unseen empire that so obsessed him. Mr Ford had come amongst them, he had set up his camp in the very heart of that hidden power that plotted relentlessly to drag his country into a foreign war. Somewhere down there Baruch, Goldman, Warburg and Rothschild were whispering together in a cryptic tongue. For a moment I wondered if he even thought of Europe at all.

"Will you look at that? The first car I ever travelled in, Samuel, was one I made with my own hands and when I drove it, it was the only one on the road. In ten days the millionth will roll off the line at Highland Park. In little more than a year another million will follow. I just . . ."

He told me these things with the tone of one announcing a bereavement and as he faltered I hoped for one last chance to reason with him.

"Surely you can help them here — direct the campaign at home while they are away?"

He seemed not to hear me.

"I just wish I could make you understand how sad money is. Show me a rich man and I'll show you a disappointed man. I think there must be some law about it — there are delays, but in the end the result is always the same. I don't know how to . . ."

He turned to me, suddenly cheered by a thought.

"Do you like this hotel, Samuel?"

I was used to his mental jumps, but this was one I couldn't follow. I shrugged and gave him a questioning look.

"Do you want it?"

"What do you mean?"

"Just that — do you want it? We can wrap it up in a few days. We'll wire the proprietors, have it valued, offer three times as much, call the lawyers in — by the end of next week it's yours. Look, there's another one over there. Why not have two? It'd make no difference to me. You just say the word, Samuel."

Any man could say these things, but when Henry Ford says this to you it is very different. There is no fantasy in such an exchange and the hair rises on the back of your neck as you grasp the power of your response. Just say the word. One says "No", of course. One says it quickly, or dismissively — whatever one needs to cover the hesitation as one brushes by that other, radically changed life, yours for the price of a single syllable.

"Do you follow me, Samuel? I am in a peculiar position. No one can give me anything. There is nothing I want I cannot have, but I do not want the things money can buy. Neither the making nor the use of money means anything to me as far as I am personally concerned. I want to live a life, to make the world a little better for having lived in it. You know, the trouble with people is that they do not think. I want to do and say things that will make them think."

The homespun school of philosophy is Mr Ford's last and most impregnable fortress. When he retires behind its walls and pulls up its drawbridge only a fool does not admit defeat.

"Well," I relented. "Busy day tomorrow — best get some sleep."

"Goodnight, Samuel."

"Goodnight, Mr Ford."

Anticipating failure, Clara had come through from Detroit two days before. If necessary she would see her husband off, but had firmly refused to go further. She had her own room two floors down, away from the disturbance and indiscretion of the campaign headquarters. Past muffled snores and a sleepy bellboy carrying a glass of whisky on a tray, I trod the thick crimson carpet as it snaked over the veined marble of the stairs — the Biltmore's advertisements talked of Italian palaces, of the luxury of experiencing Europe without ever leaving home. I knocked lightly on Clara's door — perhaps she would not hear, perhaps it could all be put off till the morning? But it opened promptly and I went in. I said at once that it was hopeless and she thanked me for trying.

Preparations for the morning were still being made, a selection of furs lying on the bed or draped over the back of the dressing-table chair. In only a few hours she would go to Hoboken with her husband, be seen by the press and the public and make a good show sending him off on the *Oscar II*. I would return with her to Detroit.

"Go with him, Samuel."

"What?"

She put her hands on my arms and drew me towards her.

"Who else can I trust? Who else can I ask? I want you to bring him back to me, whatever happens."

I made my excuses, and they were not trivial — my job, my engagements, my wife.

"This one thing, Samuel, please. If I never ask for anything again? Samuel — for me."

Is it that some women know how to be unrefusable, or that money knows how to command? I have given the question up and recline here, quite pleasantly for the moment, on the first-class promenade deck of a Danish liner that has seen better days. I am flanked by new friends. Mr Bingham on my left, a gentleman of the theatre. And on my right young Berton Braley, reporter and syndicated poet of the people, still a little dazed by the freshness of his matrimony. We are not good sailors and the swell makes it unwise for us to stand too long. By contrast, Miss Inez Milholland walks steadily by, as untroubled as a mermaid, and spares us a glance of scant respect. Helplessly, our three married heads turn to watch her pass. Inspired, poet Braley takes out a pencil and makes a note on the back of a menu card.

Theodore

Oh, sure — Ford was a dream job. In the days between my first piece in the *Free Press* and that riot on Hoboken pier you couldn't shift a spotlight fast enough to keep him out of it. The old man was as generous with his name as he was with his money — he didn't care at all how I used it and it became the biggest and best megaphone anyone could have wished for. Articles by "Henry Ford" appeared everywhere and the whole country was reading my words — *Millions Murdered by Military Parasites; Cannon and Slaughter No Part of Patriotism; Sloths and Lunatics in Military Cliques; World Cries Out Against War — Ford Takes the Lead.* Everyone was talking about it. Under other names I could syndicate inside stories about the Peace Ship right across the country. What Mr Ford paid me was maybe half of what I made in those few weeks. I did a good job for him.

I was really supposed to be back in Detroit, but I got out of that as quickly as I could and decamped to New York where everything was happening. The seventh floor of the Biltmore Hotel was an inferno and for the week before the *Oscar* slipped out of Hoboken it must have been the most exciting place in the world. The Ford office on Long Island was thrown into chaos and then just as quickly re-tooled for the new task of promoting world peace. Omnibuses arrived and decanted scores of bewildered staff — stenographers, typists, clerks, messengers, translators and cashiers who swarmed all over the place.

"Hey, buddy — you'd think there's a war on!"

No one seemed really sure what was going on, but everyone knew it was important. You could see from their faces they just knew nothing like this would ever happen to them again, however long they lived.

Mr Ford's a natural for good copy, but I learned early on he's better with one or two people at a time than he is with groups. This is, after all, the man who addressed the prisoners in Sing Sing with the phrase "Hope to meet you all here again soon." There was, accordingly, no little anxiety on the morning of the big anouncement. Forty reporters crowded round in the lobby of the hotel, their eyes focused on a dry-mouthed Mr Ford, myself, Mr Louis "the victim" Lochner, and Mr Oswald Garrison Villard of the *Evening Post* who had come at Mr Ford's invitation to lend his expertise in press matters. As it turned out, it's just as well he was there.

"We're going to try to get the boys out of the trenches by Christmas," he started. "I've chartered a ship and some of us are going to Europe."

The reporters scribbled then looked up again and waited in silence.

"You see we . . . The main idea is to crush militarism and to . . . Well, to get the boys out of the trenches. Our object is to stop war for all times, and also preparedness. War is nothing but preparedness. Those who talk of preparedness in America are nothing but warmongers, profiteers. There are hidden forces in . . ."

Mr Villard gave him a sharp nudge.

"No boy would ever kill a bird if he didn't first have a slingshot or a gun. That's what I say."

There was another pause, and when it seemed that was the end of the statement the man from the *Tribune* put up his hand.

"Mr Ford, sir. What *exactly* do you plan to do once you're over there?"

"I'll leave that to the experts."

Mr Lochner explained the international neutral commission of mediation and enquiry while Ford looked vaguely into the middle distance. When the questions came they were all for him. Mr Ford answered by saying how the ship would be armed with the Marconi equipment, "the longest gun in the world," that would keep everyone in touch with the movement. He then repeated his desire to get the boys out of the trenches.

"They don't want to fight. I know they don't. They'd be just as happy to shake hands with each other. That's what we're going to do over there, gentlemen. We're going to do the greatest good to the greatest number. Thank you."

With that he reached behind himself, found the handle of a door, and disappeared. The newsmen had plenty more to ask and we stayed on a few minutes trying to limit the damage as best we could. I got on the telephone straight after and bought a lot of drinks that evening. The next morning it was clear I had squared some of the papers, but not others. According to one yellow rag we had kidnapped Mr Ford and had him hypnotised by Madame Bolshevatsky (Rosika Schwimmer's secret sister) so he no longer knew he was an American. The *Times* thundered harmlessly above the heads of the people by calling him "a callow utilitarian".

"Now tell me, Theodore, is that a good thing or a bad thing to be?"

I reassured him on that point. He liked the *Trib* headline best of all: GREAT WAR ENDS CHRISTMAS DAY — Ford to Stop It — *Best of all Christmases Less Than a Month Away*. I got pretty nervous when he picked that up, but he read the whole thing without getting it and no one saw the need to put him right. If Mr Ford was happy, we were happy. To tell the truth, the cartoons were more of a problem than the reports. Mr Ford didn't read much but he would look at any number of pictures. In the end they started to come so thick and fast Lochner took on a boy just to cut them out and hide them first thing in the morning. "Cuttings for the archives" was the answer if anyone ever asked us. No one did, not even Mr Ford, who just looked through the holes and never gave them a second thought.

With the great industrialist installed and his purse-strings loosened, the Biltmore did a land-office business in hucksters and charlatans. Beside the herds of reporters, photographers and publicity agents there was a steady stream of vaporous enthusiasts who came to tell us we were getting this peace thing all wrong and how, by following their plan, we could get it all right. Others came to denounce the German plot they believed us to be. Some of the newspapers had fun hiring sabre-slashed Prussians from whatever Broadway theatre or moving-picture concern could spare one and sneaking them in in the hope getting a photograph of their "spy" beside Ford, Lochner or Schwimmer. Half the crowd had nothing to do with the peace campaign. Promoters of useless accessories for the Model T descended in plague proportions only to flutter hopelessly against Ray's impenetrable screen. Amongst them, failed vaudevillians not yet engaged for the Christmas season offered at a discount their morale-raising talents.

These were the souls, hopeful or sneering by turns, who populated the outer circles of the Biltmore headquarters. At the centre of the storm sat Rosika Schwimmer doing all the real work. It was her job to select the delegates who would bring peace to Europe. Thousands volunteered every day by letter or telegram and while these were all conscientiously sifted, few, I think, ever got through to the lady herself. She had other names in mind — the sort who had to be pursued rather than fended off. After long debate a text was settled on and this is what the invitees received:

> Will you come as my guest aboard the *Oscar II* of the Scandinavian-American Line, sailing from

New York December 4th for Christiania, Stockholm and Copenhagen? I am cabling the leading men and women of the European nations to join us *en route* and at some central point, to be determined later, to establish an international conference to lead to a just settlement of the War.

One hundred representative Americans are being invited, among whom Jane Addams, Thomas Edison and John Wanamaker have accepted today.

With 20,000 men killed every twenty-four hours, tens of thousands maimed, homes ruined and another winter begun the time has come for women and men of courage and energy to free the goodwill of Europe that it may assert itself for peace and justice.

HENRY FORD

Changes were soon necessary on account of the fact that none of the three named persons had accepted. Mr Ford, being admirably plain in his own use of language, had not heard the silent "but" at the end of John Wanamaker's response — "I would go to the ends of the earth with you to halt the war . . ." As for the Edisons, Ford had shared the Thanksgiving turkey with them but had returned crestfallen. It was painful to see how long he held to the hope that his great mentor and model would go with him. And the great Miss Jane Addams? Well, let's just say the truth of that one remains unclear.

Madame Schwimmer was undaunted. All signs were good, if only they were correctly interpreted, and she declared it was for the best if lily-livered, torpedo-fearing fainthearts stayed at home. These were not people any true peace-campaigner would care to share a cabin with. There were plenty more willing to take up their place, and as the image of a Peace Ark became commonplace Rosika rose magnificently to her role of the new Noah, parading through the corridors of the Biltmore with an ominous list in her hand. Early each morning I looked over the shoulder of our boy censor as he cut the caricatures of our ample, bespectacled, bun-haired leader from the papers. There she was, standing by the gangplank with list and goose-feather quill at the ready, saving friends and damning enemies to extinction as the patient line of delegates snaked away to the vanishing point. In another, the *Oscar* was already at sea (her name crossed out and replaced with *Ship of Fools*) while behind her the United States themselves were sinking. "The Good Lord be thanked!" burbled the Statue of Liberty as she went beneath the waves, "The best of America is saved." On the other side of the ocean the British Army organised a welcoming honour guard, a mustachioed sergeant shouting the order, "Squad — present straitjackets!"

"I don't fear criticism," Mr Ford liked to say. "I learn from it."

The lesson many learned from their morning papers was that the Peace Ship was fast becoming untouchable. Cardinal Gibbons down in Baltimore had started off by calling it the finest and best gift for Christmas. Mr Ford received his personal blessing and sent a cablegram to the Holy Father himself, detailing the project. A confusion over some roman numerals didn't help (not my fault), and it ended up being addressed to someone who had been dead for six hundred years. Anyway, the next we heard at the Biltmore was talk of caution and "rocks ahead" and fears that Mr Ford's sincere wishes might be prevented by unspecified obstacles. Mr William Jennings Bryan, recently departed from President Wilson's cabinet on account of preparedness, had been associated with our campaign from its earliest days. He came to see us at the hotel and spoke for an hour with Mr Ford. After, I admired the skill with which he handled the reporters:

"I have seen Mr Ford and am in hearty sympathy with the effort he is making, and hope to join the party later once it is established in Europe. Only those who want the war to continue ridicule the effort. This was to be expected. Ridicule is the favoured weapon of those who desire to oppose any movement against which they can find no rational argument. If any of the persons on the Ark had been making money out of the Flood, they would have ridiculed Noah for sending out the dove. Success to Mr Ford and his companions. May they return with an olive leaf."

In other words — I will come with you to the end of the pier, but no further.

With one exception, all the Governors of the States found excuses or were frankly opposed. Ida Tarbell came in person to give her regrets to Mr Ford. Minor ailments and "personal reasons" were reported from all quarters. Just before we were due to sail Clara Ford herself came to the Biltmore with Edsel, her son. Their presence was felt two floors above in the Stop the War Suite, and made flesh in the person of Clara's suave, creeping agent, Reverend Samuel Marquis. There were fears that Mr Ford himself would not go and it was in the middle of this anxiety that Louis Lochner put down a report on Madame Schwimmer's desk:

> JANE ADDAMS IN HOSPITAL — BUT ONLY FOR OBSERVATION
>
> Jane Addams, settlement worker and peace advocate, was taken to the Presbyterian hospital today for "observation".
>
> Dr James Herrick said that her illness is not serious. Miss Addams has not been feeling well for several days. Whether her condition will prevent her from accompanying the Ford peace party abroad depends on developments.

Schwimmer immediately headed for the lobby. At the height of her energy she drove in a taxi-cab round every hospital in the city and returned three hours later. One third furious, two thirds triumphant, she declared to Louis and me — "Just as I thought. Nowhere to be found — the rat!"

We threw our net pretty widely in this business of gathering delegates. Former presidents were by no means beyond our ambition. Theodore Roosevelt was not polite, but when we heard that Mr Taft was coming through town Schwimmer sent a messenger to catch him up and ask for his answer. This enterprising boy finally got hold of Taft and had a broad smile on his face by the time he got back to the Biltmore, still with our message in hand, though it had clearly been opened and resealed.

"Well?" demanded Schwimmer.

"I wish I knew what was in it, lady. When Mr Taft read your letter he laughed so hard he set the whole Twenty-third Street Ferry rocking."

It was about this time I started to think. I was getting to dream about ships, and most usually things didn't go too well and I'd wake up in a sweat. Maybe the rocking Twenty-third Street Ferry was a sign too.

Clergymen were easier — we had no shortage of them. Men of middling rank and advanced opinions were also bolder. Judge Ben B. Lindsey of Colorado, the fashionable juvenile judge and apostle of free love said "yes" and stayed true to his word. The old warhorse of the muckraking days, S. S. McClure, also found some space in his diary now that his business partners had thrown him off his own magazine. Those with no reputation at all were never a problem. Journalists we had to stave off like drowning men from a lifeboat — this was a story everyone wanted a part of, and no need to worry about expenses neither. We had guys from the *Times* (New York and Brooklyn), the *Eagle, The Day*, the *World*, the *Tribune* (New York and Chicago), *Harper's Weekly* and *Collier's Magazine*, the St Louis *Globe Democrat* and the *Jewish Daily News* all the way down to *Staats Zeitung* and the Spartanburg *Herald*. A quartet of photographers and three cinematograph men completed the press corps.

One other species had to be gathered together and loaded before the *Oscar* was ready for the off. Being a great despiser of education, Mr Ford felt that students would be better off going to Europe than wasting time in the classroom.

"I want fellows with sand," he explained. "Young men and women who'll quit their colleges if need be to go on the expedition."

It turned out that a very large number of students felt exactly the same way about their education, and had no lack of "sand". We soon had more than we could use and were forced to impose a quota. Struggle broke out across the most gilded campuses of the land. In the end some twenty-five Athletic Union Presidents and all-round habitual participators elbowed their way to the front and received their accreditation. A small but exquisite contingent from Vassar and Brown added greatly to the aesthetic quality of the passenger list and there was a new and more salacious outbreak of Ark metaphors. Mrs Ada Morse Clark, personal secretary to the Chancellor of Stanford, was sent precisely to put an end to all such talk. A good job had been done disinforming this formidable lady about train timetables, sailing times and the new passport regulations. Nevertheless, the chaperone cleared all obstacles and arrived from California with papers in order and five minutes to spare, only to be booed from the rail of the second-class deck by her disappointed charges and immediately christened "Policeman Clark".

Being bound for a war-torn continent, it was decided that this peace army should carry all its material with it and be as independent as possible. Accordingly, the name of Rexford Holmes was added to the payroll, an energetic character who relished the task of provisioning such a mighty expeditionary force.

"Yes, sir!" he told me. "It's a ripsnorter and no doubt about it."

Twenty thousand large envelopes were ordered, six hundred reams of paper and three hundred boxes of carbon paper, two thousand pencils, forty jars of paste and, with admirable realism, five gross of erasers. A set of rustproof Navy typewriters was acquired and a team of staff to use them. Whatever was going to happen would certainly be well recorded.

Money washed out across the city. Much of it went to the Biltmore, which provided luxury after luxury without ever being asked, or being told not to. Madame Schwimmer found the ship itself not quite fit for the noble cause of peace and ordered a $1,000 freshen-up from Wanamaker's. The lounge and cabin furnishings were redone and the drapes and lampshades changed to match. Six score of new cushions were strewn about the place to support the delegates in their post-debate exhaustion. A hot-house of palms and flowers appeared. Pigeons vanished from the public parks, were stuffed and bleached and equipped with olive branches and wired to the branches of frosted Christmas trees. A hedge of decency grew up across the corner bar in the grand saloon — prohibitionists on one side, journalists on the other.

Many of the delegates had little or no money and no one thought it reasonable that they should equip themselves for a sea voyage and European diplomacy at their own expense. Purchase orders from the Ford Motor Company became as good as banknotes. The mere mention of the Peace Expedition was enough to make a customer creditworthy. Shop assistants put away the serge and flannel in favour of *peau de soie*. Astrakhan and skunkskin gave way to seal. The merchants of life-vests, waterproof trunks and sea-sickness remedies had never known a year like it. The comedians at the Hippodrome sang that Santa Ford had come to town. In the audience, delegates, students and journalists laughed and charged their tickets to the company.

On the grounds that Peace should not go threadbare, Rosika Schwimmer herself was forced to impose upon the generosity of her patron. The pawning of her jewels for the cause was an oft-told tale and whenever we heard it we knew we were in for two hours of calm as she headed for the department stores to gather a few more items for her "peace wardrobe". This also mattered because on her return from these trips she was, for a short while, in her most malleable mood. The time to strike was as she struggled from the elevator, momentarily balanced between an equal weight of purchases in each hand. That was the moment when ideas that had been folly in the morning, or persons who had been proscribed on account of some ancient offence, might be slipped past her guard. That was how that fool Bingham got his ticket. There were all sorts of theories, but it really was just as simple as that. I was there by Lochner's side as she puffed down the corridor towards us.

"What about these fellows?" he asked her, waving a handful of letters and telegrams and decade-old signed photographs of made-up faces. "We've been talking about it in the office — maybe it makes sense after all. We could call them Entertainments Officer, or something. There are going to be a lot of opinions on that ship, a lot of very different people. It might be wise to think about the lighter side."

She took the applications and shuffled through them, quick as a card sharp, before handing them back. Surrounded by parcels and bags, economy was one objection she could not raise.

"I don't see the point of it myself, but if you like. Pick the most hopeless, the one who really needs it. At least then it'll do some good."

Rosika went into her private office and returned a few minutes later to provide us with the day's other memorable moment. She held in her hand a large, flat jeweller's case. She opened it to display a spectacular necklace of pearls.

"What do you think?"

Minor extravagance, the sort that everyone felt was too vanishingly small to trouble the Fords, had become the order of the day — people even joked about it — but this was something different. Louis and I stared stiffly at the pearls and said nothing. Rosika reacted with shock at the failure of her gesture.

"You think . . . ? I don't believe it. You think I bought them for *myself*?"

Louis and I shrugged and waited to be told otherwise.

"They are a gift," Rosika nearly shouted. "A gift for Mrs Ford, for all her support."

"You're going to give those to Mrs Ford?"

"But you . . ." Louis looked at me for some hint of how best to go on. "You bought them with . . . Oh, forget it. Whatever you think best."

Rich or poor, most of us understand there is an etiquette to money, a way of handling oneself in its presence. Madame Rosika Schwimmer has never learned those rules. Where and how she lived before getting in with Henry Ford I don't know, but she seemed not even to suspect that such things existed. Perhaps she had some theory that explained why she alone, with the privilege of her cause, was exempt. That would have been in character, but I don't know — I never heard her say it. Like the laughter of President Taft on the Twenty-third Street Ferry, the incident sounded once again the warning bell. If the torpedoes didn't get her, then the money surely would.

The day dawned. There had been worry the night before as we lost sight of Marquis and guessed what he was up to. But it all started well — not only had he failed to detatch our chief from the expedition, the net he had been sent to cut trawled him up too and we hastily arranged one more first-class cabin. I encountered him in one of the corridors as he struggled towards Madame Schwimmer's office.

"Well done Reverend!"

He had his funeral face on and ignored me as he pushed on by.

With our leading man still in place I went down to the lobby to release copies of Mr Ford's departing statement to the press. Like the others, a work of Schwimmer and Lochner, it talked of the carnage depopulating Europe and the terrible slaughter of young manhood, of the secret assurances of thirteen envoys of belligerent and neutral governments, of the certain and universal desire for peace. Hardened hacks scanned it briefly before thrusting it into their raincoat pockets.

"So where's the boss?"

"All in good time. We don't sail till two."

I checked out. Outside, the black five-car caravan that would take Mr Ford and his staff and family across the river to New Jersey had already assembled. The newsmen were gathering round it, trying to pump the drivers for information, and I had the satisfaction of having my Pierce-Arrows brought round and seeing them all follow me with their eyes as I motored off to Hoboken.

There was the *Oscar II*, her name painted in huge white letters against the middle of her black hull. White crosses were at the bow and stern and between them DANMARK in letters high as houses — visible, one hoped, through a distant periscope. Someone had already boarded and their peace banner hung over the rail showing the white knight of civilisation pacifically lancing the dragon of militarism. A red pennant fluttered from a mast with the word "Peace" in white letters. Early delegates harassed the tourist conductors hired to bring order to the embarkation, and these in turn fretted over huge mounds of luggage. The first three stowaways had been detected and were being menaced in a corner by the harbour police. The smallest had been revealed when a dropped trunk cried out in pain. A tearful ten-year-old with a German accent explained he had been given ten dollars to hide in the trunk and say he was a spy when he got out.

"He told me he was a magician," sniffed the boy.

I recognised the style.

"Sure he did, Hansel. His name's Prescott Schumacher and he works for the *Morning Herald*. You see him again you run away — got that? Here."

Overtaken by the mood of the occasion, I gave him ten more and told him to get lost before someone made him a mascot.

The crowd swelled steadily until a carnival of five to six thousand persons was in full swing. The twin spirits of Ziegfeld and Barnum hovered invisibly over the chaos and took fleshly form in Lloyd Bingham, jester and energetic MC. In beret, smock and canary yellow spats he enjoyed to the full his greatest ever success, leading the cheers for every identifiable delegate as they came up the gangway, clowning the Kaiser, shadow-boxing the monster of war and conducting the band in endless repetitions of "I didn't raise my boy to be a soldier". Wielding an enormous megaphone, he made announcements of escalating grandeur as the minutes were counted down to the moment of departure:

"The Reverend Jenkin Lloyd Jones! Hurray for Reverend Jones!"

A man with a large white beard attempted to lead a prayer for peace, but was quickly drowned out by a chorus of Santa Claus jokes.

"Mr Louis B. Hanna, Governor of the great state of North Dakota!"

Governor Hanna, grim-faced and plodding as he ascended to the ship, brightened as he saw a friend in the crowd. He cupped his hands to his mouth and shouted down — "What can I do? I've got relatives in Sweden I haven't seen for years!"

Again Bingham raised the megaphone to his lips.

"Mrs Inez Milholland Boissevain."

A tall figure seized the instrument, causing Bingham to step back in amazement. As the band fell silent a powerful female voice sounded out across the seething quay. There was a passionate response — low, masculine booing and shrill female cheers. The speaker seemed highly satisfied and handed back the bright cone of metal with a flourish.

I shook off a panic-stricken squirrel as it ran up my leg. A number of the reporters had decided to add colour to the event by bringing their own props and these included squirrels, on the ground that Hoboken was where the "nuts" were. A score of these hapless animals had been released and darted here and there, giving rise to shrieks of alarm when they tried to climb whatever dress or lady's coat most resembled a tree trunk. A dog set off in violent pursuit of one, others sped up the ropes and promptly infested the ship. A dozen remained incarcerated in bird-cages, awaiting the leading figures of the voyage. The menagerie was completed as a cloud of white doves emerged from a laundry basket only to escape the scene as fast as they were able. Women became hysterical. An epileptic had a fit.

"Mr S. S. McClure. Hurray for Samuel McClure!"

The fallen titan of the magazine business acknowledged a largely generous reception. Behind him, a brawl threatened to break out over whether "Onward Christian Soldiers" was a suitable number. The first punch was about to be thrown when an electric tremor ran through the crowd. Heads turned, a way was made. Madame Schwimmer herself appeared, borne forward on a wave of noise and excitement, holding aloft the famous black shagreen bag as she made the only entrance of the day to be reported in the fashion as well as the news pages — "Carrying her beaver-trimmed coat over her arm despite the chill and the commencing rain, Madame Schwimmer proved a model for the older woman of refinement, with a full skirt of black satin moire with a pleasing velvet ornamentation, the whole cut simply with two front gores and a plain French-gathered waist that was perhaps only a little too tight beneath the ribbon belt in the suffrage colours of yellow and white. A dove-grey blouse with a deep yoke collar of fine batiste and insets of real valenciennes completed an outfit of authority. The whole was highlighted with much passementerie of tarnished gold." Male eyes saw it differently. One thought she had come as a magpie. Another recorded that ". . . the rotund Hungarian idealist entered into the costume party spirit and came as Lady Macbeth on her way to a free lunch."

Bingham gave her the star treatment. She disappeared on stepping off the gangway, and then was seen a minute later, higher up at the rail of the first-class deck. To a storm of cheering and hooting and a certain quantity of laughter, she brandished her famous bag of secrets. Briefly, she invoked an ocean of blood and misery and the essential goodness of mankind before asking to be excused so that she could begin her work.

"The Reverend Samuel S. Marquis. Hurray for Reverend Marquis!"

Carrying in his hand a small, hastily packed valise, the joyless episcopalian climbed to the ship as tragically as to his own execution. Bingham stepped aside and presented him to the crowd with an impresario's sweep of the hand. Pilgrim Marquis was not tempted and passed on without saying a word. He spotted me and hesitated, glowering down to where I stood on the quayside, perhaps surprised and a little envious to see me still on dry land. Up to the last two or three days I had thought I would travel too. But then enthusiasm — or was it courage, or conviction? — started to slip away under cover of darkness. Each morning I awoke with diminished forces and began to wonder if I should not join the deserters myself. A more honourable course became possible when I found myself alone with Mr Ford on the last Wednesday at the Biltmore.

"You need a good man to stay behind, sir. Someone to direct the campaign at home while you're away."

There was a lengthy silence while he considered the idea.

"You don't want to turn your back on Congress, sir. You know what they're like — someone should stay back to keep things on the boil."

He began to tell me something about himself, stopped, shook his head and said, "No, no — it's too late now. Fair enough, Mr Delavigne; you stay, I'll go."

With the suggestion that my title be adjusted to Homeland Peace Secretary, the deal was done. Something deep down told me I had used up my luck with ships. The quayside was where I wanted to be and I was happy there, as the mercury plunged and the rain strengthened, as Lloyd Bingham clowned on and as Dean Marquis raised his hat to me from where he stood by the rail with his worldly, and rather sad smile. I wonder if we weren't the only two who had much of an idea what was going on. The Peace Campaign offered Henry greatness — that was its purpose — and it was Marquis's mission to take him home to his factory and make him small again. Of all the snakes in the grass they took with them on that ship, Marquis was the most dangerous and it came as no surprise to me that he was also, ultimately, the most successful.

"Mr Berton Braley, America's great popular poet. Hurray for the hayseed Homer!"

Berton scampered up the gangway, pulling after him a girl who vaguely resembled the one I had seen at the *Eastland* disaster back in the summer. He was going as correspondent for his magazine, but had just enough fame to be greeted as a delegate.

"Poem! Poem! Poem! Poem!" demanded the crowd.

The people's laureate chose his spot by the ship's rail, took a sheet of paper from inside his coat and unfolded it momentously.

From Europe we came to make a good New
World.
Now our old home groans with war's banners
unfurled.

We brought the best of Man to this land of
peace,
And now we return like well-intentioned geese.

"Boo! Rubbish! Drown him for his bad verses!" shouted the envious newsmen on the pier. Berton held up his hand and managed a modicum of quiet.

Henry Ford's our leader, getting mankind on the
move;
He knows how the car and the human heart to
improve.

Off on the Oscar we go, to snowy Christiania
Peace and love to bring by Christmas and New
Yeeah.

"Boooo!"

"Hurray! Out of the trenches by Christmas!"

Berton adjusted the arctic fox stole about the neck of his young companion, then embraced her passionately, eliciting a more general cheer.

From the pier, where he sat enthroned on his own small mountain of luggage, Dr Charles Giffin Pease looked on with a sharpened sense of injustice. He had boarded half an hour before with much hoopla from Bingham, but had now been forced to return to dry land. A pale, dominated woman stood by his side. She shivered and was occasionally tearful as Dr Pease gave the truth of the story to the clustered reporters.

"Personal reasons have frustrated my plans."

Dr Pease was well liked in the news business. The nation's leading opponent of fumimania, he appeared regularly as he rode the trains and trolley-cars of New York, plucking cigarettes from the lips of startled tobacco inebriates and dancing on the ashes as he delivered another lecture on the evils of tobacco, alcohol, coffee, tea, ginger ale, corsets, vinegar, meat, cocoa, chocolate, vaccination, excessive condiment intake, and the licking of artificially flavoured lollipops. Mr Ford is a believer in the Pease gospel and his invitation was one of the few he insisted on personally. Dr Pease was dressed as a cigar. Smoke drifted weakly from the crown of his brown plush top hat which emitted a hissing sound every time a raindrop scored a direct hit. It was discovered too late in the day that the good doctor did have one vice — her name was Annette Hazelton and she was snivelling and saying she wanted to go home. At the mention of personal reasons all eyes turned in her direction.

"Is Miss Hazelton your personal reason, Dr Pease?"

"I resent that. Miss Hazelton is my private secretary. A man of such extensive affairs as myself could not possibly do without assistance."

"Would you still be sailing, sir, if you were married to Miss Hazelton?"

"You are a cocoa degenerate, young man. It has poisoned your sense of propriety. No man with a healthy mind and body would have asked such a question. Read this pamphlet before it is too late — and if you want to be useful call me a taxi cab."

Purged of immorality, the *Oscar* was now fit to receive Mr Ford. He arrived half an hour before sailing when everything was complete and waiting only for him. From where I stood it was impossible to see the line of cars from the Biltmore draw up, or Mr Ford himself getting out. I knew it had happened because of the roar from the crowd — a huge, unanimous earthquake of noise that swept everyone together, whatever their real views of the Ford-Schwimmer project. Two minutes passed before, through a canyon of cheering people, Mr Ford appeared, blithely carrying the caged squirrel that had just been thrust into his hand. The noise grew and grew. At once solemn, ecstatic and humble, my employer's face showed what it meant to him. The joke of the squirrel failed utterly. Not only that — it was inverted, changing Mr Ford into a new St Francis. He paused obligingly for a photographer, holding up the cage to give him a better shot and peering in at the terrified animal. I looked again at the photographer as he thanked Mr Ford and moved away. It was true — there were tears in his eyes and suddenly the emotion was everywhere. Even the newsmen joined in, overwhelmed by the moment. Mr Ford shyly acknowledged the crowd. He seemed like a man reprieved, a man whose every need and prayer had been answered all at once. By his side, a disregarded and fearful Mrs Ford concentrated her attention on the squirrel. A bemused Edsel supported his mother by the arm. Behind these three Ray followed closely, with Louis Lochner two steps further back, dapper in his own new peace wardrobe and with authoritative attaché case in hand.

The Ford party embarked and took their place by the rail of the first-class deck. Rosika Schwimmer came out to join them. Reverend Marquis's hat was just visible in the background of the group. From another disturbance on the quayside an elderly Thomas Edison slowly emerged, leaning on the arm of the Great Commoner himself, the champion of neutrality, Mr William Jennings Bryan. Mr Ford seemed greatly relieved to see them and waved vigorously. After several minutes they appeared by his side on the deck, a trio of great Americans buoyed up on a new surge of acclaim. All at once I saw the *Oscar* arriving rather than departing, the buildings different and the clothes of the same huge crowd slightly strange on the other side of the ocean. This Hoboken scene was a mirror image of how the Peace Ship would arrive in Europe. I made a sudden, exhilarating discovery, like a piece of maths I had struggled and struggled with and could now see as clear as day — success was guaranteed, it really would work and — who knows? — maybe even by Christmas too. Fireworks went off, paper streamers rained down from the ship. It all made sense.

Bryan made a booming, gesture-filled speech of which little could be understood. The sailing bell rang and the call went out — "All ashore that's going ashore!" Mr Ford kissed his wife. Soon the well-wishers, a trembling Mrs Ford and the son were back on the quay. The gangway was rolled back, the hawsers cast off. A thick cone of breath shot into the air as the steam whistle shrieked, making some leap for joy and others cover their ears. The waters churned, and as the band played "America the Beautiful" the gap between the *Oscar* and the pier slowly widened. Tugs nudged in at bow and stern and started to push her further out. Mr Ford threw American Beauty roses down to his wife, the last handful of blooms falling short and floating brilliantly on the murky water. It seemed that everyone on the ship, all the delegates, the students and the journalists too, was pressing against the shore-side rail and waving and shouting down to everyone below. Lloyd Bingham held to his post, miming limp and harpoon and the sighting of distant whales as a comic Ahab set out to catch and pull in his elusive obsession. Mr Ford moved to the stern from where he could be more easily seen as the ship turned to the sea. He stood there quite still, except for occasionally raising his hat and saluting his supporters. I took my eyes from him only once when distracted by a last caprice of the crowd.

"Jump! Jump! Jump! Jump!"

A bizarrely dressed figure whirled his arms and fell into the water, paper wings torn from his shoulders by the impact. Sounds of alarm and ridicule mingled as a harbour police boat turned and lazily rowed in his direction.

The *Oscar* slipped away down Ambrose Channel and the sounds of her excited, happy cargo became faint. A hazy bar of smoke rose from the single stack, drifting slowly southward in the calm air. Above, a weakness in the clouds cast down a brighter almost-sunlight on the ship. Mr Ford stood motionless by the stern rail, picked out in an electroplated gleam, an affordable altarpiece for the Age of Innocence, shrinking away in the direction of Europe.

Zero

I sensed that something was about to happen. And I sensed too — oh, terrible thought! — that it might not happen, that the smallest part of the mechanism was also the most essential, that if it failed, if I failed, humanity would fail. But what to do? How to prophesy in the very heart of Mammon?

Messages filled the air more thickly than ever. The cars in the street chattered to me as they passed. At night, above my head, the gun-barrel apparatus of the Milholland & Batcheller Pneumatic Despatch Tube Co. hissed and thumped without a moment's rest. At last the Word came to me. It was a cold night and I was stuffing a newspaper up my vest by the Forty-Second Street soup kitchen. I reached for another sheet and then, as lightning flickered in the cloudless sky, I saw the headline — *Ford Pledges All for Peace* — and I knew that he would achieve nothing without my help.

"Talk to Henry."

"Excuse me?"

Another auto went by.

"Talk to Henry. Talk to Henry. Talk to Henry."

I got straight down to work. I danced around my hat in Central Park, I learned new tunes on my squeeze-box, I swept the stoops of the idle rich, I made a new sign — Blessed are the Peace Makers — and held out a tin cup beneath it all hours of the day and many of the night. Before long I had enough for paper, envelopes, a box of steel nibs, a bottle of ink and a sheet of two-cent stamps. As the man said — give me a lever and I'll move the world. I wrote to the names I picked out of the papers. Theodore Delavigne seemed the most hopeful at first, though I was wrong about him. I wrote to Mr Lochner many times explaining how I had been invited to bring him together with the only man who could make peace. I wrote to Mrs Schwimmer, that wonderful, good woman, that great soul, and told her the door was open. I had cleared the way for them and if only she and her friend from Chicago would ask, they would receive. Three days later — it was cold and I was on the hunt for more insulation — I read the news that all my hopes had been fulfilled.

So you see, this is my doing, whatever anyone else might tell you. I go now to give it my blessing, winged as Victorious Peace, edging through the people who smile and cheer and clap me on the shoulders and urge me on because they understand. I step aside for a man dressed as a cigar coming the other way — these events often attract the benighted. I press on, anxious that I am too late. The whistle sounds and a great shout goes up. I hear the water thrash and the engines turn. The tugs sound their horns, the bands play. At last I am at the edge. There is the ship, there the man. It is the first time I have seen him — in the flesh, that is. Everything is perfect. The people cheer me on. Hope is on every face as they chant. Through a furled newspaper I address them —

My name is Mr Zero,
A thoroughly modern hero.
To swim for peace I go.
Splash! Cheerio!

I take a great run at it, clearing people out the way. One, two, three, four, faster and faster. Too fast now. Too late. Good! And a great jump from the edge and the water's far beneath me and the nuts are falling into it from all around, a brown hailstorm of nuts from them that know not Peace, and everyone's shouting and screaming and the squirrels are running all over the place and the newspapermen are laughing, but oh! let them, 'cos they're thinking too, they're writing in their heads and it will be in all the papers tomorrow, I know it will as I spread my arms and feel the wind beneath them, I know I've done it, it's working, Zero Stops the War! And then I'm flying and the gulls are beside me and I see the *Oscar* and it's all so right as I knew it would be and the *Oscar*'s upside-down and . . .

Ouff!

Cold! Cold! Cold!

But no! I'm swimming, slapping down the holy oil and water of Hoboken, and there's Henry at the rail, Saint Henry, King Henry, the sun is on him and I'm hailing him and he turns and I give him my all and he's going to take it to that poor dark place and it's going to be all right because I know it is now because it can't not be, and the water's getting thicker and I'm kneeling on it, I'm getting up on it as it helps me because the sun is on it too now and I know what that means. I'm going to stand on this water and run across these waves, I'm going to lay my hands on the *Oscar*, on her sainted iron that from this day forth will know no rust. I'm getting to my knees on this oil and water, I'm going to stride across these waters, peace beneath my feet and put it all in the *Oscar* and up to the deck plates and up through the shoes, feet and very bones of the sainted Mr Henry Ford, automobileer of the age, and into his dollars green as leaves and I'm standing now, Peace raises up her servant and the little boats are rowing after to cheer me on and Hey! lemmygo, lemmygo I'm gonna stop the war!

Inez

The first floor of a brownstone two blocks from Washington Square, and at a rent we might not be able to afford for much longer — a domestic scene of the espoused at breakfast in a quiet, childless household. I check the papers for my own name and pretend to be relieved when it is not there. *Germans Mass 500,000 Troops on Bulgarian Frontier; Carranza Nearer to Power in Mexico; Duma Members Arrested — Plans to Forestall Popular Demonstrations; British "Blacklist" US Commerce; 10,000 Turks Wiped Out, p.2.*

"Have you read this, dear?"

"Mm?"

"A German submarine disguised itself as a British submarine and was then torpedoed by one of its own. Blew up and sank. Off Denmark."

"How do you disguise a submarine?"

"It doesn't say, flags or something I suppose."

"Under water?"

"Oh, Eugen — that's not the point. It's just terrible, appalling!"

"They certainly don't seem to have thought it through."

"Can you imagine women doing that? Can you? It just couldn't *ever* happen!"

Half a minute of silence passes. I contemplate my husband — a cheerful, dark-haired Dutchman caught and reeled in two years ago while crossing on the *Mauretania*. My father thought I had taken leave of my senses — "enamoured of an ass" was his first comment — but parents come round to these things in the end. I tell Eugen, calmly, that I will shortly be forced to throw something at him. I explain that it is probably already too late to avoid this incident, that I hope it won't do him too much harm and that when it does happen he should remember that it is really his fault. The mantel clock chimes the quarter hour and rouses him to sudden energy.

"I have to go. I'm seeing a man uptown about the coffee business. If he buys it we'll be on easy street — for a while anyway. We must go away somewhere — rest after all your excitement."

He kisses me as he shakes himself into his coat and clips a good fountain pen to his inside pocket. On leaving the room he stops abruptly.

"No, that won't do. I'll run out halfway through the afternoon and not be able to think of anything else."

He comes back and kisses me hard, pushing me until the chair tilts on its two hind legs. I put my fingers behind his head and stroke his ear with my thumb. I feel his hand on my breast, running slowly down to my waist and then over my thigh to burrow like a puppy into the warmth between. Suddenly, I'm weightless. I give a smothered cry of warning and throw my arm out to catch the edge of the table with enough force to make the knives rattle on their plates. I pull myself level as Eugen regains his balance.

"That's better. You won't make love to anyone else while I'm gone?"

"Not today," I tell him.

"Promise? I won't be any longer than I'll have to be. I think Peter's coming soon. I'm sure of it."

"Yes," I say. "Or Eugenie. Perhaps she'll come first."

"Or Eugenie."

He presses his lips to my cheek and leaves. Martha, who has been listening all the time, hears the sound of the door closing, comes in and asks if she may clear the table.

"Will there be visitors today, Mrs Boissevain?"

"No, Martha."

I settle by the window and put my feet up. I take something to read but leave it closed in my lap, preferring to look outside. In the street people hurry and hold together the lapels of their coats. The clouds are paper white and threaten early snow. I think of Eugen, somewhere out there. I have been so lucky sometimes I can cry thinking about it, and I know it is wrong not to be happier than I am. It is my time to be unwell for a few days and a cavernous, echoing mood of review settles on me — my life becomes a space I can stand in and see all at once, the house that takes shape as its first great timbers are joined. My dear parents have a cuttings file that is already Bible-thick, but what does it all amount to really?

For years now you've known my name, perhaps even my face — the ardent child activist of the International Sunshine Society who grew up to be the Gibson Girl of radical politics. The convictions, like the features, were inherited — a provincial newspaper proprietor for a father, the title sold at a profit before moving on to dabble in the progressive wing of Republican politics. Once the Napoleon of the Manhattan Eleventh Assembly District, old men pushed him aside for conservatives, forgetting that he had been the first to organise behind McKinley's candidacy. Instead, it was Police Commissioner Roosevelt who made the headlines and then, with the help of an assassin's bullet, the White House. Later, when he had made something of himself, Father recalled standing by a young Henry Ford at the presidential funeral service. He shared a train with him until the change at Philly. He said the future hero of the five-dollar day was a strange man with little to say for himself. He spent much of the time reading a three-cent pamphlet called *A Short View on Great Questions* and making notes in the margins with a pencil. He said you wouldn't have guessed the way it turned out. It could have been different, Father always said — very different.

He left the front line of politics, but kept some of his friends. One of them was honest John Wanamaker, the inventor of the department store and former postmaster-general under Harrison. Father and Uncle John had a talk about the pneumatic tubes that blew the cash takings from Wanamaker's store here and there beneath the streets of Philadelphia. He said he'd have a go and in October 1897 the Milholland family Bible, wrapped in the Stars and Stripes, whooshed from the central post office to Produce Exchange, New York City in forty seconds, rather than a messenger boy's more usual seventeen minutes. In a few years fifty-four miles of mail tubes sucked and blew half a million letters around New York every day and I was the daughter of a very wealthy family.

The family farm was bought back. And then the old country made its call and life became transatlantic. From when I was thirteen you could show me a photograph taken inside any of the better liners and I would name the ship and tell you when I had last sailed on her and in which cabin. For a year I was Daisy Miller — *the* American girl in Budapest, Vienna, Berlin, Antwerp, Paris, Edinburgh, London. We settled in 4 Prince of Wales Terrace, from where I walked to the Kensington High School for Girls and played with my brother and sister in Kensington Gardens. We went to see *The Mikado* and *Pirates of Penzance* and sang the songs at home as my mother played the piano and little Vida discovered she had a voice. We nodded to Mr Barrie in the park at the weekends and were there on the first night for Charles Frohman's production of *Peter Pan*.

Billy Marconi we met on the *Lucania* from New York to London one fall. In the middle of the ocean he could send messages to Europe and North America at the same time. He showed us how it worked and the next morning my mother and I found a message from Father back in New York pinned to the ship's bulletin board. It is a Milholland family tradition that this was the world's first Marconi-gram. For the rest of the trip we treated the wireless like a private toy.

Billy became a regular visitor to our London home. He was a frequent faller-in-love and proposed marriage when I was seventeen and he a sumptuously established thirty. I accepted as lightly as the offer was made, our engagement lasting a year until I heard that he had married an Irish baroness and gone off to sell wireless sets to the generals of the Russo-Japanese war. I learned what silliness it is to talk of broken hearts and how much better to keep on old lovers as friends.

School ended, but Cambridge was stuffy and full of old maids too abjectly grateful to be there at all. Besides, they refused Miss Pankhurst the right to make a speech there so it would have been totally impossible for me. I got back on the boat and went to Vassar, where people listened to my mid-Atlantic accent and asked which part of England I was from. Captain of hockey, record-holder for the shot put, Romeo to another girl's Juliet, I was praised in the college magazine for my passionate balcony scene. Real passion came in the last year when President Taylor banned a suffrage meeting in college and it fell to me to lead the women of the new century across the road and into the cemetery where he had no authority. There we made the speeches among the graves of those who had lived and died in a man's world, without ever once having their voices heard. My romance with the press began the very next day — *Vassar Invaded!* — *Boadicea of the*

Ballot Brigade Leads the Way, and a rather nice photograph underneath. I had found my cause.

That summer in London I marched with the suffragettes on Women's Sunday and we filled the whole of Hyde Park. Back in New York I stepped off the *Lusitania* into a crowd of eager journalists.

"Were you not afraid in such an enormous demonstration, Miss Milholland?"

"Not me, but I think some men were pretty scared. Here we come, boys, ready or not!"

It was noticed that I had a certain effect on people and I was soon put to work in the movement. I observed the pickets in the shirtwaist strike and when the women were arrested I went with them to Night Court and told them their rights and gave evidence against the police. I collected money so they could eat and keep themselves warm during the lockout, and when they were put in prison Vida and I put ladders up against the wall and sang the suffragettes' "Marseillaise" so they could hear it in the cells. In the end the employers gave in and I and my friends got all our cars together and the workers got in and we paraded through the garment district in triumph. WOMEN TAKE THE WHEEL, said the *Times*. The girls in my little 28 h.p. graduation present said it was the first time they had been in one. Only the Triangle Shirtwaist Company held out — the one that had started all the trouble in the first place. That was the one that burned down the next year, one hundred and forty-six women and girls dying behind its barred windows and locked doors. In the papers I graduated again and became "the well-known socialist agitator".

Journalism seemed an obvious second string and I covered the 1912 Women's Suffrage Association for *McClure's* Magazine, writing an account of Jane Addams speaking. All the boys were in love with me and, which was more important, the cameras too. And so when it came to choosing a leader for the suffrage parade on the eve of President Wilson's inauguration everyone was kind enough to think of me. I was dressed all in white — "the beautifullest suffragist in town" — and mounted on Grey Dawn, stallion or gelding according to the sympathies of the newspapers. I carried the suffrage banner — Forward through the darkness! Forward into light!

The parade was to go from the Capitol to the Treasury where we would perform our allegory of the suffrage struggle. Almost at once it degenerated into a riot. The crowds for the inauguration the next day were huge and we could see hardly any police. There was a strong smell of drink in the air and within a hundred yards we were pushed together almost into single file and then stopped altogether. The abuse got louder, the gestures more vulgar. I understood when I saw a police officer looking the other way. I dug my heels in and Grey Dawn leapt forward scattering the cowards to left and right.

"Shame on you! Shame on you men!"

I don't think I'd ever had such excitement. I kicked away the hands that grabbed at my ankles and rode down the drunks to clear a way for the parade behind me. In two hours of battle we had still only made half the distance. Ambulances queued to remove the wounded, the overcome and the intoxicated. At last, a troop of cavalry came from Fort Myers across the river and cleared the avenue with a single magnificent charge. As I watched them, I wondered for the first time in my life if it wouldn't also be rather nice to be a boy. Then I arrived at the Treasury and dismounted and saw the flanks of my poor horse, slick with human spittle and the ash marks where the lighted cigarettes and cigar butts had found their target.

It was a few months later, in the summer of 1913, that I walked into the dining room of Holland House in the company of my good friend and onetime fiancé Marconi and his wife, Beatrice. It was there that I was first seen by my husband, Eugen Boissevain. Billy turned out to be a mutual friend. We were introduced and sat down to share the same table. It was thunder and lightning, or so Eugen told me. This Dutch-Irish businessman, coffee planter, big game hunter and former patient of Carl Jung (he was quick to reassure me that he was completely uncured) listened to me talk over plans for a trip to England and immediately abandoned everything that had brought him to America.

"I must come with you. I will come with you! Which ship? When does she sail?"

Before we set foot in England I had proposed to him, more than once. We went with the Marconis to their estate at Eaglehurst and there, in the topmost room of the tower, in sight and sound of the sea, we made love for the first time.

"It's yes, then?"

"Yes," he said. "Yes, my wife."

We promised never to own each other, always to keep each other free. The newspapers back home were delighted — *World's Prettiest Suffragette Succumbs to Tyrant Man*.

Some sort of independence was in order and it took the form of a little two-bed flat at 35 East Thirtieth Street. Father still helped, and it was always possible to have someone come in to do my hair and nails for the evening, even though he grumbled at the bills. From there I tried to make my way as a laywer and Eugen worked hard to breathe some life into the struggling coffee business.

"We could go to Java," he suggested one morning. "Live on my family's plantations. Life is easy there."

"Easy? For whom?"

We didn't talk about it again. Eugen told me I could do anything and I think I still almost believe him.

"You know," he told me once after making love in the afternoon, "I always wanted to look up to my wife, to admire her. When people say, 'This is the husband of Inez Milholland,' I am very happy."

I don't think I could have made a better choice.

The suffrage work continued — we mobbed Senator O'Gorman's office on Wall Street, and danced the turkey trot all night at the victory party of the new pro-suffrage mayor. Freedom of the press was another front. I battled the Comstock laws for novels honest about human nature and some not very good moving pictures about the so-called white slave trade. I got myself nearly shouted down in a meeting of the NAACP when I told them that freedom for *The House of Bondage* also meant freedom for the likes of Mr Griffiths and his poisonous history of our nation. I began to feel quite grown-up, except for one thing — although I lectured on birth control I did not practise it and still no Peter and no Eugenie to join us.

I read the newspapers closer than most, but still the war was a shock. At the time I could not have been more surprised if the Black Death had broken out again, or if a dinosaur had hauled himself out of the East River and lumbered down Broadway. Jane Addams founded the Women's Peace Party and the new cause left me busier than ever. It became clear to me that war was only to be expected in a world where the women did not vote. The male was morally obsolete and incapable of restoring himself to health without help. Now, the ghastlier things get, the more desperately they need their women.

Personally, the war has cut my life in two and for now I have to live wholly as an American, stranded on one side of my transatlantic home. When it started it was the occasion of the saddest letter I hope ever to receive from Father. He wrote to me from London and explained why we had to give up our home there. He described the men loading the vans with furniture and the servants closing the shutters before being paid off and the young soldiers at drill among the daisies in Kensington Gardens.

I spoke from more platforms, marched on more parades, pressed on in the courtrooms against the prejudices of my own profession. Before, slow progress seemed better than none, but since the war started I can no longer tell myself that is enough. I could not be busier and yet I get very low sometimes and ask if there is anything a woman can do to make a difference. I must have been in that sort of mood when I thought of my little Italian adventure.

In the spring I was still hopeful that Italy would stay out of the madness. I made a reassuring story for myself about such a culture never succumbing to barbarism and was very sad indeed when this proved to be just another delusion. I tried to cheer myself up by accepting a dinner invitation from Billy and it was then he told me that "the call" had come and he was returning to direct the wireless operations of the Italian forces. As I had had a few successes in *McClure's* and *Harper's* I knew how little there was to being a journalist and I decided there and then to go with him and report the war. Eugen was wonderful — would one husband in a thousand have loved me enough to let me go just like that?

"Yes, you must go. You must fulfil your heart's desires! But I think I had better stay here and look after business."

Money was tight, but I promised to get an exclusive, an interview with a king or a prime minister. A friend had told me I could get two thousand dollars for a piece like that and I saw no reason why I shouldn't. If Mary Roberts Rhinehart could make a living writing about night patrols in no-man's-land for the *Saturday Evening Post*, I could certainly do the same. Surely, there could be nothing more modern than that. On 22 May, Eugen and my tearful mother saw me off on the *St Paul*. Inez, *correspondante de guerre* — I was as excited as a child.

Although the papers had covered his voyage, the Marconi name appeared nowhere on the passenger list and Billy gave me all his personal papers for the duration just in case. Our captain thought it entirely likely that the Germans would stop the ship and take him off if they could. He personally censored every outgoing radiogram and assured us at dinner of his thoroughness.

"You will not be betrayed by your own invention, Signor Marconi — forgive me — Mr Smith. Not on my ship."

Off Ireland we slowed. There was a service and wreaths were laid on the water where the *Lusitania* had gone down only a fortnight before. A steward told me how the *St Paul* had nosed through wreckage for an hour on her outward journey. He had seen a life-raft carrying a dead woman with her arms around a dead child. Only once we were safely in Liverpool did the Captain tell us we had been followed by a U-boat. I cabled the story to the *Tribune* and made the front page.

When we entered France the first struggle was to get press credentials from the authorities. I was a little embarrassed to discover that half of America had come with me. Seasoned veterans stood back and exchanged disobliging remarks as a younger crew of sports editors, baseball reporters, drama critics, book reviewers, gossip columnists and cartoonists waved their passports and posed dashingly in new riding breeches.

"Let me through," drawled one of the onlookers to his friend, "I'm from the *Philadelphia Ladies' Home Journal*."

"Perhaps she's researching a piece on bandages."

I asked if they were referring to me, but they just smiled, tipped their hats and walked away.

Billy, of course, knew everyone and he had agreed that we should meet up with Will Irwin as soon as the formalities were over. It was in his car that we were chauffeured all the way to Paris. My skin tingled all over as we pushed our way out of the port through fleets of ambulances and strange armoured cars. My first sight of injured soldiers lying on stretchers and the thrilling brightness of blood did something almost sensual for me and I regretted Eugen wasn't there to share it. I began to compose in my mind the passionate letter I would send him that night. We bumped over railway tracks and I looked out at the train that had just arrived. Red Cross nurses were lined up and being held back until the officers had all got off — the female repairers waiting on the male destroyers.

In the first hour we were stopped by so many sentries we nearly ran out of cigarettes to bribe them with. After that the military traffic thinned out and we passed through a succession of half-deserted villages where old men sat together on benches and young girls peered out like portraits frozen in window frames, bracing themselves for news, or hoping for life to start again in the form of a handsome German soldier. Paris was unutterably sad, hunkered down and only half alive, like an animal in winter. The streets had been thrown back to the eighteen-nineties with horses everywhere and only the occasional official or staff-officer in a car. At the sound of a motor people looked up, fearing a Zeppelin rather than an automobile. We lunched the next day at the American Embassy and coincided with a tetchy Jane Addams who had come straight from the Hague where the Women's Peace Party had just broken up. She was attempting to deliver the conference's resolution to the French government.

"We were going to post them," she complained. "A simple device allowing for both thrift and tact. The matter was nearly concluded when a brassy, rather eastern voice sounded from the back of the hall. Schwimmer is her name. I have had dealings with her before. All heart and rhetoric, I am sorry to say, and in two minutes she persuaded the conference to make personal embassies across the whole of Europe. A costly way of being ignored, I say. That is why I am in Paris, Mrs Boissevain. I am a postwoman. An emotional woman, Frau Schwimmer. Very emotional."

I commiserated and tried not to smile. There is an age for adventure and Miss Addams has passed it.

The next day a slow, halting train took us south to where Billy and I would part — he to the business of war, I to record it. In Rome my opponent was the Ministry of the Interior on whose silence I waited as they considered my letters of introduction and my commissions from the *Tribune, Collier's* and others. I wasted my time in the Grand Hotel, typing pieces on charity kitchens and the courageous efforts of the American ambassador's wife between shaking my sheets from the balcony, counting the flea-bites on my skin and slowly falling out of love with Italy.

Frustrated, I helped myself to a seat in a train of officers going north. I toured the hospitals, passed round more cigarettes, admired the pieces of shrapnel the soldiers showed me and their X-ray photographs with the sharp, white shapes inside their ghostly bodies. I hated everything I saw of the war and wrote voluminously every night about its cruel stupidity. In Vicenza I met a mother of three sons. Not one of them is able-bodied and she was angry and humiliated that they cannot go to the war. She haunts the recruiting office and harangues the officials there, spitting on their enrolment forms when they reject her offer. Patriotic demonstrations are common and are fuelled by impossible quantities of wine.

I got closer to the *zona di guerra*. Fresher casualties were carried back from the front and sometimes the sound of artillery could just be heard. I pressed on — what right did I have to protect myself from what I might see there? I felt that I had to see it and, if I could, to bear witness to the very moment at which a life is violently lost. That would be something to come home with — new passion, new words on the stump. After doing my articles I wrote to Eugen every night, how what I sought was coming close, how it would make us both safe. "Let me love myself first, Eugen. Then I will bring a child into the world."

Nearer the fighting the army controls journalists more tightly. I found myself corralled in a farmhouse with half a dozen boorish newsmen and Guido, a charming army press officer who censored our despatches and promised an escorted trip to the trenches. I had to listen to anecdotes about "correspondentesses" like the English girl supposedly found in sodden Flanders with sleeping bag, six pencils and a powder puff. I endured being told I wanted to see a battle the way a child wanted to see a pantomime. I filled my despatches with loathing for war and compliments for the gallantry of certain young Italian officers, men one would so easily fall in love with if one were not a married woman. Guido read, smiled and applied his rubber stamp before passing them on to the telegraph office.

When the day came for the trip to the front line the men squeezed themselves excitedly into two staff cars and then gleefully told me that regulations forbade women from attending the war zone. The next day notification came from Rome that I was immediately to return to the capital.

"Too bad, Sugar-Plum."

The "boys" contained their disappointment and played another hand. Guido obtained a forty-eight-hour extension for me over the weekend on which he was also due some leave. On my last night in the north, more comfortably quartered in the Hotel Vicenza, I opened my door to him and we spent a long and delicious night together. He was very beautiful, and sweetly conventional — we were already standing in each other's arms and quite naked when he stopped and took his hands off me and asked about "Mr Boissevain".

"You must not worry, Guido. I will tell him everything."

"That is all right in America? What a wonderful country."

I received a letter from him just before I was expelled — more gratitude than love and all the better for that. Briefly, the war seemed a little smaller. He says he will come to live here as soon as there is peace, if he is still alive.

In Rome the Minister of the Interior frowned at me over a stupendous desk. I accused him of conspiracy.

"It was the other journalists, wasn't it? The men put you up to it and you were happy to go along with them. Why not? Men do not want us to see what they are doing. They want to war in secret and still be welcomed home by their women. I have seen why they want to keep it a secret, and I will tell the truth. That is why you have recalled me."

The Minister pushed an extract from a *Tribune* article across his desk. I read it.

"So?"

"You tell the people of New York the only brave Italian is a drunk Italian."

"No — I tell them the drunker they are the braver they are."

"A nicety."

"You can't say you haven't seen it for yourself. Don't you ever tell the truth? Look — we're alone. Tell me now you know it is true. Who would ever know?"

"The readers of your newspaper. Signora, I have a war to fight. Let us meet again when the world is a happier place. For now, I regret that I must compel you to go home."

He stood, kissed my hand and returned my passport with ten thousand regrets and a cancelled visa.

"This will be good for you, yes? This little adventure."

He was not entirely wrong. But there was unpleasantness too — a letter from Irwin blaming me for Italy banning all correspondents from neutral countries, and another from Eugen which I read on the ship back. "Dearest Nan, I know I should be more modern. I am. I believe in it, but sometimes it is too hard. Damn that stinking Latin macaroni monkey! Damn him for taking what is mine! I see myself shooting him. And if I ever met him and really did it, I know I would be proud. I am sad and frightened. What of Peter, of Eugenie? Are they safe? Will they be mine?" The answer to that was clear before the end of the voyage — he had nothing to fear, or hope for.

So there I was, back in New York in the last week of September, walking down the West Thirty-fourth Street pier and getting more than my fair share of the scavenging newsmen. The Minister's prediction was abundantly proven — being expelled from Italy was my best ad yet. Everyone was so excited it would have been selfish to talk of failure.

"Miss Milholland!" (They still call me that here.) "Inez, Inez! Over here!"

I turn into the flashes and answer the question.

"Because men fear to make peace more than they fear war, that's why. Give me supreme command of the press of Italy, or of any warring country, and I will guarantee to turn the sentiment of that country for peace inside a month."

How desolate I felt as they wrote it down. And it was no help the next day to be back on the front pages under someone else's byline, still emptily making the news rather than reporting it.

So this is what I am, the plant that grows in this easy soil. And these are the "adventures" from which I must rest as Eugen goes uptown to sell a failing coffee-import business and I sit here with my feet up by the window, watching the first white flakes fall. Of course, there has been no end of friends to welcome me back, and when they say how good it is of me to be here for the suffrage referendum I go along with them and pretend it was all planned. I speak tonight at Cooper Union — back up on my soapbox and banging away at the forces of evil. I'll put on a good show for the cause and never let on to anyone that it is no substitute for war.

The doorbell rings and Martha goes to answer it. I feel a cold draught of outside air as I listen to the exchange and try to make out what is being said. The cadence of her words is repeated more forcefully.

"Martha?"

She comes into the room.

“Some crazy man wanting to sweep the steps for a nickel.” She raises her hand to the side of her head and makes that uncharitable gesture. “I told him I keep them clean enough, thank you, and I wouldn’t want him touching them anyhow.”

“Give him a quarter, Martha.”

She looks at me as if I must be every bit as mad as the vagrant shivering out on the stoop.

“If you say so.”

I hear the outer door close and then see the man on the sidewalk. Dressed in ragpicker’s motley he looks up to the window and doffs a green lady’s hat with the quill end of a feather just poking above the band. I return the salute as he walks out of sight.

Berton

Queen of *Herland*

*Inez, Inez, newest of New Women!
Amazon, Androgyne, Outdoor Pal;*

*To all your smilings
We are as iron filings;*

*Under your powers magnetic
Slaves quite pathetic.*

*Inez, Inez, you were loved by Marconi,
But his love was too tele-phoney.*

*You gave your heart to suffrage,
But it wasn't enoughrage.*

*Then, my dear, you married a Dutchman
And the hearts of your lovers turned to Edam;*

*Happiness for you, I hope, and a life of ease.
But for us — hard cheese!*

* * *

One of my better ones, I think — beauty brings out the best in me. Not a payer, though, not the versified World's Series or the right charm at last to crack that long dry spell at *Vanity Fair*. One for the locked cabinet. I close my notebook and slip it back into my pocket, leaving my hand in there to protect it from the cold.

A grey, steady, medium swell extends to the horizon and above it a blank sky save for one patch of half-hearted brightness where the sun is concealed. I look out on this scene, the middle of three muffled statues — a trilby-hatted padre from Detroit on one side and one of the guys who's organising this whole thing on the other. I would ask his name if he hadn't told me three times already.

"Better weather today," says one of the statues. The other two make affirmative noises.

Twenty feet along the deck Inez Milholland — or is it Mrs Boissevain? — leans on the rail and frames her profile against the western sky. Unhusbanded, fiercely suffragettical and emphatically anti-prohibition (also rumoured to be radical in matters of the heart), she has only enemies and admirers and nothing at all in between. Another glass of champagne, which she early declared to be the only effective remedy for *mal de mer*, is in her hand.

"It's still working, then?" I ask her. She smiles but says nothing. I feel foolish and look back at the sea.

A door bursts open and there appears on deck a large man making gestures as if he has just entered from the wings of a stage to the accompaniment of a drum roll and a few notes on a trombone. He is dressed to resemble a college football coach and has a stopwatch hanging from a lanyard around his neck. Despite his considerable bulk he runs energetically on the spot.

"What! Not laughing? That's not allowed. Captain Bingham's order of the day. Here."

He hands out menu cards with the shipping line's crest at the top, but the word "Entertainments" printed just below.

"Deck quoits at two — second round of the tournament. It's gonna be a hot one. Will the sophomores win a clean sweep, will wisdom prevail over youth? Charades in the smoking lounge after dinner. Plenty of time to work on your acts, gentlemen. Everyone loves charades. Say, did you hear?"

He looks behind, then leans towards us with his hand shielding one side of his mouth.

"We're off course — Miss Beautiful back there was standing too close to the compass."

He plucks my menu card from my hand and turns it over.

"Submarine competition — first one to see Fritz poking his nose out of the water, you note it down. Win a life preserver — it's the only one we got! No prizes for torpedoes. Hup, hup! Gotta go!"

He explodes with a messy sneeze, says "Oh, my" to himself and trots off, wiping his hand on his jersey.

The intervention leaves us speechless and my two companions more morose than before. The younger man checks his watch and says he has a meeting to prepare for. As he leaves, I notice that under cover of Bingham's tirade of cheerfulness someone else has arrived to take the air. The lean, life-worn figure of Samuel McClure surveys the sea from a position by Miss Milholland's elbow. They talk together too quietly to be understood, the movement of the ship moving the thick merino cloth of their coat sleeves together and apart in slow rhythm. Inez laughs and throws her empty champagne glass into the sea. Together they go inside, McClure guiding her through the narrow doorway with a fatherly hand between her shoulders. Five years ago he was a man I wouldn't have let out of my sight — one good word from McClure could make a man's career — but now I am merely curious.

I turn to the autoville bishop and nod at the empty recliner.

"That man — I can't let him tell me again — what *is* his name?"

"Lochner — La Schwimmer's second fiddle."

"That's the one. Seems a nice guy, if a little nervous."

He says nothing to this, but instead looks at the spot newly vacated by Inez and then at my pocket. He asks, and with a tone I don't quite like: "Was that inspiration you experienced a moment ago, Mr Braley?"

"Pardon me?"

"When I saw you writing in your notebook."

"Even a married man can be a poet."

"I don't doubt it. How is Mrs Braley?"

"It's the swell — it doesn't agree with her. To be honest she doesn't take to ships at all."

"That's too bad — especially on a honeymoon."

Unexpectedly, he takes a hip flask from his coat and offers it to me.

"Will you take something for the cold?"

A mouthful of good brandy slips down and starts to fan out towards my fingers and toes, and that other extremity too.

"And Mr Ford?" I ask, as if out of politeness and wishing also to avoid the question of whether there is a spouse I should be asking about.

"Well enough, last time I saw him."

I'd like to press him, maybe get a bit of a scoop here (the word is that this Marquis fellow is one of the few who really knows what's going on), but there's a warning in his tone and a fixed stare at the horizon. I should give him something.

"You know that Inez girl?"

"We were introduced yesterday."

"Rotten journalist."

"Mm?"

"Shocking. She sent pieces in to my magazine. We had to wring the tears out of every despatch before we could read them. Then we laughed so much they got wet all over again. Editor spiked every last one of them. Don't get me wrong — lovely girl, looks great on a horse. But, you know — enthusiastic."

He tells me he used to be enthusiastic and keeps on looking at the sea.

"Bet I know what you're thinking," I say.

"Slug of brandy says you don't."

I look out on the same queasy grey and think of what's to come and of what lies two decks down, waiting for me.

"You're thinking, 'What in God's name am I doing here?' — if you'll excuse the expression."

He hands me his flask. I drink and join him in the same line of thought.

Well, I suppose Mr Henry Ford had quite a lot to do with it, and pure chance too, and a war and a lack of dollars and a timid heart that needed something big to set it working the way it should. Perhaps you know that old story about John Barrymore and the San Francisco earthquake? John came to with the pieces that used to be his hotel collapsing around him. Somehow he got out alive and was wandering the streets in his nightshirt when some troopers conscripted him for a clearing gang. On hearing all about it his uncle remarked — "Just like John. It took a convulsion of nature to get him up in the morning and the United States Army to put him to work." Well, it was kind of like that with me and marriage — it took a European war and a rich man's scruples to make it happen.

I'd made a false start on the business back in the summer and ever since stammering to a halt in Chicago with the upturned hull of the *Eastland* as a backdrop I had never ceased to carry that ring with me. I had learned something about timing, but also something about myself that made me realise it might never happen without a little outside help. Nothing in the intervening months made a difference. I was still selling six or seven verses a week and getting a little more reporting work on the back of the *Eastland* story, but was nowhere near what any respectable father would consider a "prospect" for his daughter. I liked Marion just as much, and she still seemed to like me. And so along we went, smoothly enough one weekend in two.

Late in the fall the Ford story began to break and I saw my old friend's name up there on the front page of the Detroit papers. "Good for you, Theodore," I said to myself. "Nice to see someone making a living." At that time there was no reason why it should have anything to do with me and I thought no more about it. It was a good few weeks later, just after the last of the charming Inez's hymns to suffering humanity had come in over the wires from Italy and been put out of its misery, that the story seemed to catch fire in a whole new way. It wasn't clear to me exactly what had happened, but somehow someone had got through and the talk turned to money. That was interesting enough, but then the whole ship business started and the telegrams of invitation. Now there have been many "hottest tickets of the century" over the last fourteen years and eleven months — most of them heavyweight boxing bouts — but here was one that really deserved the name. As human nature is not at its best in proximity to a hot ticket, I lost out to a lesser man as far as the *Collier's Magazine* berth went. My first thought was to call my old friend Bill Hawkins at UP and remind him how much he owed me.

"Berton," he said to me, "the whole world has gone mad and I've decided to join them. As far as I can see it makes about as much sense sending a poet over there as anyone else on that damned fool ship. Good luck to you, my friend."

No dice with Bill. It was then I saw that Delavigne had done the wise thing and ditched journalism for being Henry Ford's Peace Secretary, whatever that was. I put in a call for old times' sake.

"Theo, you old devil! How you do land on your feet. What's the secret? Berton. Berton Braley. *Collier's Magazine*. Used to be staff poet for *The American Machinist*. Course you do! Oh, you had me going there for a moment."

We caught up on the last six months.

"Listen, Berton," he said to me. "It's about the ship, isn't it? It's the peace thing?"

"Glad you raised it, Theodore. Get me on and you'll always be in my prayers."

Three long seconds of silence.

"You really think it's a good idea for you to go, Berton?"

My turn to pause — translating silences can be tricky.

"You know something about this, Theo? There's something you know and I don't?"

"Nothing. It's what it seems. You've read it all already."

"U-boats? The Germans?"

"Berton —"

"You're going?"

"Absolutely. Safest ship on the ocean. You want to get over there, it's the only way to go."

"You can do it for me? To tell the truth I need this. It's the poem business — I don't know, maybe it's the war or something, but the bottom's fallen out of the light-verse market. There are other things too."

"You still got that girl?"

"Sweet as ever."

"You're not trying to escape from her, are you?"

"No, no — that's not it at all."

"So what about two tickets?"

"It's possible? You can really do it?"

"All I need is an address — oh, and her name."

The next weekend was a married weekend. We met at a little place in New Jersey and booked in as Mr and Mrs Trenton. It was there, in room 13, behind curtains half drawn on a view of the back lot and the gloom of a late November afternoon, that I moved my hand over her shoulder and down the long, sweeping dip of her back — that line of lines that she hid so very slightly under the muslins and taffetas of her fashion drawings. Over that rolling fleshscape I looked with one eye at a bleak room — my pants crumpled on the threadbare rug, my jacket hanging from the chairback with the lump in one pocket where the weight of a boxed ring was slowly wearing through the lining.

"I might be going on a trip."

"Mm?"

"You could come with me."

"Is it the weekend after next?"

"It could be several weeks, maybe months — who knows? We might never come back, Marion."

"Where?"

"Europe."

She turned over on her side before wriggling back into me. We waited while a train went by.

"Where in Europe?" she asked sleepily.

"At a location to be decided."

"Have you done something wrong, Berton? Do you have police trouble?"

"Don't be silly. It's the Ford Peace Ship, the campaign to stop the . . ."

"That thing! The *Enquirer* says they're a bunch of nuts."

"Well, there you go — you've already read about them. Nuts make good copy. It's an opportunity, Marion."

"But weeks?"

"Think of it as an adventure. Come with me on an adventure, Marion."

I kissed the back of her neck persuasively.

"You must be thinking of your other girl."

"What?"

"I have a job, Berton. I work for a living — have you forgotten that?"

"You're good at your job, aren't you?"

"Yes, I am."

"So get another when you get back."

There was a pause. She turned to face me, arranged my hair with her fingers, hooked one leg over me and squeezed.

"Will I need one?"

I looked straight into her eyes and she looked into mine with a steady, competitive stare. Had she been through my pockets? Did she know what was in there? I backtracked through our movements since we booked in. It was possible — there had been unguarded moments.

"I want you to come with me, Marion."

"Do you, Berton?"

"I do."

"I will."

"You have a passport?"

"You think I should?"

Two weeks later we paid off our cab on the edge of a huge carnival of chaos in Hoboken. Marion got into the spirit of it, delighted to have so many people to admire her. She pushed ahead and I followed on, pursuing the brilliant white flash of her fur like one rabbit on the heels of another. I'd say it took a good twenty minutes for us to fight our way through to the ship and when we got there it was no more organised. As we waited to show someone our invitations a shadow passed over us and we looked up.

"Oh, look Berton! Look! I can see one of ours."

An enormous pile of suitcases and steamer trunks was being hauled up in a rope net.

"We're going Berton, we're going. It's really happening."

She kissed me as if we were the only people there. Everyone was looking and she enjoyed that. I noticed for the first time that the whole thing was as much a fashion show as a peace campaign. Everywhere was the newest and the best and I couldn't help wondering if we were to be the poorest people on the ship. Where had all this money come from? I picked out Theodore Delavigne from the crowd. He was further away from the ship and standing on something that put him two or three feet above the other heads. I waved.

"Hey, Theo. Theo!"

He turned and saw us.

"We always meet on quaysides. D'you think there's something in it? How are you?"

He gave me the thumbs up.

"We'll see you on board," I shouted.

He smiled and brandished his hat.

We climbed up most of the gangway to where we had to wait behind a group of students as they had their invitations checked and were given directions to their cabins. They were steadily sorted by gender, the young ladies being sent forward and the men aft. It was our turn to present our credentials.

"Braley. We're together."

"Good afternoon, Mr Braley."

The strong Scandinavian accent seemed to confirm that an adventure was about to begin. Marion was behind me looking the other way and happily waving to the crowd which responded as if it knew who she was.

"This is incredible," she laughed.

I jumped as a booming voice announced my name through an enormous red megaphone. There was another indiscriminate cheer from below.

"But we have just a single cabin here. There is a mistake?"

The official was showing me a piece of paper with names handwritten in among printed Danish. I noticed his peaked cap and the single line of gold along the top of the eye-shade.

"No mistake. That's us."

I held out my hand for the return of our documents, but it wasn't going to be that easy. The man examined Marion's new passport.

"You have been married recently, perhaps. Since 23 November, yes?"

Well, sometimes a very small last push is all that's needed and that happened to be it. I got down on one knee. I felt the cold dampness of the deck seeping through my trousers as I fumbled for the ring. There really couldn't be any going back, certainly not after Marion turned around from waving at the crowd and saw me there, looking up at her with God only knows what sort of an expression on my face.

"Berton?"

"Marion Rubincam, you are indispensable to my happiness and I . . . well . . ."

I coughed and felt like I'd swallowed a hair.

"I'll do my damnedest not to disappoint you, Marion."

She pushed her finger through the ring while down on the pier one of the bands segued into the wedding march. And that was that. I have revisited the moment a good few times over the last two days. I tend to change some things — my own part, mostly, and I like to remember Marion as more surprised than she really was.

The chief steward, or whoever he was, was only partly satisfied.

"This is progress, Mr Braley, but it is not yet marriage, I think."

"Look, bud, neither were Adam and Eve — it's the thought that counts, right? Anyway, what does it matter to you? You're not telling me you haven't seen a bit of life on this ship."

"It matters nothing to me. In fact, sir, my staff would rather not have to clean the bridal cabin, but there are unusual charter conditions. Our . . ."

He flicked through his papers a trifle self-consciously.

"Yes, here we are. Mr Henry Ford wishes to run, as I believe it is said in English, a 'very tight ship'. Two passengers have already been asked to leave."

The man nodded toward the pier and I looked down on the ludicrously attired Dr Pease and the sulky young woman by his side and the hungry journalists all around them.

"He threw them off?"

"Mr Ford's bodyguard escorted them ashore."

"Oh, well — at least we'll be able to have a smoke in peace. What do you say, Marion, could there be a better start than this? Shall we go the whole hog?"

"The whole damned hog, Berton!"

She threw herself into my arms and I held her tight, pressing my cheek into the warmth of her neck as I stared into the beady black eyes of an arctic fox. From that point on I knew nothing of the remaining speeches or the last stages of the send-off or how the *Oscar* made her way out of port. Marion and I were inside, the subjects of a marriage arranged as summarily as a frontier hanging, but very strange and delightful and highly auspicious for all that.

It being a peace expedition there was no shortage of clergymen aboard. A conclave was held and a white-bearded unitarian found who was willing to do the job. The Reverend Jenkin Lloyd Jones presided over the dearly beloved who crammed tight as immigrants into the main saloon. Mr William Jennings Bryan was there, smiling on the proceedings exactly as he does from all those countless newspaper photographs. And at the last moment, just before the crucial words were pronounced, I saw the face I was looking for, the lean, American features of Mr Ford himself as he slipped in and joined the back row of the congregation. Like a child confronted with the reality of a monument after years of revering it in a schoolbook, it was all I could do not to point and exclaim and interrupt Reverend Jones in a way that could never have been forgiven. Ford was there nevertheless, his presence was with us, and his benediction.

"By the power vested in me by the states of New York and Illinois . . ."

There was a loud whisper from someone I couldn't see.

"Hey, aren't we in New Jersey?"

"Shut up for Christ's sake or we'll never get out of here."

". . . I now pronounce you man and wife."

I kissed my bride. Marion had been persuaded to part with her fox fur for the duration of the ceremony and had left it on a bench at the side of the saloon.

Mercifully, she could not see it at that culminating moment. I could, and was forced to observe a squirrel, inspired perhaps by the epithalamial spirit, crouch low over the soft white fur and knead the stuff with accelerating urgency before pressing down its trembling squirrel loins. The creature's tail reached a pitch of ecstatic vibration in the moment before it was swept from its partner's back by someone wielding a large hat.

"Shoo! Get away, you filthy little thing!" commanded an outraged Bostonian matron.

It ran up the curtains and disappeared. I quickly kissed Marion again to prevent her from turning around and because my own mind was turning hungrily to the next stage in the drama.

There was some debate about the legitimacy of our union and I feared a further delay. A harassed Captain Hempel looked at his watch and said that if anyone was worried he could do the whole thing again as soon as we passed out of territorial waters. Mr Bryan had a more practical argument — namely that the "all ashore" was being sounded and that if Marion was no legal bride he would miss the chance to kiss her before getting back to dry land. This won the day and we were man and wife by common consent whether or not in the eyes of the Lord. Mr Bryan got his kiss, but Mr Ford had already left the scene.

We were declared to be good omens, the lucky charms of the expedition. A tumultuous escort accompanied us to the bridal cabin and the key was ceremoniously handed over. Once in, we locked the door and lost no time in consummating what must be the most modern and American marriage ever made. I got an answer to a question that had been bothering me — is it different when a man makes love to a woman who has just become his wife, I mean a woman he already knows in that way? Well the answer is, surprisingly — yes.

"Well, Mrs Braley?"

"Very well, thank you, Mr Braley."

"Did you see Mr Ford there?"

"Not knowingly."

"Oh, come on, Marion."

"What do you mean — how would I know what he looks like?"

"Well, he was there. He came in specially, just at the right moment. Marion, we were damned near married by Henry Ford himself!"

Time passed, the porthole went black. Now and again there were sounds of considerable excitement from other parts of the ship, but neither of us was at all curious to know what was happening there. Eventually we were disturbed by a tentative knock. Marion put on her new silk kimono (an unreturned sample from a department store), answered the door and came back with a brown derby hat. We sat together on the bed and looked inside. There was a note that said "From the Ford Peace Delegates and Press with all best wishes for the future". We unwrapped the red-spotted handkerchief and found inside enough five-, ten- and twenty-dollar gold pieces to fill Marion's cupped hands. She picked them up and let them tumble musically back into the hat.

"How kind people are."

Marion let the kimono slip down around her ankles and got back into bed. I started at once to curl myself around the warmth of my new wife but she moved away suddenly, put her hand flat over her navel and looked up at the ceiling. There was an anxious expression on her face, as if she was asking herself a difficult question.

"Are we moving? Do you feel right, Berton?"

"It's love, gorgeous. The power of love."

I took an ear-lobe between my lips and paid no attention at all to the rising sound of the wind. She pushed me away, raised her hand to cover her mouth and groaned.

"Need a rest?"

She nodded silently.

That was two days ago and in that time I've explored everything there is to explore on this ship, human and mechanical. I've endured all manner of barely decent enquiries about the first night of my marriage, met up with a few old friends, made plenty of new ones, and a handful of enemies too. I've even radiogrammed a few reports to my employers back home. And now here I am in the company of a gloomy Dean Marquis of Detroit, somewhere in the middle of the Atlantic ocean. Lloyd Bingham's absurd talk comes back to me and I find myself squinting at a patch of sea I don't like the look of, as if a submarine really could be just beneath the surface.

"I'd be pleased if you would call me Samuel, Berton. There doesn't seem much point in talk of 'Reverend' or 'Doctor' or whatever out here."

"All in the same boat, eh?" I say lamely.

"That's one way of putting it."

"This whole thing going to work, d'you think? D'you really think anyone will listen, that the war'll stop?"

"I suppose it will have to some day."

Another mouthful of brandy goes down before I speak again.

"That marriage — was it really kosher?"

I get worried as Samuel thinks about this for a long time, like he's going through a whole list of problems in his mind.

"Well, Berton, you're here now. You really want my advice?"

"Yes sir, I do."

"Don't ever ask. You had more clergy there than a royal wedding and everyone heard you say yes. Let that be enough. Question it and all you'll do is make a lot of lawyers even richer. And good luck."

"Thank you, sir. I appreciate that. Wind's getting up again. Will I see you at dinner this evening?"

"It doesn't seem to affect me."

"Until then, Samuel."

I take his words with me down below and let myself quietly into the bridal cabin. With the shade drawn over the porthole and a single dim night light burning, Marion's sleeping form, stretched face down on the marriage bed, stops me quite still and tells me something new about beauty. I sit down by her side and peel back the sheet. The shoulders, the line of the back rising to spread in perfect buttocks — if there is one thing in the life of a man he can never tire of, this wondrous shape must surely be it, God's never-failing covenant against boredom. I put my hand there and press gently. Warmth, softness. Marion wakes and makes a noise like a cat with its tail in the door. She waves one arm violently behind herself and slaps me away.

"You're made of ice! Are you *trying* to kill me? Is this terrible ship not enough?"

I say I'm sorry. She fumbles for an empty bottle of patent medicine on the night table and it drops to the floor. She pulls up the sheet and turns to look at me. Her face is nausea-white and snake-framed in unwashed hair. But it's the voice that is more strangely changed, straight from twenty years into a spoiled future.

"Have you been drinking, Berton Braley?"

Ray

Mr Ford often sees something in a newspaperman I don't and I've never come to like that particular breed. When I first came across Mr Theodore Delavigne he wasn't much to look at or listen to. Then in no time he's going round in a fancy car and with more money than he's worth and I start to hear about his qualities from Mr Ford himself. Well, I suppose he'd crossed the line and come over to our side and so I tried to like him, but it still kind of rankled when he was the one sent to tell me.

"Ray," he said, right of the blue. "You're going to Europe."

"What? But I ain't done nothing."

"Mr Ford needs you."

"In Europe? Why? I can't even speak the language. What use . . ."

"It's all right, Ray. Mr Ford's going too. You'll be with him."

"Mr Ford's going to Europe?"

"That's right and Mrs Ford would like you to go with him."

"Oh yeah? How would you know?"

"Well now, Ray, I just heard — that's all."

"To the factory in England?"

"No, not to England."

"In France?"

"Don't think so, not at the moment anyway."

"Then where?"

"Well, we don't know yet, but it will be somewhere in Europe. He's going to stop the war."

Then it all came out and I can't say I was pleased.

"Listen," I said to him, "is that a good idea?"

Delavigne didn't seem too sure himself. In fact, he wasn't at all sure. Then I find out later that he's the one behind most of those pieces in the papers, that he writes the words, words I never heard Mr Ford use, and makes him say all those big things like he can really do it any time he wants. That's what I mean about newspapermen.

"One other thing," he tells me before he goes back into the Biltmore. He taps me on the side of my jacket. "They don't like guns."

"What're you talking about?"

"Those Europeans over there — they don't like guns."

"*They* don't like guns. Tell me it's a joke."

"I mean off the battlefield, Ray. I'm not telling you your business, just be discreet, that's all I'm saying. Mr Ford shouldn't be embarrassed."

"Well it won't be *me* who does that."

And so in no time I find myself on the deck of this rustbucket, having just fought my way through something that looks for all the world like a revival in a lunatic asylum. The papers say it's a nut house and guess what? — you get here and they don't even have the half of it. Mr Ford is out front where he can be seen and I feel better now I've got him on the ship. Young Edsel is at his side looking pretty happy at the prospect of getting out from under his father for a few weeks, or months, or — who knows? — maybe for ever. Mrs Ford is on the other side preparing to go ashore. She has an expression on her face like she's about to put her husband over her knee and spank him and the only thing stopping her is other people. I look around to see what we've got. Schwimmer is there, close enough to be intruding on the family group. Mr Lochner holds back at a more respectful distance. Then there's Dean Marquis, spotless, giving nothing away. I concentrate on Mr Ford, but can see Marquis looking at me all the time. When I look back he turns away after a fraction of a second. Delegates I don't know are everywhere, and I'm trying to keep an eye on all of them at once. Photographers start pushing over the best spot and journalists are muscling in from the lower deck — men whose luggage consists largely of hot-water bottles filled with whisky.

The whistle blows for the last time. Mrs Ford has to go and I make sure I'm by her side. Schwimmer comes forward with a simple-minded smile on her face like she's about to hand out a Bible tract. She almost stands right in her way, but Mrs Ford just goes on by without seeing her and I follow close behind.

"I'm relying on you, Ray," she tells me just before stepping off the ship. "I'm relying on you and Dr Marquis."

"Yes, Mrs Ford," I say, though without really knowing what she means.

She and Edsel walk down to the pier and almost as soon as their feet touch the ground I feel the engines start. The *Oscar* eases out from the pier and I think "Oh, Christ! It's really happening after all."

What's left of the first day goes quickly. It's hard to think of Dr Marquis and myself as a team but things seem to work out all right. He tails Mr Ford around the upper decks while I sort out the problems below and start studying the passenger list and putting faces to names. I take time to learn where the wireless operator lives and find a good-humoured American who tells me his story about how he was taken on in New Jersey at the last minute and is as surprised to be here as I am. Some joker in charge of the cabin allocation puts Marquis above the coal bunker at the far end of the ship from Mr Ford, who also has to change on account of a wedding breaking out and the use of the bridal suite messing everything up. I eventually find three cabins together at the end of a corridor and kick out a bunch of old maids and one looker who seems happy enough to move on. Now no one can get to Mr Ford without passing me and Marquis. By nine everyone's exhausted or seasick and the ship starts to quieten down, apart from the newspapermen around the bar of the second-class saloon. I go through Mr Ford's luggage with the Dean and find a miniature Model T car someone's given him. It has a little tank at the back and smells of gasoline so we drop it over the side just in case. I lay out Mr Ford's nightshirt on the bed and put the old school reader he's brought with him under the lamp. When I'm sure he wants nothing more I close the door and set my chair outside and stretch my legs out across the way. After a few minutes Dr Marquis steps over my legs, nods goodnight and double locks himself into his own cabin.

I know it's still there — the weight under my arm — but I have to put my hand inside and touch it just to get that feeling, like a shot of whisky after hours of wanting one. There's no movement anywhere and I drift off trying to work out how many hours there will be in our passage and, if somehow we can come back straight away, how many hours that will be before I put my feet back on American soil. By the time I come to an answer — I make it five hundred and twenty-eight — it's time to take one off. Five hundred and twenty-seven hours then. In another forty minutes it'll be closer to a mere five hundred and twenty-six.

This number and the roll of the ship make me sleepy and I'm caught with my chin on my chest by a young woman walking round the corner who stops sharply as soon as she sees me. I've seen her before, always in the company of Mrs Schwimmer, but I don't know her name yet. She carries an envelope and holds it like she'd rather it would disappear. I'm getting up and about to ask if she has something there for Mr Ford but she just makes a little noise, flaps a hand and runs off. Twenty minutes later her head and shoulders appear for a second and dart away again. This time I follow her to the other side of the ship and down the long corridor that gives access to the starboard first-class cabins. There she is, halfway down, sitting on her own chair just like mine, with a tray at her feet with a cup and a pot of coffee I can smell from where I'm standing. She glances at me and there's the trace of a smile before she turns to look straight ahead to concentrate on the task of guarding her leader. From inside Rosika Schwimmer's cabin comes the irregular tick of a typewriter at one o'clock in the morning.

I return to my station and find Mr Ford standing in the corridor in his nightshirt. He takes my arm nervously.

"Ray, where have you been?"

"Just checking on something, Mr Ford. Everything's fine. Is there something I can get you?"

He puts his finger to his lips and looks up and down both ways. Then he whispers — "The Dean!"

"Mr Ford?"

"Get me some dirt on the Dean."

"Yes, Mr Ford."

He goes back into his cabin. I can't stay awake for much longer and so I take the key from my pocket and quietly lock him in before going to my own bed.

Louis

One of the most extraordinary consequences of my annexation by Henry Ford was that I became for the first, and no doubt last time in my life, a *habitué* of the White House.

The first occasion had nothing to do with Mr Ford, but without him it would have remained my only experience of presidential interviews. I gained admission as the companion of Dr David Starr Jordan, illustrious peace campaigner, president of Stanford University and our nation's greatest expert on fish. Given the background and character of our current President, it was thought that Dr Jordan would be able to talk to him as one college man to another and thereby achieve better results.

We were received at ten-thirty in the morning. I noticed at once how the President and Dr Jordan, once equals, are now very far apart indeed. Mr Wilson was affable and calm and spoke in the whole meeting one or two words to our ten. Dr Jordan, constrained in a stern Prince Albert coat, was nervous and perhaps embarrassed by the great change in their relative positions. He was so painfully conscious of the situation that he began his explanations while still standing and had to start all over again after he had been asked to sit down.

A peace conference had recently been concluded in San Francisco and the resolutions sent to the President. We learned that he had read them and were encouraged to hear that he had ". . . revolved them carefully in my mind a dozen times or more". The scheme was explained — neutral mediation led by America, the world's great new power for peace, the only country that could lead, Wilson the only man who could do it. A conference in Europe when the parties were ready, Wilson in the boulevards of Paris or the great palaces of Berlin, directing the groundwork for a new and better world.

"And do they want it, Dr Jordan? Will the powers you talk of have this peace?"

The weariness of the combatants was set out, reports gained through private channels relayed. The President's objections were considered and subtle, but Dr Jordan, as he forgot where he was, became more fluent and met them all with mounting eloquence, the President himself acknowledging the force of our arguments with little noises of assent and nods of the head. Our hour was over and I was convinced that we had triumphed and that no man of reason and goodwill could withhold his agreement from what we were proposing. Success was at hand — a success which, as one of its smaller consequences, would have kept me away from Henry Ford and this ship. I spoke up confidently:

"Then, Mr President, may we take the message with us that you will act?"

The President's manner changed suddenly.

"No. That is for me to say when the right moment, in my judgement, arrives."

It was my first lesson in power.

Then a telegram, a confusion, a stroke of luck, a conversation by an empty swimming pool and holding out my hand as an express train rushed by and carried me straight back into the White House ten days later. As the President greeted me very civilly Mr Ford made his choice of armchair, sat in it before being asked and let a long, thin leg hang over one arm and swing back and forth.

"You are looking very well, Mr President — better than I have ever seen you before. You must tell me what you do to keep yourself in such good trim."

The President explained that he liked to forget about business outside business hours and always enjoyed a good joke. Mr Ford told him one and the President responded with one of his favourite limericks. These preliminaries over, Mr Ford started briskly in the same manner, I suppose, in which he orders half a million tyres or some inconceivable tonnage of iron ore.

"I don't think I need say much about the plan I favour. I have decided to back the proposal for neutral mediation. If you will take the steps to appoint a mediation commission with all the authority of your office, I will offer unlimited financial backing for the undertaking. Failure would be impossible."

"Hmm," said the President.

He went on to explain, so far as I could understand it (and heaven knows what Mr Ford made of this), that he was not necessarily of the opinion that the plan was not quite possibly the best one that had yet been offered. Commendable though this was, he had to give full regard to his position as head of a neutral country and, more particularly, to the need to retain the United States' full freedom of action in the event that a better plan might be proposed at some later date.

For a brief moment Mr Ford's expression resembled that of a dog to which someone had just read Hamlet's soliloquy — a very brief moment.

"Mr President, tomorrow morning in New York at ten o'clock precisely representatives of every newspaper in the country worth a damn will come to my apartment for a story. I will tell them I have chartered a steamship and offered it to you to send delegates to Europe. If you don't act, I will. I will tell the newspapermen I'll do it myself. One way or another, I will put an end to this obscenity in Europe."

The President blinked. He seemed about to laugh but then stopped himself, doubtless recalling that the man before him had a treasury for a bank account and no Congress to tell him how to spend it.

That was not quite the end of my second encounter with President Wilson, but as to what was said or done between that moment and me finding myself once again on the steps outside the White House, my memory is indistinct. Mr Ford pressed his hat firmly back on before shaking his head slowly from side to side in disappointment.

"Louis," he said to me, "Mr Woodrow Wilson is a small man."

The following ten days was a sort of fever. The thought of it is almost as exhausting as the events themselves. I became the passive, hollowed-out instrument of the cause and by the end, when I was looking forward to boarding the *Oscar* as my only chance of salvation, I felt something less than human. Finally resentful of these demands, I left the Biltmore hotel on the last afternoon before sailing, Schwimmer's imperious voice calling my name as the elevator doors closed and I was carried down to a few hours of freedom.

I had not picked a good hour. The city seemed to be in a state of hysteria, the streets seething with vehicles which bellowed at and threatened each other like they must be more than mere machines. Only a passing horse seemed calm, pulling a truck loaded with half a dozen iron stoves and living surely, behind its blinkers, in some remote, resigned horse world far from the city. I walked aimlessly. Was I about to embark on one of the greatest humanitarian triumphs, or on something quite stupid and futile? There were good and thoughtful people on both sides. I tired myself trying to come to a decision and felt I must be betraying my friends even to think about it that way. Madame Schwimmer never weakened — what was her secret?

New York is loud to the eye as well as to the ear. Almost every convenient surface seems to have been hired to impose some profitable idea on the passer-by — Thermos, Kodak, Waterman, Colgate all blare out.

Side by side, two peeling posters recommend the "Allah" Christmas card and Pebeco dentifrice — a third insisted that I should learn to stuff birds for a rewarding hobby. Higher, brighter and more costly, the Aetna Insurance Company issued its fiery warning — "One man in seven is accidentally killed or injured each year. You may be the one." I tried to keep that information out of my mind but couldn't stop myself from wondering if their actuaries had included the risks of being torpedoed in the western approaches. Perhaps my chances were not even as good as one in seven. Illuminated every few seconds, an angel descended onto a piano stool. Its hands remained rigid while a mechanism out of sight caused it to vigorously pedal the Angel Player Piano. After a while I came to a halt under an enormous gilded revolver that hung over an ironmonger's shop-front. Behind the glass and a steel security grille guns were laid out in careful display —

The Colt Automatic Pistol
Fire the first shot first!
Trust Colt for the Protection of Home and Family.

A cheaper model was still more sensationally advertised. The prospective buyers of the Ivor Johnson Safety Automatic Revolver were encouraged to envisage themselves confronting a crouching, distorted form in which a commercial artist had just about managed to combine the feline with the human.

> Is a cruel, lurking, murderous beast any less a beast because it is human? If your business takes you into bad or lonely neighbourhoods, there is but one way to guard against the possibility of a crushed skull and a broken body — keep your distance and cow others into keeping theirs.
>
> $6.00

I stared through the glass, mesmerised by the guns and the picture of the crouching man-beast. Another wanderer did likewise and we became aware of each other at the same time as the only two figures standing against the flow of the sidewalk. I tried to get a look at him without moving my head, only to find that he was doing exactly the same to me. I caught a jaundiced, wary eye and easily imagined us both running into the shop in a desperate hurry to be the first to buy a safety revolver.

I walked on until I found myself outside the faded Lincoln Vaudeville theatre, reading an offer that would keep me away from the Biltmore for half the evening. I bought a ticket and sat in the semi-darkness with maybe a dozen others. At length curtains parted to reveal a large white screen obscuring the disused stage. The darkness deepened. A whirring started and a hot, chemical smell as a narrow triangle of light shot through the theatre. A boy pressed a chord on a piano as the letters DG appeared on the screen along with a stern guarantee of the authenticity of what we were about to see. Words appeared advising me to consult the printed programme (absent), and then some pomposity about the liberty to show the dark side of wrong in order to better illuminate the bright side of virtue. The freedom of the written word was invoked, along with Shakespeare and the Bible — then slaves cringing in a marketplace before the pianist picked up the tempo as we were shown the domestic happiness of the Stoneman family prior to its destruction by the evils of war. In a very short time I found what I really needed — two hours of uninterrupted sleep.

After a restless night in the hotel I rose early and struggled for over an hour to find the right words for a letter to Emmy and Elizabeth. I put myself in a state of high anxiety with the thought that these might be the last words my little girl would have from her father. From 5 a.m. the noise of preparation rose beyond my door and I let two people knock and call my name and go away before giving up and sealing into its envelope a letter that was sometimes too plain and sometimes too mawkish. I decided that if I got back I would find the letter at the bottom of Emmy's drawer and secretly burn it to celebrate my return.

With no breakfast, save for the taste of stamp glue on my tongue, I was pulled back into the fray and in a few hours found myself on the deck of the *Oscar* beside my chief and his great friend Mr Thomas Edison. Mr Bryan, the recently resigned Secretary of State, was also there and communicated with the crowd with a politician's skill. Rosika placed herself carefully where she could best see all the players at once. She had a distant, visionary smile on her face and held her now famous bag high against her chest. From time to time

Mr Ford would make observations to Mr Edison and would point things out among the holiday crowd on the pier. The old man would smile and nod and lift his hat to the people below. Mr Ford put his hand on the arm of his mentor and onetime employer and spoke a few words that I believe only I could have heard.

"Come with me, Thomas. Don't go ashore. I'll give you a million dollars to come with me to Europe."

Mr Edison raised his hat and received once again the gratitude of the nation of electric light and recorded music. The fringe of white hair around his head blew in the icy wind, as fine as a baby's. At nearly seventy years of age he is a little deaf and was spared the embarrassment of responding.

The well-wishers returned to shore and as the whistle blew Mr Ford was sent on his way with a storm of cheers and hand-clapping and hurrahs. He bowed again and again and had a calm, certain smile on his face that I had not seen before any time in my short acquaintance with him. There were not a few tears of emotion.

Delegates installed themselves in their cabins and quickly reappeared in the smoking rooms and lounges in high excitement and with their names pinned to their clothes. Hardened social uplifters — mostly women of a certain age — greeted each other familiarly and separated into hunting parties to track down and shake by the hand the greatest celebrities on board. Mr Ford was the most valuable prize of all and by the end of that first evening he had charmed everyone on board with his modesty and openness. It was universally agreed that as great industrialists go, Mr Ford is the best you can get.

As might have been expected, the arrangements made so meticulously on paper did not long survive their first brush with reality. Cabin arrangements decreed by Mrs Ford herself for the protection of her husband had been overturned by Rosika Schwimmer.

"The King must be accessible to his court!" declared Rosika to a twitching and highly coloured Dr Marquis.

"If you wish to be a Queen, Madame, you may be accessible! *We* will inform you of Mr Ford's arrangements."

She lost that one.

An impromptu and farcical wedding further upset the allocation of cabins. A youthful Marion Penn was quartered with three female students. In the spirit of the voyage a debate was held in which Mr Penn argued for a pioneering attack on the outmoded taboos of the older generation.

"Rational dress for our minds as well as bodies, girls. We must take the corsets from our thoughts as well as our waists."

The girls applauded, but said they could not possibly share a cabin with a man who wore a corset. He lost the vote three to one and was sent off to find the chief purser and more suitable bachelor accommodation. Thus a line of dominoes was set tumbling which resulted in me standing at nine in the evening before a door with four names behind its isinglass cover, one of them Mrs Inez Milholland. She answered the door herself, venting an incongruous cloud of camphor and naphthalene. Her expression softened into a tired smile.

"Louis Lochner."

"Oh, yes," she said. "I know."

Inez moved out into the narrow gangway and almost closed the door behind her. She was forced to stand very close and I was struck by how the pupils of her eyes in that low light seemed as wide as coat buttons. I mumbled my explanation and wondered if she could possibly accept moving cabins even at that late hour.

"Oh, thank God!"

There was a noise from within and then, in another voice, an emphatic, "Good riddance, I say!"

Inez went back into the cabin, slammed shut a suitcase and seized her fur-collared wrap and hat.

"Ladies, I must leave you. Louis — I may call you that? — can someone send these flowers on to my new cabin? They do not agree with my friends."

There was a loud sneeze from one of the three more mature residents.

Inez's new address was twice the size of the old and reserved for her sole occupation.

"But this is wonderful!"

I tried to explain that it was also accidental. She dropped her things on the bed and kissed me on the cheek.

"Thank you."

"It's all been a bit of a mess, that's all."

"I never sleep on boats," she declared firmly. "Not properly, anyway. And I certainly won't on this one with everything being so exciting and all these fascinating people here. I just want to talk and talk and talk. I want you to come and talk to me any time, Louis. Absolutely any time at all — except just now."

The newspapermen scented their way to the bar from the off and were delighted to find it was to be free for the duration. A handful of prohibitionists started the first debate of the voyage, insisting that a peace mission was no place for strong drink. The journalists held a vote and unanimously found the prohibitionists to be "boring". The latter stormed off to Mr Ford who sternly disapproved of liquor but was unwilling to tell grown men what to do, especially men who wrote for the newspapers.

Although we have a captain — Hempel by name — his authority largely evaporated as soon as Mr Ford stepped on board. All cases are taken to him for judgement in the ancient manner and the next on the court list, after the burning issue of wet or dry, was the first great human interest story of the expedition. One Jacob "Squint" Greenberg emerged after seven hours in a lavatory cubicle and declared himself a stowaway. He had gained access to the ship with the help of an American District Telegraph uniform and a bogus, but all too plausible, *bon voyage* message for Inez Milholland. He baffled Mr Ford by enthusiastically spouting Tom Paine and Walt Whitman and spoke with confusion and sincerity about our mission. There was talk of a long sentence of potato peeling in the galley. Mr Ford took a quite different view, commending Greenberg for his determination and appointing him to the expedition staff as his personal messenger. With the addition of much colour and imaginative detail the story was quickly wired back to New York for the Sunday papers in a dozen competing versions. As soon as the wireless office got free I slipped in and spent a useful twenty minutes making the acquaintance of Robert Bastian, the wireless operator. I quickly got the story of his last-minute appointment, of the wife and two children back in New Jersey, of his love for the job and his bright-eyed enthusiasm for the future of the wireless.

"It's only just stated. You wait. In ten years everyone will have their own. You'll be able to hear your baby cry from the other side of the world."

He admits the money isn't good.

"Look," I said. "You know what we're trying to do here? You know this isn't the voyage you signed on for any more?"

He's articulate — more than most in his position — and knows a lot about our campaign. He tells me very definitely that he is with us.

"I'd like to help you out."

He hesitated just short of taking the two ten-dollar bills.

"It's Mr Ford's money," I told him. "It's all right. Official. Not everyone thinks the way we do and I need to know what's being said — to know everything that goes out over the wires."

"Wire*less*."

"Sure. I mean from the journalists. You understand?"

"Yeah, I get it. You know the captain has to censor all the messages — to keep within the neutrality regulations."

"I want to know before he does. And other things too, things that might not bother him. And not just the journalists — the delegates too."

He smiled and took the money. He said he wanted to help, but I got the feeling it would soon cost me another twenty dollars.

"Which delegates?"

I shrugged and began to feel a little grubby. Bastian was keen to play the secret agent. "Any names I should be looking out for? Who are the suspects? Makes it easy for me — that's all."

"Anything unhelpful."

Late at night I make a last round of the ship. Ray dozes on his chair outside Mr Ford's cabin while the young Rebecca Shelly mimics him on the other side of the ship. William Bullitt of the *Philadelphia Public Ledger* emerges from Rosika's cabin with notebook and heads wearily for the press room. In the lounges the other newspapermen are red-faced, unsteady and loud. Elsewhere, in a quiet corner Inez, true to her claims of insomnia, has emerged in a silk dressing gown and gives her rapt attention to an anecdote from the debonair and inexhaustible Samuel McClure. I can't match him and go below in search of my bed — or is it "bunk" now? I pass doors that emit whisky, snores, astringent life-preserving embrocations and from Lloyd Bingham's cabin, coughing.

In darkness and solitude at last, my mind plays over its old theme of power, of how to make things happen. I'm in the middle of it now, at the very heart of the mechanism that turns the world to its own beat. I've heard tell that Mr Ford, as a boy, once looked at a watch and then made one himself merely from that single glance at its workings. That is something I shall never do.

The ship's band woke us this morning with a Sunday hymn. The weather has worsened and only a handful have appeared for breakfast. The students are holding up well and Reverend Charles Aked has also joined us. An Englishman, he has some experience of peace work — his church and home having been wrecked by a mob in Liverpool when he spoke out against the Boer War. He improved his circumstances by crossing the Atlantic and ministering to the spiritual needs of John D. Rockefeller, before being dispensed with and moving on to San Francisco. As Dr Jones made a lengthy speech at Hoboken yesterday, it is Dr Aked's turn this morning. A sense of occasion has been added by the information that his entire sermon will be telegraphed back to New York. Someone has calculated the cost — in an hour's time I shall be listening to an eight-hundred-dollar, world-record-breaking radiogram.

McClure comes in, bouncy as a new puppy. He orders an enormous, high-smelling Scandinavian breakfast and begins to look over some notes ostentatiously as he eats. I catch his eye and he responds with an ambiguous wink. I know he has not always been a friend of the peace movement and decide to check his telegrams after breakfast. Other delegates and the odd hung-over journalist wander by in search of another spoonful of Mothersill's Seasick Panacæa. Some have the verdigris skin colour of the Statue of Liberty, a picture of which has been posted on the wall, redrawn as a suffering Belgium. Through the dining-room window the horizon shows, vanishes, shows again in a deep, oily rhythm. I have to look away and for a moment I fear I am about to embarrass myself. I hold the edge of the table and half rise from my chair as I stare down at the unhelpful sight of a gnawed brioche and the black circle of coffee in a cup, the scent of which is now nauseatingly powerful. My stomach contracts, I poise to run before, just as quickly as it came, the sensation passes. All this time I have been under the amused observation of Samuel McClure as he relishes his pickled herring.

My morning promises to improve as Mr Ford enters and joins me. A steward is instantly in attendance and takes an order for stewed fruit, toast and coffee. I see the thin, black lines of oil worked under his fingernails. A smell of coal diffuses from his clothes. He is in an excellent mood and explains in copious detail the workings of the steam engines down below, where he has already spent two happy hours.

"I don't suppose you can make them go any faster?" I ask.

"Not these ones. It's quite a museum down there, though don't tell the second engineer I said that — a charming fellow. You know — if this business comes to anything I might buy this ship. People can pay a dime to see the ship that brought peace to the world, and how engines used to be."

I ask him, now that he has had the opportunity to meet everyone, what he makes of his motley crew.

"They suit me exactly. It's like a community — some old, some very pretty young ones, rich and poor, men and women, prominent and obscure, able and less able. It's as though I had scooped up an average American community and transferred it straight to this ship. I like this crowd. It's representative. You see, Louis, this is what I do. I scoop up America and set it to making cars, or whatever else I want it to make. I don't care what a man knows when he walks through the gates of Highland Park. I teach him all he needs to know. Now we'll make peace instead of cars. Say — that's rather good, isn't it? Write it down for me and we'll send it out over that Marconi thing."

He talks on volubly on the subject of progress, which he ascribes to animals as well as machines, explaining how biology keeps up with engineering through the transmigration of souls. His proof is an observation on the behaviour of chickens.

"You see — when I first drove a car on America's roads most creatures, men and beasts, had never seen such a thing before. Chickens would run straight in front of me, right along the road, and would often get hit. Now, you watch next time you go driving out in the country — when you come round a corner and find yourself nearly running over a chicken you'll see it'll go left or right and save itself more often than not. And why is that? Chickens don't read history any more than I do. They don't talk to each other. There's only one explanation — that chicken was hit in the ass in a previous life and that's how it learned its lesson."

I feel a little faint as I look down at my abandoned meal. Hunger and nerves make my fingers tremble. McClure's unsympathetic gaze is upon me from across the tables. Like a bullying parent Mr Ford urges me to eat. I decide that the best I can do is to dose my coffee generously with sugar. I reach for the bowl only to be intercepted by Mr Ford's firm grip across my wrist. The most self-made of all America's great self-made men shakes his head in sombre warning.

"Don't do it, Louis."

I return an uncomprehending look.

"Have you ever examined granulated sugar beneath the microscope? I thought not. Razors! The edges of those crystals on an empty stomach have sent many a good man to his grave before now. Let me get you some honey."

"Thank you, Mr Ford."

McClure

Ah, well — even with a passenger list like this, S. S. McClure is still the biggest name here, that's always something. Then again, when you think about all those who turned the old man down maybe being here isn't such a good thing after all. At least Bryan didn't come — in his human form, anyway. God's own windbag — he really would have made me sick.

The third day out. Weather even worse, but folk are beginning to get their sea legs and be a little more sociable in the evenings. The students are delightful, though whether they are much good for the self-regard of the delegates is harder to judge. They walk about with an exaggerated respect for everyone five years older than they are, convinced they must be dignitaries of the highest order. Then, as soon as they are a few paces past one invariably asks the other, "Who was that?" It's a fair question — there are some luminaries here even I don't know.

The scribes I am all more or less familiar with. I have given most of them work in my time, and sacked one of them on three separate occasions. At the moment they are gathered round the bar, loudly celebrating the birth of their new fraternity, the Vacillating Sons of St Vitus. Behind the leafy barrier a contest is in train to decide on the Vacillating Sons' anthem. Ugly looks are piercing the palm fronds as college club voices get rough:

It's a long way to Copenhagen,
It's a long way to go.
It's a long way to Copenhagen,
We're going on Henry's dough!

Actually we're going to Christiania — but that doesn't quite fit and these aren't men to let an extra syllable, let alone the truth, get in their way.

"Ruffians!" declares someone. Or did they just sneeze? I'm not sure — *la grippe* is making its way through the *Oscar* on the heels of *mal de mer*. Meanwhile, Mrs Morse Clark keeps such a tight rein on her student charges that I doubt any other French diseases will get much of a chance.

It's a curious scene, to be sure. Herman Bernstein gives me a nod as he goes by — publisher of *The Day*, translator of Tolstoy and Chekhov and Foreman of the Brotherhood of American Yeomen. He still has enough Russian in his accent for Madame Schwimmer to have taken a shine to him — gossips are marrying them off. If benevolence, culture and sincerity can do anything, he's a good man to have with you.

The southern tones of Colonel Robert Henry remain clear, even when voices are raised. The Grand Commander of the Mississippi Masons is here because his master, the Governor of Mississippi, had a change of mind late in the day but felt he shouldn't be entirely unrepresented. I listen to him explaining why it is a woman's privilege to remain unsullied by politics, why no true Southern gentleman would foist the indignity of voting on her. His astonished interlocutor, John Jones of the Anti-War Society, sounds like just the sort of man who should be here, but I know for a fact he solicited his invitation. Estelle, his wife, has been stashed down below in case they appear too flagrantly to be a couple in search of a free ticket to Europe.

Governor Hanna of North Dakota is broadcasting through the ship, and through the ether, his intention of visiting the battlefields as soon as landfall permits. Someone has told him that pacifism is not much use in gathering votes. He has turned the Ford Peace Ship into "Hanna Heads for the War!" A neat piece of work from a man who clearly still has some ambition. He chats amiably with a colleague of South Carolina whose command of English reached its height at Hoboken when he declared to the crowd that departing the United States with Henry Ford was "an unspeakable blessing to mankind".

There is an entire synod of padres of one stripe or another and a quantity of women in La Schwimmer's image — widows or spinsters beyond marriageable age, a quartet of teachers on furlough. One presented a children's peace petition to the State Department two miles long, another thunders with the full authority of the Oregon Federation of Women's Clubs. Helen Ring Robinson, our nation's first female state senator, is here as well as the stately Mary Fels. Mistress of the Fels

Naphtha soap concern, she has perhaps a half of one per cent of Henry Ford's capital and is, therefore, a very wealthy woman indeed. She is the party's second tycoon and emits, as if a living advertisement, a reassuring odour. A pair of bewildered Finns talk only to each other. The older woman, another associate of the Hungarian, enjoys the cachet of having been exiled from her homeland by the Russian bear and, in the absence of any Belgians, holds the trump card for suffering and subject peoples. Her charming young friend, Miss Eriksson, wears her national costume this evening. With a rod of braided ash-blonde hair extending down her back she seems to have been freshly animated from the pages of Hans Christian Andersen, or some other fairy tale.

In the corner a pretty co-ed, still in her fur coat, attempts to interest the former Secretary of State in an anchovy canapé. She mashes the pastry through the bars of the cage and asks the trembling rodent in her sweet Bennington accent whether it too gets sea sick. This is William Jennings Bryan, the squirrel. Beside him in another cage, Squirrel Ford has listlessly turned his face to the corner and is talking to no one. There was a fracas the evening before and the two cages had to be moved apart in the interests of inter-squirrel peace and security. There is now a small card between the cages which reads "Buffer Zone — Do Not Cross" and there has been much earnest talk on whether the theories of international relations can be made more scientific if they are tested first on small but suitably aggressive animals. Reporters have sent another $200 of radiograms declaring the Ford Peace Expedition's first success.

Across the room, through a gap between two shoulders, I glimpse the five-foot-five frame of my old friend Ben Lindsey, the juvenile court judge the newspapers apostrophise as the man who puts a little love back in the law; the second biggest thing in Colorado after Pike's Peak, and last year's eighth greatest living American, tying for the honour with Andrew Carnegie and Billy Sunday. He seems to have pestered one of the stewards for a glass of carrot juice which he brandishes in my direction.

"Still on the wagon, Ben?"

"Clean as a whistle, inside and out!"

We last met a year and a half ago at the Battle Creek Sanitarium. We put the world to rights over a bowl of oatmeal soup and he read the galleys of my autobiography. That was before my recent difficulties which, by chance, also originated while under the care of the good Doctor Kellogg.

There are prominent absentees. The Braleys remain below. There are conflicting reports — according to one of the younger newsmen much of the ship's uncomfortable motion can be attributed to their activities; according to the Braleys' neighbours, separated from them by the thinnest of partitions, there is already trouble in paradise. From the music room comes the umpteenth performance of "Alexander's Ragtime Band" followed by the stagey booming of Lloyd Bingham, our tireless court jester who is enjoying an unparalleled success with the students and those newsmen young enough to find some novelty in a vaudeville act of the 1890s.

Madame Schwimmer's heavy responsibilities confine her to her cabin and we have seen little of our guiding genius except for a few contributions to discussion groups and a teasing presentation on the contents of her infamous bag. The earnest Mr Lochner is more in evidence. On the subject of neutral mediation plans he is endlessly informative and seems to know no doubt. One would think there is nothing more to him until the conversation finally flags and he shows you a photograph of his infant daughter and coyly mentions the expected sibling and his hopes for him or her to be born into a peaceful world. He apologises and puts the photograph away and then is at a loss for what else to say and is greatly relieved when a note comes from Schwimmer and he dashes off to her cabin.

As for Mr Ford himself, he was seen at dinner this evening — entrance to "Stars and Stripes Forever" courtesy of the ship's band — but seemed to me a little greyer and more sunken than before. He sat with only his bodyguard and Dean Marquis of Detroit who talked incessantly, but too discreetly to be overheard. Ford appeared to listen to every word with the fixed attentiveness of a mesmeriser's patient. The conversation in the dining saloon nearly stopped at one point as everyone had their eyes on this pair and was paying no attention at all to what their companions were saying. No doubt a report will already be in Madame Schwimmer's hands.

I would have listed Inez Milholland high amongst these absentees if she had not come in just this moment. A woman mostly known from newspaper photographs of a goddess on a white horse, she does not disappoint in the flesh. The beauty is unconventional — a sensuously ambiguous face, eyes pale as a husky's and a nose that would not disgrace the bust of a Roman senator; a smile that is warm and yet sufficiently reserved never to seem easy. It's a face countless thousands have turned to take a second look at without quite knowing why. She carries with her the unspoken electric thrill of scandal, a hint that a moment of guiltless and thoroughly up-to-date happiness might for once be more than fantasy. Inez is the future. When I watch our half-dozen female students I feel only fatherly, but when I see Inez, my fifty-six years become desolate. She wears a black silk gown loosely wrapped around and belted at the waist with a simple strip of the same material. A white lace bodice shows between the broad lapels, and if she did not move with such confidence it would seem that Miss Milholland had taken to walking the ship in her night clothes. She goes straight to the screened bar, jokes with the newsmen who are at once charmed and chastened by her appearance among them. She emerges with a glass of stomach-settling champagne, sees me, approaches and sits down.

"I was hoping to have such an opportunity, Mr McClure."

She laughs quietly as I kiss her hand.

"Would it be too awkward for you to call me Samuel?"

"But I have a bone to pick with you first. Why do you never print my journalism?"

"Did you send it to me?"

"I thought so — you rejected it without even reading it, all my reports from Italy, I sent them to your magazine."

"That is easy to explain — it is edited by imbeciles and no longer mine."

"Alibi," declares Inez, attorney-at-law. "The complete defence. Perhaps I shall just have to like you after all. Talk to me about anything other than politics, peace or war. Otherwise I shall go mad, I shall run to the lifeboats and cast myself adrift."

And so the question can no longer be avoided — why am I here? I am the only member of this strange crew, other than Ford himself and just possibly the soap widow, whose name is a household word. But now it runs off the presses with no trace of my mind or hand in its pages. My own name disturbs my sleep, mocking me as letters on a magazine cover and a signature on a lapsed insurance policy.

"But someone tells me you have written your autobiography," declares Inez. "Too soon, surely. Can that really be true?"

"Almost true."

"I'm fascinated — really. But oh no, I can't read at sea. Never could — even as a girl it made me just too sick."

I acquiesce and save Inez the inconvenience of having to wait for dry land before learning the life story of Samuel S. McClure. I pass briefly over the remoter episodes — the simple childhood in rural Ireland, crucible of the McClure myth; the start of school which was the start also of memory from my fifth year, the mile walk along the meandering road shut in between the blossoming high hawthorn hedges. Later in the year the whin bushes were yellow and the flax fields beyond as blue as the sky. I tell how I was kept in that school for six hours a day, fifty weeks of the year and resented only that it could not be longer. When new readers came from Dublin once a year and the box was opened and I saw the bright colours and smelled the fresh ink I could not have been happier. I rose at six each morning to study before breakfast. Ever since, I have hated rest and been a martyr to my interests. I have never derived any pleasure from putting my occupations aside even for a day or two, as so many others seem to.

Two tall monuments stand over those early years and both are stories of death. On the first occasion I was eight years old and walked into McKeever's store one evening on an errand for my mother. A group of men stood close together in the candlelight. They talked excitedly and I soon understood that President Lincoln had been assassinated. Years later, when I published Ida Tarbell's *Life of Lincoln* in *McClure's Magazine*, I talked to many people about when they first heard the news and every one recalled the circumstances with complete precision. That's how it was for me too. It was the first time the outside world had cast a shadow over my own life and I can see McKeever's store now, as perfectly as a photograph.

The second event was altogether different. Lately it has been clearer than for years — the war I suppose, and too much time on ships.

You see, I say to Inez, a warship killed my father. It was the end of the shift and the men were walking off, half blind with exhaustion. My father stepped into an uncovered hatch and fell the depth of five decks through the empty shell of steel to be broken and killed on the keel. It took a week for the news to make its way home to Ireland from the Clyde. My friends and I were stealing sweet turnips and Daniel called over the wall to me.

"Your da's dead."

That night I thought of the last week and how it had been no different from any other. I hadn't known I had no father. Then the coffin came back with his wages and we buried him. He was thirty-two years old. I began to dream of a country where such things could not happen.

My younger brother was born, my father's posthumous son. Our little farm was sold and I began to understand what poverty was. We took to reading steamship circulars and railway maps of the United States and before long made our passage on the *Mongolia*. I remember the scene of parting at Glarryford railway station. The old women wept as bitterly as at the graveside and no doubt many did not see their children again.

We landed at Quebec on 26 June 1866. The journey by rail from there to Valparaiso, Indiana, where my mother's married sister lived, took seven days. Time and again our immigrant train was laid up in sidings while passenger and even freight trains were allowed to pass ahead of us. I remember nothing of our arrival, but recall clearly the next day when we were driven to Hebron, a few miles away, where I celebrated my first Fourth of July, watched my first firecrackers explode and tasted my first lemonade. The Democratic candidate made a speech. He talked of a young country ripe for the ambitions of Youth. I suppose it seemed true in those days. I thrilled to that message, but took a dislike to the man who delivered it. I could already guess that I felt what he wanted me to feel. For no better reason than that I became a Republican that day.

There were hard times ahead and, more for money than love, my mother married again. Mr Simpson became my stepfather and I was put to work on his farm, snatching a few hours of schooling a week when the chores were done. There was nothing to read in the house but the *Agricultural Reports* and the *Farmstead Catalogue*. Later, when I was on the point of making my fortune with the newspaper syndicate, I remembered those years and the emptiness of young boys' minds all across the prairies. I put Stevenson and Kipling and Stephen Crane and Conan Doyle into their newspapers, and pieces on how to collect fossils or butterflies; all those things of which I was most starved as a child.

The debt on the farm never got any smaller and one day, when I was fourteen years old, my mother called me to her and told me to leave for the new High School in Valparaiso or I would never make anything of myself. I left with the new clothes she had made for me, a dollar in one pocket, and a great sheltering ignorance of the world. Between working as a chore-boy and as a country schoolteacher, and tramping the roads as a pedlar in the summer and with the help of the occasional act of kindness, an education was finally obtained. What defects remained were made good at Knox College, Illinois. There I completed my young mind and lost my heart to Harriet Hurd, Professor Hurd's daughter, who was promptly instructed not to see such a worthless fellow again and sent out of harm's way to a Protestant girls' school on the banks of the St Lawrence. By eavesdropping — or journalism as I would later call it — I obtained the address of this place. I wrote at once, but she was an obedient girl and I received no reply.

On graduation I found myself no taller or more decisive than before and with no great cause in view. I sternly judged my features in the mirror and could not conceive of them ever being set up in marble or bronze on a public plinth. I had one great anxiety — that Harriet's letters (which had been secretly re-established after our first break) had once again stopped. I knew that she was staying with a friend near Utica, New York. With not the slightest plan in mind I packed my bag and left the West for the last time. I located my love, but only received from her a painful dismissal which I accepted as final. I walked back to the station at Marcy and asked how soon there would be another train out. I bought a ticket without asking where it went.

I might have starved in Boston, but instead found the direction of my life. It was while wandering in that city that I discovered my one remaining asset — my connection with the Pope Manufacturing Company, makers of the ubiquitous Columbia bicycle. I say "connection" — in fact there was nothing more than the fact that I had once sold this company some advertising space in our college newspaper. On this slender pretext I presented myself at their offices at 597 Washington Street on 3 July and requested to see Colonel Pope himself. Colonel Pope explained that he did not wish to buy any more advertising that season. I replied that I wanted work, but he told me he was laying off hands. I persisted and in the end was given a position scrubbing floors at the downtown bicycle rink. Colonel Pope observed his employees closely and when he wished to start the *Wheelman*, his own cycling magazine, he called me into his office and asked me if I thought I could edit it. By this chance I found my vocation.

The new venture prospered and I liked the work well. You are too young, Inez, to recall the importance of the bicycle in those days. For people in cities, the world beyond the end of the trolley-car tracks was stranger and more exciting then than it is today — less spoiled too. The bicycle opened it up. Attorney's clerks and doctors riding for their health would send us stories of adventures that went on for days or weeks and hundreds of miles. They would read Mark Twain, then mount a Columbia bicycle and live it. I remembered my time as a pedlar in the long vacations away from college. It's only thirty-five years ago and yet, away from the railway tracks, I could spend the best part of a summer and never hear the sound of a machine.

We grew quickly and then Colonel Pope decided to take over another magazine and merge it with the *Wheelman*. He presented me one day with a co-editor acquired from this other publication. I don't doubt he was an excellent man, but I found it was no longer in my nature to have an equal. I understood that I could never be happy except as my own man. Under this impulse I sat down one day and set out every last detail of a simple idea that would give me my freedom and, for a while, no little fortune by the standards of ordinary men. I would enlist newspapers and periodicals of every sort across the continent and promise them good articles and stories on a weekly basis. I would then go to writers and tell them they could have their work published not once, but a hundred times or more from New York to San Francisco if only they would put it exclusively into my hands. It started slowly, as all new things do. I managed it from a desk in the corner of one room in our small apartment, working all the hours I could, taking papers to the library when the baby cried too much. Oh, yes — Harriet. I wore her down in the end — and her father too. After five months there still seemed no end to the losses. Would it ever work? I wandered on my own in the summer evenings and knew some of the worst days of discouragement I have ever experienced. It was a six-storey city in those days (at most). You see how old I am? The Upper West Side was still largely empty and Harlem was a country district. It was lit by gas and every car was drawn by horses, or by the little steam-engines that pulled the elevated trains. Mr Henry Ford was out there somewhere in the western darkness and there was nothing to suggest it would ever change. The city seemed complete to me, as if everything had been done and there were no further possibilities.

Well, you know what happened. Within a very few years I could offer my good friend Mr Robert Louis Stevenson $8,000 for the American serial rights to his next story. I was the one who gave him enough money to charter that yacht and sail off to the South Seas. I bought Rider Haggard, I bought the Sherlock Holmes stories for $60 a piece, I paid Rudyard Kipling $25,000 for *Kim* and still made a profit on it. The magazine was added to the syndicate. We serialised the life of Lincoln. Circulation went from 120,000 to 175,000 to 250,000 in December 1895. *McClure's Magazine* was soon bigger than *Century*, *Harper's* and *Scribner's* put together. We became a power in the land and myself the chief of the "muckrakers". Important men began to fear us as we ran the Standard Oil articles, and then Steffens' pieces on municipal corruption. We were the first of our kind to take science seriously, covering Drummond on evolution, the excavation of dinosaurs, Marconi's wireless telegraph and the Wright brothers' first flight. On the last two occasions we received many letters from professors in midwestern colleges telling us sternly that we had been imposed upon by practical jokers. Because of all this a million minds a month were less empty than they might have been.

"There you are, Mrs Inez Milholland Boissevain — the contents of my autobiography. I have done myself out of a sale. Very unprofessional."

She covers a yawn with her hand and asks if it is true that Miss Willa Cather wrote my life story for me. She says she is a great admirer of Willa Cather and I must tell all about her. The thread of our conversation goes slack. There are only a few of us left up. The ship's band disperses from the music room as Lloyd Bingham's revels melt away. And yet, neither of us seems quite ready to be alone. I almost laugh at myself as I feel the strength of my need to impress this young woman. She looks at me intently and with a very slight and inviting smile. I choose to find some compassion there, woven through the unspoken question — "That's all very well, Samuel McClure, but you're here, aren't you? Why would you be here at all if it were not for these more recent, unwritten chapters — the ones your tame Miss Cather could never have mentioned?"

"Of course," I say, "things have changed a lot since then. You see, I slaved to feed those minds and in the end it broke my health. I began to spend more time away from the office. The old restlessness came back and I wandered for months each year in Europe. At first I pretended that I was looking for new material for the magazine and the syndicate, but in truth I was in flight from something I could never quite name. The steady repetition of success wore me down as much as any routine ever did. I began to feel like I was back teaching in a country school, always planning my escape before the end of term. This was when I became a good customer of the Battle Creek Sanitarium.

"I left good men in charge of my business, but editing is personal, the impress of one man's mental thumb-print on the final product. No one else can do it quite the same way and every time I came back *McClure's Magazine* was a little less my own. Can you understand how painful that is, Miss Milholland? It is like seeing your own child run to a stranger for comfort. I would set things right, only to flee again as soon as the dust had settled. Our competitors learnt our tricks, our better writers began to look elsewhere. One day I found my business partners all on one side of the table and myself alone on the other. They offered me ten thousand dollars a year for the use of my name and a promise never to interfere again in the magazine I had created. These are the men who turned down your excellent journalism.

"And so I was unhorsed, or liberated as I prefer to think of it. I travelled, adding from time to time another lecture to my repertoire. I found myself in London for the thirteen days between the ultimatum to Serbia and the British declaration of war. All my old friends were running to the colours — Wells, Bennett, Conan Doyle, Kipling. My energy came flooding back. I wanted to work again, like a young man. But through what instrument, with what voice? Circumstance had silenced me.

"I went home and lectured for the money, struggling grimly way out in Kansas and Nebraska with audiences who shouted me down as anti-German. I wrote my life story and saw it serialised by my former colleagues in *McClure's Magazine*. People said it was the only good thing in it any more and, sadly, they were right. I proposed a biography of Henry Ford but received a terse reply telling me the project was already in hand. I went down to Mexico to cover the revolution. I got sick of staying in hotels where everyone was a journalist half my age. I went back to New York and I suppose it all ended well when . . ."

I open my hands expansively to indicate everything around us, and to include most particularly Inez herself.

"When I found myself free to say yes to a new adventure."

Inez puts her hand over mine and tells me she is very, very pleased to find me aboard.

"You know," she says, "I believe that for the first time in my life I might be about to get a good night's sleep on a ship. And I haven't felt sick for hours. You are better than champagne, Samuel McClure."

She gives me her cabin number and an open invitation adding at the end, "and I really mean that." She asks if she will see me at the preparedness debate tomorrow evening. I tell her she can be sure of it and then pat my inside jacket pocket and let her know I have something special for the occasion, a little bomb to throw, something she will not want to miss. She smiles with that appetite for trouble I recognise so well and that is so indispensable for anyone who would change the world.

"Goodnight, then."

"Goodnight, Inez."

It is a quarter to two in the morning. Drunken newsmen watch her as she goes. They turn to look at me and shake their heads in disbelief.

There was no need to tell her the rest — she must know it anyway, or all the most fatal parts that have appeared in the newspapers. That one last piece in the story started in the Battle Creek Sanitarium to which dejection and a general malaise had once again drawn me. It was in one of the cleansing suites, where I lay face down preparing for that deep relaxation I so value when the attendant eases in his instrument, that I turned my head to one side to find, being similarly treated, a young acquaintance by the name of Dr Edward Rumely. He had made a little money for himself through the manufacture of farm equipment and had asked me a year before if I would print a neutral article on how the British blockade of Germany was damaging American business, not least his own contract for the supply of diesel-engined tractors. I could not oblige, but found him nevertheless a moderate and sympathetic man whose frustrations in his business life I could understand all too easily. In the intervening period he had acquired some powerful associates and, as he explained to me over a week at the Sanitarium, they were now in a position to make an offer to buy the *New York Evening Mail* and to run it as a neutral paper propagandising neither for the

Germans nor the Allies. In Rumely's own phrase, he and his partners could not believe their luck when they heard that a man of my stature was free to take the helm of their new venture. We talked about editorial policy. I made my loyalties clear, but they were no obstacle — if they could get McClure editing their newspaper, they would have him. I was back in the saddle.

It was on Saturday 24 July that Albert Heinrich, *Geheimrat* of the German Reich, and his friend Sylvester Viereck, editor of the pro-German weekly *The Fatherland*, boarded the northbound elevated at the Sixth Avenue Station. Viereck got off after a few stops, but Heinrich travelled on, drowsing in the summer heat. He nearly missed his stop, and in his hurry to get off the train momentarily forgot his briefcase. He ran back to get it, but it was already gone, carried off into the crowd by the Secret Service agent who had been dogging his every move for days. By some unknown route these papers, which contained my name in several innocent passages, quickly made their way from the hands of the government to those of the editor of *The World* who had little love for me. The first I knew of the affair was when a journalist from that paper came to ask if it was true that secret German money backed the purchase of the *Evening Mail*, that it was a propaganda front for the Kaiser, that I had been recommended by nameless persons as a useful instrument for promoting an embargo on American arms to the Allies?

"No", I said. "None of it is true. No, I do not want Germany to win the war."

But it was too late for the truth. As I left my office that evening old friends cut me dead in the street. A few days later I was informed that my unrestricted passport had been withdrawn at the request of the British authorities. And so when I opened that unlooked-for telegram and read the high-flown rhetoric of the invitation and saw Henry Ford's name at the bottom of it, I might have laughed if only I'd had anywhere else to go.

With this all swirling in my mind I step out for a little cool air before turning in. I lean on the rail and look out on the heavy, lightless swell. Uneasily, I sense the trajectory of life, that ever steepening downward curve and the cold mathematical laws that make it so and from which there is no appeal. I tell myself, with a violent shudder, that it is just a metaphor, that it might describe quite perfectly a thrown ball falling to earth without saying anything at all about life. And yet, if it is a universal law, truly universal —

Ahead of us, where nothing else is visible and first light still many hours away, an eerie hazing of the air puzzles me. Thinking of what I have read in the newspapers, I prepare myself for the stink of chlorine. In a moment of tragic indulgence I reflect that this innovation in war has come, for me, at the right time. I will breathe deeply and cut off only a last act for which I have no great appetite. But instead, soft descending curtains of grey approach and then cover the ship. I look up and experience the dizzying illusion of moving vertically upwards through a shower of soft hail. It falls faster than snow, slower than rain. It collects in the palm of the hand before melting, as regular as ball bearings or shot from a gun, like miniature snowballs, each moulded from a single flake. In the heart of the shower the fall is so dense that every flat surface is soon covered. In fifty-six years of life and a hundred crossings I have never quite seen anything like it. We move out of the shower and the harmless, charming transformation is already over. The strangeness of the scene evokes old magazine illustrations of Ancient Mariners, Flying Dutchmen, explorers' ships trapped in Arctic ice. It quickens something in me and this, together with the conviction that I am alone, licenses a grand, confessional gesture towards the discreet blackness of the sea. I step towards imaginary footlights and strike an orator's pose.

"You clutch at straws and sink a little faster, pulled down by the weight of one more straw."

I turn to the sound of a solitary, slow handclap and become aware of the whisky-scented bulk of Lloyd Bingham no more than ten feet away and now picked out with crown and epaulettes of white.

"Sounds familiar," he says hoarsely. "Remind me."

I tell him I just made it up, but he shakes his head firmly.

"No, no — some old play. I was in it once."

Inez

The coffee business didn't sell and the suffrage meetings palled. The same old arguments, the same old people, the same excess of chiefs trying too hard to make everyone else a mere Indian. It's coming for sure — we'll get there soon — but just for now I think the cause can do without me. There was something about the Italian fiasco as well — an unsatisfactory breaking off, something very like an unfair eviction that had to be reversed. There hadn't been enough of an adventure and I knew, as I looked across the breakfast table at my dear Eugen, that an unsatisfied desire for adventure was a dangerous thing in a marriage. I waved the telegram casually over my coffee, looked at the back of it, re-read the text on the front.

"You know, I've half a mind to go."

He spoke without looking up.

"Do you think it will work? Has any war ever ended just because people asked that it should end?"

"Lots, I'm sure."

"After they got tired of killing each other."

"It's your continent, Eugen. Don't you think you should take a little more interest?"

"I know them better than you, my dear."

"Well just because you're depressed doesn't mean others can't do something worthwhile. Why shouldn't good people talking plain common sense make a difference?"

"It sounds to me like you have a whole mind to go."

He put down the letter he had been reading, placing it near the middle of the table so I could clearly see it was another bill. Keeping his eyes closed, he let his head drop back. He sighed heavily and made, all in all, a typically pathetic male appeal. I closed the door to the hall, got him to move his chair away from the table and sat on his lap. He put his head on my shoulder and I smoothed his hair and planted a kiss on his forehead. He moaned about money as I contemplated his hairline and tried to remember exactly where it had been six months before — quite the same place, or had the tide already turned?

"Why don't you go in with Father? You know he'd be happy to have you."

"*He'd* be happy."

"Don't be so proud."

"You would really prefer me not to be?"

"I'm sorry."

I told him all would be well and talked vaguely about him needing a clear run at the problem, about darkness before the dawn, about me only being in his way. By spring next year everything would look different.

"And just how will this happen?"

"You'll see. And it's all expenses paid — or at least I suppose it is."

"What is?"

"The trip. The Henry Ford Peace Ship. It does say 'guest' — look. So you see, I'll be one less mouth to feed. And I can write for the newspapers. This is the start of better things. And what if it really works — you wouldn't want me not to be there, would you? I'll miss you so much."

"Go, then," he said sulkily. "Go and do whatever it is *you* want to do."

I slipped one hand beneath myself and wriggled my fingers until they had burrowed between his thighs.

"I'll miss Simon, too. I'll have to dream of him every night in my lonely little cabin."

"Simon will miss you."

"Just think — I might be away for months. When I get back we'll be strangers. It will be like the first time again. Could anything be more exciting?"

Over the next week Eugen cheered up and was perfectly sweet on the day of departure — vigorous in bed, attentive and organised through the morning, and gallantly agreeing that I had made the right decision after all. Hoboken was frantic and it made no sense for him to come all the way to the ship with me. We parted by a brass band — intimate in the privacy of the crowd and his breath warm in my ear.

"Come back safely, Nan. That's all I ask."

I'm not so sure now, but I thought I could still see him when I reached the top of the gangway. I seized a megaphone from the outlandish figure announcing my arrival and turned back to search the crowd. What last words should Eugen hear from me if it all ended in delicious tragedy?

"Votes for Women!"

There was a gratifying response, divided about half and half, which is a lot better than we usually get.

At first I was unlucky in the cabin allocation, finding myself closely quartered with three well-seasoned followers of causes. The first presented an ample chest to the world, so densely covered in badges declaring her various loyalties that she seemed to be wearing a suit of armour. She talked too much, had unrealistic views of our expedition, and embarrassed me by repeating how excited she was to be sharing a cabin with the "famous" Inez Milholland. The other, a Mrs Neuhaus, was no less committed, venturing forth on a winter voyage despite a keen sense of danger. She quaffed Sanatogen like an addict and offered us the protection of germ-killing Formamint throat pastilles in case we should be assailed in the night by "one of the old mistakes of Creation".

"Caruso uses them, you know. And Mr Bernard Shaw."

"No, thank you."

"Be it on your own head."

On my account the tiny cabin began to fill with flowers — another threat to the survival of Mrs Neuhaus, it seemed, as she began to wheeze and waft away imaginary toxins.

"I can't wait to get to Norway," she said eagerly. "I hear it's so clean."

At the end of the evening when we were making our cramped preparations for sleep, I watched in mounting amazement as she opened her Indestructo steamer trunk and donned a Neversink life-vest over her voluminous nightshirt. She turned her back to me.

"Tie me up my dear, if you would please. You didn't bring one yourself?"

The ritual was completed with the lighting of a tiny, stinking spirit lamp. This, explained Mrs Neuhaus, was the Vapo-Cresolene night guard — it would protect us from whooping cough, sore throat, asthma, bronchitis, catarrh and spasmodic croup as well as mitigating the effects of diphtheria should that demonic condition catch hold of our fragile souls before dawn.

"Well you can't stop a war if you don't get there first," reasoned Mrs Neuhaus, pulling a thick stocking over her head and falling asleep as instantly as a parrot in a draped cage.

There was an apologetic knock on the door. I opened it to find a harrassed Louis Lochner — one of the expedition's organisers. I had spoken to him earlier on the subject of accommodation and he had now come, as it appeared from his anxious expression and stumbling words, to disappoint me. I was so tired myself that I was hardly able to understand him and when at last I grasped that he had come to escort me to my own stateroom I fear I made my relief a little too obvious. I and my first-night companions parted coldly.

"Make her take the flowers," demanded Mrs Neuhaus, resentful at being woken and now with her stocking over one eye like a pantomime pirate.

My new quarters were very superior and have already proved convenient. I wrote to Eugen with the last of my strength before settling for a night of that sleepless rest which is the best I ever get at sea.

The next day I discovered a strange assemblage indeed. Ardour was everywhere, poured out in a ceaseless intensity of conversation — the single tax, women's suffrage, the solution to youthful delinquency, prohibition, free love, the outlawing of war, the removal of everything red from elementary schools. A group of female students created a wide, empty space about themselves in the first-class lounge by discussing contraception with commendable frankness. Even the war was discussed.

"Agendas for sale! Who'll buy my sweet agendas? Agenda, madam?"

"Get away from me, you stupid oaf."

Poor Lloyd Bingham made few friends with that one, though my heart began to go out to him as I discovered just how humourless many of my fellow travellers are. In four days I have changed my mind on his inclusion which I now see as very necessary indeed.

Just at the moment we are a little sore and shy with each other after last night's explosions. In the time leading up to what is already referred to as the Great Preparedness Debate we have talked and been talked at on a heroic scale. I have listened to Miss Rebecca Shelly's account of her spiritual rebirth, Reverend Dr Aked tell me I was on a journey no less significant than that of St Paul himself, a Miss Wales describe the detail and theory of neutral mediation and the splendid Dr

Lloyd Jones lecture on the perfectibility of mankind and the modern battleship. On Monday evening I got my first sight and sound of Madame Schwimmer as she addressed us stirringly on The Purpose of this Journey. She is a small, energetic and passionately sexless woman who has whittled away her existence to nothing but the doing of good. Her speech is vigorous and full of imperatives and high moral seriousness, her manner enthralling to those apt to be enthralled. She is the finished version of a type I know well. They can be effective, no doubt, whenever simplicity and relentlessness can win the day. She seems but narrowly to have missed the masculine gender and would, I think, in other circumstances have made an excellent general. Actor and politician complete her portfolio and in both she does exceedingly well. She achieved quite an effect with her locked black bag and was adept at avoiding the issue of its precise contents.

"Friends, these documents were given to me only because I was trusted. Can I not ask you to trust me the same way? In time of war there are things men can only say to women. With each other they are paralysed by the fear of weakness, but to me they told the truth, to me they opened the better, feminine heart of humanity . . ."

"Hear, hear!"

"*What* did she say?"

There was a snort from among the newsmen.

"What these men dared not say to foreign ambassadors, or to heads of government and ministers of war they dared say to me. And yet, if these secrets are exposed to the harsh light of day before their time they will only be disowned and our chance lost."

She gestured airily, a slight fluttering of raised fingers, the hand's hopeless dying away suggesting the evaporation of a volatile diplomatic opportunity. There was a sudden silence. Needle stares fixed on the great mystery of the bag. She held it high and for a moment it seemed to be the only thing in the room. We looked like bears, stupidly gazing up at a meatsafe dangling from the branch of a tree. I can't say I know quite what to make of her, but the next time I speak in public I'm sure there will be a few changes.

Through all this Mr Ford passes serenely, taking no part in the debates himself. At his approach the students and more impressionable delegates fall silent and make way. For his own part, Mr Ford seems not to have the slightest consciousness of rank. He is affable with everyone and pleasingly ordinary. If one was not forewarned of his name or did not recognise that much-photographed face, one would not at all suspect the extraordinary truth of his life. According to one anecdote he makes good use of this plainness when on motoring trips through country districts. When he finds one of his cars that needs repair he talks with the owner about the weather or the price of corn that year before moving on. A few days later a team of Ford factory mechanics appear from nowhere. Some, it is said, awake to find shining new automobiles in place of the old and are never quite sure what disguised god has blessed them. He has spoken with me twice, remarking on both occasions how pleased he was to meet me.

Neither then nor any other time in my hearing has he mentioned the war and it is impossible to say whether he is uninterested in the subject or merely reticent. His opinions generally are a mystery and at times his face suggests an oriental detachment from the affairs of the lower world. I half expect to discover him cross-legged in an attitude of meditation. If he died the engines would stop and we would drift endlessly and never be heard of again.

One thing counters this image and reminds the casual observer what Mr Ford really is. He is accompanied everywhere by two other men. The first is his bodyguard, a large and unreflective character who is known only as Ray and who frequently puts his right hand inside his coat. The other is usually a few paces behind and it is not clear, at first sight, whether the Reverend Samuel Marquis is a retainer or a pursuer. His features suggest permanent anxiety and he has the look of a detective from an English magazine story, hot on the heels of his quarry. It is his habit never to let Mr Ford dine alone and while at table he talks and talks but gets little in the way of answers from the great engineer, who seems either to ignore him or winces as if suffering some sharp discomfort. The newsmen tease with rumours of Marquis's sinister hold over Mrs Ford back home, or of her hold over him — she is the true director of the whole show, he is her secret agent, her *eminence grise* and perhaps even more than that. None of which, I suppose, contains a single word of truth.

For the rest I must say I am a little disappointed, though I have been lucky to find something of a soul-mate in Samuel "SS" McClure, the big magazine publisher of ten or twenty years ago. He talks too much about himself (the students say his initials stand for Seldom Silent) but it is not an uninteresting story and he keeps me up late enough to give me some chance of rest in the small hours of the morning. He has his own rather pressing reasons for being here. Poor man — toward the end of one evening I thought he was about to propose some business venture or even solicit a loan of money. There are differences in our politics which I ought to care about more than I do, but they never seem to matter much when we talk. We share an appetite for trouble and in the last few hours he has certainly made some, as he warned me he would. I should say he is a few years short of sixty, an age in men I find more interesting the more I experience it.

It is now five o'clock in the morning and about half an hour since Samuel and I agreed it was safe for him to go back to his own cabin. We are, I would guess, some 50 degrees west or thereabouts. That is to say, in the middle of the Atlantic Ocean and as far away from settled humanity as any modern person ever gets. Since girlhood it has been for me the most philosophical of locations. Drowsing to the beat of engines, unimaginably far from anywhere, the great questions at last came within reach, preoccupations shrank to nothing, impossibilities unravelled like slipknots leaving life brilliant and simple. All my most passionate diary entries were written in the middle of the ocean. There were nights when everything became clear and I thought I would be President by now, and there would be nothing more to do in a perfected world.

Not much became clear last night, though it was certainly one of the more memorable I have ever spent at sea. It was the preparedness debate that put an end to our harmony. The delegates packed the first-class dining room, and as we had calm water even those laid low by seasickness were able to join us. Everyone seemed happy and excited by the prospect of the rousing rhetorical exercises to come, the joyful affirmation of self-evident truths. Men and women of good will would come together.

"I see the snakes have left the garden," remarked Mrs Clark.

It was true. Meyer Block of the *Jewish Morning Journal* had drawn the short straw and was the only journalist present to cover the meeting — controversy was not expected. I looked round for a glimpse of Mr Ford but couldn't find him, or either of his two constant companions.

Reverend Jones opened proceedings with a homily, advising that when Cain raised up his hoe in the field and slew his brother this was the first instance of the great preparedness lie. Ever after, no peace-loving man or nation went prepared for conflict without the mark of Cain on his heart. The proof of America's closeness to God was that she bore no arms worth mentioning. General murmurs of approval, except among the students where a discussion started on whether a hoe, having a dual purpose and being arguably essential for life, was the equivalent in modern international law of the armed merchantman and therefore subject to special rules. Someone hissed angrily and the future Supreme Court Justice fell silent.

Madame Schwimmer ascended the dais, her head becoming visible above the throng for the first time. She adjusted her spectacles.

"I can spare only a few minutes to be with you before returning to our diplomatic preparations."

Suppressed laughter from an unknown quarter. Disapproving scowls. She recounted her odyssey — the struggle up from the depths of *mitteleuropa*; ceaseless, predestined wandering in the cause; her work for women's labour unions and universal suffrage. She sketched for us the groaning, enslaved nations of Austria-Hungary, how their hearts and minds were kept dull by endlessly fretting over ancient wrongs. And yet, even as they wandered on the dark seas of moral confusion (signs from some of returning nausea here), they looked outward to the light that was America, to the twin beams of peace and reason — "I refer, of course, to the hopeful voices radiating from that tower of American enlightenment, President Woodrow Wilson, and his good friend Mr Henry Ford."

Cheers here, and an abortive chorus of "For He's a Jolly Good Fellow". A perspiring Lloyd Bingham blew a rhythm on his whistle before quickly running out of breath. A shadow came over Schwimmer's face. Her audience fell silent. A sudden pain struck at her, or perhaps a memory of some deep grief.

"And what is this light that is now so threatened? Yes! — threatened I tell you. Is it the light that comes from more dreadnoughts, from more guns, from poisoned gas and the submarine? Some would have the Great Republic equip itself with these things — preparedness they call it, and who could doubt they mean preparedness for war? It'll never happen, they say. Or if it does it won't be our fault. And when it does we should be ready for whatever comes. But think, my friends — what approaching menace could this be? Will we poor, squabbling Europeans drain the Atlantic and attack North America ourselves one night? Will the waves of the Pacific turn warlike, or Canada's polar bears cast a covetous eye on the plains of Illinois? Perhaps the Mexicans will stop fighting each other for long enough to notice their neighbour to the north? Not likely, I think. And yet, those who talk of preparedness push and push for America to spend money on arms even though she has no enemies, no part, as President Wilson says, in this war. No war, say the preparers — but let us prepare for war. Do you believe them?"

Boos and loud denial from all sides. Calls of "warmongers" and "jingoes". Block begins to make some notes as two or three more journalists come in from the smoking room. The heat rises from the press of bodies. As I look across the heads, packed as close as in the morning train, I see where Sam McClure finds something to stand on and suddenly appears above the rest. There is a look in his eye as he slips his hand inside his jacket. I can see the white corner of the paper he lightly touches with his fingers, the promised apple of discord. On the dais Madame Schwimmer, eyes closed, mouth slightly open, head upturned, awaits a message from beyond, from something greater than herself.

"What is America to be? A man who leaves his own safe and lawful home at night to go abroad with a knife in one pocket, a gun in the other, a bludgeon in his pants and lockpicks in his vest, all bought and paid for from the public purse? One who looks at you straight and tells you, 'No, Sir, you mistake me. I go equipped for burglary and robbery not to do these things, but only so that the town may be safer.' It *can't* be true. I speak as a woman, as the suffering sex, as one of the age-old onlookers to human violence. Take it from me, gentlemen, from your wives, lovers, daughters, sisters, from those who know your nature better than you know it yourselves — give a man a sword and he *will* use it, as sure as a dog is given teeth to bite.

"This is not the America war-torn Europe looks to. You may have heard that the preachers of preparedness have an English accent, or sometimes French. Perhaps it is so, but all these siren voices can do is drag America down into their own hell. They say America must defend herself, but what they mean is that America must come to their defence. And when they talk of defence, they mean war. This is not what the peoples of Europe want. Europe wants peace. I know — she has told me . . ."

The bag is held forth, a capacious envelope of black shagreen with two long, looped handles of the same material. They hang down like ears as Madame Schwimmer cradles the treasure from beneath.

"I have her deepest desires here, close to my chest. Peace! she cries out. Peace, oh peace, won't you lead me to peace! It is the America of peace that Europe needs — the vision of Henry Ford and the wisdom of President Wilson. If the preachers of military preparedness carry the day, the light of America, which is the light of peace, will go out. My friends, true America is here, on this brave ship in the middle of the ocean. True America has heard and sends, in us, her new pilgrims. We come not with any avenging army, but pure of heart and with the greater power of empty, harmless hands."

A storm of cheering and clapping, of waving of arms, of *God Bless America*, of fainting — one near, one actual. Collars were loosened and menu cards waved as fans. Down the glass of the little windows moisture beaded and ran. Madame Schwimmer regretted that she had already taken too much time away from her duties. She begged to be excused and left triumphant, detained briefly by an applauding Louis Lochner who bent down to give his congratulations intimately into her ear.

"Stay on, please, Mr Lochner, and report to me later every word that is said."

There were half a dozen more speeches, none of which can have given Madame Schwimmer any concern. They were orthodox and loyal and not very brilliant. One got the sense that the professional musician had left her instruments on the stage and that we were now being entertained by a succession of children and apprentices getting whatever sound out of them they could. Someone attempted too literal a demonstration of his argument when he produced a meat cleaver and brandished it menacingly at the audience.

"Don't worry — I'm only 'preparing' for diplomacy and international law."

Meyer Block scribbled rapidly in his notebook as a steward impassively relieved the speaker of his prop and returned it to the galley. All that was needed was a comic turn from Lloyd Bingham, and he seemed about to oblige when a heavier pitch toppled him into a well-placed chair and he thought better of it, his supporters flapping at his pale, sweat-sheened face as if he were an exhausted boxer sticking to his corner.

Lesser figures had their moment, adding to the warm glow of consensus. The preponderance of Americans steered the gathering in a patriotic direction and President Wilson came in for much praise as the man who would always keep us out of the war, the man who taught his people that there was such a thing as being "too proud to fight". Louis Lochner stepped forward and spoke of his personal acquaintance with the President and of his complete faith in his judgement and moral strength. There was another hearty cheer and a ragged chant of "Peace! Peace!", in the dying away of which Samuel McClure unfolded the paper I had glimpsed two nights before. He held it up and waited for silence.

"It might interest you all to know what is in the President's State of the Union address to Congress."

A pause to let this phrase have its full effect as he hooked out his reading spectacles from his vest pocket and put them on.

"I received my usual advance copy and . . ."

An artful consultation of his pocket watch.

"As the President is probably about halfway through his remarks by now, I think the embargo can fairly be said to have lifted. I will summarise."

Newsmen gathered more thickly from the smoking room and soon there was a dozen of them clustered together by the door. It started well, with Sam putting on Wilson's rhetoric like a costume and beginning to swagger in its grand style. You could see the hope in everyone's eyes. Surely he would mention us, out here on the darkness of the sea doing something about the peace he so loved to talk about. Something oblique would do — we listened intently for the coded phrase, the word of half-approval that would strengthen our hand with the chancelleries of Europe. He was our man, and we knew that only discretion held him back from saying so.

"We have stood apart, studiously neutral. It was our manifest duty to do so . . . no part or interest in the causes that have brought the conflict on . . . neutrality, to which we were bidden by our habitual detatchment from the politics of Europe and a clear perception of international duty . . . moral partnership . . . common sympathies. Ah, thank you."

The Voice of the Republic accepted a glass of water, tendered ceremoniously by Reverend Lloyd Jones.

"Where was I? Yes, he goes on — United States as guardian of the republics to the south of her against encroachments from the other side of the water; disinterested enthusiasm for freedom; unmolested self-government of independent peoples; misconceptions of our motives put behind us; unabated spirit of President Monroe; common cause of national independence and political liberty in America; no selfish purpose or taking of advantage. All governments of America on a footing of genuine equality; been put to the test by Mexico and have passed that test; no imposition on her; drinking at the true fountains of principle and tradition; Virginia Bill of Rights dum de dum de dum . . ."

"A little more respect, if you please," interjected Governor Hanna.

"Just getting to the juice, Governor. Now I've lost my place. Here we are. Pan-Americanism, no spirit of empire but law, independence and mutual service; bonds of honourable partnership and common advantage. Americas destined to play part together in the adjustments of the next generation before peace resumes its healthful tasks — blah, blah, blah. Ah, yes — here we are. Good Lord, the man has clearly never worked for a newspaper. Climb aboard this sentence and hold on to your hats, ladies and gentlemen — 'I am interested to fix your attention on this prospect now because unless you take it within your view and permit the full significance of it to command your thought I cannot find the right light in which to set forth the particular matter that lies at the very front of my whole thought as I address you today. I mean . . .' "

A pause here, with exaggerated breathlessness, a gulp of water, a visible straightening of the spine and expansion of the chest and, in my direction, a distinctly mischievous hint of a smile.

". . . 'national defence.' "

There was a rustle through the tightly packed audience, the wave of alertness that ripples out from the leading edge of a storm.

There was first a brief nod to not maintaining a standing army beyond peacetime needs, but only as a preamble to the right of the people to bear arms and the farmers at Lexington rising to take care of themselves. What patriot could object to that? Things moved swiftly on, McClure so enjoying his presidential performance that it was hard to believe he hadn't once nurtured hopes in that direction, or at least dreams.

" 'To fight effectively upon a sudden summons; to play the great role in the world for which we are qualified by principle and chastened ambition.' "

Anxiety remained within bounds and pacifist hopes just alive so long as it was nothing more than words. The presidential stand-in pressed on.

" 'These seem to me the essential first steps — an increase in the standing force of the regular army of fifty-two companies of coast artillery, fifteen companies of engineers, ten regiments of infantry, four regiments of field artillery, and four aero squadrons. In addition, by way of making the country ready to assert its real power promptly and on a larger scale the plan contemplates supplementing the army by a force of four hundred thousand disciplined citizens . . .' "

The murmuring had started right away, but that last, monstrous figure was too much. The spectre of a nation permanently in arms, poised for violence, struck the listeners as a sickening physical blow. A high, female voice rang out.

"Treason! Nothing less than treason!"

"Hey, it's Mrs Wilkes Booth. Get that good lady a gun."

"Who said that? How dare you! Show yourself if you're a gentleman."

Our little family began to divide. Half began to chatter about universal humanity, those deepest calls of nature that go beyond the lesser loyalties of tribe, class and country. Others, either in their hearts or in their more calculating brains, felt and answered that little twitch on the thread of nationhood. Whatever their opinions might have been half an hour before, they could not now knowingly go against their leader in a time of danger. Gloomy silence returned as McClure read on.

" 'The programme which will be laid before you by the Secretary of the Navy is similarly conceived. It contemplates the construction within the first year of two battleships, two battlecruisers, three scout cruisers, fifteen destroyers, five fleet submarines, twenty-five coast submarines, two gunboats and one hospital ship; the second year two battleships, one scout cruiser, ten destroyers, four fleet submarines, fifteen coast submarines, one gun boat and one fuel oil ship; the third year . . .' "

"Stop! Stop, for pity's sake."

I couldn't see who was shouting. Sam was only encouraged.

"Oh, but there's more." He fanned through the pages of the speech. "Don't you want to hear it all?"

Someone must have jumped — I could see the hand, high and isolated just before the crumpling noise and the swift disappearance of the speech as it was snatched away. Confusion broke out from all quarters. The newsmen looked like children at Christmas.

"Hey, I've got it," declared one. "Wilson only let these nuts out here so they couldn't cause any trouble."

He turned to an outraged Mrs Morse Clark who looked as if she might abandon her principles for the pleasure of hitting him over the head with her evening bag.

"Try lobbying your senator now, lady."

He threw his head back and laughed delightedly. He called to one of his colleagues who was already sidling towards the exit, notebook in hand.

"Hey, Hirsch! You better get 'em to make this boat go a little faster or they'll turn you into a soldier before we even get there. First ashore and straight *into* the trenches by Christmas. There's your story."

Louis Lochner, pale with the shock of a personal betrayal, tried to quell the disorder.

"Please. Ladies and gentlemen, please be calm."

They began to pay attention as he proposed that the expedition leaders would draft a resolution condemning military preparedness and that everyone who still wanted to be associated with the aims of the Henry

Ford Peace Ship would sign it. Internationalists cheered, patriots growled. Lochner's temper deserted him.

"Anyone who doesn't put their name to the resolution has come on this voyage as nothing more than an enormous joyride."

Uproar resumed. Lochner waved his arms in despair.

"German!"

He turned as if someone had slapped his face — only to find the insult was directed at someone else.

"A mouthpiece for the Kaiser, a propagandist — have you given the Kaiser his money back yet, McClure?"

As an accusation it made no sense, but as the dirtiest thing within reach I suppose it had a certain inevitability. Sam had no chance to reply before being confronted by a more immediate danger — Jenkin Lloyd Jones in an extremity of passion.

"You have misled the young people on this ship. You have preached armament and war from the outset."

Reverend Jones' face was a festive scarlet and his beard more snowy white than ever. He seemed almost literally to burn as he held his features inches away from McClure's and shook his fist at him. For the space of a few words he became incoherent. I feared a fatal apoplexy.

"Go to bed, sir!" was what he ended up with. "Go to bed!"

The newsmen beamed with joy. I watched as Max Swain of the *Herald* played that old trick with one of his cronies. His friend smashed his knuckles hard into the palm of his hand while Max shouted "Fight!" The word made it so — in the news reports at least — and it was already too late for Lochner as he climbed on a serving table and made a last-ditch attempt to rescue the situation.

"Delegates of the Ford Peace Expedition — let us remember why we are here!"

He rapped a wine glass with a knife, only to smash it in his eagerness and then drop both to the floor. The knife skittered and span across the polished wood. The glass crunched under milling heels.

What happened next was a little unclear. The newspapermen and a trio of photographers bolted for the door with a single mind. I would not like to suggest that Mr Lochner deliberately tripped one of them up, but one way or another the formidable and loudly complaining bulk of Theophilus E. Montgomery of the Union Press Association found itself flat on the floor, blocking the progress of his colleagues. Lochner nimbly cleared the barrier and got a head start. The news posse briefly tugged at Theophilus' heels, then gave up all thought of moving him in preference for trampling him flat as they got after Lochner. I followed, guessing where they were going and determined to get every last detail for the feature story that would re-launch me as a journalist. We tumbled down steep stairs and then dashed back along a lower corridor. Lochner's voice sounded from ahead.

"Mr Bastian! Will you lock the door, Mr Bastian!"

We ran into each other in an excited, jostling heap. I was at the back and had to jump to see what was happening. There, in the brief instants in which I could keep my head above the others, was poor Louis Lochner, crucified across the entrance to the wireless telegraph office.

"Censorship!"

Lochner appealed for calm.

"You're dealing with the press, Lochner!" shouted someone in a strong New York accent. "Patience is unconstitootional."

Our little community was so stirred up that half the long night had gone before there was any peace. Lochner instilled some order in the newsmen by reminding them that regulations for neutral shipping required all messages to be cleared with the captain first. They agreed to wait while he went for consultations, but by the time he returned Mr Bastian had sold his command and many of their dispatches had already been sent, hopping from ship to ship all the way back to New York in time for the next day's evening editions.

Lochner went to bed in despair, the journalists to the bar in the first-class lounge. There they celebrated the fulfilment of their hopes and gave themselves energetically to a mock trial of the absent Samuel McClure on a charge of corrupting the morals of youth. Lloyd Bingham presided, it being agreed that he would be asleep throughout the proceedings and therefore even-handedly deaf to all submissions. The trial was called to order by the banging of a stuffed dove on the whisky-spattered bar and the witnesses' hands placed solemnly on a tobacco tin as they swore to tell nothing but lies. The star prosecution witness, Reverend Jones, was dismissed as incompetent on the grounds that he was indeed Santa Claus and so did not exist. A journalist spoke for the defence, testifying that McClure could take years to pay for a manuscript and was therefore a stranger to preparedness of any sort, military or otherwise. The jury pronounced the bar closed and brought in a verdict of not guilty just as Bingham finally toppled from his stool.

These details I heard later, but I was there in the gangway of the first-class deck as the fallen actor was carried past — two straining newsmen under his shoulders and another in front, holding his legs like the poles of a stretcher. He was given a stateroom of his own, much to the relief of his former cabinmate who had complained widely of Bingham's coughing and snoring through the night. I passed that way half an hour later and saw, drawn round the number on the door with a finger dipped in borrowed rouge, a star and beneath it the words — "at last".

There were huddles of debaters throughout the ship and much coming and going from cabin to the Schwimmer staff stateroom as opinions were lobbied, votes firmed up, divisions solidified. Mr Ford slept on, so far as anyone knew, at the far end of the upper passenger deck, beyond the double barrier of the light-sleeping Dean Marquis and the taciturn Ray, ever watchful on his chair with his long legs stretched out across the way and his toes touching the opposite wall.

McClure survived his mock trial only to be summoned to a real one before Madame Schwimmer.

Delegates loitered outside, pretending to converse with each other or to be waiting for their own interviews. No one quite had the effrontery to put their ear to the door, but they were all too curious to move on. Much of what passed between the two remained inaudible, but at the end the eavesdroppers were satisfied.

"I never trusted you — never! I've seen your type at work before. What have you ever made, Mr McClure? We all know what you've destroyed in your life, but tell me one thing you have built, just one thing."

"Listen Schwimmer, I've known a good few martyrs in my time and last I heard they were all doing pretty good business and so far I don't see that you're any . . ."

"Why don't you destroy yourself?"

"Oh, that's nice. You're a real piece of work, aren't you? You know what I think? I think if you hadn't led such an unnatural life maybe you could tell the difference between a rational argument and a fit of hysteria."

"Men and war, men and war — it never changes. No men, no war — that's what I say."

"Tell that to the new Mrs Braley, you frozen old bat."

"Get out!"

"I'm going, don't worry. Just remember this — you were born in your country and you left it. I chose my country and I'm sticking by it."

Then the door opened and there was Samuel standing in the corridor pursued by Madame Schwimmer's voice in its full stage volume.

"And that's why I'm better than you are, you . . . you . . . *follower!*"

He walked towards me, away from the astonished audience. I made sure our eyes met. He seemed tired, as we all were then, and a little unsure of his triumph.

"Well, Samuel," I said to him. "You certainly had an effect."

He looked over his shoulder. An even number of supporters and enemies returned his gaze. Sam had a more dramatic assessment, though it was not one that displeased him.

"I'm a hunted man, Inez."

I moved aside and held open the door to my cabin.

"Asylum?"

He hesitated — his old-fashioned, gallant concern making me smile.

"Oh, don't worry about that," I told him. "I already have a reputation and I'm perfectly happy with it."

I don't how long we spent together before that strange night was finally over. I broke the seal on my special brandy, telling the story of its acquisition in Paris and how I liked to think of myself as taking it home, preserving it for the victory celebration.

"Victory?"

"You think it's as well we should drink it now?"

We talked over the Wilson speech and I heard about the other parts there had been no time to read out. Scarcely conceivable sums of money were demanded to pay for these grand plans. Hundreds of millions loomed in my mind as I thought miserably on all the better things they could not now buy. There was polished rhetoric — for a moment it was almost like Schwimmer talking — about threats from within, citizens born under other flags, the poison of disloyalty in the very arteries of national life, how we would once have been ashamed to suspect our neighbours but must now prepare to crush out such creatures of passion and disloyalty.

Sam performed these solid phrases with a flourish and then a wistful dying away.

"And they can cast that net pretty wide. As wide as they want to."

"Is that why you're for it?" I asked him. "Because of what people will go on saying about you if you're not?"

"Inez, you do me an injustice. I never held a position for selfish motives and I won't now. No, it's worse than that. I believe the President is right. He is choosing the lesser of two evils."

I told him how I hated war, the ease with which men fell into it, the slickness of their endless excuses, not one of which through the whole of history I had ever believed.

"I suppose I should hate you too."

"Do you? Can you?"

I refilled our glasses, holding the little bottle upside-down for the last drop before pushing back the cork and letting it slip into the waste-paper basket.

"Maybe it's just as he says," I offered hopefully — "a precaution for something that will never happen."

"No, your lot are right — don't give that up now. It's war. It's a certainty. They'll lie and lie and lie all the way down to the last week before the mobilisation orders. Then they'll tell you they changed their minds last Tuesday for whatever reason they feel like and that everything's different now. America is arming for war. The decision has been made and whatever else is said or done we'll all look back and say this was the day. Schwimmer's not all mad, you know."

"I never thought she was."

"She's right about the dog and its teeth. The dog is not an animal to make idle threats. America, in peacetime, is arming for war. But I'll stick with her."

He raised his glass to the invisible object of his loyalties, then emptied it.

"I just don't know if she'll ever find her way back."

For a long time we were still. No voices, no sounds of argument or debate came from without and even poor Mr Bingham appeared at last to have found some peace. I felt there was a moment when something might be said. I tensed, primed for something meaningful, either word or movement. The silent crisis passed and a deep common sadness settled on us both.

Sam exhaled heavily, stretched the tiredness out of his spine and ran his palms over his face.

"Well, I suppose . . ."

He stood up.

"I should go now."

I kissed a rough cheek.

"Goodnight, Sam."

Rosika

Spies are everywhere, perhaps assassins too. Rebecca herself brought me confirmation of this within the first twelve hours of our voyage, referring breathlessly to our patron.

"There's a man outside his door. It looks like he's going to stay there all night and . . ."

The last part of her report was whispered as though the walls themselves were not to be trusted.

". . . they say he has a gun."

I remarked on the irony.

"You laugh in the face of danger, Madame Schwimmer, but if Mr Ford's life is in danger, think how much you must be at risk — you without whom we could not go on."

I bowed to the logic of this argument and an arrangement was soon in place by which Rebecca and Elli Eriksson, companion to the exiled Madame Malmberg, now share the duties of night-watchwomen. As I permit myself only four hours sleep a night, four guilty hours through which the hideous slaughter continues, their sacrifice is not too great. That we carry our enemies with us is an excellent sign — they take us seriously, they know we are on our way to achieving something. As for what Rebecca or the charming little Elli with her white linen cap and her embroidered bodice, her china-blue eyes and spun-gold pigtails, would do to preserve my life against a determined opponent I can't say. Neither do I fret much over the issue, being at that free and happy point in a leader's life where she knows that martyrdom can only speed the day. I expect my enemies know this too. Indeed, they think they are being clever by letting me live and I might be safer now than I have been for years. I did not explain this to Rebecca. She is too earnest, too passionate. It is kinder to let her serve. In a few minutes I will hear some quiet words outside my door and the slight shifting of a chair as the guard changes. It is strange, but in only a few days this has gained the force of a lifelong habit. I must stay awake for it, like they say children must for a parent's kiss. Only then, and almost at once, is there sleep.

The early histories of great causes have a regularity that comes very near to being a law of nature. Sometimes these seasons unravel over years, or even decades. We, vanguard of the century of speed, have rushed through the first few phases in a matter of days. One starts with the cheerful, thoughtless send-off. So it was at the pier at Hoboken. My detractors say I am part of this; that I share the optimisim of the crowd, the simple conviction that whatever they set themselves to has already been achieved, that it is never too early to celebrate a victory which will come as surely as tomorrow. They are wrong. I was carried back from that moment to another crowd with the same gestures, shouts, faces. It was London, not quite eighteen months ago. The people were happy then too — it was the start of the war.

On the deck of the *Oscar* I touched Mr Ford's elbow and he overcame his shyness, stepping forward to where everyone could see him. Was there a tremor in that narrow, thrifty body as he met the hopeful roar of thousands? He turned a little to his side, indicating that I should come forward to stand beside him. There we stood, the twin pillars of the world's best hope — he the gold, I the genius without which nothing much can ever be achieved. I saw how powerfully Mr Ford was moved by the acclaim that surged up from the pier.

From even earlier, that day at the Belasco theatre, I had begun to guess what the great assembler needed and why this was such a secret desire, how he could reach out for it only haltingly and with a fear that few would ever guess at. Mr Ford needed to have cars taken out of his life. He needed them to be replaced with men and women, but was powerless to bring this about, paralysed. Who could deliver him? Not even Mrs Ford, evidently. She stood behind us, glum with her own small thoughts. I understood her homely worries, but can only be relieved that I am not weighed down by such distractions myself. In times like these it is nothing less than a humiliation for the thinking person to care too much about individuals. As I waved at the excited mass of well-wishers it was clear to me that I had grasped something about Mr Ford not even his wife had seen. There are great men who have everything they need to fulfil themselves, while others are held back by some obscure want that leaves only a latency of greatness which might never come to fruition. Mr Ford is of the latter sort — he has been, until now, a seed in a dry desert. I recall his features as the steam whistle sounded and as the ropes were cast off. Our eyes met and he conveyed to me as certainly as through the simplest spoken declaration — "Madame Schwimmer, you have changed my life as much as I have changed yours."

It is true — I have rained on Henry Ford.

In such high spirits we set off. An office was organised at once. Daily bulletins were issued, instructional and uplift programmes organised hour by hour. All was harmony and optimism. I, naturally, held myself apart. Accustomed to the solitude of leadership, I observed these first innocent forty-eight hours from afar, preparing myself for the troubles that would come. I received and collated reports on the journalists and began to work out which of them were not quite what they seemed. At that time they were still humorous rather than poisonous, but I know their nature well and was determined to be ready for the change. I puzzled over the presence of the mysterious Dr Marquis, watching closely as he followed Ford and as Mr Ford's valet followed him. I sorted the faithful from the self-seeking and the merely accidental. Who is Lloyd Bingham, why is he here? Louis Lochner tells me I made the decision myself but I'm sure I'd never heard of the man before he was introduced to me on board. Surprisingly, Mr Ford finds him acceptable and I have seen them talking together more than once. That young man, supposed to be a poet and who very nearly turned our departure into a farce, has also been given more than his due. Untaxing company I suppose, and a barrier to keep the relentless Marquis at bay.

There are other types sure to fall by the wayside at an early stage — earnest doers of God's work, disappointed politicians giving it one last try, energetic burnishers of their own conscience. I wondered about Mrs Boissevain (I gather she is styling herself Miss Milholland for the duration of the trip), but in the end have been disappointed. I can almost hear the words aloud when she passes me — "I polish and polish and polish. Look! Is my heart not now as beautiful as I am?" That old fool McClure certainly thinks so. Anyway, I've put a stop to him. Rebecca brought me a report of his lecture this afternoon — audience much diminished. And then there's young Mr Louis Lochner himself, with his commitment and his peace pedigree and his education and yet — how much really do I know about him? All the history books tell us that intimates make the best assassins. You can win the war (I mean metaphorically of course) and return in triumph, but when it's Clytemnestra lurking at home it all comes to nothing in the end. I was reflecting on these lessons while making an early visit to the wireless room only to find that Louis had got there first. He was just leaving and seemed very pleased with what he had achieved.

"Everything's fine," he smiled a conspiratorial smile. "Shall we have a word about it later?"

I went in myself on the pretext of sending a personal message. I found the operator to be an engaging young man employed, I would say, rather below his station. He was of sound views and surprisingly well informed, explaining that his late father had inculcated the habit of reading a good newspaper every day and that this took the place of the education his family had never been able to afford.

"And I hardly ever need pay for them neither. There's not much worth knowing you can't find in the bins of any decent railway station or steamer quay. All you need is the curiosity. I even read about you and seen a big picture too. First time I've met a news story. Can you really do it, mam?"

"If goodwill and sanity prevail."

"Yes, mam."

"Was Mr Lochner sending a message?"

There was a pause and a sly look I rather respected. I explained that I had no objection to Louis sending messages, or to him reading over other people's.

"He said he wants his finger on the pulse, that's how he put it. I'm with you. Said I'd do anything to help."

I felt inside the hidden pocket of my purse and eased out a ten-dollar gold piece.

"Can you see that I get everything first? A separate copy, mind you."

"And Mr Lochner's own messages?"

And so I sit at night going through the endless magnetic chatter, the yellow journalism and the self-promotion and the broadcast billet-doux of Louis Lochner who, after a day of following Mrs Boissevain around the ship, sends sparks of love back to Emmeline and little morse-coded kisses for the baby. Sometimes it's hard to understand why he came. A continent in flames and still his heart is elsewhere — perhaps our work can never be completed until we have a world without men.

And so we moved on to the next stage — the first testing storm. I admit the particular provocateur who stirred it up came as a slight surprise. On the first night when I addressed the delegates it was McClure who jumped forward and declared, "I'm with you there, Madame Schwimmer. I have seen those documents and they convinced me." I can't say I recall ever showing them to him, but I let it pass at the time. There he was again at the preparedness debate. I made my speech and he had no objection to it as long as I was in the room. Not half an hour later, as I was in my cabin composing another of Mr Ford's wireless bulletins to the press, Rebecca burst in to report that chaos had broken out. There was wild talk of mutiny and even the suggestion that we should turn right around and return to New York before America "stabbed peace in the back". I calmed her down and understood the situation as soon as I could get some sense out of her. Having made it my business to know all about Mr McClure's recent difficulties I realised an antidote was close to hand. Rebecca was sweetly uncomprehending.

"But what do you mean? I don't understand."

"Just say it — others will understand."

I sent her up all the same, carrying her one-word message to be delivered in perfect innocence. I got her report about midnight, which was highly satisfactory — perhaps it made things a little worse at first, but when it comes to catharsis there must be no half measures. If it is necessary to portray McClure as a German sympathiser, he is the one who has made it necessary. Later I received a sheaf of the latest telegrams. Years of police court sensationalism had gone into them and they made colourful reading — "War on the Peace Ship"; "Mutiny on the *Oscar*" — "Pistol Shots Believed Fired"; "Ford Locked in Room — Chained to Bed by 'Secretary'". There was a message from a westbound liner — "Do you need assistance?" Captain Hempel's reply came next; an apology and terse explanation that the "mutiny" was metaphorical. All in all it was not good, but the news was flying to New York and Washington, not to Europe where our business is now. It can do no harm. Besides, I was sure at the time, and have been proved entirely right, that within twenty-four hours of this upset we would know who is truly with us and who against. The immediate affair ended with me being intruded upon by McClure in the early hours. He came, so he said, to "state his position". The interview quickly deteriorated into him storming about reputation and integrity. He demanded that I should enquire into who had so direly insulted him. I asked if he cared about his reputation more than about the war. Like all his sex, he considers righteous anger a virtue and regrettable things were said before the door finally slammed shut. To give him his due, I received an apology before breakfast the next day, though not a recantation.

It is always better to get such unpleasantness over sooner rather than later. When we land in Christiania we can now be more certain of success than ever. Some of those same guns that fire in brutish cruelty will be melted and cast into statues to be set up in the public squares of every city in Europe. Children will come with flowers in spring and lay them by the peace memorial steps as doves flutter up from their cages. I now know the faces that will be on those statues, and the faces that will not; the names of the peacebringers carved on the plinths below, and the names of the forgotten.

Mr Ford's name, I suppose, will have to be there. Those in the future who can ever find out the truth of this adventure will note it as one of the minor ironies of history. In reality our manufacturer slept through these debates and reacted to reports of them the next morning with such calm as usually comes only from not understanding what has been said. Copies were made of President Wilson's speech and distributed throughout the ship. One was sent to Mr Ford with his breakfast, carried by Dean Marquis. I should add that Marquis has taken the precaution of sending no telegrams on any subject at all and will discuss nothing other than opera and novels, leaving me in ignorance of his true beliefs. If he took the opportunity to influence Mr Ford against us, the situation could have been distinctly awkward. Both Louis and I asked to see Ford early but were sternly repulsed by his bodyguard, a man who discusses nothing with anyone. We waited anxiously for a response and it was Marquis himself who brought and read out a brief note. Firstly, the auto-maker forbore under any circumstances to censor "my friends in the press". Then the note drew attention to a sentence late in Wilson's speech which no one had yet noticed. It was proposed that his monstrous list of weapons be paid for by taxing gasoline at the rate of one cent per gallon. Mr Ford deplored this suggestion as an attack on the freedom of the American road and mused as to whether a country that taxed movement itself would truly be worth defending.

"And, eh . . ." concluded Dr Marquis, folding the paper and replacing it in his pocket, "that's it."

Since departing the United States this is the first statement issued by Ford not written either by myself or Mr Lochner. It was almost a surprise to hear his voice. I would not for the world let anyone hear me say it, but it seemed to me very plain that he makes a better puppet than a man.

I am exhausted. I lie back and let my papers slip to the floor. I hear a snatch of drunken male song and recognise two of the journalists. Their emptiness is almost enviable at times. At its extreme it reaches to a sort of invulnerability — quite simply there is nothing there to hurt. But think of their deaths — I don't envy them that. Think of being conscious at the last and having nothing more to look back on than the ephemera of having been a newsman. Not life, but a report on life. Not this great peace we will make, but merely a record of what others did to achieve it. Death for them will be a crumpled sheet of newspaper blowing down an empty street.

The coloured cabin night light glows dimly as a candle. I have explained what will happen. Tomorrow, in the afternoon, we will approach the Orkney Islands. Once in territorial waters we will come under Britannia's sway and must satisfy her navy before going on. We will then steam through the war zone under our flag of peace and begin our mission at Christiania. Norway worries me — still no response to my messages. Mr Bastian in the wireless room tells me the atmosphere is bad. I will ask again first thing in the morning. I check my father's pocket-watch, holding it close to the night light so that I can read the face. I begin to sink down sweetly to sleep. I can just hear the quiet, caring voices outside my door. It is that time — the changing of the guard, for myself just as it is for Mr Ford. Rebecca has come for the late watch. One guard gently hushes the other. I have enough strength only to raise my head and see the handle of my door turn, the lock tested and safe. The cares of leadership, the cares! The loneliness! But now, all the lead in my life turns to feathers, to breath. My fingers loosen from around the handle of my bag. Weightless in sunlight, I walk in the dream of my life where my work is done and the world is as it should be.

Louis

The sick list grows. Lloyd Bingham is said to be giving some concern and now Mr Ford has a worsening cold. The ship's nurse (a formidable and highly Scandinavian woman) bossed him into accepting a rub down with alcohol and pronounced the matter trivial. He appeared early in the afternoon and whispered hoarsely in my ear.

"Lochner, swear to me on your life you will never let that woman near me again. If I am revived it was only because of the need to defend myself. I'm going to get some heat in my bones. Don't give me away, will you?"

Off he went, down to the engine room where he spends endless contented hours watching things rise and fall and needles tremble on the faces of pressure gauges. He talks to the men about steam engines, the machine whose empire he did more than anyone to destroy. There is a story among the journalists that one of them was stopped by a stoker up for air one evening and asked, "That man — who is he?"

The cause of Mr Ford's indisposition is supposedly dramatic, but was witnessed only by Berton Braley. Our ardent bard alleges that he alone was strolling outside the principal stateroom when Ford emerged for an early-morning constitutional only to be engulfed by a freak wave. It is already an oft-recounted incident, with Berton casting his pen and notebook to the savage flood as he sprang into action to save the struggling titan. We are to believe that Mr Ford was in the process of being swept away as the waters drained from the deck and it is certainly true that his lean frame would easily slip between the railings and the lifeboat davits. Berton conjures an image of himself fighting through the billows, able to see nothing but a brown derby hat and the gleam of Ford's gold-topped walking cane.

"Oh sure — *now* I believe him," opines Tom Seltzer of *The Call*. "He was going for the cane and got old Henry's ankle by mistake."

"There's a Model T waiting for you when you get home, Berton."

"You think?"

General laughter.

We are promised a versified Saving of Henry — a work of perfect poetic equipoise, says its excited author, somewhere between Hokusai's *Great Wave, Moby Dick* and Sherlock Holmes's headlong flight down the Reichenbach Falls, although with a happier ending.

There appears to be some truth in the story, though only some. Mr Ford is reluctant to enter into details (the image of frailty cannot appeal), but has explained that he has been forced to change to his second-favourite hat on account of a white crust of salt developing around the ribbon of the first. I have not yet found an opportunity to ask, but am madly curious to know whether the proprietor of one of the world's greatest industrial concerns has brought with him only two hats — which would be considerably fewer than Rosika Schwimmer, I might add. Knowing the man, as I am slowly beginning to do, I think it is only too likely — quite charming, really. More significantly, he confirms that his cold is on the wane and that he looks forward to landfall in Norway as keenly as the rest of us.

With respect to our internal dissensions some sort of truce has finally been declared. Rosika claims it as a victory for her methods but I wonder if there was not an easier way. I admire her as much as ever — her tenacity, her courage against the odds, but I think my feelings for her will not go beyond admiration. On one thing I remain quite clear in my mind — I could not play her role and she is as essential to this effort as Mr Ford himself.

President Wilson's speech on preparedness — let me call it what it is — on the arming of America, came as a heavy blow to me. As McClure droned on through that horrible list of weapons I was aware that I was the only one in the room who had actually spoken with Wilson, who had sat and talked peace with him twice in the last few weeks. Now I know what he was thinking as he listened to us and nodded and said so little in reply. He must have been writing that speech at the very same time!

"Yes, gentlemen, how wise you are — *two battlecruisers or three?*"

"Indeed, Mr Lochner, I have often thought so myself — *two hundred thousand for the citizen militia, or four hundred thousand?*"

And then my foolish question at the end and his laconic "No, that is for me to decide," except that he already had decided.

I have made altogether too much of my meetings with the President. I spoke of them several times to Miss Miholland and then, when McClure was relishing the worst of the speech and could still be heard and the riot had not yet started, I suffered all the more when I found her eyes on me and that entrancing, transatlantic smile which said, surely — "The more fool you, Louis, for ever believing him in the first place."

My own loyalties are comfortably undivided. I hardly know how properly to express the strength of my feelings on this. There is a strangeness to it, a slightly feverish sense of remoteness, as if my own country had all at once become foreign to me. It is as if I had awoken to find myself speaking with an outsider's accent and struggling to make myself understood to people who are now, though faultlessly polite, a little more formal than before and stand six inches further away. I have read the President's message over many times. It is a deep disturbance in American tradition, all the more so as we are asked to arm ourselves against no specified enemy and to defend against a threat of no certain reality. It is Mr Wilson himself who has described the European conflict as, "a war with which we have nothing to do, whose causes cannot touch us." And yet the question must be asked — if we are now at peace and with no enemy in sight and even so are asked to live and spend as warriors, shall we ever be farmers again?

While I am entirely with Rosika in putting peace before everything, other Americans feel differently and she finds this hard to understand. She is harsh on all matters of national sentiment, insisting that it is a sort of intellectual failure, a purely emotional excuse for abandoning principle. She trusts too much to reason. I have raised the subject with her several times in quiet moments and tried to steer her gently away from making things worse, but with little success. She now holds herself out to be a perpetual wanderer, a citizen of no country, unencumbered by any of these loyalties she dismisses as "all flags, anthems and hatred". She cannot see that while she promotes this rootlessness (objectivity is her word for it) as a great modern virtue, a good part of her audience, and most particularly Americans, on the hook of Wilson's rhetoric, see it as the most ghastly and unnatural of defects. For them it is as if Rosika is a child proudly declaring its lack of love for its parents. Governor Hanna, his mind on elections back home and drink having been taken, recommended pregnancy as the cure for her ills and pronounced expertly on "having seen this sort of thing before". Others in the patriotic camp do not hesitate to diagnose the envy of the Jews for those who have a country of their own and say so frankly in front of me, as if I also should not be offended. She is now reputed to be a ceaseless plotter applying her shadowy "Dual

Monarchy" mind to the destruction of whoever disagrees with her.

"It is nothing, Louis, nothing at all. I have borne it all my life. It has never much harmed me before and it certainly won't now. Remember, Louis, that everything really important is simple. One must not let the small-minded confuse things unnecessarily. I am a partisan of humanity and whoever cannot say the same has no business being here. You mustn't worry — as soon as we land the dross will take care of itself. I expect that Milholland woman will disappear into the nearest department store and never be seen again."

All very forthright, all very clear — admirable qualities in a field marshal, but she wins few friends and, worryingly for one on an expedition such as this, she is no diplomat. Besides myself only one American shares the open grandeur of her vision — Mr Ford.

"She's right, Louis. She's ahead of them all. In a hundred years there won't be any countries left. All there'll be is customers and they'll be the same all over the world. Our problems will be over then."

It was Mr Ford who came up with the method for calming the upset caused by the preparedness debate. He proposed a moratorium on taking firm positions and suggested instead that working parties be set up to consider all the issues before coming together in three days to settle on a common platform everyone could accept. For these three days there was peace as the delegation settled down to what it does best — talk. The *Oscar* became a floating university of peace. We put war under a powerful collective microscope, we defined its structures, designed and prescribed the vaccine that will permanently remove it from our world. I smile a little, it is true, but I believe it all the same. In the future war will be a crime just as murder is today. When diplomacy fails, the peaceful blockade will be as far as any country will be allowed to go in pursuit of its own ends. A growing, and finally world federation of nations will teach everyone their common interest and make war seem as antique and barbarous as the Colosseum games of Rome. Briefly, in our cockleshell upon the seas, we became the prototype of that future world of reason.

This grace period ended Friday when a more general meeting was called in the evening finally to heal the rift. Rosika had been busy in the meantime, inventing a Resolutions Committee and packing it with her most pliable friends. This produced a document that boldly declared opposition to the growth in American arms and called on the citizens of every state of the Union to unite against it. I put my own name to it without difficulty, but was not surprised when several of my older countrymen were outraged. Worse was to come when it became clear that the new resolution was intended to be a test of faith and a ticket for the rest of the journey — signatories would continue as accredited members of the peace delegation, dissenters would be excluded.

It was Reverend Aked who announced the new arrangements, his English accent suddenly more prominent and less tolerable than before.

"If there is anybody who cannot sign the resolution we are very sorry. Copies are being distributed for signature by those who are with us."

A forlorn attempt was made to adjourn the meeting. McClure — who else? — was instantly on his feet. Everyone supported the peace mission, he explained, and everyone hoped it would lead to international disarmament in due time. But to oppose the weapons of his own country, to "impugn the course laid out by the President" — that he could not do. He stuck his thumb in his vest pocket and looked upwards before concluding with some plangent line on conscience and martyrdom that might almost have come from Rosika. He sat down with that look of self-loving sternness by which a man says, "Of these things I have spoken, I shall never speak again" — though of course he did, and at inexhaustible length.

There was plenty of support. Judge Ben Lindsey ruled that accepting an invitation did not mean accepting the host's opinions. Governor Hanna declared that he would return by the first available boat so that he could be with his country in its hour of need. Inez Milholland said the whole thing was undemocratic. Others talked of railroading, while our leading prohibitionist deposed an oath that he would not sign the Golden Rule itself if it were presented in such a way. Thus Rosika's old-world methods reignited the issue and made it burn more fiercely than before.

"The situation is positively European," one wit wirelessed back to his paper.

The weekend, pencilled in for reconciliation, was given over to more preaching and bickering. Some two dozen signed right away and got the name "Rosika's people". Many of the rest tumbled all the way back down the hill to wallow in loud talk of the "my country right or wrong" type. Once everyone had argued themselves to a standstill it was accepted that only authority could break the deadlock. The matter was carried up to Mr Ford, our silent idol. Pale and weary, swaddled in two coats and muffler in his over-heated stateroom, the tycoon sat vacantly through lengthy presentations. Dean Samuel Marquis took care always to be present, observing the suffering of his employer with no sign of sympathy. In the end Mr Ford turned to me, almost pathetically.

"But what difference does it make? They came on a peace expedition, the resolution is against war — let them sign it."

I explained again that no one questioned the support for a negotiated peace, or the call for general disarmament in the future.

"It's just the last clause, Mr Ford — the one deploring America's new weapons. The American delegates — they feel . . ."

"A gun's a gun. What does it matter who's holding it? If you're against them, you're against them. I'm against them."

This is what some call his saintliness, others his mere ignorance of all things not connected with the automobile, others again his fitful genius for cutting through to what is hidden from more cluttered minds. Mr Ford shuddered and blew his nose.

"I can see where this is going. Those bastard Dodge brothers and that bastard Walter Chrysler will make the guns and their Jew bastard bankers in New York'll give them the money to do it. Why not? They're already giving it to England and Germany and France."

I glanced at Marquis. We three were alone in the room. With something between a weak smile and a twinge of physical discomfort he looked away to the sluggish, grey heave of the Atlantic through which we churned with unbearable slowness.

"The Ford Motor Company is not a democracy," Mr Ford added unnecessarily.

He began to ramble about tractors again, indulging a new whim about travelling to Moscow to sell them to the Russians.

"Put the Russian steppe under the plough with Fordson tractors — that'll solve their problems. Why do they want to be mixed up in this anyway? Oh, Louis — can you ask the ship's nurse to call on me again?"

On Saturday, then, Mr Ford was immovable and I was sent back to make a futile plea for obedience. Rosika was delighted and chattered that evening in her cabin about future schemes to which she could hitch the willing Ford engine after the war.

"Captive Greece has captured Rome. It's for the best, Louis. Many a time in history great powers have been misdirected or left idle, unquickened by any directing vitality. An unused power is no power at all — for a generation the cause of humanity drifts simply because brain and muscle have not come together in the right way."

She lay back on the narrow cabin bed and arranged the folds of her kimono. She sipped a glass of schnapps she had just had brought to her by one of the stewards.

"Have you ever wondered what would have become of Henry Ford if he had not met me?"

She paused to work up her *aperçu* — a line, no doubt, in an autobiography.

"The engine would race, Louis, but the wheels would not turn. What would be left in the end but a name enamelled on a radiator grille?"

Elsewhere, stubborn resisters bustled from meeting to meeting, determined to dig their heels in against anything that would put them on the wrong side of their own government as the war drums began to sound. At the worst we risked leaving America as a peace expedition only to arrive in Europe talking half about peace, half about war and making little sense about either. Impending farce made my thoughts turn timidly back on myself — what of my reputation, my career? Should I scurry home and issue Petrine denials — "The Ford Peace Ship? No, no — you must have someone else in mind. I never had anything to do with it." I have a long letter to Emmy ready for posting at Kirkwall (a Marconigram would be seen by too many eyes). I try to explain what is happening and tell her not to read the newspapers.

There was no point in talking to Rosika any more about compromise. I did what I could on my own, spending Sunday making the best of quiet moments of conversation alone with our newly inflamed patriots. Without an audience McClure was reasoned and patient. In half an hour I felt him draw me in to his own way of seeing things. Only the thought of the pleasure he would gain from making a convert held me back.

"You know," he told me with a confidential air, "Inez Milholland thinks just the same way I do. Wouldn't a little compromise be so much easier?"

"Mr Ford's concern is what is right, not what is easy."

He almost derided the mention of Ford's name and suggested casually that I could talk him round to anything I wanted.

"After all," he claimed archly, "that's how this whole thing got started, isn't it?"

I said he might be underestimating our patron.

"You see," I explained, "Mr Ford tells me his motor company is not a democracy. He is very firm on that point. He has a way of doing things which, we have to admit, has done pretty well so far."

McClure objected that we were hardly his employees and that such an idea could only make relations with the delegates worse.

"Maybe so, but he does rather see you as on the payroll. He gets the bills, you understand. It colours his viewpoint."

"*You're* on the payroll, Lochner. Look, don't get me wrong. I want this thing to work, as much as it can, but don't you see how what Wilson's said to Congress changes things? I don't know what's going to happen, but signing up against preparedness could be a millstone around these people's necks. Most of the people on this boat are going to have to go home and earn a living after this. Not Ford or Mrs Fels with her soap factories, but the rest will — opinion matters to them, they're not so free. Why don't you try telling him that? Make it a matter of money rather than principle — easier for him to understand."

I objected to that last remark and he withdrew it with an easy smile.

"Just change a few words," he pressed. "Just take out anything about Wilson, preparedness, anything about America. I'm sorry, but I can't stay with it otherwise."

"Don't the words matter, or at least the meaning?"

It sounded jejune as soon as I had said it and it certainly amused McClure.

"Listen, Louis — words are my business, my life. When I was your age I used to think as you do. Now I'm a little older things are clearer. So why don't you benefit from my advice and wise up a few decades before your time? Write anything you like to keep people on board — just keep them on board. It's what people do that matters."

"And Madame Schwimmer?"

"Ah," said McClure, "Madame Schwimmer."

He ran his thumb to and fro through the greying wire of his moustache, looked distant and frowned.

"Well, she's your problem."

Resignations were threatened and through the day the rumoured list of names grew longer. McClure came first with Inez Milholland, taking a stand on democratic methods, close behind. Newsmen paired them and hummed wedding tunes whenever Inez passed by on deck or in the smoking lounge. Before long their political consciences were worked up to a scandalous elopement, the lurid details of which I could read in Mr Bastian's copy telegrams.

I saw Mr Ford again that afternoon with the intention of telling him the peace expedition was about to split, that President Wilson's blast on the trumpet had left too few Americans still willing to sign up to a universal principle. His stateroom is on the upper deck and second only in scale and elaboration to that of the Braleys. A triple window looks out to the front and allows the same view of the bow and the featureless direction of travel as that enjoyed by Captain Hempel from the bridge immediately above. I found him sitting by this window, his narrow legs pressed together and covered with a plaid travelling blanket, an illustrated magazine unregarded in his lap. The wicker chair creaked with his every slight movement and a silver spoon tinkled in a glass as Ray stirred powder into a steaming cold remedy, handing it to his employer before going out to stand guard in the corridor. Marquis, in a leather easy chair, looked up from a sheaf of papers and offered a brief, consoling smile.

"I'm better," said Mr Ford. "My guests must think me a very poor host to shut myself away like this. You can tell them I'll be fully recovered tomorrow."

I was not so sure. There was a darkness around his eyes and a tremor in his hands I had not seen before. For the first time it occurred to me that his condition might be dangerous and an appalling prospect opened before me. He coughed several times, each dry hack connected to the next by a long, convulsive wheeze that pressed all the breath from his body. He waved dismissively when I expressed concern.

"I know my own mechanism, Louis. Tell me about yourself. How is my victim? How goes the world outside?"

I explained the situation, though he seemed to hear none of it as he gazed down at the ocean and endlessly worried at the corner of a page in his magazine.

"Well, just make them sign it," he said at length. "People have to be in step, to work to the same beat. There's always some that don't like it at first, but they come round when they see what it can do — I learned that early on."

I looked at Marquis with a silent question — was there a fever, was his understanding affected? The Dean's eyebrows rose very slightly, but with no hint of an answer. I started to list the delegates likely to resign.

"You see," Mr Ford interrupted, "nothing much good ever went down the stream of life without a ripple."

He worked his theme erratically, finding links to the prohibition of alcohol, the health-giving effects of old-style dancing and the corrosion of the will accruing from too much education. He mused on his likely future adoption of vegetarianism, recommended a study of the habits of birds as a more reliable guide to life than that available from any human philosopher and regretted that the boys — by which he meant the journalists — drank too much and were thus apt to uncharitable opinions contrary to their better natures. They were all good fellows really.

Marquis attempted to interrupt but was run down by a vertiginous tour of the Ford plans for world improvement after the "European business" had been dealt with.

"The book-learned tell you there are civilised societies and primitive ones — the poorest and most benighted they call 'unspoiled'. Well, they're going to have to write their books all over again because in the future the two societies will be motorised and unmotorised. Maybe *I* should write a book. Louis, would you like to write a book? You could do it for me, I'll tell you what to say. Yes, that's the problem of the world today — how to motorise the unmotorised. The men who do that will change the world more than presidents and kings. Perhaps I'll stop over in Europe a while once we're done. My German agents tell me Poland is the place to look — the market's bound to be good once this war business is over. And then further east too — did you know, Louis, there are whole continents with hardly a mile of road fit for good Firestone rubber? My Cairo concessionaire writes a letter four times a year telling me to look south. In Africa, where there is no rail-road and no river for boats to ply, there is no trade. Men live in a perpetual prison, the cells of which are measured by how far they may carry a load in a day on their own feet. I will throw them the key to their prison. Have you ever operated an automobile tractor, Louis?"

"You were good enough to show me the factory, Mr Ford."

"A child can master it in an hour and be taught to maintain it in five. Your Hottentot with the latest Fordson tractor beneath him will bow to no man. Africa will burgeon, her displaced sons and daughters will abandon their cotton sacks and their shoe-shine stands and take ship again, returning to fulfil their homeland's promise, ending a historic injustice."

The theme was pursued until all the world was covered and the mechanically assisted perfection of man complete. Only Australia was excepted (all sand) and Japan (all mountains). Antarctica he forgot.

Dr Marquis, who showed no surprise at any of this, put aside his papers and leaned forward to speak.

"Best, don't you think, to put the present war behind us first?"

Mr Ford drank the last of his cold remedy and returned his attention to the sea. He spoke quietly to himself — "Get the boys out of the trenches by Christmas."

I was unsure of what to expect from Marquis. He is not a delegate on the peace expedition and no one seems quite sure what he is. His conversations with me have been courteous but restrained, as if he were a diplomat from an opposing power, a gentleman to his glove-tips but careful all the same not to give away the slightest detail of policy. I know from Mr Bastian's reports that the newsmen have cast him as the urbane Rasputin of the Ford Empire and Mr Ford has frankly described him to me as "a disappointment". I believe he is a thorough sceptic on the matter of our mission, privately he may even find it laughable. What remains a particular mystery is the nature of the bond between Marquis and Mr Ford, who seems obliged to accept his company for almost every waking hour, though it clearly brings him no pleasure. Ordinarily, I would have preferred him not to be there but on this occasion, whatever his intention, he was not unhelpful.

"This statement," continued the Dean, "does it have to be so specific — I mean, to single out a particular country, the policy of a particular man? If we raise the tone to a more general level?"

"There are no generalities!" snapped Mr Ford. "I don't make general cars, my customers don't generally buy them and young men in Flanders aren't generally killed. Men who talk like that are the problem. We must cut through them."

He gestured incisively. The glass was knocked from the arm of the chair and shattered on the floor. Thoughtlessly, I moved forward but was curtly ordered not to. I sat down unhappily, like a schoolboy who had failed to ingratiate himself with a master.

"Mr Woodrow Wilson does not generally intend to waste the American people's money on battleships. I didn't take to the man — I wouldn't give him a job neither."

"I'm sure you're right," smoothed Marquis. "Perhaps it's just a matter of how people see things, of perspective?"

Mr Ford's eyes narrowed, his nose wrinkled as if he were about to sneeze. Marquis, glancing in another direction, pressed on.

"It is hardly surprising if a man whose whole life takes place in a single region of a single country has a narrower, let us say, a more simply patriotic view of things than a man who manufactures in a dozen countries and under a dozen governments. To see and feel equally about the whole map of the world at one time is given to few men. Practically speaking, one has to make allowances for the smallness of the ordinary man."

"Dr Marquis, I will say you have a remarkable way with words. You could describe one of my own cars to me so that even I would not buy it. The fact is I always feel insulted when a man tries to flatter me. I thought you would know that by now."

Marquis was unperturbed. He had the air of one who knew how to handle a familiar situation.

"I'm worried — and not just about you. Think of Clara . . . of Mrs Ford."

"What does *any* of this have to do with my wife?"

"I mean what Mrs Ford will have to read in the newspapers."

"She's seen worse."

"Are you sure? And more than that — your own position once you return. If the United States should end up fighting in this war you will be the most prominent person to have been against her preparing for such an ordeal."

"You take our failure for granted?"

"Not at all. I just mean that . . . Well, to put your own name to such a bold statement might make no difference in the end and do you some harm."

"Harm? Speaking the truth does no harm. War is harm. Putting your taxes up and giving you back your son in a coffin is harm. Say, Louis — make a note of that one, will you?"

I patted my pockets in search of a pen and in the end accepted a pencil stub held out by Marquis. Mr Ford became enjoyably agitated. The orator, so deeply hidden at the Belasco Theatre, began to rise to the surface. In time, we might make quite a fine campaigner out of him.

"Wilson will do harm and I aim to stop him. And as for me, Samuel Marquis, do you think I am the sort of man to fold up his principles and pack them away as soon as someone runs a flag up a pole?"

He suppressed another fit of coughing while signalling enthusiastically that I should record this too.

"Damn! I make such good sense when I'm angry."

Marquis jumped to his feet.

"But Mr Ford, Please — to go against your President?"

There was a hesitation in the older man, an attentive stillness as if better to hear his inner voice. Marquis seemed hopeful of a breakthrough. I looked on as Mr Ford's expression changed into that hard, distant grandeur all his intimates know and that I had first seen in the winter gloom by the edge of an empty swimming pool. Henry Ford was thinking, not in any ordinary way (even for him), but labouring intensely to bring forth a precise and novel conception, perhaps even a new turn on his life's road.

"You know," he said quite simply, "I think you might be right. Presidents come and go after all, and I don't think the American people should have to tolerate a man in the White House who would tax gasoline."

At that moment I believe Mr Ford could clearly see the outline of the Supreme Court Chief Justice before him, and hear the murmuring reverence of the crowd as he spoke the oath of office. And why not? Why not, indeed? Marquis turned pale. His eyes flickered upwards as if truly about to faint and he looked just as a man should look the moment after he has committed the most fatal and irreversible error of his life. He said no more.

My problem remained and as the awesome quality of the silence ebbed away I returned to it as gently as I could. It was hard to regain Mr Ford's attention and I'm not sure I ever quite succeeded. He did not look at me for the rest of the interview, but continued staring at the sea and the gradually lightening sky. At length I arrived back at the issue of resignations.

"Miss Milholland, I fear, will also go. She would be a particular loss, I feel."

The patient, hollow-cheeked and with his steel-grey hair now seeming white and thin, drifted in his own thoughts and gave no sign of having heard.

"Such a small, indeed a barely noticeable change of wording would solve the whole problem."

I went on to explain how these resignations from the peace delegation would not be like dismissing an employee.

"There would be consequences, sir. These people will talk to the press. Whatever the truth, the delegation will be seen to be divided. Our enemies will make mischief."

He stirred at the word "enemies", but was not sufficiently roused to speak.

"If only the platform was voluntary — if no one actually *had* to sign it."

It seemed barely honest to ask for the abandonment of everything Mr Ford had insisted on over the last five days. If I had been speaking to Rosika there would have been shouting, statuesque poses, grand phrases and the slamming of doors. The facts had not changed, neither had the arguments and neither, I suppose, had anyone's principles. And so I was slow to understand when Mr Ford, shifting to relieve some slight discomfort and still not looking at me, spoke a few quiet words.

"Well, what does it matter in the end?"

The phrase was discouragingly close to the one he had used five days before to insist on the opposite position. But the tone now — the actions, the sense, the feel of it, everything but the actual, dictionary-defined words was so different that it had the effect of a sudden, unexpected insertion of a foreign language. The whole grounds and foundation of the fight were now being given up as if they had never mattered in the first place, as if all that had been gone through might just as well not have happened. What did it mean?

I was speaking — saying something irrelevant no doubt, something hesitant and puzzled, when Marquis caught my attention and gave me that look that so clearly urges, "Go on, do it now, take your chance."

"Delegates *don't* need to sign the resolution, then?"

I worried that I had made it too much of a question, or that I had sounded astonished. Mr Ford continued to look out of the window. The bow dipped and rose gently against the wintry sea. I rose slowly from my chair and began to edge towards the door, stealthy as a burglar, or as an exhausted parent creeping from a sleeping child's bedroom. My nerve could not quite hold and I spoke again.

"I'll let everyone know, shall I?"

My hand was on the door — he had another chance to stop me or, as in fact happened, to let me take his silence as an instruction and to slip out without another word being said.

Thus Atlas shrugged and what had mattered so much no longer mattered at all. The Ford Peace Expedition platform was voluntary — you could sign it if you wanted to, or ignore it completely without the slightest consequence. By the end of the day, thirty-five had signed. Inez refused but conceded that "as the demands of conscience are now being respected" she could stay with us and lend her weight to bringing peace to Europe. McClure, having won what he had fought for, resigned anyway, immediately appointing himself to the press corps as an ordinary newsman and announcing that he could still come with us in this more neutral role. Whether anyone has noticed a difference I can't say.

The sense of relaxation throughout the ship was enjoyed by everyone. The dissolution of the dispute was so complete there was not even any sense of victory or defeat to disturb the newly restored peace. Rosika alone held back from the general rejoicing. She has kept more than ever to her stateroom, claiming that arrangements for our arrival in Norway are taking all her time. When we are together there have been no openly harsh words, but a new coolness and a miserliness with information. She feels herself undermined. Miss Rebecca Shelly's loyalty to her mistress has remained absolute and she also now looks on me with a suspicious eye. Our outbreak of peace has had one other effect — the working of a small healing miracle. Lloyd Bingham rallied that evening and was seen outside his cabin and on his feet for the first time in two days. He demonstrated his recovery by drawing deep, athletic breaths and declaring that the air was much improved. It would be fair to say that he has not always been to everyone's taste, but on that peace-making evening he brought off an unmitigated success. All the talents were marshalled for the Bingham Follies, the ship's band was roped in and, after a certain hour, no one was above making a fool of himself for the general good, myself included. With Lloyd's comic songs and ten-year-old jokes the night ended with laughing until it hurt and abandonment and empty bottles rolling in the gangways.

It was timely. The *Argosy*, our little shipboard news-sheet, was pushed under our doors in the early hours. We awoke with sore heads and swung our feet down from our bunks to place them on the fresh ink of its four gossipy pages. There was an outline map of the Atlantic, a little cartoon *Oscar* and a dotted line tracing our passage from New York. We approached Scotland's Orkney Islands and were at the point of intersecting another line that bulged around them, a line neatly labelled with two words in a bold black box — WAR ZONE.

It is midnight now, or a little past. A while ago, just as in olden days, the bell rang to change the watch, though now the sound has a less musical, electric trill to it. On either side there is the North Sea — flat as a new shop window, mirror-bright under a three-quarters moon. The *Oscar* makes her steady, purposeful way while on her back is played out a scene of unutterable strangeness, something one could only believe on the stage, a swirling musical interlude in a faery play, a midwinter night's dream of romance and transformation. We are there, everyone says to themselves, so very nearly there.

Only a few hours ago we were released from out three days' captivity at the hands of the British Navy. It was on Monday last that war became real for many of us for the first time. Captain Hempel, though no alarmist, issued orders that sobered everyone and frightened quite a few. The watch was doubled, and these men no longer wandered about their posts or chatted with each other or tried to charm the female students as before but worked hard, staring through large binoculars for a trace of a periscope or the turbulent wake of a torpedo. Steel brackets with electric lights were extended over either side so that the *Oscar*'s name and country of origin and her large Danish flag would be unmistakably clear in the eye of any U-boat commander. The lifeboats were swung out on their davits, ready to be lowered. We watched excitedly as teams of crew members went from boat to boat loosening the tarpaulins that covered them and equipping each with extra drinking water, food, flares, storm lanterns and gallon tins of paraffin fuel.

"Hey, Sven," called out the man from the Brooklyn *Eagle*, "which one has the whisky in it? There are fates worse than death, you know."

"Never mind that," says his friend, "which one's Schwimmer in?"

"Now you're really spooking me. Can you imagine? A hundred days adrift and then a committee to decide who gets to drink whose blood and that Rosika dame in the chair. Hell already!"

Soon everyone was a gallows joker. The inhabitants of lower cabins moved above the waterline to squeeze in with top-deck friends. The more nervous ladies risked pneumonia by living almost permanently on the promenade deck benches. I would pass rows of them perching there, almost unchanged in their order and aspect from morning to afternoon. Squeezed in the middle, the mature Miss Severine Mylecraine of the San Francisco Women's Peace League explained that she was wearing her new rubber-soled easy walkers to protect against the effects of lightning and so that she might benefit, in case of an even greater misfortune, from their superior buoyancy in salt water. Determined not to go silently to the deep, Miss Mylecraine rolled up her political testament and sealed it in an empty champagne bottle which she then hurled a quite remarkable distance over the side.

"School discus champion," she responded to the heartfelt applause, "eighteen ninety-two."

Along the deck, resting on a steamer chair under a blanket and ready for a quick escape, Berton Braley furrowed his brow and scribbled all afternoon in search of the deathless lines the occasion demanded. Elsewhere a brief religious revival was experienced with excellent attendances at contrasting services of prayer and song. Traditionalists favoured Reverend Lloyd Jones, looking for all the world as if he had just been peeled from one of the more Old Testament panels of the Sistine Chapel ceiling. A narrow victory, nevertheless, was said to have been scored by Reverend Charles Aked, a brilliantined entrepreneur of God as modern and simply effective in his field as one of Mr Ford's automobiles. A handful of the most pious were seen at both events and were duly teased by their fellow travellers. Rosika kept to her cabin, drafting speeches and growling about the opium of the people.

The first excitement of the day was caused by the appearance of a vast battlecruiser about half a mile off our left-hand side. Some were for immediately abandoning ship before word got round that the monster was British and should have no more sinister intention than enforcing the blockade regulations. We were followed for some two hours in the afternoon. The newsmen were thrilled. Those with moving-picture cameras set themselves up and eagerly cranked away at this authentic image of Europe. Others took their drinks from the bar and stood by the rail. They gestured and called out pointlessly to the warship and engaged in boyish arguments about the size of her guns and the effortlessness with which she could destroy us. Mr Ford joined us briefly. He scowled at the bristling outline and called it a waste of good steel before pulling his collar tight about his neck and hurrying back to the warmth.

I was there among the other watchers late in the afternoon when we were all caught off guard and made to jump out of our skins. A rib-shaking crack of thunder rolled over us out of a clear sky. Here was the traditional shot across the bows. Captain Hempel stopped the engines and we rolled in the swell, feebly awaiting capture. I looked eastwards, hoping to get some sight of land through the gloom. At first there was nothing I could make out and then a few points of light that indicated another approaching ship. A liner appeared, converted for war. She circled us then let down a boat with ten men, four of whom worked the oars to bring themselves across the short gap of sea to bump against our plates and climb aboard. A middle-aged reserve Lieutenant Trevithick was in command. Without any order being given, six of his men lined up and shouldered their rifles. Lieutenant

Trevithick adjusted his bearing better to convey the authority of the British Empire. He swept us with a look of stern regret — the peace delegates, the newsmen, Lloyd Bingham who resembled him somewhat in his roundness and the touch of feverish colour in his cheeks, the short, dark, bespectacled and bun-haired intensity of Rosika Schwimmer and myself. He shook his head sadly before pronouncing his judgement.

"They're a villainous lot, Wilhelm, to be sure. It's a wonder you're still alive at all. Are all these the mutineers?"

The Captain offered a brief explanation which Lieutenant Trevithick accepted with no great show of interest.

"Ah well then," he said equably, "here was me and my lads getting all excited and it was nothing but a lot of newspaper talk after all. There you go."

He extended a cigarette to his friend and the two men chatted for a while about what the sea-going life had brought them since the last of their regular encounters. The butts were thrown over the side and the Lieutenant gave a lackadaisical order.

"Righto lads, let's get on with it. Too cold to hang about here."

It is a war, I suppose, but very much the edge of one.

Trevithick's men sealed the wireless transmitter and installed a pilot on the bridge to guide us in to Kirkwall. Just before leaving us they pulled down the Danish flag and hoisted in its place the Union Jack. No one was pleased to see it — a fact not lost on Trevithick as he took his leave.

"Don't worry, ladies — you've got the Empire with you now."

There were dark looks in reply as our captor turned to the journalists.

"Oh, and you gentlemen of the press — it won't be so funny next time. I wouldn't send any more messages like that if you don't want to go swimming."

The fourth estate shifted guiltily and mumbled their promises of better behaviour.

"Jesus!" exclaimed one of them as soon as it was safe. "Makes you wonder if they're worth saving."

Our engines turned for forty minutes and then stopped again as we reached our anchorage outside the harbour, invisible in the darkness and guarded for the night by its gate of mines. Judge Ben Lindsey lectured on the law of the sea and found much to interest him in the issue of whether we could now, temporarily under a belligerent flag, be lawfully killed by a declared combatant. He thought it an uncertain area, lacking in any clear precedent. Otherwise, it was a dull evening and most retired early with thoughts of the morning and the first sight of land in ten days.

Orkney is a low range of grass-covered hills populated largely by sheep and devoid of interest as a landscape. At one point in its past all the trees were removed the better to allow the uninterrupted passage of the winds over its surface and no one has since thought to put them back, preferring instead to weigh down the roofs of their houses with stones so they do not blow off quite so often. The houses of Kirkwall are low and tenacious in appearance and seem to have no purpose other than the mere sheltering of their inhabitants who, presumably, have such long winters and short days that they care little what they look like from the outside. Frankly, on my first morning in Orkney harbour, land seemed less exciting than I remembered it.

The authorities — a combination of the Royal Navy and the amiable but determined Kirkwall harbourmaster — proved ingenious at coming up with excuses for searching, questioning and delaying us. It wasn't long before the word "incarceration" was being used freely. There were compensations, nevertheless, and the first of these was the delivery of a large packet of newspapers on our first morning. We fell upon them like starved animals and breakfast was a wordless affair as we scanned them with that special intensity readers reserve for when they are the news.

"There's nothing here."

"This can't be right. How old are these papers?"

I looked through my own copy of *The Times* — Slander Action: Butcher Called "German" by Fishmonger; Horatio Bottomley says No Peace Piffle!; See how it becomes new again with the correct use of Fels-Naphtha Soap, give your Family the Fels-Naphtha smile! Below the soap ad a young man with a steel plate strapped to his chest smiled at the reader:

Send at Once a
DAYField Body Shield
to Father, Brother, Son or Friend
to save his Life

Sir Hiram Maxim heartily endorsed the product, which could be sent directly to the front for twenty-two shillings and sixpence.

"Censorship!" declared someone. "Not a word and it's nothing but downright censorship."

"Hold on — here's something. Bottom of page five. 'Ford Peace Party at Kirkwall, arrived yesterday. Understood that faddists will not be allowed to land.' "

"Faddists!"

"What else?"

"I think that's it."

"Just as I told you — naked censorship."

A thorough search revealed a second mention of our project deep in a parliamentary report. A certain Lord Rosebery had amused the upper house with talk of a ship fraught with peace, financed by an American gentleman believed to be a manufacturer of perambulators. A statement from Rosika's office welcomed this evidence of our growing success — "My fellow humanitarians — if we did not have the power to stop the war, governments would not feel the need to ignore us. A true peacemaker must have the courage to have the right enemies as well as the right friends. Mr Ford and I are in possession of information we cannot yet share with you. All is well."

"Louis," he said to me later.

"Yes, Mr Ford?"

"What is it I know that I mustn't tell you?"

"I couldn't say, sir."

"You'll be sure and stop me if I'm going to say something I shouldn't, won't you Louis?"

"You can rely on me, Mr Ford."

The newsmen rattled off dispatches to their papers back home all about the spinelessness and the low moral standards of their English colleagues — U-boats Torpedo English Liberty; Sufferings of a Hoodwinked Europe — Where Ignorant Armies Clash by Night.

"Hey, nice one, Schulzy — your own?"

"Sure is, my friend. You're talking here to the muse of the news."

Such creativity may not have travelled far. These dispatches and the sack-loads of other mail that was hurriedly written had to be collected unsealed by the harbourmaster and rowed back to his office on the quayside. There was grumbling from the British and talk of further censors being taken on just for us, and the great expense to His Majesty's Government. On the first night after our arrival, as I walked round the *Oscar*'s tight circumference, I could see the lights in that office burning late into the night as bleary-eyed and yawning censors waded through all our hopes, boasts, lies, reassurances, uncertainties, yearnings and declarations of love, searching for the least trace of hidden enmity.

The ship was examined as thoroughly as our correspondence. Suitcases of unwashed clothes were rifled for secrets or the material of war. Uniformed men and guns were everywhere. I came upon three rifles propped in a corner, apparently forgotten by their owners as they searched a hold. Newsmen harried the young sailors with questions, but they held loyally to their orders to say nothing. They did have one area of weakness and that was their curiosity about the great man himself. They had seen his name on motor cars and vans and on advertisements in newspapers and magazines — was he real, what did he look like, sound like, could he really do it? These are the men whose lives Mr Ford, and all of us, haD come to save and he was every bit as keen to meet them. Several interviews were held while officers were looking the other way and I was at one of these, watching as three ratings stood in a line with their hats in their hands. Mr Ford asked their names, where they were from and how they liked their work. He learned of brothers and fathers serving elsewhere and was pleased to hear that none of them had yet lost a family member. There was a short silence before one of them spoke up.

"We're all with you, sir. The boys all agreed to tell you, everyone here and at home too. We know what you're doing and everyone's with you."

Mr Ford smiled serenely.

"I appreciate that, son, I really do."

"It's hard, sir, you see with a wife and kiddies back home you haven't seen for six months and no end to it. We hate it, to tell the truth. Can you do it, sir? Do you really think you can do it?"

Here was a tonic straight to the heart of my chief. His eyes filled with brightness and the colour came back to his cheeks.

"Now I want you boys to trust me and all the good people on this ship. Whatever humanity and common sense, brain-power and a good deal of money can do, we're going to do and we won't stop till you get those orders to go home where you're needed."

In that moment his enthusiasm and faith in our journey were fully revived.

"We must let everyone know about this, Louis. Put it in a press release and get it straight out as soon as those limeys have given us our radio transmitter back. You'll know what to say — the full hundred horsepower!"

Outside, a frustrated mob of newsmen lay in wait.

"Hey, bud, how come you get an interview and we don't? Cigarette? What did he say? Did he tell you not to obey orders — isn't that what he said, huh? Could you use five dollars, my friend?"

The newsmen were to receive a much greater blow on the morning of our last day in Kirkwall harbour. The alarm was raised, very calmly at first, when it became clear that one of our number was indeed going ashore, whatever the blockade regulations said. Bob Doman of the *Morning Telegraph* was the first to notice.

"Aw — are we losing our radio man? He was a really nice guy."

There was the personable and ever helpful Robert Bastian sitting in the bow of a tiny dinghy, looking back at us over the shoulder of another man who rowed vigorously in the direction of an iron ladder set in the wall of the harbour. At the rower's feet lay two large sacks and something shiny.

"What's he got there? Is he turning mailman?"

More people gathered to wave at Mr Bastian — he had done them all favours, including favours of a highly confidential nature. The other man picked up the pace with the oars and they both turned to look at the ladder and up to the little Hotchkiss car that waited above it.

"What *is* he doing?"

The newsmen fell quiet and concentrated anxiously on the diminishing figures. The dinghy bumped the ladder and there was an ungainly scramble as the two men made their way up with their various items of cargo. A bright metallic flash signalled back to us through the chilly sunlight. Lloyd Bingham had pushed his way to the front and was standing beside me. His shoulders began to shake and I could hear the beginnings of rumbling, phlegmatic laughter.

"It can't be!" said someone.

Speechless journalists began to gape like fish. On the quay Bastian's friend cranked the little car into life and got behind the wheel. Bastian himself struck a triumphant pose and held up two gleaming, round mirrors — cans of movie film.

"The bastard!"

His voice travelled to us across the water, weak and half-strange as in a phonograph recording. There was a new and unfamiliar accent.

"My name is James Joseph Cooper and you won't ever forget it! I was born and raised in London and in ten hours' time I'll be back there. I'll be walking down

Fleet Street with copies of every message you've ever sent and photographs of everything you've ever done and I'll be the richest and most famous journalist in the whole of Europe!"

"Shoot that man! God damn it — shoot both of them!"

Two startled sailors broke off from their leisurely search for contraband.

"Those men in the car, sir?"

"Yes, those men in the car! Quick, they're getting away. In the name of the freedom of the press, shoot them now! For Christ's sake, can't you at least shoot the car?"

The sailors looked thoughtfully at the disappearing Hotchkiss.

"If you was an officer, sir, we could oblige. But seeing as you aren't, I don't think we can help. I'm sorry you're upset."

Hats were thrown on the deck and trampled in impotent rage. The car vanished, leaving only a trail of blue smoke dissipating slowly in the winter air. Bingham was convulsing with delight.

"You know what that was?" he asked me. "That was the first half-decent piece of organisation I've seen since I fought my way out of the lobby of the Biltmore Hotel."

Doman was alone among the journalists in seeing the funny side. He shook his head slowly and smiled.

"Shall I tell you a better joke, boys? A bigger one? That crumb gets to Fleet Street, he walks up and down all day, in and out of every office he can think of and when it's over he can't sell the whole damned lot for a dime — now *that's* funny!"

A movie cameraman was unconsoled. He put his head in his hands and groaned.

"Oh, Jesus! This was my first foreign assignment. What am I going to tell my boss?"

McClure stepped up and put a fatherly arm around his shoulders.

"Don't worry about it, young fellow — there's plenty better ways of making a living. Gentlemen, I believe the bar has been restocked."

The search of the *Oscar* finally came to an end. The whole procedure ended with a pleasing farce. Three hundred sacks of parcel post had been discovered in Hold no.5. These consisted for the most part of brightly wrapped Christmas presents, brought by the delegates and Mr Ford, for the children of Norway. The very innocence of these packages aroused the suspicions of the customs officers and the outrage they provoked when some were found knee-deep in brown plush bears and wooden aeroplanes and china dolls and clockwork racing cars was all the confirmation they needed that hidden somewhere in that huge mound of good will there must lurk something harmful.

"That's it, lads — it'll all have to go."

The journalists, the delegates and even members of the *Oscar*'s crew gathered by the side of the ship to witness the crime and abuse the perpetrators. The *Pax Vobiscum* and the *Good Shepherd*, two elderly steam-powered tenders, puttered away through the early northern gloom. Uniformed men stood guard over the sacks of presents — a cartoon of war's evil, humourless Santas stealing Christmas itself.

"Thieves!" shouted our most fiery co-ed.

Someone urged caution but Inez, looking on happily at one of the next generation's fighters, nudged her with an elbow and whispered encouragement.

"Common thieves!"

"Remember the Boston Tea Party!" shouted another.

One sailor turned to make an indecent gesture before being ordered to ignore us.

The *Oscar* received her licence to proceed and these strange theatricals somehow came together. The sea is as Captain Hempel has never seen it before. His first officer tells me it is because we are tiptoeing our way across a graveyard. He says I should listen for a scraping sound — the wrecks of our predecessors clutching at our still living hull. Tonight no one could hear it. We are crowded together on what, for other latitudes and seasons, is known as the sun deck. Hats and thick coats are our evening dress, our breaths whiten in the icy air as we dance, the ladies are buxom in their life-vests and the unfaded stars above as new to my city eyes as to a child. Stewards weave through us and as we pick glasses of champagne from the salvers they seem to come down from the moon itself. The band plays lustily to keep itself warm. We swirl to up-tempo renditions of "By the Beautiful Sea", "They Didn't Believe Me" and "Roamin' in the Gloamin'". Mr and Mrs Berton Braley are seen in each other's arms for the first time in three days. The white fox is about Marion's shoulders, brilliant under the white light of the moon. As they turn I see first Berton's peaceful features and then Marion's and then the black button nose and glinting glass eyes of the fox as it crouches by the warmth of her neck. The music changes. Marion spins away to deliver herself to a delighted Samuel McClure.

"Poem! Poem!"

Berton feigns reluctance then jumps onto a life-raft and silences the band. He fumbles with three slips of paper, rearranging them in different pockets before finding the right one.

Hail, Argonauts of Peace Sailing from America's
golden Hesperides!
We come, we come to raise despairing Europe
from her knees.

There to seek and find the gleaming secret of
Peace,
Humanity's hyperborean gilded Fleece.

Henry of the Fjords labours at our oars,
Soon to triumph over the war god, floored.

Together in the Oscar, *brimful with benevolence,*
We come to drive all that is evil from men's
hearts thence.

Hurray for the Oscar! *Hurray for Henry Ford!*
We fight on till war be universally deplored!

* * *

"Drivel, did he say? We come to drivel?"

"Genius! Hurray, carve it in stone!"

Everyone cheers wildly and claps. Marion is about to burst with pride. Her husband bows a dozen times and then, quite overcome, is helped to make a shaky descent from his platform. Mr Ford, sitting to the side in two coats, a lady's sable muffler and a quantity of travelling blankets around his knees, orders the verses to be sent out over the wireless. At the very same moment Rosika Schwimmer comes upon us in high excitement. She has been working our new wireless operator hard. She is breathless as she gains the sweating, gyrating sun deck. She carves a route through the dancers, holding a white sheet of paper as high as her stature permits. She ascends a bench and signals for the music to stop. As "The Aba Daba Honeymoon" crashes to disorder, Rosika stands there quite still, darkly clothed as ever, her dark arm held up against the cloudless night and at the end of it, bright as fire, the moonlit and slightly fluttering brilliance of her sheet of paper.

"The Prime Minister of England will discuss serious peace terms. Asquith is with us, the English are with us. My friends — it's peace!"

Delirium, ecstasy, a deluge of champagne. The stars spin round, the band plays "For He's a Jolly Good Fellow", the notes thumping through the *Oscar*'s hull, snaking away through the deep dark waters to hum, mysterious and hallucinatory, in the ears of homesick submariners. I turn from partner to partner, hoping, sure that it must be. Here is Inez, her left hand falling into my right as neatly as a well-caught ball, her right hand on my shoulder, pressing firmly. Her features, marble-pale, are those of a quizzical female Antinous, her grey eyes more arresting than ever.

"A polka!" demands someone. "A polka to warm us up."

The band begins at once and we are off at a gallop. Everything is colour and movement — black sky, swirling winter coats, cold air and warm breath, faces champagne-bright. Inez is my compass point, the only clarity.

Captain Hempel climbs up to see the strangest thing ever to happen in the long years of his command. He stands by Mr Ford, whose face is very white and serene. He presides over the magical, impossible scene like the Prospero of the industrial age, sustaining everything he sees by his will alone. The polka comes to an end and we slow to a breathless halt beside the two old men. Mr Ford is applauding, his face beaming with delight.

"The old dances are the best," he shouts. "You young folks don't have as much fun as we used to."

Inez pulls me close and kisses me on the cheek. With eyes, the turn of her head and fingers moving around my waist she communicates, with no possible ambiguity, the scandalous offer that is her heart's creed. Statuesque, exquisite, scented, she smiles down at the seated Mr Ford.

"We're going to do it. By heaven, I'll wager the *Oscar* to a penny we're going to get those boys out of the trenches by Christmas! I'll buy her and set her up as a museum in Detroit. People will come from all over the world to see where war was ended. What do you say to that, Captain?"

Lloyd

Amelia, Amelia — I am with you in spirit. At least I think I am, it's just that I don't know where to send my spirit at the moment. In all the excitement of departure I did a foolish thing — I told myself over and again to pack your engagements list, but forgot it in the end all the same. I went through my valise and all my pockets a dozen times before giving up and then kicked the wall of my cabin hard enough to break a hole in it. And so, my dear, I don't know where you are. I while away the hours as I lie here trying to remember the theatres and the dates. I try to unfold in my mind that maddening sheet of paper — is this an engagements list I see before me, the words towards my eyes? Come, that I may clutch thee. I have thee not . . . dum, de-dum, de-dum. How does it go? I'm wandering.

Where are you, Amelia? I get as far as the words — I know I'm on the right track because I recognise your secretary's typing mistakes. Then they start to move around and I get so frustrated it tires me out. Is it Philly tonight, or Frisco? Are you charming the roughnecks out in Bismarck or Cheyenne, or have you flown south for the winter to Mobile or to that new vaudeville in Galveston, relaxing on the balcony, looking out over the Gulf? Are you back in the Bijou where you first made it big in the east? I can smell that place. I don't know what it was but the Bijou always had its own smell, like no other theatre. I breathe it in now and I'm there. You are too, your face flickering from limelight to shadow as you run into the wings, flowers falling as you open your arms — "Oh Lloyd, Lloyd, thank you. I could never have done it without . . ." Amelia, my darling, perhaps you are closer, perhaps you are in London — why not? If the call came just after I left you would have crossed quicker than we did in that rusting old cockle-shell Ford hired. You could be here in two days, or I could come to you — what does this gloomy Swedish sawbones know? The Lyceum is it, Wyndhams?

So you see, my dear, because of my forgetfulness all I can do is guess. I must broadcast. That's what they call it now — scatter in all directions, though whether I can make myself heard through the babble from all these Marconi machines these days, I don't know. Sometimes I think the world will never be quiet again. At least you know where I am. When was the last time my name was in print more often than yours, my dear? Twenty years ago or more, I should think. Now you will be reading about me every day — or at least about my new friends. I can't tell you what a complete triumph everything has been. The great days are come again, and it's true after all what they say about talent — you can misplace it, but you can never lose it. Just wait till I get home — this thing is the greatest comedy in fifty years. I've thought it all through — you and me together again. The parts are perfect — I swear no one in the world can do them better than we can. We're going to pack the houses from coast to coast, and then they'll make a moving picture of it. You'll be Clara Ford and Rosika Schwimmer. Don't worry — I'll explain everything and no quick changes needed. So keep the faith, my dear, for our reward is coming. Pick my love from the air and send your thoughts back to me, Mr Lloyd Bingham, room 317, Grand Hotel, Christiania, Norway. Oh, oh — here comes Dr Grimgloom. I'll pretend to sleep. Amelia . . . are you there? I don't want to frighten you, my girl, but if things don't work out you'll receive a letter from Mrs S. R. Meissner of 1524 Thirty-First Street, Georgetown — she specialises in our sort.

Better today. I outlasted old Sawbones and got some peace in the end. You know I think he doubles as the undertaker. Normally I'd call that a conflict of interest, but this place is none too big a town. The hotel is pretty fine — colossal room, big picture window all winter clouds where I can see through and green above where the blind is pulled half down. The light makes me look jaundiced. It snows most of the time. The furniture is classy, little bits on it everywhere, very European. There's everything here for a historical drama. I can see you now, stopping by that fancy table under the window to deliver your lines. There's heavy paper with the letterhead stamped on so thick you could read it blindfold, and a pen tray with a big crystal inkwell. I think I ask for these things, but either they don't understand or that Swedish quack has got some idea about writing being bad for my health. They don't seem to get the heat right — always too hot or too cold. Strange that — with everything else just so.

Sad news, my dear, which I doubt the newspapers will bother to inform you of — Henry Ford is dead. He was poorly much of the way, but very nearly made it across. I witnessed a most affecting burial at sea when we were already within sight of land. None of the clergy aboard were willing to officiate, but Berton composed a delightful funeral ode. At the words "nearer my hazelnut to thee" the little chopping board was tipped up and the furry peacemaker slipped from beneath a handkerchief to his eternal rest. Unsure whether this was a squirrel of the Christian persuasion, Poseidon was also offered a few glasses of whisky to ease the passing of this toothy soul. An evergreen corsage was plucked from a lady's breast and thrown on the waters. You'll call me a fool, but there was quite a tear in my eye by the end. William Jennings Bryan remains in robust health and now gets twice the attention and twice the food. There has been talk of foul play — but on a peace ship? The human Ford is still with us and I'm sure has no intention of ascending to the great dealership in the sky any time soon. Like me, he has had a little seasickness, a slight cold, but that is all. I hear someone coughing in the room above — that could be him.

So this letter — I shall think you a letter. It's barely two weeks since I ambled downstairs after a late breakfast to tackle the mail. You know how it's been lately — for me at least. It's getting so I like a bit of lunch too before taking the first blows of the day. Bill, bill, first reminder, second reminder, final demand, Dear Mr Bingham, The commencement of proceedings in the District Court of . . . Oh, by the way, did I get your cheque last month, my dear? I suppose I must have done. This time, in amongst all the threats and the ingratitude, a telegram too. I fortified myself and tore it open with a flourish — do your worst, telegram! Some sort of joke, obviously. One of my old friends trying to make a laughing stock of me. Even after I confirmed by telephone I was still a little suspicious. The *what* expedition? Henry Ford — *the* Henry Ford? I certainly hadn't volunteered for this — in fact, it would be no exaggeration to say I hadn't heard anything about it. Then I realised. Amelia, my darling, my guardian angel — you had been looking after me all the time. You called them — or, more likely, they called you.

"Mrs Bingham, I wonder if you would be so good as to advise us. We need an exceptional man for a most unusual position. We appreciate of course that you could not do it yourself, but . . ."

What else could you say? How things turn, my dear, how they turn. I was a good agent for you and now you return the favour. You know, I'm still a little unclear about the fees for this job, but I suppose you've wrapped all that up. But don't you think it a bit strange that no one has mentioned money? A lot of these folks seem to be giving up their time for nothing and I'm just hoping there hasn't been some dreadful misunderstanding. Perhaps I shouldn't complain — I haven't spent a dollar of my own since leaving Hoboken.

Oh, you should have seen me that day. Perhaps you did? If I missed you in the crowd, my dear, I can only apologise — it *was* the biggest I had ever had. Nothing could have done me more good. So there I was — the new Noah welcoming these strange creatures aboard. How they lapped it up! Apparently it was raining, apparently it was freezing cold — I stayed out there to the end and didn't notice a thing. The theatre, my dear one, is the only miracle cure I ever believed in and it didn't let me down. You know, part of my audience was so enthusiastic he came swimming after me. How's that for a review?

I guess you'll have read a fair bit about the characters on this jaunt. Among the women there is more than the usual quota of twitchers and blinkers. One is never seen in daylight and jumps out of her shoes whenever you meet her coming round a corner. Another is on her honeymoon and is never seen outside her cabin. The queen of them all is Madame Schwimmer. She looks just like she sounds — you half expect her to ask for a quarter to tell your fortune — sort of cross between Pandora, Lady Bracknell and a serio-comic middle-aged Hedda Gabler. She's a scream — one hundred per cent pure comic potential. Do you remember a girl on a white horse causing a riot at some suffragette thing a few years back? Well she's here too! She's the honey — think Cleopatra ten years before she had that last fling. Amelia, my darling, by the time we've put this farce on stage where it belongs it'll be as big a success for you as it's already been for me. Good parts for the boys, too. We brim with padres of every conceivable hue — one is an Englishman with a hidden past and looks like a salesman, another has clearly been abducted from a department store grotto and finds it impossible to get himself taken seriously. A third, Marquis by name, personally attends the great man himself, though whether he conveys messages from God to Henry Ford or from Henry Ford to God, no one is entirely sure. The newsmen swell the cast and chorus drunken prophecies of doom. A sprinkling of ingénues from the best colleges look on wide-eyed and agonisingly untouchable. Oh, you know me, my darling — nothing to worry about there. Not these days, anyway. Not now.

I shall play Henry Ford myself. Sacrifices will be required — the man doesn't eat much. You'd think with all that money he'd enjoy himself more but he looks like a few rags on a broomstick. Amelia, is that you? "You could lose a few pounds, Lloyd, you know you could. You look puffy in the mornings." Ah, sweetness, you could be here in this room! Well, you got me a job, my guardian agent, and now it's payday for both of us — I tell you, this is a hit. I got the whole thing in my head. Hire a stenographer, my dear, when I get home I'll talk for three days solid and we'll have a script by the weekend. Charlie Frohman will come back to life to produce this one.

I suppose you'll have heard about some disagreements. What the papers might not have told you is who set it right, who the hero of the hour was. Yes indeed, my dear — yours truly, the only tried and tested, bona fide peacemaker on this here expedition to date. Don't ask me what it was all about — half the folks on this ship talk like a convention of college professors and no sane man would go near them without ear plugs. Whatever it was, in the space of a few hours one evening they worked themselves into a powerful hatred of each other. At the time I was laid up, but they came and knocked on my door anyway and begged for help. What else could they do? It was nothing really — the Muse cured me in an instant and, though I say so myself, I improvised a pretty fine cabaret. Peace was restored and I was the toast of the ship. Mr Ford acknowledged me the next day. I have a new theory, Amelia — that if anyone is going to stop this war it's as likely to be people like you and me as anyone else. All the same, I'm getting to like these people. They sort of belong together and in ten short days I've come to feel at home with them.

Then we got captured by the British Navy and taken to some island and searched high and low like we were smugglers. Are you following this, my dear? It's important — I want you to know how it was. There must have been another argument about that time — things were a little worse with me and I was in my cabin for much of the day, but I could hear raised voices and doors banging. The next thing was music and laughing and rounds of applause as I drowsed and woke, and the feet drumming on the deck above as everyone was dancing. Well what happened next was a peach, a juicy, fat, sweet peach. You know, I've been called a genius before and I will be again, but sometimes all a man needs to do is sit under the tree of life and let the good things fall into his lap. This was one such occasion and I tell you, Amelia, when I think of what you're going to do with material like this I get sore laughing. No doubt about it — this scene is a show-stopper.

It's all about the bag. I did explain the bag, didn't I? — no matter. The bag's the whole damn thing, that's all you need to know. Get the bag and you've got the whole chase and the thing you've got to know about the bag is how it got under the skin of the newsboys before anyone even cast off from Hoboken. Whatever was in it, the public had a right to know and they were determined to get it any way they could. It wasn't easy — Schwimmer was rarely seen without it, two girls guarded her cabin day and night and on the few occasions when they were able to try the door in the early hours of the morning it was always firmly locked. But everyone dancing under the moonlight and Schwimmer up there too vapouring about some message from the Prime Minister of England was just what they had been waiting for. Picture the scene, my dear — there I am, a little revived by the sound of all this merry-making and wondering if I should go up myself to join in when a distinctly suspicious noise comes to my ears. There is a rattling in the corridor, the sound of effort and the self-conscious attempts of three or four strong men to stay quiet. The very sounds, put another way, that would make a policeman's ears prick up and all of them coming from the direction of the boss-woman's cabin. There was a grunt, a hushed demand to be careful and then the bang of something being forcibly opened. By the time I was decent and in the corridor the boys were coming the other way, young Hirsch holding up the bag itself like a captured standard.

"Why, Lloyd!" exclaimed another. "How are you? You catch us at a glorious moment — rescuing the truth from its abductors."

The prospect of a little fun did wonders for my head and in no time we were all together in the smoking room crowding round as someone forced the bag lock with a knife. Pop! — it opened, cavernous and black. Did we fear to look inside? Who was the man for the job? The place was full of newsmen by this stage and some instinct made them all turn to me. So I got straight into character and there I was, balancing bellydown on a barstool "schwimming" an Atlantic of tears.

"Don't panic, don't panic!"

Heavy garment-district accent.

"Ich kommt to make ze peas. I eff everyzing vee need right eear!"

I stir around inside, averting my eyes until my hand falls upon one of those all-important secret dispatches. The boys get the idea, but they're tense too. Like me, they can't quite shake the idea that there might really be something there, that if everything they know about the world and everything they believe turns out, just this once, to be wrong that'll be the bigger story. They want to be wrong. For a second, they're all leaning toward me and the bag, hoping for a revelation.

Crash goes the cymbal — and there's the first piece. I wave it in the air.

"A lady's handkerchief, embroidered RS, lightly soiled."

"Something to wipe away her tears with."

"No way — she's going to rip it in two and each side's going to use it to surrender to the other."

We're a double act, we get a rhythm going. Oh, Amelia — is anything better? Throw physic to the dogs; I'll none of it.

"A small powder compact — a very dainty piece, gentlemen."

"To make the human animal look better than it really is — essential rainbow-chasers' kit."

"Get on with it, fat boy. Where's the beef?"

Ah, to be heckled again — how it did my heart good. More averting of the eyes, more stirring of the hand in the stygian darkness of the bag.

"Here it is — something on paper anyway."

I pull out a scarlet notebook, closed with a bronze clasp.

"Now we're getting there."

"An address book? A blackmail list?"

"Recipes for putting spells on elderly auto-makers," suggests another.

"No," says a third, "it's her secret diary. Who's she in love with? Toss it here, Bingham."

The book flies, is caught and violated.

"It's in foreign. Hey, Hirsch, you read this stuff, don't you?"

There is a moment's hush as the pages are quickly gone through.

"What you got there, hot-shot? Don't you dare hold anything back."

Hirsch is already at the end and is flicking back for another look. He shrugs.

"It's nothing."

"What! No Asquith, no Lloyd George, no Clemenceau, no Bethmann Hollweg?"

"Personal stuff. Nothing at all."

The book is snatched away.

"Hey, dopey — you missed a bit. My dearest little Austro-Hungarian Rose, how I recall your words from last summer. I see now you are right. War is silly and together we will stop it at once. Oh, how I yearn to be in your short, thick arms again. Your ever loving Paul von Hindendindenburg, your cuddly Prussian bear and general of the Imperial German forces — kiss, kiss. What do you know, she does have some charms!"

"Shut up, Hiram — you're not funny. Lloyd — get on with it. Is there anything in there or are we wasting our time?"

I go fishing again. She can't have lied completely — surely there's got to be something.

"Hold on. Here's another book."

I bring out a tiny English-Hungarian dictionary. The boys start to hook up.

"Oh, Grandma," says one, "what a large vocabulary you have."

"All the better to fool you with, my dear."

"Here's another one — 'Travel and Accommodation Guide to Northern Europe With Railway Timetables'."

"Give it here. Maybe there are some notes in it. There might be clues."

"Check out the timetables for secret codes."

I bring out, one after the other, a near-empty bottle of seasickness pills, a magnifying vanity mirror, a lipstick and a small tortoiseshell jewel case which, when opened, reveals a single gleaming false tooth. Schwimmer is successively accused of hoarding essentials, having a distorted view of the world, trying to paint over the truth and disguising her true identity.

That seems to be it, but I'm back in the bag for a last check. I dive in there.

"Oh, can this be all?" I moan. "Tell me it's not true."

I straighten up. The bag is stuck on my head. I'm half man, half bag-monster and I do the blind schtick — arms out, blundering around, carefully knocking into all the things I've memorised. It started out fine and then there was that sublime moment when there's only one guy on stage who doesn't hear the silence — really we couldn't have rehearsed it better. I plough on for a few seconds, still working for the next laugh. Then I realise it hasn't just gone quiet out there, it's a damned funeral. I take the bag off my head and there she is — Schwimmer herself, towering, outraged, basilisk eyes, bust poised for attack. The audience can't contain themselves and the scene is held until their applause dies away. Meanwhile, the newsboys have been struck dumb and are all looking at each other and then at me

— me, who they dragged in and put up to the whole thing! But get this. Here's the clever bit — she brandishes . . . yes, you guessed it — THE BAG! We look from bag to identical bag. It's the comedy of errors with bags rather than people. Are we being fooled, is there real treasure anywhere? Schwimmer triumphant.

"You faithless imbeciles, you cynics, you hypocrites. Not even a decent thief among you."

"Hey, easy, lady — we're just doing our job."

You storm magnificently.

"Infants — not knowing right from wrong, not knowing what you do!"

No comeback from the boys this time — just a conceding droop of the shoulders. Only one has the spunk to speak up.

"Say, Rosika, how many of those bags you got?"

"Ha!" replies the idealist. "One more than you could ever steal. That's all *you* need to know."

Amelia Bingham's dazzling portrayal of Madame Schwimmer gathers herself for a magisterial departure. And then . . . Ah, my dear, something we really didn't expect at all. Something that was entirely, shockingly unnecessary. She stops, turns, sweeps us with a baleful, contemptuous gaze — the gaze of the microscopist on the squirming forms of her infinitely insignificant subjects. She inhales. We wait. We are all ears.

"And one other thing, gentlemen, before I go — Henry Ford and I are *not* lovers."

Well, this was new — and I tell you, Amelia, when the Israelites watched the waters part and looked down on whalebones and shipwrecks and the snarled nets of their grandfathers, they could only have had an expression of the mildest surprise by comparison with the look on those newsboys' faces. No one had ever suggested such a thing. I would guess that no one had conceived of it other than Schwimmer herself. A shudder started somewhere and ran through the whole group as if they had, with a single appalled sense, sucked on a whole barrel-load of pickled limes. Schwimmer had already swept out and got no idea of the full catastrophe of her mistake.

"Oh well," said J. J. O'Neill, lighting another cigarette. "If you've gotta deny it, it's gotta be a story."

I suppose I blotted my copy-book with Madame with that little performance, but I'll say one thing for her — she's no bearer of grudges. I had a visit this morning and she spoke as if nothing had ever happened. No, sir — whatever you read, my dear, there is no smallness of heart in Rosika Schwimmer. The flowers on my side table are hers too — the bill, as ever, Henry's. Reverend Marquis has been as well. After a few minutes he forgets the obligations of the sickroom visitor and drones on about his own problems. I have had some surprising confidences, Amelia, and will be very popular with the newsboys once I am on my feet again. The man is a puzzle. Of all the great excess of clergymen we brought with us I sometimes wonder if it isn't Marquis who has most completely mistaken his vocation. He hasn't got the bedside thing at all and always seems a little sadder after seeing me — and I certainly feel a little sicker. Dr Glumsmussen is here. I asked him just now if that was a tape-measure sticking out of his pocket in place of his stethoscope, but he is a humourless man. He stands by the window, a frock-coated silhouette of mourning paper, casting my dark water against a bleak light. I think the damned furnace has broken again. Amelia, my dearest, I fear the snowball fight was a mistake.

Next morning we saw beautiful, snow-capped land. The *Oscar* coasted northward all that day and through the following night. The students shouted at fishermen and waved their banner. Schwimmer practically camped in the radio office, sending out dozens of messages to all her pre-war friends and making a big deal out of the few replies. As the early darkness fell we met up with the Norwegian coastguard and took on their pilot. There was great excitement in the dining room. Appetites were off and we all hurried away to pack and to look out the one clean set of clothes we had been saving for disembarkation. The newsboys made their final attack on the bar and swore a fraternal oath never to set foot on European soil before they had drunk it dry.

"I was overcharged for a replacement drive-belt in 1911," swayed Teddy Pockman of the *Tribune*. "If I don't get myself a full refund tonight I never will. Hey there, Lloyd, you're looking better. How's that famous wife of yours doing?"

Trunks and suitcases began to stack up in the gangways. Matrons twittered and ran from cabin to cabin brandishing passports hours before they were needed.

"Grace, Edith — call me at once if anything happens. I'll not be sleeping."

At four in the morning we gathered before the approaching lights of a harbour. The *Oscar* crept into her berth, a team of her own crew climbing down to secure the cables. The scene lifted our shivering spirits — the homes and workshops of landliving creatures, the smell of it, steep roofs thick with snow and all the charm and strangeness of a department-store window at Christmas. An annunciation painted on a stolen bedsheet was unrolled over the side while a student played a hymn on a trumpet.

"Hey — there's someone. Ask him."

A man packing fish in wooden boxes was, beside ourselves, the only life to be seen. One of the newsboys spoke up.

"*Entschuldigung*, Bud — you know anything about these fruits? Peace Ship, Henry Ford, mediation, stopping the war, anything at all?"

There was a shrug and a reply of several words in the middle of which only a heavily accented "Ford" stood out as meaningful. We looked to Madame Malmberg, our stately and many-tongued Finnish exile.

"He says he used to have one and it was all right although sometimes it wouldn't start in the winter. He now drives a Renault. You can get more fish in a Renault."

"That's all?" asked Rosika.

"That's all."

"Well," explained someone, "it *is* four in the morning."

"And it *is* twelve degrees below zero."

"And he *is* only a fisherman."

"And it's Sunday, too."

All would still be well. Five hours later, as the Norwegian day struggled out of darkness, we were indeed welcomed by a small delegation of local campaigners. The women all looked like Schwimmer's long-lost sisters and the handful of men bore a discouraging likeness to our various padres. Some local journalists came with them and, after asking forlornly if they could see Mr Ford, were guided away by their American colleagues to the discretion of the palm-screened bar and a great deluge of advice as to what they should put in their papers. There was talk of a reception in the evening — arrangements were in hand, the students of the university were highly excited and the townspeople agog for their first sight of the great man. The manager of the Grand Hotel plucked the dust sheets from his fifty best rooms, the occupation of which he had not hoped to see again before the end of the war. Spring came early to the hearts of high-class provisioners, tip-starved waiters and general vendors of the unnecessary. In short, as the sun rose over a cloudless, crystalline scene and we put our feet on the salted stones of the quayside, the circus had come to town.

"No, no, no."

Ford waved away the taxi Marquis had summoned for him. The curate of industrial souls looked worried. He went aside with the impassive bodyguard and had a few words with him. Their mutual master would not be moved.

"Nonsense! A walk is exactly what I need. Walking is a powerful medicine. Walking is what I haven't had enough of these last ten days."

It's a strange thing, my dear, but I have come to feel oddly connected to Henry Ford. When he weakens, I too weaken. When he is up, the same energy surges through me. There are times when he seems to have more than any one man can contain and it spills out to everyone around him. People sort of tune up with him — they feel like him, think like him, they fall into step by his side and are carried along that bit faster as they get a little of what it must be like to be Henry Ford. So you see, Amelia — you really mustn't worry. Even if I should not write or wire for a few days you only have to look in the paper to see how I am. If our Henry is doing well, you'll know that I'm just fine.

"Here's one, girls!"

Schwimmer invaded the taxi Ford had just turned down. She summoned Madame Malmberg, Mrs Fels and Rebecca Shelly to join her. The magnetic Miss Inez Milholland took a step in their direction, then looked elsewhere as the door on the inner sisterhood slammed shut. We heard an umbrella being stoutly rapped on the roof and the words "Grand Hotel!" falling on the driver like the stroke of a whip. The car jumped and made off with a spurt of slush from its hobnailed tyres.

"It must be this way."

The miraculously refuelled Ford followed in its tracks with an entourage of people half his age struggling after. Around me there gathered a jam of taxis and luggage sleds drawn by shaggy, steaming ponies. No Hoboken this — no freaks, bands, fainters, thieves, swimmers after publicity, self-seekers, chaos or squirrels, with the single honourable exception of little William Jennings Bryan shivering in his cage as he dangled from the lilac-gloved hand of the new Mrs Braley.

"This was your idea, Berton. *All* yours. Where the hell is this place, anyway?"

Instead, the calm tagging and loading of luggage, the steady bearing away of the Ford Peace Party by taxi-loads of threes and fours as if our sort arrived from America twice a week and had done for as long as anyone could recall. I squeezed into a horse-drawn sled beside the Braleys and a heap of suitcases. Off we went, jingling through snow-banked streets, gaps cut in the white walls wherever there was a door. Halfway, we ran up behind Ford, Marquis, the bodyguard, a ruddy Louis Lochner, a dozen of the newsboys and the magic bearded Reverend Jones. Ahead of them McClure strode out, his perpetually overwound mechanism stamping into the snow. The intrepid Inez Milholland straggled between the two, skipping every third step to keep up with the fallen magazine king. Braley stood up and cracked an imaginary whip between the ears of our plodding, one-horsepower engine.

"Huzzah! Clear the way there."

An elated, humorous Ford shook his fist at us.

"Roadhogs."

"Come on!" shouted Inez.

She picked up her skirts and ran, quickly outpacing McClure and very nearly us too. The whole thing descended into a preposterous race to the hotel and I laughed until I couldn't breathe.

By the time we arrived at the hotel a couple of dozen had got there before us and the local press made up the numbers until the lobby was crammed with bodies and shouting. Ford's arrival, as usual, set a match to the whole thing. The warmth sort of got to me all of a sudden and I toppled into the nearest chair as the journalists threw questions and a happy Ford fired out all the grand phrases he had been saving, ten to the dozen. Lochner waved his hands and tried to get some order in it all.

"No, he didn't mean that. Mr Ford is very tired. Interviews later, please — there'll be plenty of time for everyone. Interview requests to the Peace Party Staff, please."

Only no one was paying the blindest bit of attention and the local reporters started to fight each other for the three telephone cabins. While this entertainment developed nicely a worried young man with brass on his tunic tried to explain that I had tumbled by sacriligious mischance into the ever-to-be-empty chair of the late Henrik Ibsen, onetime habitué of the Christiania Grand Hotel. This no doubt accounted for the sensation of a thread breaking beneath my ample rump as I restored some human warmth to the great playwright's station.

"Ah, Ibsen," I declared. "The source, you know, of some of my wife's finest triumphs."

I went on, of course. I gave him your full due, my dear, you may be sure of that, but it required more English than he had at his disposal and I soon settled for being moved to a leather sofa closer to the fire.

Keys flew through the air and just failed to blind me.

"Hey, Lloydy-boy! Room 102 — the best in the west. Come on."

I struggled to the edge of the sofa and failed to stand — tremulous, hamstrung.

"Give me a hand here."

So there I was — half dragged to the elevator between two uncaring pillars of health.

"You need a rest, Lloyd, a good long rest — that's all."

Everyone around me is a doctor now. Ah, my dear, what a scene it was — affecting would not be too strong a word. And yet my hopes now are brighter than for years. I am on the very threshold of my late, great phase. I ripen into the full measure of good John Falstaff's costume. Amelia, my love, just wait till I get home — what a terror it will be. For a generation no one will dare play the part after me — if only I can shake this thing, escape this bed and this damned Norwedish coffin-carver coming at me with his stolen stethoscope. At least this will be something for you to savour, Amelia. The irony will not be lost — ready for Falstaff, trapped instead in some interminable Scandinavian stage-wake any sane man would take poison not to have to sit through. Pay no attention, Amelia. I talk nonsense, I fumble with the sheets and play with flowers.

Two days ago I still had strength. After a half-hour's rest on this bed I was up again and in the flow. The corridors filled with laundry bags, steam billowed from bathrooms as we washed away the voyage. We mobbed the dining room, devastated the larders. At least the young people did. We older ones were still queasy and my own long-suffering stomach would take nothing more than a few crackers, a horse-trough of coffee and a balloon of best French brandy.

"Put that on my bill, Olga."

Everyone agreed it was not the time to start skimping on universal peace. The man with his name on the world's biggest hotel bill sat at a round table in the middle of us all, serene in the sunlight, objecting to nothing. Then Lochner was on his feet calling for quiet. Some nonsense about refreshing hearts and minds, rebuilding harmony, clearing metaphorically cluttered metaphorical desks for the great task ahead. What it all amounted to was that before getting down to work there would be an expedition up a mountain and a chance for everyone to get their land legs back.

The idea seemed a little less ridiculous once I learned we were to take an electric railway to the top. A festival atmosphere quickened to near hysteria as we gathered outside the hotel.

"Has someone read the papers today?"

Fingers were jammed childishly into ears.

"Not listening, not listening, not listening, not listening!"

No one had.

"We'll miss the train."

The train, chartered just as the *Oscar* had been, was waiting for us. Like factory workers on their annual day of forgetting, we jammed into this elaborate toy. Its electric motors hummed, the air filled with ozone and lightning crackled from the power rail. Up front, Mr Ford leaned from a window, charmed by the mechanism and talking all the time to himself about its good and bad points and what he would improve and what would never catch on. Gears meshed and slowly we began to move. We ticked and whirred our way up an impossibly sugar-white mountain, past the gingerbread Holmenkollen church and on into a perfect, Christmas-card blue. At the top, a Norwegian Sunday — everything white and blue and the deep green-blackness of the trees, everyone young and beautiful and impossibly healthy, blond hair whizzing by on skis, girls exotic in tinted snow goggles, and ourselves, the Ford Peace Expedition on our improving mission, out of place, unequipped, skittish as the snowballs started to fly. Was the air too thin, Amelia? Should I have eaten more for breakfast, or have I been away too long from you, my strength? Was it the well-aimed shot from — from who knows? — that finally tipped my balance, setting off that private earthquake beneath my feet as I bent to scoop up a retaliatory handful only for the world to turn sideways and the blue sky to fill everything and a dark circle of heads to gather round and talk in distant voices.

"Jeez! His face is the same colour as the snow."

"You're going to be all right, Lloyd. You're going to be just fine."

Shifting, grunting, cracks about my weight. Then I'm shoulder high and being borne down to the boardwalk halt where the train waits to unwind itself back down the mountain. A taxi, the welcome, blessed heat of the hotel, a practised commotion among the staff as the doctor is summoned. I find my tongue and tell everyone not to bother, not to make such a fuss. The diamond-patterned grill of the elevator gates closes across my face. There is movement, but my legs feel light.

"He's going," says someone right in my ear. "He's going."

I found myself here, in this soft bed, in this hot and cold Scandinavian room so very far away from the only thing that could bring me comfort. I'm sorry, my dear, I was about to break our old rule — whatever happens, definitely no self-pity. And for how long in this room which now bores me more than I have ever been bored before? I can't count. Is it day or night?

Marquis was here a while ago — to do his duty. I spoke to him the two words I most wanted to say in the world. I beckoned with a finger, with the expression on my face and he leant close and turned his ear to my dry mouth. Marquis, you should know, is a proud and a dull, dull man. He doesn't think anyone like me can tell him anything. But I did. Oh, my dear Amelia, I did.

I wonder what time it is with you. Is it evening yet? Are the house lights dimming, is the curtain about to rise? I think it must be that time again, for here comes our comedy doctor with a mirror in his hands. Not so close — how can I see?

My dear, it's the strangest thing — I don't believe I even have the strength to close my eyes.

Marquis

My mind worries endlessly at a scene I dread, but that must come soon. I am home in America, on the train to Detroit travelling to that painful meeting. Will it be in the town house, or out at Dearborn with me splashing across the track to the half-built mansion, Clara standing in the cold to greet me? Inside everything is proper, dignified exactly as I would expect. Edsel is there, of course, standing throughout as the man of the house. He is weighed down but shows no emotion. Clara is the strongest of the three.

"I don't blame you, Samuel," I have her say to me. "There was nothing more you could have done."

There, with such an unsatisfactory self-acquittal, my imagination fails.

The truth is, if it goes badly I will be more to blame than it appears from the outside. I have known for some time that one of Mr Ford's axioms is to do the perfect opposite of whatever I suggest to him. I believe he is attempting to escape something in his own life, and it is my misfortune to remind him of whatever that thing is. And so when I urged him on the freezing quayside to take a taxi to the hotel it was decided that he must walk. When the others prepared for their winter train-ride and I pleaded with him to stay behind and regain his strength, I might as well have pushed him up that mountain myself.

Two days here and I already look back on the crossing as a period of relative sanity. With a fresh infusion of local press and Madame Schwimmer perched recklessly in the driving seat we have returned to the near-continuous frenzy of Hoboken pier and the Biltmore Hotel. After the unnecessary walk to the Grand Hotel things deteriorated further with an impromptu press conference by the check-in desk. Unfortunately, Mr Ford had been thinking up some new phrases.

"If we can save just one boy it will all have been worth while."

"One by Christmas, Mr Ford?"

Louis Lochner tried to limit the damage, but it did little good. The least sympathetic of the Norwegian newspapers distributed lottery tickets with its morning edition, advising readers to send them to the front so the lucky Ford soldier could be fairly chosen. An accompanying cartoon showed the winner of life returning to a Carl Larsson family on Christmas morning in his complimentary Model T while the fire and smoke of war still billowed over a distant horizon.

While Schwimmer got down to the business of organising the first publicity events a stupendous landfall breakfast took place, by the end of which I had suffered my second failure of the day. I don't know how the project started, but by the time any reasonable advice could be given it had gained a juvenile momentum of its own and was impossible to stop. Mr Ford showed little interest in the mountain trip until he learned that it involved an electric train. Then, in my efforts to dissuade him from going, I made a mistake in risking too bold a use of Mrs Ford's name. When he was at his weakest on the ship he was amenable and willing to listen, but with the excitement of arrival and the prospect of new mechanical experiences he drifted once again back into the world of Schwimmer and young Lochner. I confessed to him my secret purpose — that I had not come out of any belief at all in the prospects of success, but solely because his wife had asked me, charging me, at all costs, with bringing him home alive and well.

"It is all she cares about, Henry, and right now it is all I care about too."

I compounded my mistake by referring to his son. As we waited in the lobby of the hotel I had to endure his response, certainly loud enough to be overheard.

"You won't tell me what is good for me, Dr Marquis, and by God you won't tell me what is good for my wife."

Patience was needed, as well as what the generals far to the south of us might call a tactical withdrawal. Mr Ford boarded the train at the front, I at the back. There we were — as harshly exposed in that too-brilliant northern light as at any time since the whole miserable idea was planted in Mr Ford's mind. Our leader lectured us on why electric power had no future and instructed the fawning Lochner to arrange meetings with local manufacturers. Mr Bingham, sporting something like an engine-driver's cap, pulled an imaginary cord and made chesty impressions of a steam whistle. Off we went, to a destination no one had ever heard of and for an obscure purpose on which none of us could agree. No one mentioned the war. My depression deepened when I remarked obliquely on this fact to Samuel McClure and even he seemed not to have the slightest idea of what I was talking about. The old campaigner has found his own way to make a fool of himself. He has become inseparable from his new companion Miss Milholland, a woman already assumed by the hotel staff to be his daughter and one who, according to the journalists' gleeful rumour, is prepared to pay more than just a financial price to get into print.

So there I was, as solitary and joyless as the one sober man in a party of drunkards, silent and sullen and adding, no doubt, to the overall comedy of the scene. At the top, I should think no more than fifteen minutes passed before poor Mr Bingham collapsed. After another short delay while it was established that this was not a joke, disordered attempts at rescue began. I watched these from a distance (there were already too many hands), and thought more about my own light-headed unconcern than the events themselves. They struck me as disasters must have struck the ancients, unforeseen to be sure, but always vindicating prophecy.

The journalists formed a team and gave orders and pushed the others away as they got beneath their helpless friend. I followed them down to the train station, dawdling to let Mr Ford go ahead so that I could keep him constantly in sight. I thought of home and all that would have to be done to get back there, and what story I would have to tell. Was Mr Ford paler than usual, was that a stumble, was that cough sinister? My nerves frayed. Mentally, I worded telegrams I prayed I would never have to send.

By the time we regained the hotel Bingham had rallied and there was jocular talk of too much whisky at breakfast. His legs moved weakly as two of the newsmen held his weight and guided him towards the elevator. He rambled through a mixture of jokes and apologies, making little sense in either vein. I concentrated on Mr Ford and found him, as he cast his own fearful eye on the stricken entertainer, willing to be shepherded up to his room and straight to bed.

I was reassured to make the acquaintance of Dr Rasmussen, the hotel's excellent physician. He moved quickly from one sickroom to the other, drawing me aside in the corridor for a confidential word on Bingham before attending to Mr Ford.

"I have concerns, sir, I will not conceal them from you — but perhaps we may yet avert a crisis. I am glad you did not wait any longer before consulting me. Can I ask you, is there money for a nurse?"

A nurse was engaged immediately and two others retained in preparation for the night and early shifts.

Dr Rasmussen is a perfect dictator in medical matters and he cleared Mr Ford's room of all unnecessary persons with a few words and an emphatic gesture. He scowled at me as I lingered in closing the door, looking past him to where his patient lay on the bed, very pale and ready, it seemed to me, to be under another man's authority if only for a few minutes. A large and indecently curious crowd assembled in the corridor outside. The journalists shifted like runners waiting for the gun. They consulted their watches, never changed from New York time, and calculated distances to the telephones — some loitered by the stairs, others put their money on the elevator. Anecdotes of newsworthy deaths were exchanged — how that old fox J. P. Morgan had scooped them from beyond the grave, his mortal remains cooling in a Roman hotel bedroom long past the evening deadline on the other side of the world. They looked suspiciously at the door to Mr Ford's room — what story was breaking on the other side of it, what dastardly plot being cooked up to deny the newspaper readers of the world their rights? Dr Rasmussen emerged and cast an expressionless eye over us all before finally settling on me.

"You are in authority here?"

He drew me apart and gave a brief résumé of what he had found before handing over a note of his fees and heading for the stairs.

"He's fine," I said to the journalists. "It's nothing but a cold and the chest is clear. There is no cause for concern."

There was a general exodus in the direction of the bar, where death would no doubt draw a line under their credit as well as Mr Ford's life.

Lochner and I went in to find the bed empty and steam drifting through the open doorway of the bathroom. Mr Ford gave instructions to his bodyguard, who had clearly been admitted also to the intimacies of the valet, while we sat outside in the main room of the suite. From my position, the narrow neck and greying head could just be seen in misty outline above the rim of the bath.

"What did I tell you?" he demanded. "Nothing to worry about."

"Dr Rasmussen told me you must rest. He said it was absolutely essential."

"I knew he was a charlatan. What doctor ever says you don't need him?"

"He recommended a sanatorium. A few days would put you right."

"Small men always think great men are mad. You know you're on the right track when small men say you're mad."

"A *sanatorium*, Mr Ford — for your health. It's in the mountains."

"Jesus Christ! Have I not just come down from a mountain? Does he think I didn't spend enough time up there?"

There was vigorous splashing and a terse order for a towel. I looked away just too slowly to avoid seeing the naked billionaire standing in his bath before gingerly stepping out and into the enveloping whiteness held out for him by Ray. A moment later he emerged tying the belt of a blue silk dressing gown just as young Lochner finished noting down his thoughts on madness.

"Whose fool idea was that anyway — the mountain thing?"

Neither of us knew.

"Well, it doesn't matter now. I expect Rasmussen owns the sanatorium. I expect it's the Rasmussinovitch sanatorium, the Rabinovitch sanatorium more likely. You've got to be on your guard against these things. Anyway, I'm better now."

At that moment, still pink from the heat of his bath, it seemed true.

Lochner started on a report of what he and Madame Schwimmer had arranged with their local supporters. The first great public event was only hours away. The Ford Peace Party was to be the guest of the university students' association — the biggest hall in town had been hired and tickets were selling fast. Everyone of substance in Christiania was certain to be there and they had all been promised sight of the famous Mr Henry Ford. I interrupted at once, before Lochner could say another word.

"It's impossible. You can't, you absolutely can't — at night, in these temperatures, in an unheated hall. Listen to Dr Rasmussen if not to me."

I glared at Lochner, forbidding him to suggest anything that might lead Mr Ford to put himself in danger. He lay on the bed and extended his neat, bath-softened, dancer's feet to Ray, who covered them with a pair of slippers.

"It doesn't look good," he told me. "You know there's nothing I hate more than disappointing people."

Lochner jumped in with the solution.

"People will understand, Mr Ford."

"You think so?"

"Oh, yes — there's great good will towards you, sir. No one would want you to risk your health."

"You might be right. But all the same . . ."

"A day's rest, Mr Ford sir . . ."

"Two days," I interjected.

"Yes, just two days, it's all we ask. No one could ask for more than you have already given."

Lochner had quickly learned the ways of his employer. With these and a handful of similar phrases he worked like a masseur on the needs and fears of Henry Ford. The maker of three hundred thousand cars a year lay back on his pillows and allowed surrender momentarily to ease his features. Lochner persisted.

"It's all a matter of how it's handled. With the right words it's no problem at all. You must send the people a message, Mr Ford. Tell them — well, tell them you will look the people of Norway in the eye and talk to them of peace before you move on."

"That's good. Yes, tell them I said that."

His words became vague at the end and he seemed suddenly to be very tired.

"Square it with the boys downstairs, won't you, Louis? No misunderstandings."

Lochner was leaving when he was given one further instruction — to get the desk clerk to send up the Wall Street closing prices from the wires.

When the door closed I was entirely alone with Henry for the first time since the night before our departure from New York. I had failed then to put any doubt in his mind and he now gave me a look that conveyed how ashamed I should feel for finally having run him to ground. I decided to be ruthless.

"Do you think you should send a telegram to Mrs Ford? I know you get on well with the reporters but they are apt to exaggerate. I'm concerned that she shouldn't read something unduly worrying in the papers. Perhaps if I found the right words . . . ?"

"Sure," he said to me. "Say something fancy so she knows it comes from you."

"I really think it would be a good idea — for Edsel too. For the company."

"Well, do it! Where is this damned war, anyway? Did someone make it up?"

"The papers are full of Turkey, Baghdad."

"Why? Why don't they report the war? I know why they don't report the war — it's too profitable, that's why — and you know who for, don't you?"

My hopes rose. I knew from occasions in the past how he would return to harping on old themes and how these oubursts would often precede moments of weakness or, as others saw it, of reluctant reasonableness. I saw how he suffered from the sudden, chilly withdrawal of romance, from the intrusion of questions too long held at bay by excitement and novelty and thoughtless optimism — what was he *really* doing here, just how many miles was he from home and how in God's name had this whole cockeyed thing happened at all?

The day had clouded over and the light was already dying. From the window I looked down on a scene of blue-grey bleakness and people hurrying away to shelter. From its damp edges, crystals of ice had started to grow across the glass. I switched on another table lamp, the effect of which was only to give the impression that night had fallen with the abruptness of the close of an eye. Mr Ford gathered his robe around his shoulders and gloomily regarded his surroundings.

"You go ahead and do that telegram home. Sign it for me."

I was about to leave when he started on a question, then halted after the first word and said at once that it was nothing.

"There's something else I can do for you?"

He glared at me resentfully, accused me of enjoying the situation and then asked, "How is Gingham?"

"Mr Bingham? He's . . ."

I recalled Dr Rasmussen's words and decided that their blandness, their hint of encouragement were not at all what was needed. Some embellishment was in order — for the common good. I shook my head in grim resignation.

"Very grave, I'm sorry to say, very grave indeed. It's a sad state of affairs — he is hardly older than I am, a few years younger than yourself. Still a young man, some would say, and then comes a sudden chill on the chest and what can be done . . .? Sad indeed — but I must let you rest."

I left my employer to stew in mortality.

As there seemed, in truth, nothing about the condition of either man to keep me at the hotel, I wrapped myself in half the clothing I had and joined the others tramping through the streets of Christiania to the first great public announcement of the plan to end the war. Madame Schwimmer had begun her work earlier in the afternoon, returning from a private meeting with the Norwegian chapter of the Women's International Peace League bearing tidings that would have made the angel of the annunciation a miserable pessimist by comparison. Reason had returned to Europe the moment her own dainty, Ford-funded foot had stepped off the *Oscar*. A new light shone from the heavens and was already doing its humane work. The evening meeting was to be an altogether larger affair and, I assumed, a tougher test. I was keen to witness it for myself and to make sure that Mr Ford received my version of events as well as others.

In the company of a sombre Reverend Lloyd Jones (he claimed to have some knowledge of the next morning's newspapers), I followed the flow, turning the last corner to find the place already full and a crowd of mostly young people milling around outside. The advent of Mr Ford had not failed to bring with it an entrepreneurial spirit and we had to part with two kroner to be allowed in. The better sections of Christiania society packed the interior. It may have been true that there was nothing much on at the theatre that evening, but the turnout was impressive all the same and the audience just dense enough to bring a little warmth to the air. Standing in a side aisle I recognised the American Minister to Norway, looking apprehensive and perhaps a little bemused by how his obscure office had been so suddenly thrust into activity. I regarded him with sympathy as he endured his own minor case of what can only be described as the Ford effect. He had brought his stenographer to make a record of this private diplomacy and would no doubt be exchanging more telegrams with Washington over the next week than in all the last six months together.

His account of what followed will have caused no great anxiety in the State Department. Things started badly when Lochner explained Mr Ford's absence. There was politeness and concern and unconcealed disappointment. Ford was the image they had come to gaze on and without him the price of admission weighed more heavily on the audience's mind. The affair deteriorated further as Reverend Jones led prayers in a manner suspiciously unfamiliar. An earnest lecture on the Christian duty to be a peacemaker recovered no ground at all. Miss Wales followed with a technical account of continuous mediation. May I be forgiven for recording it, but the truth is she is a woman of rare dullness and the translator clearly did an excellent job in conveying this to her listeners. There was a steady crescendo of shifting and sighing. There was folding of the arms and glances over shoulders towards the exit. There was thought, no doubt, of the many small and necessary tasks that remained to be done at home, of the warm beds that are man's supreme pleasure on a winter's night. I looked across at the American Minister. All anxiety had left his face and his stenographer had ceased to write. The Ford peace expedition looked set to be the most complete and untroubling failure. I do believe he even smiled as he contemplated the phrases with which he would fill out his confidental report. Perhaps he would get Paris next time, or Berlin? Some reward would be in order for these good tidings, surely.

It was left to Madame Schwimmer to turn the tide. She laboured mightily and had a certain effect, there's no denying. But even she struggled, nearly losing her poise altogether as she stood with arms outstretched, breathing heavily in a moment of pregnant silence only for the gap to be filled by a burst of laughter from the back. You would have thought that Schwimmer alone had not heard this disastrous interruption so smoothly did she carry on, but I was close enough to see the sweat run down her face and the heart-racing tremor in her hand. She and her sort are not for me — all the same, as I watched her work to pull back everything she had lost in that savage moment and make the whole hopeless dream seem possible again, she forced no little admiration from me and I willingly joined the applause at the end.

It was Lochner who saved the day. Tempering passion with reason, he found the right tone for his sceptical Scandinavian audience. His explanations were credible without being tediously detailed. He did not shed tears, clutch at his heart or contort his features with a personal agony. He frightened no one and could just about be imagined sitting in a foreign ministry conducting a conversation with men of power and being listened to. The people of Christiania concluded there was only one Rosika Schwimmer in the Ford Peace Party and gave it their blessing.

At the end, those who had spoken came to the front of the stage, joined hands and bowed like actors. The applause swelled, the students shouted and cheered. People were already leaving when Schwimmer called for quiet and astonished everybody, not least those in the inner circle of the Peace Party, by declaring that Mr Ford had decided to donate ten thousand dollars to good causes in every city they visited and the students could do with this money whatever they thought best. Then came a bizarre coda to the evening's events. Singing broke out and the spaces left by the older members of the audience were filled as the young crowd pushed in from where it had been waiting in the cold for the last two hours. The smell of strong drink suffused the air. Chanting started as there emerged from the back of the hall the gilded effigy of an enormous pig carried on poles by four students. The bearers made the pig dance as the chanting and the clapping and the stamping grew louder. The golden pig approached the stage and bowed in gratitude for Henry Ford's ten thousand dollars. Madame Schwimmer bowed to the pig. For a few moments the war, if not stopped, had at least been forgotten.

At the hotel I found a solemn Dr Rasmussen waiting for me in the lobby. Upstairs in Bingham's room the transformation to hospital was complete. The air was stifling and pungent with antiseptic. White-uniformed nurses were changing shift and moved about their work with an ominous, studied quiet. Bingham lay on his back, his face and neck very red and with a sheen of perspiration. He snored, but strangely.

"He is asleep," I said hopefully.

"No, he is unconscious."

Dr Rasmussen applied his stethoscope.

"I am sorry, but there is an infection in your friend's lungs. In both of them. Listen."

He tapped Bingham's chest in several places, so firmly that I was sure his patient would wake up and object.

"You hear that?"

"I don't . . . I know nothing about medicine."

"You know an empty bottle sounds different from a full one — it's the same. There should be air under here, but there is fluid. When I first examined Mr Bingham there was fluid only here, but now it is here and in a few hours . . ."

His hand moved further up Bingham's chest and then he shrugged and turned to look at me to make sure I understood.

"It was already serious a few hours ago, but little is certain, even in science, Reverend Marquis, and I have seen strong men survive such things. You understand why I said less than I might have done? But now, with weakness, with other illnesses . . ."

"Other illnesses?"

"Your friend has not been well for a long time. Did he not tell you that?"

"I don't know Mr Bingham well."

"I see."

"There's no chance?"

Dr Rasmussen glanced briefly at his patient to check, I suppose, that he had not regained consciousness.

"Oh, no — none at all. This man has been dying for the last week. Is it true, what I heard — that he was up at Holmenkollen this morning? Now *that* is remarkable. His case is typical in other respects, but to be on a mountain when it is already so advanced is something I have never heard of before."

I stared at the rotund and seemingly peaceful form on the bed. My mind turned to practicalities.

"How long?"

"I would say twelve to twenty hours, not likely more than a full day, though I am often wrong about these things. There could still be periods of consciousness, but they will be shorter and more widely spaced as time goes on. The breathing will become shallower and more rapid. The lungs will progressively lose their function and so it is the lack of oxygen in the blood that will be the specific cause of death. If he is aware near the end there will be nothing more than a little dizziness. It is like, well perhaps it is like how you feel if you stand up too quickly in the morning — you know?"

I nodded.

"Nothing more than that. A quarter to half an hour later death will follow. But I don't need to explain — as a clergyman you have seen this many times."

"Well, actually . . ."

"Then perhaps you will see it now, if you wish to."

He snapped his bag shut and spoke briefly to the nurse before turning back to me.

"I will look in from time to time. Your friend will not be neglected."

I followed him into the corridor and put the question that really worried me.

"And Mr Ford?"

"Ah, yes," asked the doctor. "How is he?"

For an hour I was the only member of the Peace Party to know of Bingham's certain death. I was disturbed by the conviction, however unfounded, that there must be some connection between his fate and Mr Ford's. At first I wanted to reassure myself by visiting him at once — but what if there was some contagion, or I disturbed his rest and weakened him? Was that possible, or mere nonsense? As Dr Rasmussen no doubt meant to convey, a minister of religion is not always a very useful thing to be. I had lurid thoughts of Lloyd Bingham as a dead body, weirdly multiplied in size and weight. What on earth was one to do? Who was to be informed of a dead American entertainer in a Norwegian hotel room? I had some vague notion that his wife was an actress but knew no more than that. Where was she, what would this mean to her? How, more strangely still, had he come to be involved in this? I paced my room and steeled myself for a meeting with Rosika Schwimmer.

In a suite of rooms two floors up the arrangement mimicked that of a government office. Outer chambers were filled with secretarial activity, the salt-proof typewriters already unpacked and ticking away at innumerable reports and press releases. There were new faces — young, local staff, serious as they worked on translations or reports of the Scandinavian and other continental press, the less interesting parts of which lay ankle-deep in shreds about the floor. Six telephones had been installed but perhaps not yet connected — in any case none of them rang when I was there. Room service came and went, feeding and watering those who had no right to a moment's rest. Someone I had not seen before signed for an elaborately garnished lobster. Further in, the more domestic pieces of furniture had been stacked to one side with the peremptoriness of an occupying army. Through this clutter one approached the former master bedroom, now the cabinet of Madame Schwimmer. The door was ajar and her voice could be heard in the steady rhythm of dictation. There was a pause, a thud, a flash and a curl of white smoke drifting into the outer room as the words started again. I stepped aside to let pass a pair of photographers with their bulky equipment.

"Reverend Marquis — come in, come in. Thank you, Rebecca, we'll finish this later."

Schwimmer strode rapidly to and fro before her desk. She wrung her hands energetically and looked in a vague upward direction, though not at anything in particular.

"What a triumph — a triumph! Let the doubters fly."

I asked her when Mr Ford had agreed to make his very generous donation. The question seemed trivial to her, quite without implication.

"Mr Ford is a great man. But I have more news for you — it gets better. We have momentum — what all struggling causes need, what transforms them from hopeless to unstoppable in a single day — momentum. Mr Ford has an appointment to meet the Norwegian

Foreign Minister tomorrow. There is talk of a meeting with the Prime Minister, perhaps even the King. Interest is growing in Copenhagen — I have excellent reports from our friends there. Peace is coming. It is close."

She held out her hands to beckon the timid, invisible creature that hovered just out of reach.

"I am negotiating our passage through Germany as we speak. Dr Marquis — we are Europe's new dawn come from the west."

A telephone rang.

"Excuse me, that must be Berlin now."

She returned a minute later, only a little crestfallen but with no visible loss of momentum. I didn't ask about the telephone call.

"We must get into the German newspapers and the French — we must speak to the people directly. I will handle Hungary myself, of course. Do you know people in Russia? We must have Russia!"

Madame Schwimmer had ascended to her destiny — the Napoleon of peace.

"There is something you should know."

In her elation, all news was good news and she was eager to hear it.

"Lloyd Bingham is dying."

She seemed not to have understood and I started on an explanation.

"So," she interrupted, "our vaudevillian is leaving us. I am sorry."

We were, of course, talking about the man who had ridiculed her, the man who had collaborated in the journalists' theft and rifling of her bag, the identical twin of which stood on the table at our side. A warm response was hardly to be expected.

"He must have his due and I will make sure he gets it. Peace has its casualties as well as war. Let me see now — does he know, has he said anything?"

"He's sleeping. He might not wake again."

"Then he must trust to us. I shall prepare press releases immediately. Something along the lines of — 'I die in a foreign land, far from home but with hope in my heart. I die for the greatest cause possible. I die in joy on the eve of Peace.' "

"It doesn't sound like him."

"People can change. And quite frankly, Dr Marquis, they can also be useful. A dying man should be happy to be made use of — what other compensations can he have for his condition? I think there's a wife somewhere. I'm sure a good collection of press cuttings will ease the pain. They say she is an actress, after all."

"That's what I wanted to ask you about. Where do we send the telegram, how do we ask her for instructions? I mean — does she want him back? You must have an address."

The bureaucracy over which Madame Schwimmer presided had been concentrating on other things and she thought it unlikely there was any information.

"But why was he here at all? I've never quite understood that. What was the connection, how did it happen? If it's going to end this way I just feel I should understand something."

"You know — there's something strange there. He told me once his wife had arranged it."

"Is that true?"

"No. I never heard of her before he went on and on about her. He had been drinking."

"He always seemed out of place."

"You saw yourself how it was in New York. There was a score of them or more. Mr Bingham was chosen at . . ."

She stopped and looked upwards again, vaguely scanning the cornice.

"He was drafted. Yes, that's it — a soldier for peace. Do you think he would object to being photographed?"

It all happened exactly as Dr Rasmussen had predicted. Bingham did wake from time to time and he talked good clear sense as late as four or five in the morning of his last day. Then there were ramblings and the tiring frustration with others who were too slow-witted to understand him.

"Say, Reverend — you haven't come to give me my last rites, have you? Tell the truth, I don't much hold with that sort of thing."

I denied any such intention and agreed entirely when he said he might be unwell for quite a while. I don't believe the poor man ever understood his situation and I'm glad of that. I was with him frequently, sometimes for a quarter-hour, sometimes for just a few minutes. A nurse was always there and Rasmussen kept his promise, calling in several times and making sure that he was present at the end. Reverend Lloyd Jones proved stalwart. Miss Milholland came with flowers she had found at a most unsociable hour and talked on cheeringly for a good long time, though without a word of response.

When the morning came and the hotel began to stir I was surprised that we were so completely left alone. The reason was soon clear — the rest of the party was in the dining room and the lounges downstairs already mourning Lloyd Bingham. The translated digest of the local press brought them the news that Madame Schwimmer had not been able to wait for her first martyr. An unknown Bingham was described, his passing the close of one of the great humanitarian careers of the last fifty years. The return of his corpse to the United States, it was confidently predicted, would be the occasion of national grief on a quite unprecedented scale. The temptation was understandable — who in Norway knew anything about any of us? With the exception of Mr Ford we can be whatever we please. In the last hours of Madame Schwimmer's happiness I saw no point in raising the issue with her. I was sure I knew already what her position would be. She would retreat to the possibility of shortening the war by a single day. She would ask how mere honesty could compare with the saving of one, two or five thousand young lives or whatever the last day's toll would be. Who could begrudge anything to the bearer of such an infallible moral pass-key as that? Besides, I also had my uses for the unfortunate Mr Bingham.

I spent the day busy with my own preparations, breaking off whenever I could to check in on Bingham and on my employer too. Mr Ford's physical condition improved steadily and I began to put my most exaggerated fears behind me. His mind remained dark, however, and it was no part of my plan to cheer him up. I kept him closely informed of Bingham's decline and of our difficulties in finding any relative to contact. I firmly approved the cancellation of his appointment with the Foreign Minister and generally remarked as often as I could on all matters relating to cold, dullness and discomfort. I allowed myself the occasional positive note about how well the peace campaign seemed to be doing — how well, that is, without his active participation. In spare moments I studied railway timetables and steamer schedules. I pumped the desk clerks for advice on the availability of taxis at all hours and bribed them handsomely to say nothing to anyone. I left a note for the senior night porter who, I was told, possessed the only key to the hotel safe between the hours of midnight and five a.m.

When it was learned that the entertainer still lived, his sickroom became the social centre of the Peace Party. The newsmen were the most frequent visitors, each offering lame jokes about surviving one's own obituary as if they might have the power of a spell, or what seemed to them the only sort of prayer that might work where all earthly power had failed. Several of these new acquaintances wept. All promised him an honourable mention in despatches and I feel sure that if any comfort is to be had for the widow, it will be from these brief lines wired back to the American papers rather than anything Schwimmer has had a hand in. Another public meeting in the town drew them away and so it was quiet in the afternoon when I received what were, for all I know, Lloyd Bingham's last words. I could see from the nurse that nothing more had been expected. She was surprised and quickly active about her patient as soon as there was movement in one arm, a noise in the throat and an opening of clear blue eyes. She spoke in her own language, then asked in English if he was in pain. Bingham made no response but instead, with a vast effort raised a hand from the sheet and laid it on my arm. He turned his head towards me as slowly as if it were made of lead. I believe there was recognition.

"What is it, my friend — is there something we can do for you?"

He started to speak and I leant closer to hear the words . . .

"More clowns. If only you had brought more clowns."

His hand slipped back and his eyes closed.

The nurse thought there were still some hours to go. I spent the time packing, at one point standing immobile before a half-filled suitcase as someone knocked on my door. How could I explain it if they came in? It was, undoubtedly, a crime scene and I waited until they left before silently turning the lock.

I envisaged what might happen — going though each of the possible obstacles and adjusting my plan point by point until they were all smoothed away. I practised glib answers to awkward questions. Where mere ambiguities would not do, I crafted lies in advance so they would be ready for immediate use. I rehearsed them to a mirror, my ears sharp for the over-eager intonation or the unnatural cadence of deceit. I drilled myself until there was no danger of stopping for a conscience-stricken swallow between one syllable and the next. I would eat with the pacifists in the evening and take an interest in what they thought tomorrow would bring. Perhaps I would add how much I was looking forward to our journey to Stockholm and then to The Hague where we would settle to our task of ending the war, turning the moral force of Henry Ford's billions on the great mystery of human self-destruction. I would drink with the newsmen in the saloon bar, share their worn opinions and agree that the best of the comedy was yet to come. To keep them all blind for another few hours was the essential thing. All that was required was a little organisation, a taxi and ten unwitnessed minutes just after four in the morning. It would be best for everyone.

I called in on Mr Ford again just to make sure there was no change in his mood. All seemed well — other appointments had been cancelled and he blew his nose frequently and complained of every little thing. He rambled on about great mechanical projects and told me he had, in the last half-hour, decided that he would start to make aeroplanes as soon as he got home.

"Aeroplanes are the future, Samuel. There will be a great demand for aeroplanes in the future. Mechanical man ascends through the elements — from land to air to . . . whatever. With the right machines man can be at home anywhere. In ten years I'll make them as cheap as cars. In thirty you'll be able to drive all the way up to heaven just for the weekend and be back in time for work on Monday morning. What do you say to that?"

The old love was reasserting itself, and in Henry Ford's heart there is only room for one at a time.

"How's that man whose name I can never remember? Is he dead yet? Are there children?"

I said I didn't know.

"Well, find out. Tell someone to find out. Is there a widow? I mean, will there be . . .?"

"A famous actress, they say."

"I'm going to do right by these people. Remind me of that, Samuel. Don't let me forget."

"They say she earns the money."

"I'll send her a car. A car is always acceptable."

I glanced again at the railway and steamer timetable I had brought in with me. Mr Ford had looked at it pointedly several times, but I had said nothing and there was now an understanding that neither of us would. I had marked it in pencil — slightly vague marks and certainly without words. They were marks one could interpret any way one pleased. They might not have any meaning at all. I laid the timetable down at the foot of the bed and forgot about it.

"You'll let me know when . . . When it's over?"

I stepped outside to find Ray close by. He confirmed that through the afternoon he had kept everyone away, twice telling Lochner that Mr Ford was asleep and once fending off Samuel McClure's demands for an interview.

"No one must see him now, do you understand? Mr Ford will be fine, but he does not want to speak to anyone — is that clear?"

"Clear enough for me."

"Just you and me, Ray — no one else."

He nodded definitely, but had no curiosity as to the purpose of these instructions.

"Tell me, Ray — are you a sound sleeper?"

"You'll have no trouble waking me, sir — any time you need me."

"I would try to get some rest early tonight. Try to get a couple of hours before twelve."

I waited for a second or two before leaving him. Surely he must have a question now, I thought, and for a moment I desperately wanted him to ask it. But, no — nothing but another nod of assent and silence. Whatever happened, Ray would be sharing none of the blame.

For half an hour I went over things in my room and listened to the soft tread of feet in the corridor outside and the dulled, recriminatory voices of the Braleys from the floor above. I paced and checked my watch and made primitive attempts to catch some hint of death in the air. What if Bingham survived against all the odds? What if he rose from his bed and told a joke and danced a jig and was taken for a sign and the life flooded back into Mr Ford too and the whole pointless cavalcade rolled on to Stockholm, Copenhagen, Berlin or the trenches on the Somme or whatever damn fool plan she had? Did such things ever happen? I prayed like a child — Oh God, why can't people just see things the way they are?

It was five o'clock. I splashed a little water on my face and stood before the mirror to straighten what needed straightening. I stepped out and turned left toward Lloyd Bingham's room, detecting the disturbing scents of illness long before arriving and finding the door open by a few inches. Inside, there was only Bingham, Dr Rasmussen and the nurse. Rasmussen leaned over his patient with a stethoscope in his ears. I hoped it was over, but as I came further into the room I could hear the faint rasping of breath and see the rise and fall of the chest. This survival exhausted me, and as there was nothing that remained to be done anywhere else I found a chair and sat down, determined to stay till the end. Dr Rasmussen sympathised with my tiredness and told me, in tones proper for the delivery of good news, that it would not be long. Checks were made every few minutes. Breathing diminished to the barely visible, then the invisible. The nurse moistened his staring eyes and closed the lids with her fingers, but still the breath laboured on.

"Has he said anything?"

The doctor smiled at my foolishness and shook his head.

Rasmussen sat at the writing table and opened his bag. He took out a form, a traveller's inkwell and an old-fashioned pen. He took his pocket-watch from where it hung at his black waistcoat and set it, face open, on the table. He sat down to write. If there was a moment, I missed it. Whether I slept or daydreamed I can't say and the next time I was aware of the room nothing seemed to have changed. Bingham lay peacefully on the bed, the whiteness of the sheets and pillow the only bright thing to be seen. Dr Rasmussen continued to fill in his form until the nurse called him over. I too went slowly to the bedside, approaching as the pulse was checked, the stethoscope applied to the rash-red skin of the chest and the eyes, once again open, closely examined. The doctor returned to his bag and took out a metal mirror which he polished on his sleeve. He held it above Bingham's face, flashing its bright reflection in his eyes before holding it steady above his nose and mouth.

"You see?" he asked as he turned its unmisted surface towards me. "It is over."

The nurse pulled up the sheet. Rasmussen checked his watch and completed his form before pushing it towards me and indicating the last blank.

"If you would be a witness, please."

I signed.

"You will need this if you wish to remove the body from the country. If you permit me, I will talk to the manager of the hotel. I know him well — he is an excellent man in these matters and will make whatever arrangements you wish. If there is property of value a notarised inventory can be useful — I have known customs officials to be difficult, particularly these days."

We both looked at the bedside table. There was an old leather pocketbook and the nickel wristwatch he had shown me on the ship. I heard his voice telling me, "I'm mad for anything new."

"Well," said the doctor as he packed up, "I will leave these things to you."

The problem of where to send the telegram bothered me again and I hoped something in the pocketbook might provide an answer. I opened it, all too conscious of the intrusion, but found nothing save a single crisp five-dollar bill and, tucked in an inside pocket where it had pressed its shape into the leather over the years, a picture card. My heart felt the shock as I eased it out and held it under the light. There was a young woman in a short brocade jacket with cuffs and lapels trimmed in white fur, a very full lace blouse and a voluminous black bodice skirt very tight about the waist. She held herself carefully in three-quarter profile with her face turned further to the right, darkening one cheek and eye which she directed coquettishly at the camera lens. Tight curls were crowned with the most extravagant millinery. In her gloved hands a parasol was opening. At her feet was the name "Amelia Bingham" and beneath, in gold cursive against the black frame — *Ogden's Guinea Gold Cigarettes*. I turned it over hoping for an address. There were only a few words handwritten over the print and a date nearly twenty years in the past.

Madame Schwimmer hoped that good things would come of Bingham's demise and I had the same intention as I carried news of it up the stairs and along the corridor, past the ever-watchful Ray and into Mr Ford's room. My parishioner has little taste for religion, being guided in his observances more by a sense of social propriety than by belief. It is not a subject he discusses, but if prompted he would explain to me how my convictions are an outmoded machine, a tangle of old horse harness in an age of automotive miracles. He would tell me how much he had created — more than any man naturally could — how his name was on every street in the civilised world, whatever gods they prayed to, how his workers eat or starve according to what he decides and how he will stop the war. In Mr Ford's religion death is never seeing his factory again, and of this he has an immeasurable fear. I found him in bed, five-day-old American newspapers scattered about and a mess of ticker-tape on the floor.

"Well?"

"Mr Bingham passed away a few moments ago. It was a very peaceful end."

He had nothing to say about this, but observed instead that the hotel was quiet and asked what he was missing.

"Another public meeting. The town hall this time — some local councillors are attending and professors from the university, I hear."

Mr Ford particularly deplores professors. He removed the spectacles he usually pretends not to need and let them drop on the coverlet.

"Were they told I would be there?"

"They know not to expect you. Your illness is in all the papers — everyone is concerned."

I was holding Lloyd Bingham's death certificate — just a piece of paper which I folded at that moment and discreetly put away. Mr Ford's eyes were rimmed with darkness, his narrow features depleted. I looked for the steamer timetable and saw a corner of it beneath one of the newspapers. There was an understanding, but would that be enough? I agonised over whether I should risk another word. Mr Ford greatly values the belief that he is the author of his own life and I have seen before how the most persuasive case comes to nothing only because it is tainted with the opinions and will of another man. Any hint that a return to America was more my idea than his would condemn us both to weeks or even months in Europe, and possibly to no return at all. I waited. I prayed. I felt for him as I watched the long, boyish adventure of not being himself slowly drain away.

"Samuel," he said to me, "I guess it's time to go home to mother."

Ray

I got this theory about men of religion. Think how it is when you're in sight or earshot of one of these characters — there are things you don't say, words you don't use, things you don't do until you're round the corner. Well, after a few years of that your average padre must end up with a pretty partial view of what folks really are. I never did yet meet one without gaps in his knowledge, or who didn't hold to notions a half-witted child would long since have given up on. Now a man in my line of work sees all the things they never catch sight of, and to my mind that gives me no little advantage in the judgement of situations. This Marquis fellow dresses well and talks even better — whatever the subject it's never long before you know about the books Reverend Marquis has read and the operas he's been to. When he says something you don't understand he seems to like it, as if he never meant you to get his drift in the first place or doesn't much care whether you do or not. But I started to wonder if he was any different from the others I've known and I guessed pretty soon he wasn't. And then he came out of Mr Ford's room not twelve hours ago and said to me, "Ray, I can trust you, can't I? It's tonight — everything's arranged, it'll all go smoothly. Just be ready for when Mr Ford needs you."

Well, then I knew there must be gaps in his knowledge too — and on more than one count. You see, it's just not in the nature of these things to go smoothly and I wouldn't have bet you a cent to a dollar it had any chance of doing so. There are contrary passions in the world, and they just are what they are. Well-meaning folk can talk them away as long as they like, but it never makes any difference that I can see. There they still are, as hot and senseless as ever. And sometimes they come together, and then there has to be a fight and all you can do is be ready for it. Marquis thought he could get round all that. He thought sneaking away in the middle of the night would be the better way. The whole thing must have been his idea — it had Sunday and sermons and "God bless you, mam" written all over it, but it ain't my gospel. Now I'm not saying that I can tell the future — it's just that I knew what was going to happen because I was the one that went and told Madame Schwimmer all about it.

"Yes, sir," I said to Reverend Dr Marquis of the Detroit Episcopal Church. "You can trust me."

But to do what? I don't believe the question ever entered his mind.

When I went to see the lady herself I cleared everyone else out of the room and shut the door and sat down without being asked and folded my arms so she couldn't see me shaking.

"Oh!" she says — I had interrupted her in the middle of making up another speech. "Oh! It's poor Mr Bingham, isn't it. Tell me the worst."

"Bingham's problems were over three hours ago — half a day after you buried him in the newspapers, from what I hear."

"That's unkind, Ray. Excuse me — I don't think I ever learned your surname. You must understand that I have always acted for the best. There are bigger things at stake and I am one of those whose role in life is to be burdened by bigger things."

"That's as may be, lady, but it's not Bingham I've come to talk about. It's Mr Ford."

"Not Mr Ford too! Oh, monstrous war — are you never satisfied?"

"Mr Ford is going to be just fine. In fact, I'd say that within a week or so he'll be back to normal."

"I thank God for it. I must talk to him, I want to tell him how well everything is going."

"Listen, Schwimmer — you're never going to talk to Henry Ford again. You're never going to get within five secretaries of him again, your calls will never be returned, your letters will come back unopened and if anyone catches you anywhere near his home without a damned good explanation you're going to end up in a police station because that's what happens to people Henry Ford doesn't want to see any more."

What followed was the longest period of silence I ever heard from Madame Schwimmer. She felt her way round the huge desk and slumped into a chair where she seemed, just for a moment, very small and beaten.

Perhaps I hadn't said any of it. Perhaps the things you didn't like about the world could be made to go away if only you were good enough at ignoring them. That was the rule all along with these people, and for Schwimmer I guess it had to be worth one last try.

"But what are you saying? I don't understand."

"I want you to get this first — what I am about to do is give you the power to destroy me. When I walk out of here all it'll take from you is one word and I'll be back where I was ten years ago just as if nothing had happened. I'll be back on the docks at four-thirty in the morning pushing old men out of the way to get a day's work at thirty cents an hour, but I'm going to do it anyway. It's simple — he's doing a runner. Marquis has arranged the whole thing. Four o'clock tomorrow morning they flit for the early boat train to Bergen. No looking the people of Norway in the eye, no spending his fortune to stop the war, no nothing. It's over."

It just wouldn't go in.

"It's not true. You hate him, I can see that. You don't care about what we're trying to do. I know him — he is a good man."

"Listen, Rosika. When Henry Ford doesn't feel like talking to his marketing director he climbs out the window of his own goddamned office. And don't tell me it isn't true — I'm the guy who sits in his car all day at the bottom of the fire escape to take him home. That's my job and in a few hours I'm going to do it again."

"It's a misunderstanding. Let me talk to him, let me give him a little strength. Someone has poisoned his mind, but when I tell him how close we are . . ."

"It's too late. He's lost interest in you, he's lost interest in the war. This is how it always is. Don't you see? None of this was ever supposed to happen. There are men whose whole purpose in life is to stop people like you getting anywhere near Henry Ford — not because they're "small people", but because they know what he's like. Normally they're pretty good at it, then someone messes up or a crank gets lucky and we all go on a jaunt. There were others, now there's this one and there'll be more in the future. He doesn't care, Rosika — he just gets bored."

There's one thing you can't take away from Rosika Schwimmer — she can take a blow as good as any eighteen-stone bare-knuckle prizefighter and press on through to the bell like it was nothing. I saw that when she picked herself up after Bingham ridiculed her in front of all those newsmen, and I saw it again just then as she got her breath back and her mind right on the job.

"So," she says to me, "what about the money?"

I shrugged, said I knew nothing about it, that I kept away from all that. She pressed me, asking if I had heard anything at all about it, had it been mentioned, would Mr Ford really cut off the cause of world peace without a cent?

"You really want my advice? Say nothing about the money. There's an even chance that whatever you're getting now you'll still be getting in six months' time, if only because no one back in Detroit notices the cost of half a dozen cars a day out of a couple of thousand. Let him forget about you and he'll forget about the money too. People don't get the money, Rosika. They think it's commitment, but that's not it at all. To Mr Ford it simply isn't worth anything."

We were standing together by the door. She asked one more time if she could speak to him but showed no surprise when I refused. I began to make my excuses, telling her it would be better for everyone if I got back before questions were asked. She half opened the door and then closed it again and took a step closer so that I had to look straight down on her small, unnerving form. She put her hand on my arm.

"You believe in us, don't you, Ray? You believe we can make peace. Why don't you come with us?"

"You really want to know why I'm here? It wasn't part of my plan, but you asked so I'll tell you. It's got nothing to do with you or your rainbow-chasing peace project. I came here because you and I are a pair. Before Henry Ford took me up I was nothing and when he's finished with me I'll be nothing again, just like you. What he's going to do to you tomorrow morning, he'll do to me one day, sure as death. When that happens I'll want to tell myself there was five minutes in the whole damned ride when I wasn't owned. Well, that was my five minutes."

"Come with us, Ray. It can be more than five minutes."

That's another thing about Rosika Schwimmer — she can deal out the blows just as well as she can take them. I guess that was how she got her whole strange crew together in the first place, Mr Ford included — stirring them up, then promising each one she had the balm for what ailed them. I tried to look as if it hadn't got through, but I reckon everyone who's lived a bit has got that spot — that special place so that however cleverly you say it isn't there, the words still come out like a cry of pain.

"You can't afford my services, Rosika. You don't need them neither — you'll never be important enough for anyone to assassinate. Goodnight."

I spent time in my room, counting off the minutes until the journey home could start. Dulled voices came through the wall — Marquis mostly, and the occasional word from the captive Mr Ford. I got to thinking — why did it have to be this way, why not a speech to everyone, thanks, a big fat cheque and best wishes for the future? Why not in daylight? Then again, why does he still climb out of his window rather than call through to his secretary and cancel the appointment? Things way back, I suppose — the things that make folk as they are. You need more than a billion dollars to change that.

I slept a little and tried to forget Rosika's words and that look on her face as she said them — ". . . more than five minutes." You got to ask yourself — who else but Rosika Schwimmer could have brought us here, to this? The woman's got qualities. What you would call them exactly, I don't know — but she's got them. Was it so impossible — going with them and making peace, or at least feeling good while we tried? I started to see the moment. The taxi door would slam with me still on the outside and I make some big-sounding speech through the window.

"Mr Ford, sir — you may have all the money in the world but I've got what you ain't — principles, a heart, love for my fellow man, and I'm staying."

People love that stuff. I could look real serious and wag my finger at him and then someone would hold the words up on a board and everyone would cheer. I started to think maybe I should go west and get a job in the pictures — they say all you have to do is look human. How hard can that be? My mind wandered to places it hadn't been for ten years and I found myself again and again pulled back to the moment it all changed. There are the railings and the batons, the fire-hoses and the rank steam rising from the crowd of men on the other side. There is the face of that scrawny guy I've got by the collar — not pushing him away any more like the others but pulling him towards me, dragging his miserable features hard up against the iron of the railings till we're damn near skin to skin as I swing at him and he's calling me everything evil he can think of and I turn to see why they're opening the gates and there, in that fixed, powder-flash clarity is all I can remember of my first sight of Mr Henry Ford. What did I think then, and what did I think a day later when I came out of his office feeling like . . . well I don't know — something like what those big tent preachers go on about when God has been talking to them? I felt like I would never be on the wrong side of those railings again. And that, I suppose, is the heart of it. Own myself for more than five minutes? I like to talk that stuff, but the truth is I owned myself for thirty years up till that day. I just didn't make anything of it — not like Mr Ford has.

I awoke stiff and seedy from sleeping in my clothes and thinking I must have heard something. There was another timid knock at the door and the sound of Marquis hissing my name. I checked the time — twenty after three. The door handle turned furtively and there he was with his coat buttoned up and his hat and gloves on and an unhappy Mr Ford by his side, clutching his lapels around his neck and starting to shiver with nerves.

"Ray, are you ready?"

He froze for a few seconds, testing the silence.

"Come on, everything's fine," he told me. "The taxi should be waiting. We'll be at the station in no time."

He reached out to call the elevator, pushed the button a second and then a third time and swore. A few minutes passed as we retreated into Mr Ford's room and Marquis summoned night porters and organised an eight-man baggage train down the main staircase. They were hardly clumsy, but Marquis made things worse by loudly shushing them and wincing with every tiny noise.

There was something comical about it as I watched them creep down. What was waiting for Mr Ford and his friend in the lobby? I couldn't be sure and didn't even know what to hope for — an easy end to it, or the full melodramatic works. What would Rosika Schwimmer choose?

Either way there was another thing Marquis didn't know. His habits always took him early to bed and he never understood that the Ford Peace Party had quite a night life, whether it be in the form of newsmen drinking and arguing, political and social debaters who never knew when to stop, or the young folks sneaking from room to room when there was no one but me around to see. All in all I reckoned his chances of getting clean away were no better than zero.

"You go on," I said to them both. "I'll give the room one last check."

They went out of sight around the turn of the stairs, inching down a step at a time behind two porters with a steamer trunk. I leaned back, lit a cigarette and waited. What would the first sound be? The farce of a trunk falling down the stairs and sleepy people coming from all directions to see what was up? Or would it be the opening phrases of Rosika's great speech as she put some steel into the boss and changed his mind for him? It turned out a little different in the end.

It was Marion Braley who set the fireworks off. Everyone knew the first few days of married life had been a disappointment to this young lady. Her voice was shrill and often carried beyond the walls of cabin or hotel room as she made her complaints. Even at four in the morning it was not unusual to hear her, and so I paid no attention at first. Then I realised she was really letting it rip and if there had ever been a chance of a clean getaway Marion was about to ruin it. I start to go down and I'm just getting to the first floor when the Braleys' door bursts open. There's Marion in her nightdress not giving a damn about anything. She's crying and screaming all at once and I duck as a shoe flies by and bounces off the wall.

"You bastard, Berton Braley! Ten days — ten days married and *this*, you bastard."

I try to get past her, but she doesn't even see me and wanders in my way as she tears this piece of paper to shreds and throws them back towards the room. Berton shouts something I don't catch, but it only makes Marion more mad.

"It is *not* a work of art, Berton Braley. It's not even a poem, you bastard — it's a love letter!"

Berton comes stumbling out, half tripping over himself as he stuffs his shirt tails into his pants.

"For Christ's sake, Marion, do you want to wake the whole damned . . ."

He sees me and freezes. Doors are opening everywhere, lights are coming on, ordinary folks coming out and asking questions or complaining in several languages. Half a flight of stairs down Marquis is shouting, "Go on, go on." Someone stumbles over a valise and for a few seconds they go nowhere. Berton notices them for the first time and walks past his new wife to look over the bannister. Twenty other assorted guests of the Christiania Grand Hotel do the same. They find the Reverend Dr Marquis of Detroit and Mr Henry Ford in a jam of baggage, dressed for escape and looking back up at them with two of the worst poker faces in the whole history of the world, caught like they were no more than a couple of bums who couldn't pay the bill. Berton forgets all about his domestic troubles and tries instead for a career-making story.

"Would you say something to the readers of *Collier's Magazine* before you go, Mr Ford? Have you changed your mind about peace? Were your critics right all along? Should America join the war?"

Foreigners mill about trying to find out what's going on, Marion speechifies about her louse husband and the worst mistake of her life, Berton hustles for a quote from the boss as Marquis bullies the porters.

"Pick it up, get a move on!"

They do exactly that and go down out of my sight, turning to the last flight of stairs where they can be seen from the lobby. There's an ambush of noise and camera flashes. Rosika has elected for the big scene and it's her voice that cuts through the chaos.

"Be strong, Mr Ford. Be all you can be — don't be dragged down by the little people!"

Lochner's voice is in there somewhere too and I can pick out six or seven of the newsmen all shouting questions at once. The bearded reverend starts to sing. Pretty much the whole damned expedition has been lying in wait — thanks to me. Marquis's voice is suddenly loud — he's losing his grip.

"Get away from him you stupid woman — haven't you done enough harm already? Ray, Ray, where the hell are you?"

I can hear the panic and go down to be with the old man. I push the newsmen out of the way and tell Marquis to go ahead. I get such a hold on Mr Ford I nearly lift him clean off the floor and drag him to the door. The Hungarian gets there first and plants herself in our way.

"Oh, Mr Ford, don't do this, I beg you. We're so close to success. We *can* stop the war, we really can, and there'll never be another, and it'll be the greatest thing anyone has ever done. The future of mankind is a future of peace. Mr Ford, you can put your name on it for ever!"

Well, that Rosika Schwimmer is one smart lady and she knows just what Mr Ford likes to hear. And the strangest thing is it almost worked. No one else will ever know it, but I felt his skinny arm stiffen and his body push back against mine and for half a second I feared he might stop and say — "Just wait a minute, Ray, maybe this whole thing isn't so stupid after all."

Rosika might have learned something about Mr Ford, but she'd got me all wrong. I tell her to get out the way and before she has the chance to think about it I lay a hand on her and yank her aside so hard she falls over. She shrieks with alarm, little feet kicking out the end of her petticoat as her glasses go sliding over the polished floor and find their end somewhere under the feet of a photographer. She makes a meal of it, of course, and gentlemanly types come running to help.

"Outrageous! How dare you!"

But I don't give a damn for any of them. And just at that moment, working at what I know best, I didn't give a damn for Rosika either. She had had her chance, Marquis was getting his punishment and I had my job to do. I step over her and drag a trembling Mr Ford out of the hotel. The cold drops on us like an anvil. It's snowing heavily — everything is thick white and I can see from the lack of tracks that there have been few visitors to the hotel in the last hours. It's not even clear where the driveway is and I think for a nightmarish moment there just isn't one there at all, this is all there is of the world and we'll be re-running this farce night after night for ever.

The only marks in this field of snow curve round to a large laundry truck which has just pulled up. Two guys are getting out and starting to ask questions I can't understand. There's no sign of the taxi Marquis promised, but then I hear his voice from the other side of the truck and I go round with Mr Ford to see him picking his way through the snow towards oncoming lights.

"Here it is," he calls back to us.

The taxi slithers to a halt as soon as it meets Marquis, thirty yards or more from the doorway of the hotel. Mr Ford's hat and shoulders are already white with snow. His face is bluish and he's shivering violently as I rush him towards the taxi. All the time the scene is getting brighter as the last few people asleep in the hotel wake up, turn on their lights and pull back the curtains to see what's happening. We have stage shadows as we run about, Marquis now going back the other way as he remembers the baggage and the porters at whom he shouts and waves a handful of banknotes. I get Mr Ford into the back of the cab. He's dazed, listless — he doesn't seem to know where he is. I bellow, "Station, train station, railway," until there's some sign of understanding from the driver. What has he been told, has anything been organised at all? The man clearly has no experience of emergency getaways and starts to help with the bags. Two suitcases are bundled in the back beside a rigid Mr Ford, another is slammed on the roof. A luggage rack overhangs the back of the vehicle and here there is a confused struggle involving hotel porters, Marquis, a steamer trunk and too many leather straps. It's all bad news, and I realise just how bad as I look back towards the hotel and see the posse coming our way. All the hard cases are there — Lochner, Fels the soap widow, Madame Malmberg the Finnish exile and her tasty pig-tailed sidekick, Judge Ben Lindsey, State Senator Robinson, a whole pack of reverends, two comedians off to one side who fight and fall over as they try to set up a moving-picture camera, even Berton Braley has found some more clothes and is heading our way with a notebook and pencil. To the fore is Rebecca Shelly and at the head of them all the dumpy, relentless darkness of Rosika Schwimmer herself, wrapped up in her new fur coat.

Someone is shouting from a hotel window and I guess "politi" must be Norwegian for the cops. I make a quick count of the peacettes and realise we're in serious trouble. I get the notion they're going to surround the car. Marquis will crack for sure and the whole idea of a breakout will fall apart. At this moment he's concentrating on a second trunk.

"Leave it," I yell at him. "For Christ's sake, leave the damned thing and get in the car!"

He turns to see Schwimmer and the gang advancing on him. Marquis isn't made for this. His thinking gets stuck on the trunk and he goes back to the straps and tells me just another second or two and it'll be fine, like we're all off on a goddamned picnic.

It's an emergency. I put my hand to my inside jacket pocket. Marquis lets the trunk fall on his toes and then jumps in front of me, holding his arms out wide and shouting like a madman.

"Oh, God — not that, Ray. For pity's sake, don't let it come to that!"

People get the strangest ideas. I take it out anyway — what Mr Ford gave me in the Biltmore Hotel. "Now you keep that out of sight, Ray. That's just a little reserve for you and me in case we should need it." It's given me a queer feeling all along, a man like me carrying a thing like that and having to put my fingers in there to touch it all the time to see that it's not vanished somehow, as if it could. It's the same for the others — they stare intently as though a curtain has just risen on something they've never seen before. Only Mr Ford, shivering in the car, pays no attention to the neat block of two hundred fifty-dollar bills still in their cashier's wrapper fresh from the bank — a lifetime's work for Joe, in the palm of one man's hand. I yell again at Marquis to get in the car and at last he does what he's told. The trunk and the other cases are left where they lie. I peel off a thickness of money and hand it out to the nearest hotel porter.

"You send these on, understand? Mr Henry Ford, United States of America — they'll get there."

The man hesitates and I let the bills flutter down to the snow. I catch myself despising him, almost as if the money is mine, then there's no time to think of anything.

Marquis is in the front seat. Mr Ford is in the back at the right-hand side and I jump in at the left. We might have made it just then, had anyone been behind the wheel. There's an outburst of profanities and shouting and the driver gives up on the bags and runs for his cab. It's too late. Rosika catches us and starts banging on the window and screaming and crying like someone's stealing her baby. She does all this six inches from Mr Ford's face, but he looks ahead so still and pale and like he's frozen solid there I wonder if it's all for nothing.

"Drive, drive!" shouts Marquis.

The engine sings, the wheels spin against the snow and we go nowhere. People are trying to haul Rosika back, but she's losing control. She grabs for the door handle and gets it half open before I can lean across and slam it shut again. She's got a new tune to sing, all about how much she cares for Mr Ford.

"Don't do this. Mr Ford, don't let them take you — you're too ill to travel. Stay with us until you're stronger."

She goes for broke.

"Murder! Kidnap! Somebody stop them."

Now I'm yelling at the driver too, praying he can find some grip. Rosika is coming round to the other side and the cab lurches forward just as she's behind it. I can't quite see what happens — maybe she stumbles, maybe she reaches for it, I don't suppose I'll ever know. The cab jumps again then picks up some speed, slewing this way and that across the soft snow. Marquis thanks God and urges the driver on. I look back through the tiny rear window. The Peace Party delegates, the newsboys, the hotel, the laundry truck and the moving cameramen shooting the night all get smaller — only Rosika's panic-stricken face stays the same.

I look down and see her white hands paralysed on the luggage straps. Her feet draw tramlines within the cab's wider tracks as she's pulled along.

"Can't you go any faster?" asks Marquis, who is looking ahead and thinking of home.

The driver says something angry but opens the throttle all the same. Mr Ford is still a statue and even a strangulated shriek from Rosika doesn't shake him. Marquis looks back at the noise just as I say, "Brake, brake!" The driver does his best, but we glide on over the snow, twisting sideways. Marquis is saying she must be mad. Rosika, now pressed up against the rear glass by the loss of momentum, is yammering away in her mother tongue. It occurs to me that this white, soft-edged world we are escaping through is padded, momentarily safe for the insane.

"Give it some gas, Mac. Shake her off."

The driver lifts from the brake and steers into the slide. We pick up speed and Rosika is plucked from the luggage straps and deposited as a dark, furry mound in the middle of the snowbound driveway. We slide to a halt. Except for Mr Ford we're all looking backwards. The driver and I hold our breath. Marquis laments — "We've killed her. Oh, my God. Oh, Jesus, we've killed her."

But the helpers come running and there is movement. The scene freezes in my mind as Rosika is helped to her feet and, deeper in the lit background, the laundry truck stands with its wing doors open as it receives, discreetly as they must have thought at this godforsaken hour, the mortal remains of Lloyd Bingham. Lochner dusts the snow from the standing, unharmed conscience of the world. I follow his gaze upward and see that in all this we have barely gone beyond the length of the hotel itself. Directly above, through a bright open window, cut out against the darkness, there tolls over us all, as unanswerable as Cinderella's midnight bell, the beautiful laughter of Inez Milholland.

Clara

One afternoon, when Henry was still away, I remembered who I was — Clara Bryant of Dearborn, Michigan, daughter of farming folk, sister to two sisters and seven brothers, descendant of Warwickshire stock, good at baking and with a neat quilting stitch. What more was there to know about me? I was like the others and can look back on four or five young men who might have been my husband. I'm sure Henry can do the same and think of half a dozen from our small field of friends and acquaintances who might have done well enough had a dance, or a glance, been different. We married, we had few choices — good enough was good enough. I wonder what those other brides would have become — changed versions of themselves or just me, the Mrs Henry Ford, slightly different raw materials in at one end but the same reliable product out the other?

Sometimes I want to ask him how much he foresaw. Did he know what a long, strange journey he would take, and me with him, dragged along farther and faster than I could ever have imagined? I don't say I was ever reluctant, but there are days when I wonder if less might have been happier. The invoice from Altman's has come. I look over the list of carpets and rugs I have ordered for Fair Lane and write a cheque for fifty-seven thousand one hundred and five dollars and eighty-one cents. I carefully transfer the number into my account book, never failing to hear my mother's advice on the importance of looking after the cents. Two people look at the number — one still astonished, but the other unstirred by anything except perhaps a sense of unlooked-for responsibility and a guilty sadness.

I quickly learned that it is the vocation of Mrs Henry Ford to be alone — alone across the dinner table from her husband, alone in the same bed, alone with our lonely only son, alone when reading to him by the fire only to discover that he has been somewhere else for the last five pages. Twenty years ago, I secretly tried to teach myself engineering. I hid a primer beneath the mattress for fear that he should find it and laugh at me. I felt it like the princess felt her pea as I lay awake and listened to the sound of machinery coming from his workshop through half the night. I planned to ask him a question one evening about vanadium alloys — the words are all I can remember now. I imagined we could talk together for hour after hour like he did with the men, but I never had the courage to start that conversation.

I contented myself with the things I understood, all the things Henry does not outwardly care for or know about, or even much notice, as long as they are still there when he comes home, whistling his little tune in the hallway. I built my own machine — until recently it has turned my husband's world so smoothly he has never suspected its existence. This domestic machine does many things, but the most important of all has been to keep my Henry safe from himself and from all the cunning and cleverness of the world that a man who only knows one thing could easily fall prey to. The worst times when he was away were when I thought of him not coming back at all. When I learned that one delegate had indeed died, the idea of widowhood grew in my mind almost to a certainty as if it had already happened. With it came the thought that it would be my fault, the result of a breakdown in my machine. I don't believe I have ever been more miserable than when I returned from New York and that disaster on the Hoboken pier. Edsel stayed with me for a couple of days and I went on as if nothing had happened. Then he went golfing in Virginia and I sent the staff away and wept from morning till night. Who were these strangers Henry was so keen to follow, why was my house suddenly so empty? This was a new way of being alone, and in the middle of the winter too. I heard bird calls as voices and when the wind blew and the timbers creaked it was the sound of a car pulling up and Henry opening the door, just as they say it is when you know someone is never coming back. I am still angry with him for that.

There are, of course, expectations of the Mrs Henry Ford. Her married name rolls down every Main Street in the country and proclaims itself from every fourth billboard in the world — or at least in all those parts of the world I have visited. She is durable and easily repaired. She is never off the road for long. I busied myself with completing the house, choosing the fabric for the curtains and sorting through the player rolls that had been sent for the organ, deciding which to keep and which to send back. I endured a visit from Mr Liebold, such an unsympathetic man. He pestered me for an invitation and I was forced to find half an hour for him in town. He wanted to talk about his concerns for me at this worrying time, but quickly moved on to an explanation of where he had been when Madame Schwimmer and Mr Lochner first came to call on my husband. He repeated how firmly he had been against the whole peace scheme. I fell quiet before the end of his visit and allowed the maid to show him out. I really don't know what Henry sees in him.

I thought ahead to spring and drew and redrew plans for the new gardens. Hours could pass this way almost entirely without anxiety. The men from Willens came to review the construction of the glasshouses and then Mr Jensen himself from Chicago. We wrapped up warm and walked the grounds for a whole afternoon until I could see exactly how it would be.

"In ten years," he told me, "it will be exquisite."

We understood each other so well and he described everything so beautifully that it became quite real to me. I could see and smell the summer even as we stood among the dripping trees and the dreary, melting snow. But in my daydreams it was only myself I could see walking by the brilliant banks of peonies.

Back at the house the hall table groaned under letters and newspapers and telegrams too terrible in my imagination for me even to touch. I opened a parcel one morning — it was the day the *Oscar* steamed into the restricted zone where the U-boats hunt. Inside was a jeweller's case, and inside that a string of pearls paid for with my husband's money. I would like to forget that day.

The newspapers have been a burden and one, surely, that no earlier generation has had to bear in quite this way. Young Mr Delavigne has been scathing about his former colleagues and tells me I mustn't pay attention to a single thing they say. He says he knows for a fact that a full two thirds of everything in the papers is just plain made up, but I suppose he is just trying to be kind. It is strangely hard to keep away from what people write about you and your family, and what others read all over the country in their hundreds of thousands, in their millions I suppose. Privacy is wrecked, a single harsh word withers the day and yet one is drawn back to it again and again, peace as much spoiled by ignorance as by knowledge. Friends send consoling notes — dreadful, they say, outright lies, rise above it all. And yet, their well-meaning letter is the first one hears of it — gunfire in the dining room, my husband a deranged prisoner in his own cabin, a Pittsburgh steel-worker's dream of the *Oscar* torpedoed and sinking in mid-Atlantic. At such times everyone is a bearer of bad news. Henry knows nothing of these things. It is against his principles to notice backward steps. When he talks of the future, and I love it when he does, all is progress and improvement and I'm sure that part of the picture he sees will come together exactly as he says. But I think we make new pains for ourselves too. The newspapers are a new pain, and the tar on the country roads that kills the fish when it rains. We get what we want faster and easier, and electric trains crash into stalled automobiles and Victor Nicholson, returning from an orphanage outing, dies at five years of age and is forgotten as I fold his name out of sight. Something always holds us back.

I would not go to New York when Henry came home. My experience of the Biltmore Hotel and the departure from Hoboken is something I swore I would never repeat. I read of my husband's return in the newspapers, but let him and his companions take the train to Detroit from where Samuel and Mr Delavigne brought him out here to Dearborn. It was near a month since I had last seen him, our longest ever separation, but at first sight it could have been ten years and I had to try hard not to let him see how worried I was. At first all I wanted was to keep everyone away from him, the whole bruising world if I could. I managed it for a while, intercepting letters and telegrams, fending off the company's managers and secretaries and even lying to Mr Liebold on the telephone about all his messages I had not, in fact, passed on. Henry never questioned it — he seemed to believe everything I told him and for a while there was peace such as we have not enjoyed for many years.

I should not have been so anxious about his physical condition. Within a few days it was clear that it was nothing more than his usual winter cold made worse by tiredness and nerves. But he suffers still in his mind, his thoughts endlessly returning to the events of his misadventure, redrawing them a thousand times as if they are a puzzle or a machine that can finally be made to work.

I talk to him of ordinary things, the domestic tasks of the day, nothing that is not within sight or reach. We oversee the work on Fair Lane, settling the last details of the design and choosing the furniture from the catalogues and pattern-books the tradesmen bring. Mostly I make suggestions and Henry distractedly agrees. It is good for him not to make decisions. We still live in the old farmhouse and in the evenings when the staff have finished and we are alone we sit either side of the fireplace like a picture of our parents from forty years ago. I read *Good Housekeeping* while Henry looks through *Scientific American* before falling asleep. These are happy moments for me and I can imagine that the last few weeks never happened. I think of a future of twenty years or more just the same — the company sold, the newspapers read only for recipes or the latest fashions, grandchildren, being no one but ourselves. I conduct imaginary conversations in which Henry gradually comes to understand me and lays down these pointless burdens that have made him so pale and lined. But this was never more than a private game, and one I treasured as I watched him recover, knowing that every day he strengthened and cleared his mind was a day closer to it starting all over again.

The first room to be habitable in the new house is our wonderful sun parlour facing the river. On good days it gets as warm as a greenhouse and Henry is happy to be planted there for hours on end. He sets himself up with his telescope and keeps his eye on the bird boxes in the woods. Three years ago, when we were travelling in a peaceful Europe, Henry stopped suddenly one morning and said, "Listen — don't you think these birds sing more sweetly than the ones at home?" I suggested they might just be different, but he was very sure and found an aviary in London to put six hundred thrushes, finches, skylarks, linnets, warblers and nuthatches into cages and ship them across to America. The survivors were released here the following April. From time to time Henry still thinks he sees one of them or hears a foreign call, but to me the birds in Dearborn seem just as they always did.

It was in the sun parlour that I found him a fortnight ago drowsing in a recliner, happy for having seen a grey jay, but with the outside world washed up around him in a litter of newspaper pages. I put the tray down on the table and sat beside him. He took my hand and we were quiet for a long time.

"Callie," he said at last. "Who was King Canute?"

"I don't know, dear."

"Don Quixote?"

"I don't know dear, I really don't. You shouldn't be reading those terrible things. What good can it do?"

King Midas he does know, the story recalled in every detail from one of his old school readers. He nudges one of the newspaper sheets with his foot.

"It's true what they say about me here — I have been a failure at everything except making money."

I tell him right away I don't like to hear such talk. For a moment he seems distant and shocked and infinitely regretful as if he suspects that money, gold if you will, and any amount of it, can do no good so long as it is in his faulty hands. I refuse to talk about this. I refuse to be interested in any of it and say the only thing in my mind.

"You married me, Henry."

I watch the sun inch across the new carpets as the long, slow thought forms.

"Callie, if I were to die and come back to another life I would change everything except my wife."

We have reached the middle of March and the early signs of spring are certain. There are as many difficulties as before, but we are stronger in bearing them. There now seems to be no subject of discussion other than preparedness for this terrible conflict. Mr Wilson speaks of little else, Congress votes money, some say it was always going to be this way, there was never anything anyone could have done. The people ask, "How can we be safe?" A man on Brooklyn Bridge is arrested with a bomb in his suitcase. It is hard for Henry to see all this. He shouts at the newspapers and there is hardly a single page he can now read without some upset — health tonics to make you fighting fit, boots good for marching, corsets that promise a shape that will please embarking soldiers. The flag is everywhere and he has come to hate it — "Flags are for fools," he tells me. "What are they but something to rally round? I'll pull the flag down from the factory and never raise it again. Why should I not? Men born in fifty countries go to work there every day." I spoke to Samuel and Mr Delavigne and they dissuaded him, for now at least. Somehow his opinions reached the press and there are those who openly call him a traitor. For others he is a hero and his name has appeared on the Republican presidential nomination, though only in Nebraska. Henry will not admit to knowing how this has happened, but I have told my dear husband that if he runs for President I will divorce him. He smiled.

Fair Lane is now fit for guests, on the ground floor at least. Henry has decided it is fit for business too. He has had a long table set up in the sun parlour and he is there now, alone after a tiring day. Outside, men are talking and engines starting. Henry is in his recliner holding his field glasses to his eyes. I stroke his hair and ask him if he has seen anything interesting. In reply he puts his finger to his lips and says — "Not a word, Callie. Not a single word."

I sit with him and together we look out across the river. I see the bright blue of Mr Delavigne's automobile as it splashes down the half-made road towards town. In the back sit the men from the War Office. They hold their briefcases on their laps. In one of them there is my husband's contract for ten thousand ambulances.